Affinity

Also by Sarah Waters

Tipping the Velvet

Affinity

Sarah Waters

RIVERHEAD BOOKS
a member of Penguin Putnam Inc.
NEW YORK
2000

This is a work of fiction. Names, characters, places, and incidents either are the product of the author's imagination or are used fictitiously, and any resemblance to actual persons, living or dead, business establishments, events, or locales is entirely coincidental.

RIVERHEAD BOOKS
a member of
Penguin Putnam Inc.
375 Hudson Street
New York, NY 10014

Previously published in England by Virago Press.
First American edition published by Riverhead Books, 2000.

Published simultaneously in Canada

Library of Congress Cataloging-in-Publication Data

Waters, Sarah, date.
Affinity / by Sarah Waters.
p. cm.
ISBN 1-57322-156-2
1. Millbank Penitentiary (London, England)—History—19th century—Fiction. 2. Women prisoners—England—London—Fiction. 3. London (England)—Fiction. I. Title.
PR6073.A828 A69 2000 99-087554
823'.914—dc21

Printed in the United States of America

3 5 7 9 10 8 6 4 2

This book is printed on acid-free paper. ∞

To Caroline Halliday

Affinity

3 August 1873

I was never so frightened as I am now. They have left me sitting in the dark, with only the light from the window to write by. They have put me in my own room, they have locked the door on me. They wanted Ruth to do it, but she would not. She said 'What, do you want me to lock up my own mistress, who has done nothing?' In the end the doctor took the key from her & locked the door himself, then made her leave me. Now the house is full of voices, all saying my name. If I close my eyes & listen it might be any ordinary night. I might be waiting for Mrs Brink to come & take me down to a dark circle, & Madeleine or any girl might be there, blushing, thinking of Peter, of Peter's great dark whiskers & shining hands.

But Mrs Brink is lying quite alone in her own cold bed, & Madeleine Silvester is downstairs weeping in a fit. And Peter Quick is gone, I think for ever.

He was too rough, & Madeleine too nervous. When I told her I could feel him near she only shook & kept her eyes shut. I said 'It is only Peter. You are not frightened are you, of him? Look, here he is, look at him, open your eyes.' But she would not do that, she only said 'O, I am terribly afraid! O Miss Dawes, please don't have him come any closer!'

Well, many ladies have said that, having Peter come near them for the first time, alone. When he heard her he gave a great laugh. 'What's this?' he said. 'Am I to come all this way, only to be sent back again? Do you know how hard my journey is & how much I have suffered, & all for your sake?' Then Madeleine began to cry – of course, some do cry. I said 'Peter, you must be kinder, Madeleine is only afraid. Be a little gentler & she will let you come close to her, I am sure.' But when he did step gently to put his hand on her, she gave a scream & grew at once very stiff & white. Then Peter said 'What's this, you silly girl? You are spoiling it all. Do you want to be made better or not?' But she only screamed again, & then she fell, she fell upon the floor & began to kick. I never saw a lady do that. I said 'My God, Peter!' & he looked once at me then said 'Now you little bitch', & he caught her legs & I put my hands across her mouth. I did it only to make her be quiet & stop jerking, but when I took my hands away there was blood upon them, I think she must have bitten her own tongue or made her nose bleed. I did not even know it for blood at first, it looked so black, & seemed so warm & thick, like sealing-wax.

And even with the blood in her mouth she shrieked, until finally the row brought Mrs Brink, I heard her footsteps in the hall & then her voice, that was frightened. She called 'Miss Dawes, what is it, are you injured, are you hurt?' & when Madeleine heard that she gave a twist, then cried out clear as anything 'Mrs Brink, Mrs Brink, they are trying to murder me!'

Then Peter leaned & hit her on her cheek, & after that she lay very quiet & still. Then I thought we really might have killed her. I said 'Peter, what have you done? Go back! You must go back.' But as he stepped to the cabinet there came a rattling at the handle of the door & Mrs Brink was there, she had brought her own key with her & had opened the door with that. She was holding a lamp. I said 'Close the door, here is Peter look & the light is hurting him!' But she said only 'What has happened? What have you done?' She looked at Madeleine lying stiff upon the parlour floor with all her red hair about her, & then at me in my torn petticoat, & then at the blood upon my hands, which was not black now but scarlet. Then she looked at Peter. He had his hands before his face & was crying 'Take the light away!' But his gown was open & his white legs showed, & Mrs Brink would not take the lamp away until at last it began to shake. Then she cried 'O!' & she looked at me again, & at Madeleine again, & she put her hand upon her heart. She said 'Not her, too?' & then 'O Mamma, Mamma!' Then she laid the lamp aside & turned her face against the wall, & when I went to her she put her fingers upon my bosom & pushed me from her.

I looked once for Peter then, but he had gone. There was only the curtain, dark & shivering, & marked with a mark of silver from his hand.

And after all, it is Mrs Brink that has died, not Madeleine. Madeleine had only fainted, & when her maid got her dressed she took her to another room & I heard her walking about & crying there. But Mrs Brink grew weaker & weaker, until finally she could not stand at all. Then Ruth came running, calling 'What is the matter?', & she made her lie upon the parlour sofa, all the time pressing her hand & saying 'You will soon be well, I am sure of it. Look, here am I, & here is Miss Dawes, that love you.' I thought that Mrs Brink looked then as if she longed to speak but could not, & when Ruth saw that she said we must send out for a doctor. Then she stayed holding tight to Mrs Brink's hand while he examined her, weeping & saying she would not let it go. Mrs Brink died soon after. She never said another word, Ruth said, except to call again for her mamma. The doctor said that dying ladies very often do become like children. He said her heart was very swollen & must always have been weak, he thought it a wonder she had lived so long as this.

He might have gone then, & not thought to ask what startled her, but Mrs Silvester came while he was here & she made him go & look at Madeleine. Madeleine has marks upon her, & when the doctor saw those his voice grew quiet & he said this was a queerer business than he thought. Mrs Silvester said then, 'Queer? I should say it is criminal!' She has made a policeman come, it is for that reason they have locked me in my room, the policeman is asking Madeleine who hurt her. She is saying Peter Quick did it, & the gentlemen are answering 'Peter Quick? Peter Quick? What are you thinking of?'

There isn't a fire lit in all this great house, & though it is August I am awfully cold. I think I shall never be warm again! I think I shall never be calm again. I think I shall never be myself, I look about me at my own room & see nothing in it that is mine. There is the smell of the flowers in Mrs Brink's garden, & the perfumes on her mother's table, & the polish on the wood, the colours of the carpet, the cigarettes I rolled for Peter, the shine on the jewels in the jewel-box, the sight of my own white face in the glass, but it all seems strange to me. I wish I might close my eyes & open them & be at Bethnal Green again, with my own aunty in her own wooden chair. I would rather even be in my room at Mr Vincy's hotel, with the plain brick wall outside my window. I would rather be there a 100 times than be here where I am now.

It is so late, they have put out the lamps at the Crystal Palace. I can see only the great black shape of it against the sky.

Now I can hear the sound of the policeman's voice, & Mrs Silvester is shouting & making Madeleine cry. Mrs Brink's bedroom is the only quiet place in all the house, & I know that she is lying in it, quite alone in the darkness. I know that she is lying very still & straight with her hair let down & a blanket about her. She might be listening to the shouts & weepings, she might still be wishing she could open her mouth & speak. I know what she would say, if she could do that. I know it so well, I think I can hear it.

Her quiet voice, that only I can hear, is the most frightening voice of them all.

Part One

24 September 1874

Pa used to say that any piece of history might be made into a tale: it was only a question of deciding where the tale began, and where it ended. That, he said, was all his skill. And perhaps, after all, the histories he dealt with were rather easy to sift like that, to divide up and classify—the great lives, the great works, each one of them neat and gleaming and complete, like metal letters in a box of type.

I wish that Pa was with me now. I would ask him how he would start to write the story I have embarked upon to-day. I would ask him how he would neatly tell the story of a prison—of Millbank Prison—which has so many separate lives in it, and is so curious a shape, and must be approached, so darkly, through so many gates and twisting passages. Would he start it with the building of the gaols themselves? I cannot do that, for though I was told the date of it this morning I have forgotten it now; besides which, Millbank is so solid and so antique, I can't believe that there was ever a time when it did not sit upon that dreary spot beside the Thames, casting its shadow on the black earth there. He might begin it, then, with Mr Shillitoe's visit to this house, three weeks ago; or, he might begin it at seven this morning, when Ellis first brought me my grey suit and my coat—no, of course he would not start the story there, with a lady and her servant, and petticoats and loose hair.

He would start it, I think, at the gate of Millbank, the point that every visitor must pass when they arrive to make their tour of the gaols. Let me begin my record there, then: I am being greeted by the prison porter, who is marking my name off in some great ledger; now a warder is leading me through a narrow arch, and I am about to step across the grounds towards the prison proper—

Before I can do that, however, I am obliged to pause a little to fuss with my skirts, which are plain, but wide, and have caught upon some piece of jutting iron or brick. I daresay Pa would not have bothered with the detail of the skirts; I will, however, for it is in lifting my eyes from my sweeping hem that I first see the pentagons of Millbank—and the nearness of them, and the suddenness of that gaze, makes them seem terrible. I look at them, and feel my heart beat hard, and I am afraid.

I had a plan of Millbank's buildings from Mr Shillitoe a week ago, and have had it pinned, since then, on the wall beside this desk. The prison, drawn in outline, has a curious kind of charm to it, the pentagons appearing as petals on a geometric flower—or, as I have sometimes thought, they are like the coloured zones on the chequer-boards we used to paint when we were children. Seen close, of course, Millbank is not charming. Its scale is vast, and its lines and angles, when realised in walls and towers of yellow brick and shuttered windows, seem only wrong or perverse. It is as if the prison had been designed by a man in the grip of a nightmare or a madness—or had been made expressly to *drive* its inmates mad. I think it would certainly drive me mad, if I had to work as a warder there. As it was, I walked flinchingly beside the man who led me, and paused once to glance behind me, then to gaze at the wedge of sky that showed above. The inner gate at Millbank is set at the junction of two of the pentagons and so, to reach it, one must walk along a narrowing slip of gravel, and feel the walls on either side of one advancing, like the clashing rocks of the Bosporous. The shadows there, flung from the jaundiced bricks, are the colour of bruises. The soil in which the walls are set is damp and dark as tobacco.

This soil makes the air there very sour; it grew sourer still, as I was shown into the gaol and had the gate made fast behind me. My heart beat even harder then, and continued to thump while I was made to sit in a plain little room, watching warders cross the open door, seeing them frown and murmur. When Mr Shillitoe came to me at last, I took his hand. I said, 'I am glad to see you! I had begun to worry that the men might take me for a convict just arrived, and lead me to a cell, and leave me there!' He laughed. There were never confusions like that, he said, at Millbank.

We walked together then, into the prison buildings: for he thought it best to take me straight to the female gaol, to the office of the governess or principal matron there, Miss Haxby. We walked, and he explained our route to me, and I tried to match it with my memory of my paper plan; but the organisation of the prison, of course, is so peculiar, I soon grew lost. The pentagons that hold the men, I know we did not enter. We only passed the gates that lead to those gaols from the hexagon-shaped building at the prison's middle, the building in which they have their store-rooms, and the surgeon's house, and Mr Shillitoe's own offices, and the offices of all his clerks, and the infirmaries and chapel. 'For you see,' he said to me once, nodding through a window at a set of yellow smoking chimneys he said were fed by the fires of the prison laundry, 'you see, we are quite a little city here! Quite self-sustaining. We should do very well, I always think, under a siege.'

He spoke rather proudly, but smiled at his own pride; and I smiled when he did. But if I had grown fearful, having the light and air shut out behind me at the inner gate, then now, as we passed further into the gaol, and that gate was put behind us at the end of a dim and complicated path I should never be able to retrace alone—now, I grew nervous again. Last week, sorting through the papers in Pa's study, I came across a volume of the prison drawings of Piranesi, and spent an anxious hour, studying them, thinking of all the dark and terrible scenes I might be confronted with to-day. Of course, there was nothing to match the things I had imagined. We passed only along a succession of neat, whitewashed corridors, and were greeted at the junction of these by warders, in dark prison coats. But, the very neatness and the sameness of the corridors and the men made them troubling: I might have been taken on the same plain route ten times over, I should never have known it. Unnerving, too, is the dreadful *clamour* of the place. Where the warders stand there are gates, that must be unfastened, and swung on grinding hinges, and slammed and bolted; and the empty passages, of course, echo with the sounds of other gates, and other locks and bolts, distant and near. The prison seems caught, in consequence, at the heart of some perpetual private storm, that left my ears ringing.

We walked until we reached an antique, studded door that had a wicket in it, which proved to be the entrance to the female gaol. Here we were greeted by a matron, who made Mr Shillitoe a curtsey; and, she being the first woman I had encountered there, I made sure to study her carefully. She was youngish, pale, and quite unsmiling, and dressed in what I was soon to see was the uniform of the place: a grey wool dress, a mantle of black, a grey straw bonnet trimmed with blue, and stout black flat-heeled boots. When she saw me gazing at her she curtseyed again—Mr Shillitoe saying, 'This is Miss Ridley, our chief matron here', and then, to her: 'This is Miss Prior, our new Visitor.'

She walked before us, and there came a steady *chink*, *chink* of metal; and I saw then that, like the warders, she wore a wide belt of leather with a buckle of brass and, suspended from the buckle, a chain of polished prison keys.

She took us, via more featureless corridors, to a spiral staircase that wound upwards through a tower; it is at the top of the tower, in a bright, white, circular room, filled with windows, that Miss Haxby has her office. 'You will see the logic of the design of this,' said Mr Shillitoe as we climbed, growing red and breathless; and of course, I saw it at once, for the tower is set at the centre of the pentagon yards, so that the view from it is all of the walls and barred windows that make up the interior face of the women's building. The room is very plain. Its floor is bare. There is a rope hung out between two posts, where prisoners, when they are taken there, are obliged to stand, and beyond the rope is a desk. Here, sitting writing in a great black book, we found Miss Haxby herself—'the

Argus of the gaol', as Mr Shillitoe called her, smiling. When she saw us she rose, took off her spectacles and, like Miss Ridley, made a curtsey.

She is a very small lady, and her hair is perfectly white. Her eyes are sharp eyes. Behind her desk, screwed tight to the limewashed bricks, there is set an enamel tablet bearing a piece of dark text:

> *Thou hast set our misdeeds before Thee, and our secret sins in the light of Thy confidence.*

It was impossible, on entering that room, not to long to walk at once to one of its curving windows and gaze at the view beyond it, and when Mr Shillitoe saw me looking he said, 'Yes, Miss Prior, come closer to the glass.' I spent a moment then, studying the wedge-shaped yards below, then looking harder at the ugly prison walls that faced us, and at the banks of squinting windows with which they are filled. Mr Shillitoe said, Now, was that not a very marvellous and terrible sight? There was all the female gaol before me; and behind each of those windows was a single cell, with a prisoner in it. He turned to Miss Haxby. 'How many women have you on your wards, just now?'

She answered, that there were two hundred and seventy.

'Two hundred and seventy!' he said, shaking his head. 'Will you take a moment, Miss Prior, to imagine those poor women, and all the dark and crooked paths through which they have made their way to Millbank? They might have been thieves, they might have been prostitutes, they might have been brutalised by vice; they will certainly be ignorant of shame, and duty, and all the finer feelings—yes, you may be sure of it. Villainous women, society has deemed them; and society has passed them on, to Miss Haxby and to me, to take close care of them . . .'

But what, he asked me, was the proper way for them to do that? 'We give them habits that are regular. We teach them their prayers; we teach them modesty. Yet, of necessity, they must spend the great part of their days alone, with their cell walls about them. And there they are—' he nodded again to the windows before us '—perhaps for three years, perhaps for six or seven. There they are: shut up, and brooding. Their tongues we still, their hands we may keep busy; but their hearts, Miss Prior, their wretched memories, their own low thoughts, their mean ambitions—these, we cannot guard. Can we, Miss Haxby?'

'No, sir,' she answered.

I said, And yet, he thought a Visitor might do much good with them?

He knew it, he said. He was certain of it. Those poor unguarded hearts, they were like children's hearts, or savages'—they were impressible, they wanted only a finer mould, to shape them. 'Our matrons might do this,' he said; 'our matrons' hours, however, are long, and their duties hard. The women are sometimes bitter with them, and sometimes rough. But, let a lady go to them, Miss Prior, let a lady do that; let them only know that she has left her comfortable life, solely to visit them, to take an interest in their mean histories. Let them see the miserable contrast between her speech, her manners, and their own poor ways, and they will grow meek, they will grow softened and subdued—I have seen it happen! Miss Haxby has seen it! It is a matter of influence, of sympathies, of susceptibilities tamed . . .'

So he went on. He had said much of this before, of course, downstairs, in our own drawing-room; and there, with Mother frowning, and the clock upon the mantel giving its slow *tut-tut*, it had sounded very well. *You must have been sadly idle, Miss Prior,* he had said to me then, *since your poor father's death.* He only called to take a set of books that Pa had once had from him; he didn't know that I had not been idle, but ill. I was glad he did not know it, then. Now, however, with those bleak prison walls before me, and with Miss Haxby gazing at me, and Miss Ridley at the door, her arms across her breast and her chain of keys swinging—now I felt more fearful than ever. For a moment I wished only that they might see the weakness in me, and send me home—as Mother has sent me home sometimes when I have grown anxious at a theatre, thinking I should be ill and have to cry out while the hall was so still.

They did not see it. Mr Shillitoe talked on, about Millbank's history, about its routines, its staff and its visitors. I stood and nodded at his words; sometimes Miss Haxby also nodded. And then, after a time, there sounded a bell, from some part of the prison buildings; and hearing that, Mr Shillitoe and the matrons all made a similar movement, and Mr Shillitoe said that he had spoken longer than he had meant to. That bell was the signal that sent the prisoners to the yards; now he must leave me to the matrons' care—he said I must be sure to go to him another time, and tell him how the women seem to me. He took my hand, but when I made to walk with him towards the desk he said, 'No, no, you must stand a little longer there. Miss Haxby, will you come to the window and watch with Miss Prior? Now, Miss Prior, keep your eyes before you, and you shall see something!'

The matron held the door for him, and he was swallowed by the gloom of the tower staircase. Miss Haxby had drawn near, and now we turned to the glass, Miss Ridley stepping to another window to gaze from that. Below us stretched the three earth yards, each separated from its neighbour by a high brick wall that ran, like the spoke on a cart-wheel, from the governess's tower. Above us hung the dirty city sky, that was streaked with sunlight.

'A fair day, for September,' said Miss Haxby.

Then she gazed again at the scene below us; and I gazed with her, and waited.

For a time, all was still: for the yards there, like the grounds, are desperately bleak, all dirt and gravel—there is not so much as a blade of grass to be shivered by the breezes, or a worm or a beetle for a bird to swoop for. But after perhaps a minute or so I caught a movement in the corner of one of the yards, and then a similar movement in the others. It was the opening of doors, and the emergence of the women; and I don't think I ever saw such a queer and impressive sight as they made then, for we watched them from our high window and they looked small—they might have been dolls upon a clock, or beads on trailing threads. They spilled into the yards and formed three great elliptical loops, and within a second of their doing that, I could not have said which was the first prisoner to have entered the ground, and which the last, for the loops were seamless, and the women all dressed quite alike, in frocks of brown and caps of white, and with pale blue kerchiefs knotted at their throats. It was only from their poses that I caught the humanity of them: for though they all walked at the same dull pace, there were some, I saw, with drooping heads, and some that limped; some with bodies stiff and hugged against the sudden chill, a few poor souls with faces lifted to the sky—and one, I think, who even raised her eyes to the window that we stood at, and gazed blankly at us.

There were all the women of the gaol there, almost three hundred of them, ninety women to each great wheeling line. And in the corner of the yards stood a pair of dark-cloaked matrons, who must stand and watch the prisoners until the exercise is complete.

Miss Haxby, I thought, gazed at the plodding women with a kind of satisfaction. 'See how they know their places,' she said. 'There must be kept a certain distance, look, between each prisoner.' If that distance is breached, the offending woman is reported and loses privileges. If there are women who are old or sick or feeble, or if there are very young girls— 'We have had girls in the past—haven't we, Miss Ridley?—of twelve and thirteen'—then the matron sets them walking in a circle of their own.

'How quietly they walk!' I said. She told me then that the women must keep silent, in all parts of the prison; that they are forbidden to speak, to whistle, to sing, hum 'or make any kind of voluntary noise' unless at the express request of a matron or Visitor.

'And how long must they walk for?' I asked her then.—They must walk for an hour. 'And if it should rain?'—If it should rain, the exercise must be forfeited. Those were bad days for the matrons, she said, for then the long confinement made the women 'fidget and turn saucy'. As she spoke she peered harder at the prisoners: one of the loops had begun to slow, and now turned out of sequence with the circles in the other yards. She said, 'There is'—and here she named some woman—'making the pace of her line grow slack. Be sure to speak with her, Miss Ridley, when you make your round.'

I thought it marvellous that she could tell one woman from another; when I told her that, however, she smiled. She said, that she had seen the prisoners walking the yards every day of their terms there, 'and I have been seven years as principal at Millbank, and before that was chief matron here'—before *that*, she told me, she was ordinary matron, at the prison at Brixton. All in all, she said, she had spent twenty-one years in gaol; which was a longer sentence than many convicts serve. And yet, there were women walking down there, too, who would outsuffer her. She had seen them come; she dared to say she would not be there to see them leave . . .

I asked if such women didn't make her work the easier, since they must know the habits of the gaol so well? She nodded. 'Oh yes.' Then: 'Is that not true, Miss Ridley? We prefer a longer-server, do we not?'

'We do,' answered the matron. 'We like the longer-servers, with the one offence behind them—that is,' she said to me, 'your poisoners, your vitriol-throwers, your child-murderers, that the magistrates have turned kind on and kept from the rope. Had we a gaolful of such women, we might send our matrons home and let the convicts lock themselves up. It is the petty regulars, the thieves and prostitutes and counterfeiters, that vex us most—and they are devils, miss! Bred to mischief, most of them, and look for nothing better. If *they* know our habits, they know only what they can get away with, know what tricks will trouble us the most. Devils!'

Her manner stayed very mild, through all this speech; but her words made me blink. Perhaps it was only the association of the chain of keys—which still swung, and sometimes tumbled unmusically together, on the chain of her belt—but her voice seemed to me to be tainted with steel. It was like a bolt in its cradle: I imagine she might draw it back, harsh or gently; I am sure she could never make it soft. I looked at her for a second, then turned again to Miss Haxby. She had only nodded at the matron's words, and now she almost smiled. 'You may see,' she said, 'how sentimental my matrons grow over their charges!'

She kept her sharp eyes upon me. 'Do you think us harsh, Miss Prior?' she asked after a moment. She said I would, of course, form my own opinion of the characters of her women. Mr Shillitoe had asked me to be Visitor to them, and she was grateful to him, and I was to pass my time with them as I thought proper. But she must say to me, as she would say to any lady or gentleman who came to walk her wards: '*Take care*'—she gave the words a dreadful emphasis—'*Take care, in your dealings with Millbank's women!*' She said I must take care, for example, of my possessions. Many of her girls were pickpockets in their former lives, and if I were to place a watch or a handkerchief in their way, then I would tempt them into their old habits: she asks me therefore *not* to place such items in their way, just as I would 'keep my rings and trinkets hidden from the eyes of a servant, so as not to worry her with the prospect of the taking of them'.

She said, too, that I must take care in how I speak to the women. I must tell them nothing of the world beyond the prison walls, nothing of what happens in it, not even so much as a notice from a newspaper—especially not that, she said, indeed, 'for newspapers are forbidden here'. She said I might find a woman seeking me out as an intimate, a counsellor; and if she does that, then I must counsel her 'as her matron would—that is, in thinking shamefully on her crime, and in making her future life a better one'. But I must make no woman any kind of promises while she is kept in the gaol; nor must I carry objects or information between a woman and her family or friends outside.

'If a prisoner were to tell you that her mother was ill and about to die,' she said; 'if she were to cut off a lock of her hair and plead with you to take it, as a token, to the dying woman, *you must refuse it*. For take it, Miss Prior, and the prisoner will have you in her power. She will hold the knowledge against you, and use it to make all manner of mischief.'

She said there had been one or two notorious cases like that, in her time at Millbank, that had ended very miserably for all concerned . . .

Those, I think, were all her cautions. I thanked her for them—though, all the time she spoke, I found myself terribly mindful of the smooth-faced silent matron who stood nearby: it was like thanking Mother for some piece of hard counsel, while Ellis took the plates away. I gazed again at the circling women, saying nothing, thinking my own thoughts.

'You like to look at them,' Miss Haxby said then.

She said she had never had a visitor yet that didn't like to stand at that window and watch the women walk. It was as curative, she thought, as gazing at fish in a tank.

After that, I moved from the glass.

I think we talked a little longer, about the routines of the gaol; but soon she looked at her watch and said Miss Ridley might now take me on my first tour of the wards. 'I am sorry I cannot show you them myself,' she said. 'But look here,'—nodding to the great dark volume on her desk—'here is my work for the morning. This is the prisoners' Character Book, that I must fill with all the reports my matrons make me.' She drew on her spectacles, and her sharp eyes grew sharper. 'I shall see now, Miss Prior,' she said, 'how good our women have been this week—and how wicked!'

Miss Ridley led me from her, down the shady tower staircase. On the floor below we passed another door. I said, 'What rooms do you keep here, Miss Ridley?' She said that those were Miss Haxby's own apartments, in which she took her dinners and also slept—and I wondered then how it must be, to lie in that quiet tower, with the gaol outside one's windows, rearing up on every side.

I look at the plan beside my desk, and see the tower marked out upon it. I think I see, too, the route Miss Ridley took me on now. She walked very briskly, picking out her unswerving way through those monotonous passages—quite like a compass needle, continually swinging north. There are three miles' worth of such passages across the prison as a whole, she told me; but when I asked her, were the corridors not very difficult to tell apart?, she snorted. She said that when women come to Millbank to be matrons, they put their heads upon their pillows in the night and seem to be walking, walking, walking down the same white corridor. 'That happens for a week,' she said. 'After that, the matron knows her way all right. After a year, she wishes she might grow lost again, for the novelty.' She herself has been matron there longer even than Miss Haxby. She could be blinded, she said, and still perform her duties.

Here she smiled, but very sourly. Her cheek is white and even, like lard or wax, and her eyes are pale, with heavy lashless lids. Her hands, I noticed, are kept very clean and smooth—I should say she takes a pumice-stone to them. Her nails are clipped neatly, quite to the quick.

She didn't speak to me again until we reached the wards—that is, until we arrived at a set of bars, which admitted us to a long, chill, silent, cloister-like passage, that held the cells. This passage was, I think, about six feet wide. There was sand upon the floor of it and, upon the walls and ceiling, more lime-wash. High on the left—too high even for me to gaze from—there was a row of windows, barred and thickly glassed; and all along the opposite wall were doorways: doorway after doorway after doorway, all just the same, like the dark, identical doorways one sometimes has to choose between in terrible dreams. The doorways let a little light into the passage, but also something of an odour. The odour—I had caught it at once, in the outer corridors, and I smell it even now, as I write this!—it is vague, but terrible. It is the stifled reek of what they call there 'nuisance-buckets', and the lingering exhalations I suppose of many ill-washed mouths and limbs.

This was the first ward, Ward A, Miss Ridley told me. There are six wards altogether—two to each floor. Ward A houses the newest set of women, that they term Third Class.

She led me then into the first of the empty cells, gesturing as she did so to the two doors fixed at the mouth of it. One of these was of wood, with bolts upon it; the other was an iron gate, with a lock. They keep the gates fastened during the days, and have the wooden doors thrown back: 'That lets us see the women as we walk,' said Miss Ridley, 'and keeps the air of the cells less foul.' As she spoke, she pushed both doors closed, and the room at once grew darker and seemed to shrink. She put her hands upon her hips, and gazed about her. These were very decent cells, she said: good-sized, and 'built quite solid', with a double layer of brick between them. 'That stops a woman from calling to her neighbour . . .'

I turned away from her. The cell, though dim, was white and very harsh upon the eye, and so bare that, if I close my own eyes now, I find I see again all that was in it, very clearly. There was a single small high window, made of wire and yellow glass—this was one of the windows, of course, that I had gazed at with Mr Shillitoe from Miss Haxby's tower. Beside the door was an enamel plaque bearing a list of 'Notices to Convicts' and a 'Convicts' Prayer'. Upon a bare wood shelf there was a mug, a trencher, a box of salt, a Bible and a religious book: *The Prisoner's Companion*. There was a chair and table and a folded hammock and, beside the hammock, a tray of canvas sacks and scarlet threads, and a 'nuisance-bucket' with a chipped enamel lid. Upon the narrow window-sill there was a prison comb, its ancient teeth worn down or splintered, and snagged with curling hairs and crumbs of scalp.

The comb, it turned out, was all there was to distinguish that cell from the ones about it. The women may keep nothing with them of their own, and what they are issued with—the mugs and plates and Bibles—must be kept very neat, and laid out in line with a prison pattern. Walking the length of the ground-floor wards with Miss Ridley, gazing in at all those bleak and featureless chambers, was very miserable; I found I was made giddy, too, by the geometry of the place. For the wards, of course, follow the pentagon's exterior walls, and are queerly segmented: each time we arrived at the end of one white and monotonous passage, it was to find ourselves at the beginning of another just the same, only stretching off at an unnatural angle. Where two corridors meet there is a spiral staircase. At the junction of the wards there is a tower, where the matron of each floor has a little chamber of her own.

All the time we walked there came, from beyond the windows of the cells, the steady *tramp*, *tramp* of the women in the prison yards. Now, as we reached the furthest arm of the second ground-floor ward, I heard another ringing of the prison bell, that made the marching rhythm slow, then grow uneven; and after a moment there came the banging of a door, the rattling of bars, and then the sound of boots again, crunching on sand this time, and echoing. I looked at Miss Ridley. 'Here come the women,' she said, without excitement; and we stood and listened as the sound grew loud, then louder, then louder still. It seemed, at last, impossibly loud—for we of course had turned three angles of the floor and, though the women were near, we could not see them. I said, 'They might be ghosts!'—I remembered how there are said to be legions of Roman soldiers that can be heard passing, sometimes, through the cellars of the houses of the City. I think the grounds at Millbank might echo like that, in the centuries when the prison no longer stands there.

But Miss Ridley had turned to me. 'Ghosts!' she said, studying me queerly. And as she spoke, the prisoners turned the angle of the ward; and then they were suddenly terribly real—not ghosts, not dolls or beads on a string, as they had seemed before, but coarse-faced, slouching women and girls. Their heads went up when they saw us standing there, and when they recognised Miss Ridley their expressions grew meek. Me, however, they seemed to study quite frankly.

They looked, but went neatly to their cells, and then sat. And behind them came their matron, locking the gates on them.

This matron's name, I think, is Miss Manning. 'Miss Prior is making her first visit here,' Miss Ridley said to her, and the matron nodded, saying, they had been told to expect me. She smiled. I had taken on a pretty task, she said, calling on *their* girls! And should I like to speak with one of them now?—I said I might as well. She led me to a cell she had not fastened yet, and beckoned to the woman that had entered it.

'Here, Pilling,' she said. 'Here is the new Lady Visitor, come to take a bit of interest in you. Up, and let her see you. Come on, look slippy!'

The prisoner came to me and made a curtsey. Her cheek was flushed and her lip slightly gleaming from her brisk circling of the yard. Miss Manning said, 'Say who you are and why you are here', and the woman said at once—though stumbling slightly, over the pronunciation of it—'Susan Pilling, m'm. Here for thieving.'

Miss Manning showed me then an enamel tablet that hung from a chain beside the entrance to the cell: this gave the woman's prison number and class, her crime, and the date she was due to be released. I said, 'How long have you been at Millbank, Pilling?'—She told me, seven months. I nodded. And what age was she? I thought she might be two or three years short of forty. She said, however, that she was twenty-two; and I hesitated at that, then nodded again. How, I asked next, did she care for the life there?

She replied that she liked it well enough; and that Miss Manning was kind to her.

I said, 'I am sure she is.'

Then there was a silence. I saw the woman gazing at me, and think the matrons also had their eyes upon me. I thought suddenly of Mother, scolding me when I was two-and-twenty, saying I must talk more when we went calling. I must ask the ladies after the health of their children; or after the pleasant places they had visited; or the work they had painted or sewn. I might admire the cut of a lady's gown . . .

I looked at Susan Pilling's mud-brown dress; and then I said, how did she like the costume she must wear? What was it—was it serge, or linsey? Here Miss Ridley stepped forward, and caught hold of the skirt and lifted it a little. The gown was of linsey, she said. The stockings—these were blue with a crimson stripe, and very coarse—were of wool. There was one under-skirt of flannel, and another of serge. The shoes, I could see, were stout ones: the men made those, she told me, in the prison shop.

The woman stood stiff as a mannequin as the matron

counted off these items, and I felt myself obliged to stoop to a fold in her frock and pinch it. It smelt—well, it smelt as a linsey frock *would* smell when worn all day, in such a place, by one perspiring woman; so that what I next asked was, how often were the dresses changed?—They are changed, the matrons told me, once a month. The petticoats, under-vests and stockings they change once a fortnight.

'And how often are you allowed to bathe?' I asked the prisoner herself.

'We are allowed it, m'm, as often as we like; only, not exceeding two times every month.'

I saw then that her hands, which she kept before her, were pocked with scars; and I wondered how often she was used to bathing, before they sent her to Millbank.

I wondered, too, what in the world we would discuss, if I was put in a cell with her and left alone. What I said, however, was: 'Well, perhaps I will visit you again, and you can tell me more about how you pass your days here. Should you like that?'

She should like it very much, she said promptly. Then: did I mean to tell them stories, from the Scripture?

Miss Ridley told me then that there is another Lady Visitor who comes on Wednesdays, who reads the Bible to the women and later questions them upon the text. I told Pilling that, no, I would not read to them, but only listen to them and perhaps hear *their* stories. She looked at me then, and said nothing. Miss Manning stepped forward, and sent her back into her cell and locked the gate.

When we left that ward it was to climb another winding staircase to the next floor, to Wards D and E. Here they keep the women of the penal class, the troublesome women or incorrigibles, who have made mischief at Millbank or been passed on or returned from other institutions for making mischief there. In these wards, all the doors are bolted up; the passage-ways, in consequence, are rather darker than the ones below, and the air is more rank. The matron of this floor is a stout, heavy-browed woman named—of all names!—Mrs Pretty. She walked ahead of Miss Ridley and me and, with a sort of dull relish, like the curator of a wax museum, paused before the cell doors of the worst or most interesting characters to tell me of their crimes, such as—

'Jane Hoy, ma'am: child-murderer. Vicious as a needle.

'Phœbe Jacobs: thief. Set fire to her cell.

'Deborah Griffiths: pickpocket. Here for spitting at the chaplain.

'Jane Samson: suicide—'

'*Suicide,*' I said. Mrs Pretty blinked. 'Took laudanum,' she said. 'Took it seven times, and the last time a policeman saved her. They sent her here, as being a nuisance to the public good.'

I heard that, and stood gazing at the shut door, saying nothing. After a moment the matron tilted her head. 'You are thinking,' she said confidentially, 'how do we know she ain't in there now, with her hands at her own throat?'—though I was not, of course, thinking that. 'Look here,' she went on. She showed me how, at the side of each gate, there is a vertical iron flap which can be opened any time the matron pleases, and the prisoner viewed: they call this the 'inspection'; the women term it *the eye.* I leaned to look at it, and then moved closer; when Mrs Pretty saw me do that, however, she checked me, saying that she oughtn't to let me put my face to it. The women were that cunning, she said, and they had had matrons blinded in the past. 'One girl worked at her supper-spoon until the wood was sharp and—' I blinked, and stepped hurriedly back. But then she smiled, and gently pressed the flap of iron open. 'I daresay Samson shan't harm *you,*' she said. 'You might just take a peep, if you are careful . . .'

This room had iron louvres across its window and so was darker than the cells below, and instead of a hammock it had a hard wood bed. On this the woman—Jane Samson—was seated, her fingers plucking at a shallow basket that she had placed across her lap, that was heaped with coir. She had unpicked perhaps a quarter of the bundle; and there was another, larger, basket of the stuff beside the bed, for her to work on later. A bit of sun struggled through the bars across her window. Its beams were so clotted with brown fibre and with swirling particles of dust, she might, I thought, have been a character in a fairy-tale—a princess, humbled, set to work at some impossible labour at the bottom of a pond.

She looked up once as I observed her, then blinked, and rubbed at her eyes where the coir-dust prickled them; and then I let the inspection close, and stepped away. I had begun to wonder, after all, whether she might not try to gesture to me, or call out.

I had Miss Ridley take me away from that ward then, and we climbed to the third and highest floor there and met its matron. She proved to be a dark-eyed, kind-faced, earnest woman named Mrs Jelf. 'Have you come to look at my poor charges?' she said to me, when Miss Ridley took me to her. Her prisoners are mainly what are termed there Second Class, First Class and Star Class women: they are permitted to have their doors fixed open as they work, like the women on Wards A and B; but their work is easier, they sit knitting stockings or sewing shirts, and they are allowed scissors and needles and pins—this is considered, there, a great gesture of trust. Their cells, when I saw them, had the morning sun in them, and so were very bright and almost cheerful. Their occupants rose and curtseyed when we passed by them, and again seemed to study me very frankly. At last I realised that, just as I looked for the details of their hair and frocks and bonnets, so they looked for the particulars of mine. I suppose that even a gown in mourning colours is a novel one, at Millbank.

Many of the prisoners on this ward are those long-servers about whom Miss Haxby had spoken so well. Mrs Jelf now also praised them, saying they were the quietest women in the gaol. Most, she said, would go on from there, before their time, to Fulham Prison, where the routines were a little lighter. 'They are like lambs to us, aren't they, Miss Ridley?'

Miss Ridley agreed that they were not like some of the trash they kept on C and D.

'They are not. We have one here—killed her husband, that was cruel to her—as nicely-bred a woman as you could ever hope to meet.' The matron nodded into a cell, where a lean-faced prisoner sat patiently teasing at a tangled ball of yarn. 'Why, we have had ladies here,' she went on. '*Ladies*, miss, quite like yourself.'

I smiled to hear her say it, and we walked further. Then, from the mouth of a cell a little way along the line there came a thin cry: 'Miss Ridley? Oh, is that Miss Ridley there?' A woman was at her gate, her face pressed between the bars. 'Oh, Miss Ridley mum, have you spoke in my behalf yet, before Miss Haxby?'

We drew closer to her, and Miss Ridley stepped to the gate and struck it with her ring of keys, so that the iron rattled and the prisoner drew back. 'Will you keep silence?' said the matron. 'Do you think I don't have duties enough, do you think Miss Haxby don't have business enough, that I must carry your tales to her?'

'It is only, mum,' said the woman, speaking very quickly and stumbling over the words, 'only that you said you would speak. And when Miss Haxby came this morning she was kept half her time by Jarvis, and would not see me. And my brother has brought his evidence before the courts, and wants Miss Haxby's word—'

Miss Ridley struck the gate again, and again the prisoner flinched. Mrs Jelf murmured to me: 'Here is a woman who will pester any matron that passes her cell. She is after an early release, poor thing; I should say, however, that she will be here a few years yet.—Well Sykes, will you let Miss Ridley pass?—I should step a little further down the ward, Miss Prior, or she will try and draw you into her scheme.—Now Sykes, will you be good and do your work?'

Sykes, however, still pressed her case, and Miss Ridley stood chiding her, Mrs Jelf looking on, shaking her head. I moved away, along the ward. The woman's thin petitions, the matron's scolds, were made sharp and strange by the acoustics of the gaol; every prisoner I passed had raised her head to catch them—though, when they saw me in the ward beyond their gates, they lowered their gazes and returned to their sewing. Their eyes, I thought, were terribly dull. Their faces were pale, and their necks, and their wrists and fingers, very slender. I thought of Mr Shillitoe saying that a prisoner's heart was weak, impressionable, and needed a finer mould to shape it. I thought of it, and became aware again of my own heart beating. I imagined how it would be to have that heart drawn from me, and one of those women's coarse organs pressed into the slippery cavity left at my breast . . .

I put my hand to my throat then and felt, before my pulsing heart, my locket; and then my step grew a little slower. I walked until I reached the arch that marked the angle of the ward, then moved a little way beyond it—just far enough to put the matrons from my view, but not enough to take me down the second passage. Here I put my back to the lime-washed prison wall, and I waited.

And here, after a moment, came a curious thing.

I was close to the mouth of the first of the next line of cells; near to my shoulder was its inspection flap or 'eye', above that the enamel tablet bearing the details of its inmate's sentence. It was only from this, indeed, that I knew the cell was occupied at all, for there seemed to emanate from it a marvellous stillness—a silence, that seemed deeper yet than all the restless Millbank hush surrounding it. Even as I began to wonder over it, however, the silence was broken. It was broken by a *sigh*, a single sigh—it seemed to me, a *perfect* sigh, like a sigh in a story; and the sigh being such a complement to my own mood I found it worked upon me, in that setting, rather strangely. I forgot Miss Ridley and Mrs Jelf, who might at any second come to guide me on my way. I forgot the tale of the incautious matron and the sharpened spoon. I put my fingers to the inspection slit, and then my eyes. And then I gazed at the girl in the cell beyond—she was so still, I think I held my breath for fear of startling her.

She was seated upon her wooden chair, but had let her head fall back and had her eyes quite closed. Her knitting lay idle in her lap, and her hands were together and lightly clasped; the yellow glass at her window was bright with sun, and she had turned her face to catch the heat of it. On the sleeve of her mud-coloured gown was fixed, the emblem of her prison class, a star—a star of felt, cut slant, sewn crooked, but made sharp by the sunlight. Her hair, where it showed at the edges of her cap, was fair; her cheek was pale, the sweep of brow, of lip, of lashes crisp against her pallor. I was sure that I had seen her likeness, in a saint or an angel in a painting of Crivelli's.

I studied her for, perhaps, a minute; and all that time she kept her eyes quite closed, her head perfectly still. There seemed something rather devotional about her pose, the stillness, so that I thought at last, She is praying!, and made to draw my eyes away in sudden shame. But then she stirred. Her hands opened, she raised them to her cheek, and I caught a flash of colour against the pink of her work-roughened palms. She had a flower there, between her fingers—a violet, with a drooping stem. As I watched, she put the flower to her lips, and breathed upon it, and the purple of the petals gave a quiver and seemed to glow . . .

She did that, and I became aware of the dimness of the world that was about her—of the wards, the women in them, the matrons, even my own self. We might have been painted, all of us, from the same poor box of watery tints; and here was a single spot of colour, that seemed to have come upon the canvas by mistake.

But I didn't wonder, then, about how a violet might, in that grim-earthed place, have found its way into those pale hands. I only thought, suddenly and horribly, What can her *crime* have been? Then I remembered the enamel tablet swinging near my head. I let the inspection close, quite noiselessly, and moved to read it.

There was her prison number and her class, and beneath them her offence: *Fraud & Assault.* The date of her reception was eleven months ago. The date of her release was for four years hence.

Four years! Four *Millbank* years—which must, I think, be terribly slow ones. I meant to move to her gate then, to call her to me and have her story from her; and I would have done it, had there not come at that moment, from further back along the first passage, the sound of Miss Ridley's voice, and then of her boots, grinding the sand upon the cold flags of the ward. And that made me hesitate. I thought, How would it be, if the matrons were to look at the girl as I had, and find that flower upon her? I was sure they would take it, and I knew I should be sorry if they did. So I stepped to where they would see me, and when they came I said—it was the truth, after all—that I was weary, and had viewed all I cared to view for my first visit. Miss Ridley said only, 'Just as you wish, ma'am.' She turned on her heel and took me back along the passage; and as the gate was shut upon me I looked once over my shoulder to the turning of the ward, and felt a curious feeling—half satisfaction, half sharp regret. And I thought: Well, she will still be here, poor creature! when I return next week.

The matron led me into the tower staircase, and we began our careful, circling descent to the lower, drearier wards—I felt like Dante, following Virgil into Hell. I was passed over first to Miss Manning, then to a warder, and was taken back through Pentagons Two and One; I sent a message in to Mr Shillitoe, and was led out of the inner gate and along that wedge of gravel. The walls of the pentagons seemed to part before me now, but grudgingly. The sun, that was stronger, made the bruise-coloured shadows very dense.

We walked, the warder and I, and I found myself gazing again at the bleak prison ground, with its bare black earth and its patches of sedge. I said, 'There are no flowers grown here, warder? No daisies, no—violets?'

No daisies, no violets, he answered; not even so much as a dandelion clock. They would not grow in Millbank soil, he said. It is too near the Thames, and 'as good as marshland'.

I said that I had guessed as much, and thought again about that flower. I wondered if there might be seams between the bricks that make the walls of the women's building, that a plant like that might thrust its roots through?—I cannot say.

And, after all, I did not think of it for long. The warder led me to the outer gate, and here the porter found a cab for me; and now, with the wards and the locks and the shadows and reeks of prison life behind me, it was impossible not to feel my own liberty and be grateful for it. I thought that, after all, I had been right to go there; and I was glad that Mr Shillitoe knew nothing of my history. I thought, His knowing nothing, and the women's knowing nothing, that will keep that history in its place. I imagined them fastening my own past shut, with a strap and a buckle . . .

I talked with Helen to-night. My brother brought her here, but with three or four of their friends. They were on their way to a theatre, and very brilliantly dressed—Helen conspicuous amongst them, as we were, in her gown of grey. I went down when they arrived, but didn't stay long: the crowd of voices and faces, after the chill and stillness of Millbank and of my own room, seemed awful to me. But Helen stepped aside with me, and we spoke a little about my visit. I told her about the monotonous corridors, and how nervous I had grown being led through them. I asked her if she remembered Mr Le Fanu's novel, about the heiress who is made to seem mad? I said, 'I did think for a while: Suppose Mother is in league with Mr Shillitoe, and he means to keep me on the wards, bewildered?' She smiled at that—but checked to see that Mother could not hear me. Then I told her a little about the women on the wards. She said she thought they must be frightening. I said they were not frightening at all, but only weak—'So Mr Shillitoe told me. He said I am to mould them. That is my task. They are to take a moral pattern from me.'

She studied her hands as I spoke, turning the rings upon her fingers. She said I was brave. She said she is sure this work will distract me, from 'all my old griefs'.

Then Mother called, why were we so serious and so quiet? She listened shuddering when I described the wards to her this afternoon, and said that I am not to tell the details of the gaol when we have guests. Now she said, 'You mustn't let Margaret tell you prison stories, Helen. And here is your husband waiting, look. You will be late for the play.' Helen went straight to Stephen's side, and he took her hand and kissed it. I sat and watched them; then slipped away and came up here. I thought, If I may not talk of my visit, then I can certainly sit and write about it, in my own book . . .

Now I have filled twenty pages; and when I read what I have written I see that, after all, my path through Millbank was not so crooked as I thought. It is neater, anyway, than my own twisting thoughts!—which was all I filled my last book with. This, at least, shall never be like that one.

It is half-past twelve. I can hear the maids upon the attic stairs, Cook slamming bolts—that sound will never be the same to me, I think, after to-day!

There is Boyd, closing her door, walking to draw her curtain: I may follow her movements as if my ceiling were of glass. Now she is unlacing her boots, letting them fall with a thud. Now comes the creak of her mattress.

There is the Thames, as black as molasses. There are the lights of Albert Bridge, the trees of Battersea, the starless sky . . .

Mother came, half an hour ago, to bring me my dose. I told her I should like to sit a little longer, that I wished she would leave the bottle with me so I might take it later—but no, she wouldn't do that. I am 'not quite well enough', she said. Not 'for that'. Not yet.

And so I sat and let her pour the grains into the glass, and swallowed the mixture as she watched and nodded. Now I am too tired to write—but too restless, I think, to sleep just yet.

For Miss Ridley was right to-day. When I close my eyes I see only the chill white corridors of Millbank, the mouths of the cells. I wonder how the women lie there? I think of them now—Susan Pilling, and Sykes, and Miss Haxby in her quiet tower; and the girl with the violet, whose face was so fine.

I wonder what her name is?

2 September 1872

Selina Dawes
Selina Ann Dawes
Miss S. A. Dawes

Miss S. A. Dawes, Trance Medium

Miss Selina Dawes, Celebrated Trance Medium,
Gives Séances Daily

Miss Dawes, Trance Medium,
Gives Dark Séances Daily – Vincy's Spiritual Hotel,
Lamb's Conduit Street, London WC.
Private & Pleasantly Situated.

DEATH IS DUMB, WHEN LIFE IS DEAF

& it says that, for an extra shilling, they will make it very bold & give it a border of black.

30 September 1874

Mother's injunction against my prison stories did not, after all, last long this week, for every visitor we have had has wanted to hear my descriptions of Millbank, and of the prisoners in it. What they have asked for, however, are dreadful details to make them shudder; and though my memories of the gaol have stayed very crisp, those are not at all the kind of points that I recall. I have been haunted, rather, by the *ordinariness* of it; by the fact that it lies there at all, two miles away, a straight cab's ride from Chelsea—that great, grim, shadowy place, with its fifteen hundred men and women, all shut up and obliged to be silent and meek. I have found myself remembering them, in the midst of some plain act—taking tea, because I am thirsty; taking up a book or a shawl, because I am idle or cold; saying, aloud, some line of verse, merely for the pleasure of hearing the fine words spoken. I have done these things, that I have done a thousand times; and I have remembered the prisoners, who may do none of them.

I wonder how many of them lie in their cold cells, dreaming of china cups, and books, and verses? I have dreamt of Millbank this week, more than once. I dreamt I was among the prisoners there, straightening the lines of my knife and fork and Bible, in a cell of my own.

But these are not the details people ask me for; and though they understand my going there once, as a kind of entertainment, the thought of my returning there a second time, and then a third and fourth, amazes them. Only Helen takes me seriously. 'Oh!' cry all the others, 'but you cannot mean really to *befriend* these women? They must be thieves, and—worse!'

They look at me, and then at Mother. How, they ask, can she bear to have me go there? And Mother, of course, answers then: 'Margaret does just as she pleases, she always has. I have told her, if she wants for employment there is work that she might do at home. There are her father's letters—very handsome letters—to be collected and arranged . . .'

I have said I plan to work upon the letters, in time; but that for now, I should like to try this other thing, and at least see how I do at it. I said this to Mother's friend Mrs Wallace, and she looked at me a little speculatively; I wondered then how much she knows or guesses about my illness and its causes, for she answered, 'Well, there's not a better tonic for dismal spirits than charity-work—I heard a doctor say that. But a prison ward—oh! only think of the air! The place must be a breeding-ground, for every kind of illness and disease!'

I thought again of the white monotonous passage-ways and the bare, bare cells. I said, on the contrary, the wards were very clean and orderly; and my sister said then that, if they were clean and orderly, why did the women in them need sympathy from me? Mrs Wallace smiled. She has always liked Priscilla, she thinks her more handsome even than Helen. She said, 'Perhaps *you* will think of charity-visiting, my dear, when you are married to Mr Barclay. Have they prisons, in Warwickshire? To think of your dear face amongst those convict women's—what a study *that* would make! There is an epigram for it, what is it? Margaret, *you* will know it: the poet's words, about women and heaven and hell.'

She meant:

> *For men at most differ as Heaven and Earth,*
> *But women, worst and best, as Heaven and Hell*

and when I said it she cried, There! how clever I was! If she had been put to read all the books that I had, she would have to be a thousand years old at the least.

Mother said it was certainly true, what Tennyson said about women . . .

That was this morning, when Mrs Wallace came to breakfast with us. After that she and Mother took Pris for her first sitting for a portrait. Mr Barclay has commissioned it, he wants a picture of her hanging in the drawing-room at Marishes for their arrival there after the honeymoon. He has found a man to do the work, who has a studio at Kensington. Mother asked me, Would I go and sit with them?—Pris saying that, if anyone should like to look at paintings, I should. She said it with her face before the glass, passing one gloved fingertip across her brow. She had made the brow a little darker with a pencil, for the portrait's sake, and wore a light blue gown beneath her dark coat. Mother said it might as well be blue as grey, since no-one was to see it save the artist, Mr Cornwallis.

I did not go with them. I went to Millbank, to begin my proper visits to the women in their cells.

It was not so frightening as I had thought it might be, to be led, alone, into the female gaol: I think my dreams of the prison had made its walls higher and grimmer, its passageways narrower, than they really are. Mr Shillitoe advises me to make a weekly trip there, but lets me choose the day and hour of it: he says that it will help me understand the women's lives if I see all the places and habits they must keep to. Having gone there very early last week, to-day I went later. I arrived at the gate at a quarter-to-one, and was passed over, as before, to dour Miss Ridley. I found her just about to supervise the delivery of the prison dinners; and so I walked with her, until this was completed.

It was an impressive thing to see. As I had arrived there had come a tolling of the prison bell: when the matrons of the wards hear that they must each take four women from their cells and walk with them to the prison kitchen. We found them gathered at its door when we went up to them: Miss Manning, Mrs Pretty, Mrs Jelf and twelve pale prisoners, the prisoners with their eyes upon the floor and their hands before them. The women's building has no kitchen of its own, but takes its dinners from the men's gaol. Since the male and female wards are kept quite separate, the women are obliged to wait very quietly until the men have taken their soup and the kitchen is cleared. Miss Ridley explained this to me. 'They must not see the men,' she said. 'Those are the rules.' As she spoke there came, from behind the bolted kitchen door, the slither of heavy-booted feet, and murmurs—and I had a sudden vision then of the men as *goblin* men, with snouts and tails and whiskers . . .

Then the sounds grew less, and Miss Ridley lifted her keys to give a knock upon the wood: 'All clear, Mr Lawrence?' The answer came—'All clear!'—and the door was unfastened, to let the prisoners file through. The warder-cook stood by with his arms folded, watching the women and sucking at his cheek.

The kitchen seemed vast to me, and terribly warm after the chill, dark passage. Its air was thick, the scents on it not wonderful; they have sand upon the floor, and this was dark and clogged with fallen fluid. Down the centre of the room were ranged three broad tables, and on these were placed the women's cans of soup and meat and trays of loaves. Miss Ridley waved the prisoners forward, two by two, and each seized the can or the tray for her ward, and staggered away with it. I walked back with Miss Manning's women. We found the prisoners of the ground-floor cells all ready at their gates, holding their tin mugs and their trenchers, and while the soup was ladled out the matron called a prayer—'*God-bless-our-meat-and-make-us-worthy-of-it!*' or some rough thing like that—the women seemed to me almost entirely to ignore her. They only stood very quietly and pressed their faces to their gates, in an attempt to catch the progress of their dinners down the ward. When the dinners came they turned and carried them to their tables, then daintily sprinkled salt upon them from the boxes on their shelves.

They were given a meat soup with potatoes, and a six-ounce loaf—all of it horrible: the loaves coarse and brown and over-baked as little bricks, the potatoes boiled in their skins and streaked with black. The soup was cloudy, and had a layer of grease upon the top that thickened and whitened as the cans grew cool. The meat was pale, and too gristly for the women's dull-edged knives to leave much mark upon it: I saw many prisoners tearing at their mutton with their teeth, solemn as savages.

They stood and took it readily enough, however; some only seemed to gaze rather mournfully at the soup as it was ladled out, others to finger their meat as if with suspicion. 'Don't you care for your dinner?' I asked one woman I saw handling her mutton like this. She answered that she didn't care to think whose hands might have been upon it, in the men's gaol.

'They handles filthy things,' she said, 'then jiggles their fingers in our soup, for sport . . .'

She said this two or three times, then would not talk to me. I left her mumbling into her mug, and joined the matrons at the entrance to the ward.

I talked a little with Miss Ridley then, about the women's diet and the variations that are made in it—there being always fish served on a Friday, for example, on account of the large number of Roman Catholic prisoners; and on a Sunday, suet pudding. I said, Had they any Jewesses? and she answered that there were always a number of Jewesses, and they liked to make 'a particular trouble' over the preparation of their dishes. She had encountered that sort of behaviour, amongst the Jewesses, at other prisons.

'You do find, however,' she said to me, 'that nonsense like that falls away in time. At least, in *my* gaol it does.'

When I describe Miss Ridley to my brother and to Helen, they smile. Helen said once, 'You are exaggerating, Margaret!', but Stephen shook his head. He said he sees police matrons like Miss Ridley all the time, at the courts. 'They are a horrible breed,' he said, 'born to tyranny, born with the chains already swinging at their hips. Their mothers give them iron keys to suck, to make their teeth come.'

He bared his own teeth—which are straight, like Priscilla's, where mine are rather crooked. Helen gazed at him and laughed.

I said then, 'I am not sure. Suppose she wasn't born to it, but rather sweats and labours to perfect the role. Suppose she has a secret album, cuttings from the Newgate Calendar. I am sure she has a book like that. She has put a label on it, *Notorious Prison Martinets*, and she takes it out and sighs over it, in the small dark hours of the Millbank night—like a clergyman's daughter, with a fashion paper.' That made Helen laugh louder, until her blue eyes brimmed with water and her lashes grew very dark.

But I remembered her laughter to-day, and thought of how Miss Ridley would gaze at me, if she knew how I used her to make my sister-in-law smile—the thought made me shudder. For on the wards at Millbank, of course, Miss Ridley is not comical at all.

Then again, I suppose that the matrons' lives—even hers, even Miss Haxby's—must be very miserable. They are kept as close to the gaol, almost, as if they were inmates there themselves. Their hours, Miss Manning assured me to-day, are the hours of scullery-maids: they are given rooms in the prison in which to rest, but are often too exhausted from their day's patrolling of the wards to do anything in their leisure time but fall upon their beds and sleep. Their meals are prepared in the prison kitchen, just like the women's; and their duties are hard ones. 'You ask to see Miss Craven's arm,' they said to me. 'She is bruised from her shoulder to her wrist, where a girl caught her a blow, last week, in the prison laundry.' But Miss Craven herself, when I did encounter her a little later, seemed almost as coarse as the women she must guard. They were all 'as rough as rats', she said, and she was disgusted with the sight of them. When I asked her would the work ever be so hard as to drive her to some other occupation? she looked bitter. 'I should like to know,' she said, 'what else I am fit for, after eleven years at Millbank!' No, she will be walking the wards, she supposes, until she drops down dead.

Only Mrs Jelf, the matron of the highest wards, seems to me to be really kind, and half-way gentle. She is desperately pale and careworn, might be any age between twenty-five and forty; but she had no complaint to make of prison life, except to say that many of the stories she must hear, upon the wards, were very tragic.

I went up to her floor at the end of the dinner-hour, just as the bell was sounding that sends the women back to their work. I said, 'I must begin really to be a Visitor to-day, Mrs Jelf, and I hope you will help me do it, for I am rather nervous.' I should never have admitted such a thing at Cheyne Walk.

She said, 'I will be happy to advise you, miss', and she took me to a prisoner she said she knew would be glad to have me go to her. This proved to be an elderly woman—the oldest woman in the gaol, indeed—a Star-Class prisoner named Ellen Power. When I went into her cell she rose, and offered me her chair. I said of course that she must keep it, but she would not sit before me—in the end both of us stood. Mrs Jelf watched us, then stepped away and nodded. 'I must lock the gate on you, miss,' she said cheerfully. 'But when you are ready to move on, you must call me.' She said a matron can hear a calling woman, wherever she is upon the ward. Then she turned and drew closed the gate behind her; and then she fastened it, I stood and watched the key turn in the lock.

I remembered then that it was she who had had the keeping of me in my frightening dreams of Millbank, last week.

When I gazed at Power, I found her smiling. She has been three years at the gaol, and is due for release in four months' time; she was imprisoned there for managing a bawdy-house. When she told me this, however, she tossed her head. 'Bawdy-house!' she said. 'It was a parlour only; boys and girls would sometimes like to come and kiss in it, that's all. Why, I had my own grand-daughter running in and out of there, keeping it tidy, and there was always flowers, fresh flowers in a vase. Bawdy-house! The boys must have somewhere to take their sweethearts, mustn't they?—else, they must kiss them in the very road. And if they was to hand me a shilling when they went out, for the kindness, and the flowers—well, is *that* a crime?'

It didn't sound like much of one, when put like that; but I remembered all the matrons' cautions, and said that sentencing of course was something I could have no opinion on. She lifted her hand, which I saw was very swollen at the knuckle. She answered: Yes, she knew it. It was 'a subject for the men'.

I stayed with her for half an hour. Once or twice she drew me back again towards the niceties of bawdiness; at last, however, I nudged her to less controversial topics. I remembered drab Susan Pilling, the prisoner I had spoken with on Miss Manning's ward. How, I asked Power, did *she* like Millbank routines, and the Millbank costume? She looked thoughtful for a second, then tossed her head. 'The routines I cannot answer for,' she said, 'as never having been inside another gaol; but I imagine they are harsh enough—you may write that down' (I had my note-book with me), 'I don't care who reads that. The costume, I will say right out, is very nasty.' She said it bothers her that they send their suits to the prison laundry, and never get the same set back a second time—'and some come very stained, miss, yet we must wear them or go cold. Then again, the flannel under-things are awful *rough*, and tend to scratch; and they are that washed and beaten that they ain't like flannel at all, but like some awful thin stuff, what don't *warm* you but, as I say, only makes you *scratch*. The shoes I have no quarrel with; but the want of stays, if you'll pardon my saying it, is a trial to some of the younger women. It don't bother an aged creature like me so much, but the little girls—well I should say they do feel the want of stays, miss, rather bad . . .'

She went on like this, and seemed to like to talk to me; and yet, too, talking was troublesome to her. Her speech was halting. She sometimes hesitated, and often licked her lips or passed her hand across them, and sometimes coughed. I thought at first that she did this out of some sort of consideration to me—who stood before her, now and then setting her conversation down, long-hand, upon the pages of my book. But then, the pauses came so queerly, and I thought again of Susan Pilling, who had also stammered and coughed and seemed to grope for ordinary words, and whom I had guessed to be only rather simple-minded . . . At last, as I moved to the gate and wished Power farewell, and as she again stumbled over some common word of blessing, she placed her swollen hand against her cheek and shook her head.

'What a foolish old creature you must think me,' she said.

'You must think me hardly able to say my own name! Mr Power used fairly to curse my tongue—said it was quicker than a whippet with the scent of a hare. He'd smile to see me now, miss, wouldn't he? So many hours, and not a soul to speak to. Sometimes you wonder if your tongue ain't shrunk up or dropped clean off. Sometimes you *do* fear you will forget your own name.'

She smiled, but her eyes had begun to gleam, and her gaze was miserable. I hesitated—then said that she would think *me* foolish, for not guessing that the silence and the solitude were so hard. 'When you are like me,' I said, 'you seem to hear nothing about you but chatter. You are glad to be able to go to your own room and say nothing.'

She said at once that I must go *there* more often, if I wanted to say nothing! I told her I would certainly go to her, if she wished it; and that then she must talk to me for as long as it suited her. She smiled again, and again she blessed me. 'I shall watch out for your coming, miss,' she said as Mrs Jelf unlocked the gate. 'Let it be soon!'

I visited another prisoner, then, and again the matron picked her out for me, saying quietly, 'This is a poor sad girl I am very afraid for, as finding the habits of the prison very hard.' This girl *was* sad, and trembled when I went in to her. She is named Mary Ann Cook, and has been sent to Millbank, for seven years, for murdering her baby. She is not yet twenty, was put in there at sixteen, may have been handsome once but is now so white and wasted you would not recognise her for a girl at all, it is as if the pale prison walls have leached the life and colour from her and made her drab. When I asked her to tell me her history she did so dully, as if she has told it so many times before—to the matrons, to Visitors, perhaps only to herself—that the telling has made a kind of story of it, realer than memory but meaning nothing. I wished I could tell her that I know what such a story feels like.

She said she had been born to a Catholic family, that her mother had died and her father remarried; and that then she had been put to work as a maid, with her sister, in a very grand house. There, she said, were a lady and a gentleman and three daughters, who were all very kind, but there was also a son—'and he, miss, was not kind. While he was a boy he used only to tease us—he used to listen at our door while we lay in our bed, and call into us, to frighten us. We didn't mind that; and soon he went to school, and we saw him hardly at all. But after a year or two he came back, quite changed—as big as his father, nearly, and slyer than ever . . .' She claims he pressed her into meeting him in secret, offered to set her up in a room as his mistress—she wouldn't have that. Then she found that he had begun to offer money to her sister and so, 'to save the younger girl', she had submitted to him; and soon she found herself with child. She left her place then—says that, after all, her sister turned against her for the sake of the young man. She went to a brother, whose wife would not take her, and was confined in a charity-ward. 'My baby came, but I never loved her. She looked so like *him*! I wished she would die.' She took the baby to a church, and asked the priest to bless it; when the priest would not, she says she blessed it herself—'We may do that,' she said modestly, 'in our Church.' She took a room, passing herself off as a single girl, hiding the baby in her shawl to stop its cries; but the shawl fell too close about the baby's face, and killed it. Her landlady found the little body. Cook had placed it behind a curtain, and it had lain there for a week.

'I wished she would die,' she said again to me, 'but I never murdered her, and when she was dead, I was sorry. They found the priest I went to and made him speak against me at my trial. It looked then, you see, as if I had meant to harm my baby from the start . . .'

'A terrible story, that one,' I said to the matron who released me from her cell. This was not Mrs Jelf—who had been obliged to chaperon some prisoner to Miss Haxby's office—but Miss Craven, the coarse-faced matron with the bruised arm. She had come to the gate when I called, and gazed at Cook, and Cook had gone meekly back to her sewing and lowered her head. Now, as we walked, she said briskly that she supposed some people might call it terrible. The prisoners that were like Cook, however, and hurt their own little children—well, she never wasted her tears on *them*.

I said that Cook seemed very young; but that Miss Haxby had told me that sometimes they had girls, in the cells, that were little more than children?

She nodded: They had, and that *was* a sight. They had had one there once that used to weep every night for the first two weeks, for her dolly. It was cruel to have to walk the wards and hear her. 'And yet,' she added, laughing, 'she was a demon when the mood was on her. And her tongue—what a foul one! You would never hear such words as that little creature knew, not even on the men's wards.'

Still she laughed. I looked away from her. We had walked almost the length of one whole passage, and ahead of us was the archway that led to one of the towers. Beyond that was the dark edge of a gate, and now I recognised it. It was the gate at which I stood last week, the gate to the cell of the girl with the violet.

I slowed my step, and spoke very quietly. There was a prisoner, I said, in the first cell of the second passage. A fair-haired girl, quite young, quite handsome. What did Miss Craven know of her?

The matron's face had grown sour when talking of Cook. Now it grew sour again. 'Selina Dawes,' she said. 'A queer one. Keeps her eyes and her mind to herself—that's all I know. I've heard her called the easiest prisoner in the gaol. They say she has never given an hour's trouble since she was brought here. Deep, I call her.'

Deep?

'As the ocean.'

I nodded, remembering a comment of Mrs Jelf's. Perhaps Dawes, I said, was something of a lady? That made Miss Craven laugh: 'She has a lady's ways, all right! Yet none of the matrons, I think, much care for her, excepting Mrs Jelf—but then, Mrs Jelf is soft, and has a kind word for everyone; and none of the women will have much to do with her, either. This is a place for "palling up", as the creatures call it; yet no-one has made a pal of *her*. I believe they are leery of her.

Someone got her story from the newspapers, and passed it on—stories *will* get passed, you see, for all our pains! And then, the wards at night—the women fancy all kinds of nonsense. Someone gives a shriek, says she has heard queer sounds from Dawes's cell—'

Sounds . . .?

'Spooks, miss! The girl is a—a spirit-medium they call them, don't they?'

I stopped, and gazed at her, in surprise and also a kind of dismay. I said, a spirit-medium! And then, again: a spirit-medium—and there, in gaol! What was her crime? Why had they got her there?

Miss Craven shrugged. A lady, she thought, had been harmed by her—also a girl; and one of them afterwards had died. The harming, however, had been of a peculiar sort. They hadn't been able to make it out as murder, only as assault. She had heard, indeed, as the charge against Dawes was all trumped-up nonsense, all put together by a clever barrister . . .

'But there,' she added with a snort, 'you *do* hear that, at Millbank.'

I said that I supposed you did. We had begun to walk again along the passage, and as we rounded the angle of it I saw the girl—Dawes—herself. She was seated, as before, with the sun upon her, but this time her eyes were lowered to her lap, where she was teasing a single thread from a tangle of wool.

I looked at Miss Craven. I said, 'Might I, do you think—?'

The sun grew brighter as I stepped into the cell, and after the shadowy monotony of the passage-way its whitewashed walls were dazzling, and made me put my fingers to my brow, and blink. It took me a moment, then, to realise that Dawes had not stood and curtseyed, as all the other women had; nor had she set her work aside, nor did she smile, or speak. She only raised her eyes to gaze at me in a kind of patient curiosity—her fingers all the time plucking slowly at the ball of yarn, as if the coarse wool was a rosary and she was telling off the beads.

When Miss Craven had fastened the gate on us and moved away I said, 'Your name is Dawes, I think. How do you do, Dawes?'

She did not answer, only stared at me. Her features are not quite so regular as I thought them last week, but have a slight want of symmetry—a little tilt—about the brows and lips. One notices the faces of the women of the gaol, because the gowns are so dull and so regular, and the caps so close-fitting. One notices the faces, and the hands. Dawes's hands are slender, but rough and red. Her nails are split, and have spots of white upon them.

Still she did not speak. Her pose was so still, her gaze so unflinching, I wondered for a moment if she might not after all be simple, or dumb. I said I hoped she would be glad to talk with me a little; that I had come to Millbank to make friends of all the women . . .

My voice sounded loud to me. I imagined it carrying across the silent ward, saw the prisoners pausing in their work, lifting their heads, perhaps smiling. I think I turned from her, to her window, and gestured to the light that glanced from her white bonnet and from the crooked star upon her sleeve. I said, 'You like to have the sun upon you.'—'I may work,' she answered quickly then, 'and feel the sunlight too, I hope? I may have my bit of sunshine? God knows, there is little enough of it!'

There was a passion to her voice that made me blink, then hesitate. I looked about me. Her walls were not so dazzling now, and even as I looked I seemed to see the patch of light in which she sat grow smaller, the cell grow greyer and more chill. The sun, of course, was edging on its cruel way, away past Millbank's towers. She must watch it do so, fixed and mute as the post on a sun-dial, earlier and earlier each day as the year moves on. One whole half of the gaol, indeed, from January to December must be dark as the far portion of the moon.

I felt awkward, realising this, standing before her while she sat still pulling at her wool. I moved to her folded hammock and placed my hand upon it. She said then, that if I was only handling that for curiosity's sake, she would rather I handled something else, perhaps her trencher or her mug. They must keep the bed and blankets in prison folds. She said she wouldn't like to have to fold them all again, after I had left her.

I drew my hand away at once. 'Of course,' I said again. And: 'I am sorry.' She lowered her eyes to her wooden needles. When I asked, what was she working at? she showed me, listlessly, the putty-coloured knitting in her lap. 'Stockings for soldiers,' she said. Her accent is good. When she stumbled over a word—which she did, sometimes, yet not quite as often as Ellen Power or Cook—I found myself flinching.

I said next, 'You have been here a year, I think?—You may stop your knitting while you talk to me, you know: Miss Haxby has allowed it.' She let the wool fall, but still gently teased it. 'You have been here a year. What do you make of it?'

'What do I make of it?' The tilt to her lips grew steeper. She gazed about her for a second, and then she said: 'What would *you* make of it, do you think?'

The question took me by surprise—it surprises me again, when I think of it now!—and made me hesitate. I remembered my interview with Miss Haxby. I said that I should find Millbank a very hard place, but I should also know I had done wrong. I might be glad to be so much alone, to think on how sorry I was. I might make plans.

Plans?

'To be better.'

She looked away, and made no answer; and I found that I was rather glad of it, for my words had sounded hollow, even to my own ears. A few dull gold curls showed at the nape of her neck—her hair, I think, must be paler even than Helen's, and would be very handsome if properly washed and dressed. The patch of sun grew bright again, yet still inched on its remorseless way, like a counterpane sliding from a chill and troubled sleeper. I saw her feel its warmth upon her face and raise her head to it. I said, 'Won't you talk a little to me? You might find it a comfort.'

She did not answer until the square of sun had faded. Then she turned, and studied me a moment in silence, then said, that she didn't need *me* to comfort her. She said she had 'her own comforts' there. Besides, why should she tell me anything? What would I ever tell her, about my life?

She had tried to make her voice hard, but had not managed it, it had begun to tremble; and the effect was not of insolence but of bravado and, behind it, plain despair. I thought, If I were to be gentle with you now, you would weep—I did not want to have her weep before me. I made my own voice very brisk. I said, Well, there was a variety of things I was forbidden, by Miss Haxby, to discuss with her; but so far as I knew, myself was not one of them. I would tell her any little detail she cared to hear . . .

I told her my name; and that I lived at Chelsea, at Cheyne Walk. I said, I had a brother that was married, and a sister who would be married very soon; that I was not married. I told her I sleep badly, and spend many hours reading, or writing, or standing at my window looking out upon the river. Then I pretended to consider. What else was there?—'I think you have it all. There is not much . . .'

She had been blinking at me. Now, at last, she turned her face away and smiled. Her teeth are even, and very white—'parsnip white', as Michelangelo has it; but her lips are rough and bitten. She began to talk with me, then, more naturally. She asked me, how long had I been a Lady Visitor? And, why did I want to do it? Why did I want to come to Millbank, when I might stay idle in my house at Chelsea . . .?

I said, 'You think ladies should stay idle, then?'

She would stay idle, she said, if she was like me.

'Oh,' I said then, 'you would not, not if you were really like me!'

My words made her blink: they had sounded louder than I meant them. She had let her knitting fall at last, and sat carefully watching me; and I wished, then, that she would turn her head, for her gaze was very still and somehow unsettling. I said, the truth of it was, idleness did not suit me. I had been idle for two years—so idle, indeed, that I had grown 'quite ill' with it. 'It was Mr Shillitoe suggested I come here,' I said. 'He is an old friend of my father's. He came to visit at my house, and spoke of Millbank. He spoke of the system here, of Lady Visitors. I thought—'

What had I thought? With her eyes upon me I did not know. I looked away from her, but still felt her watching. And then she said, quite evenly, 'You have come to Millbank, to look on women more wretched than yourself, in the hope that it will make you well again.'—I remember the words very clearly, because they were so gross, and yet came so close to the truth, that I heard them and blushed. 'Well,' she went on, 'you may look at me, I am wretched enough. All the world may look at me, it is part of my punishment.' She had grown proud again. I said something to the effect that I hoped my visits might serve to ease the harshness of her punishment, not add to it; and she answered at once—as she had before—that she didn't need *me* to comfort her. That she had many friends, who came to comfort her whenever she required it.

I stared at her. 'You have friends,' I said, 'here?' She closed her eyes, and made a theatrical kind of pass at the front of her brow. 'I have friends, Miss Prior,' she answered, '*here*.'

I had forgotten about this. Now, remembering it, I felt my cheek grew cool again. She sat with her eyes quite shut; I think I waited until she had opened them and then I said, 'You are a spiritualist. Miss Craven told me as much.' Here she tilted her head a little. I said, 'So, the friends that visit you, they are—spirit-friends?' She nodded. 'And they come to you—when?'

There are spirit-friends about us always, she said.

'Always?' I think I smiled. 'Even now? Even here?'

Even now. Even there. They only 'did not choose to show themselves,' she said; or perhaps 'had not the power . . .'

I looked about me. I remembered the suicide—Jane Samson—on Mrs Pretty's ward, her air turned thick with swirling motes of coir. Is that how Dawes believes her cell to be—teeming, like that, with spirits? I said, 'But your friends find the power, when they wish to?'—She said they draw it from her. 'And then you see them, quite plainly?' She said sometimes they only speak. 'Sometimes I only hear the words, here.' Again she placed a hand upon her brow.

I said, 'They visit you, perhaps, when you are working?'—She shook her head. She said they come when the wards are quiet and she is at rest.

'And they are kind to you?'

She nodded: 'Very kind. They bring me gifts.'

'Really.' Now I certainly smiled. I said, 'They bring you gifts. Spirit-gifts?'

Spirit-gifts—she shrugged. Earth-gifts . . .

Earth gifts! Such as . . .?

'Such as, flowers,' she said. 'Sometimes a rose. Sometimes, a violet—'

She said that, and a gate slammed somewhere on the ward, and I jumped, though she stayed steady. She had watched me smile, and only gazed levelly at me; and she had spoken simply, almost carelessly, as if it was nothing to her what I thought of her claims. Now, with that one word, she might have put a pin to me—I blinked, and felt my face grow stiff. How could I say that I had stood and studied her, all secretly, and seen her hold a flower to her mouth? I had tried to account for that flower then, and could not; I believe I quite forgot it between last week and to-day. I looked away from her, saying, 'Well—', and then, again, 'Well—', and finally, with a ghastly kind of sham jollity, 'Well, let us hope Miss Haxby does not hear about your visitors! She will think it hardly a punishment, if you are here, receiving guests—'

Not a punishment? she answered quietly then. Did I think that anything could make her punishment less? Did I think that, who had a lady's life, and had seen how they must live there, how they must work, what they must wear, and eat? 'To have the matron's eye,' she said, 'forever on you—closer, closer than wax! To be forever in need of water and of soap. To forget words, common words, because your habits are so narrow you need only know a hundred hard phrases—*stone, soup, comb, Bible, needle, dark, prisoner, walk, stand still, look sharp, look sharp!* To lie sleepless—not as I should say *you* lie sleepless, in your bed with a fire by it, with your family and your—your servants, close about you. But to lie aching with cold—to hear a woman shrieking in a cell two floors below, because she has the nightmares, or the drunkard's horrors, or is new, and screams because—because she cannot believe that they have taken her hair off and put her in a room, and locked the door on her!' Did I think there was anything that could make her bear that better? Did I think it not a punishment, because a spirit sometimes came to her—came and put its lips to hers, then melted away before the kiss was done, and left her, with the very darkness darker than before?

The words seem still very vivid to me; and I seem still to hear her own voice, hissing them, and stumbling over them—for of course, she would not shout or shriek, for fear of the matron, but smothered her passion so that only I might catch it. I did not smile now. I could not answer her. I believe I turned my shoulder to her and gazed out, through the iron gate, at the smooth, blank, limewashed wall.

Then I heard her step. She had risen from her chair and was beside me and—I think—had raised her hand to touch me.

But when I moved away, nearer to the gate, her hand fell.

I said I had not meant my visit to upset her. I said that the other women I had spoken with were perhaps less thoughtful than her, or had been hardened by their lives outside.

She said: 'I am sorry.'

'You must not be *sorry*.' How grotesque it would be, if she were really *sorry*! 'But if you would prefer for me to leave—?' She said nothing, and I must have continued to gaze into the darkening passage-way, until at last I knew she would not speak again. Then I gripped the bars and called out for the matron.

It was Mrs Jelf who came. She gazed at me, then past me; I heard Dawes sit, and when I looked at her she had taken up her ball of yarn again and was pulling at it. I said, 'Good-bye.' She did not answer. Only as the matron locked the gate did she raise her head, and I saw her slim throat working. She called, 'Miss Prior,' and looked once at Mrs Jelf. Then: 'We none of us sleep soundly here,' she murmured. 'Think of us, will you, the next time you are wakeful?'

And her cheek, which had been pale as alabaster all this time, flushed pink. I said, 'I will, Dawes. I will.'

Beside me, the matron put her hand upon my arm. 'Will you come down the ward, miss?' she said. 'Can I show you Nash, or Hamer—or Chaplin, our poisoner?'

But I did not visit any more women then. I left the wards, and let myself be taken to the men's gaol.

There, by chance, I met Mr Shillitoe. 'How do you find us?' he asked.

I said that the matrons had been kind to me; and that one or two of the prisoners had seemed glad to have me go to them.

'Of course,' he said. 'And they received you well? What did they talk of?'

I said, of their own thoughts and feelings.

He nodded. 'That is good! For you must, of course, secure their confidence. You must let them see that you respect them in their station, in order to encourage them to respect you, in yours.'

I gazed at him. I still felt unnerved, from my interview with Selina Dawes. I said I was not sure. I said, 'Perhaps, after all, I have not the knowledge or the temperament that a Visitor should . . .?'

Knowledge? he said then. I had a knowledge of human nature; and that was all the knowledge that was required of me there! Did I think his officers more knowledgeable than myself? Did I think their temperaments more sympathetic, than mine?

I thought of rough Miss Craven, and how Dawes had had to hide her passion for fear of her scolds. I said, 'But there are some women, I think—some troubled women—'

There were always those, he said, at Millbank! But, did I know, it was often the most troublesome prisoners who responded best, at the last, to ladies' interest; because the troublesome prisoners were frequently the most susceptible. If I encounter a difficult woman, he said, I must 'make her my special object'. It will be she, in all the gaol, who will require a lady's attentions most . . .

He had misunderstood me; but I could not talk further with him then, for as he spoke a warder came, to call him away. There was a party of ladies and gentlemen just arrived, that he must guide across the prison. I saw them gathered on the slip of gravelled earth beyond the gate. The men had stepped to one of the pentagon walls and were studying its yellow bricks and mortar.

The day, after the closeness of the women's wards, seemed pure to me, as it seemed pure last week. The sun had slipped beyond the windows of the women's block, but was still high enough to make the afternoon a fine one. When the porter made to step into the road beyond the outer gate and whistle me a cab, I stopped him, and I crossed to the embankment wall. I had heard that there is still the pier there from which the prison ships took convicts to the colonies, and I went to look at it. It is a wooden jetty, with a dark, barred arch at the back of it: the arch leads to an underground passage, which connects the pier to the prison. I stood a while and imagined those ships, and how it must have been for the women who were confined in them; then, still thinking of them—and thinking again of Dawes, and Power and Cook—then I began to walk. I walked the length of the embankment, and only paused again before the house, where there was a man fishing in the water with a hook and line. He had two slim fish strung from a buckle at his waist, and their scales were silver in the sunlight, their mouths very pink.

I walked, because I guessed that Mother would still be busy with Pris. When I went home, however, I found that she was not out as I had supposed, but had been back for an hour, and had been watching me. How long was it, she wanted to know, that I had been going about the city on foot? She had been about to send Ellis over for me.

I had been a little moodish with her, earlier; I was determined not to be moodish now. I said, 'I'm sorry, Mother.' Then, as penance, I sat and let Priscilla tell me about her hours with Mr Cornwallis. She showed me again her blue gown, and how she is posed for the sake of the portrait—she sits as a young girl awaiting her lover, clasping flowers and with her face turned to the light. She said that Mr Cornwallis gives her paintbrushes to hold; but they will be lilies, in the final picture—I thought of Dawes then, and those peculiar violets. 'The lilies and the background are to be done,' she said, 'while we are abroad . . .'

Then she told me where they are going. To *Italy*. She said it without a hint of self-consciousness; it's nothing to her, I suppose, what Italy might once have been to me. But when I heard it, I thought my penance was certainly complete. I left her, and only went down again when Ellis struck the supper-bell.

Cook, however, had sent up mutton. It arrived at table rather chill, and with a film of grease upon it; I looked at it, and remembered the sour-smelling soup at Millbank, and how the women were suspicious of the unclean hands through which it had passed, and I had no appetite for it. I left the table early, and spent an hour looking through the books and prints in Pa's room, and then another hour here, watching the traffic on the Walk. I saw Mr Barclay come for Pris, swinging his cane. He paused for a moment at the steps and put his fingers to a leaf to make them damp, then smoothed his moustache. He didn't know I stood at my high window, gazing at him. After that I read a little, and then I wrote in here.

Now my room is very dark, my reading-lamp the only light in it; but the glow of the wick is taken up by a dozen gleaming surfaces, and if I was to turn my head I would see my own face, lean and yellow, in the glass upon the chimney-breast. I do not turn. I look instead at the wall here, where to-night, beside the plan of Millbank, I pinned a print. I found it in Pa's study, in an album from the Uffizi: it is the Crivelli picture I thought of when I first saw Selina Dawes—except, it is not an angel, as I seemed to remember it, but his late *Veritas*. A stern and melancholy girl she is—she carries the sun in the form of a blazing disk, and a looking-glass. I brought it up, and shall keep it here. Why shouldn't I? It is handsome.

30 September 1872

Miss Gordon, for a queer pain. Mother to spirit May '71, *heart.* 2/-

Mrs Caine, for her child Patricia – P*ixie* – lived 9 weeks, to spirit Feb '70. 3/-

Mrs Bruce & Miss Alexandra Bruce. Father to spirit Jan, stomach. I*s there a later will*? 2/-

Mrs Lewis (*not* Mrs Jane Lewis, crippled son, Clerkenwell) – This lady did not come for me, but Mr Vincy brought her up, saying he had gone a little way with her but modesty forbade he should go further, besides he had another lady waiting. When she saw me she said 'O! How young she is!' – 'But quite a star,' said Mr Vincy at once, 'quite a rising star in our profession, I assure you.' We sat for half an hour, her sorrow being –

That at every night at 3 o'clock she is woken by a spirit who comes & puts his hand upon the flesh above her heart. She never sees the spirit's face, only feels the cold ends of his fingers. He has come so often she said the fingers have left marks on her, it was these she had not liked to show to Mr Vincy. I said 'But you may show them to me', & she put her gown back & there they were, plain as day, 5 marks red as boils but flat, not raised or weeping. I looked at them for a long time, then I said 'Well it is perfectly clear, isn't it, that it is your heart he wants? Can you think of any reason why a spirit would come for your heart?' She said 'I cannot think of any reason, I only want it to go away. My husband sleeps beside me in the bed & I am afraid when the spirit comes that it will wake him', she has been married only 4 months. I looked hard at her & said 'Take my hand & tell me truly now, you know very well who this spirit is & why he comes.'

Of course, she did know him, it was a boy she said she would marry once, & when she threw him over for another he went to

India & died there. She told me this, weeping. She said 'But do you really think it can be he?' I said she ought only to find out the hour he died at. I said 'I will lay my life that it will prove to be 3 in the morning by an English clock.' I said sometimes a spirit might have all the freedoms of the other world, yet still be a prisoner of the passing of the hour it died by.

Then I put my hand over the marks above her heart. I said 'He had a name for you, what was it?' She said it was Dolly. I said 'Yes, now I see him, he is a gentle-looking boy & he is weeping. He is showing me his hand & your heart is in it, I can see Dolly written on it quite plain, but the letters are black as tar. He is kept in a very dark place by his yearning for you. He wishes to move on, but your heart is like a piece of lead holding him down.' She said 'What must I do, Miss Dawes, what must I do?' I said 'Well, you gave your heart to him, you shouldn't weep now because he wants to keep it. But we must persuade him to let go. Until we can do that however, I think that every time your husband kisses you the spirit of this boy will come between your mouths. He will be trying to steal your kisses for himself.' I said I will work to see if I can't loosen his hold a little. She is to come back Weds. She said 'What can I pay you for this?' & I told her that if she cared to leave a coin she ought to leave it for Mr Vincy, since she was more properly his lady than mine. I said 'In this sort of establishment, where there is more than one medium practising, we must you know be very honest.'

When she had gone however, Mr, Vincy came to the door & gave me the money she had left. He said 'Well, Miss Dawes, you must have impressed her. Look what she has paid, a whole *shiner*.' He put the money in my hand. It was very warm from his own hand, & as he gave it to me he laughed, saying it was a *hot one*. I said he ought not to give me the money, since Mrs Lewis had really been his. He said 'But you, Miss Dawes, being up here all alone & having no-one, you make a man remember his gentlemanly responsibilities.' He still held my hand, that had the coin in it. When I tried to take it from him he held it tighter, saying 'Did she show you the marks?' I said then that I thought I heard Mrs Vincy in the passage.

When he went I put the coin into my box, & the day passed very dull.

4 October 1872

To a house at Farringdon, for a lady Miss Wilson – brother to spirit '58, *fell in a fit & choked.* 3/-

H*ere*, Mrs Partridge – 5 infants to spirit, namely Amy, Elsie, Patrick, John, James, none of which lived in this world longer than a day. This lady came wearing a black lace veil, which I made her put back. I said 'I see your babies' faces close to your throat. You are wearing their shining faces like a necklace, & don't know it.' The necklace had a space in it however, there was room on the thread for 2 more jewels. When I saw that, I dropped the veil about her again, saying 'You must be very brave' –

I grew sad, working with that lady. After her, I told them downstairs to say I was too tired for any more, & I have kept to my own room. It is 10 o'clock. Mrs Vincy has gone to bed. Mr Cutler, who has the room below this, is exercising with a weight, & Miss Sibree is singing. Mr Vincy came once, I heard his feet upon the landing & the sound of his breaths outside my door. He stood breathing there for 5 minutes. When I called 'Mr Vincy, what do you want?' he said that he had come to look at the carpet on the stairs, since he was afraid it was loose & might catch my toe & trip me. He said a landlord must do that sort of work, even at 10 o'clock at night.

When he went I put a stocking in my key-hole.

Then I sat & thought of Aunty, who tomorrow will be dead 4 months.

2 October 1874

We have had rain for three days—a cold, miserable rain, that turns the surface of the river rough and dark, like crocodile-skin, and makes the barges roll and bob so restlessly upon it, it tires me to watch them. I am sitting with a rug about me, and wear an old silk bonnet of Pa's. From somewhere in the house comes Mother's voice, raised, scolding Ellis—I should say Ellis has dropped a cup or spilled water. Now there is the banging of a door, and the whistles of the parrot.

The parrot is Priscilla's, and was got for her by Mr Barclay. It sits in the drawing-room on a bamboo perch. Mr Barclay is training it to say Priscilla's name; so far, however, it will only whistle.

We are a discontented house to-day. The rain has made the kitchen flood, and there are leaks in the attics; worst of all, our girl, Boyd, has given us her week's warning, and Mother is raging at the prospect of having to engage another maid, so close to Prissy's wedding-day. It is a curious thing. We all supposed Boyd content enough, she has been with us for three years; but yesterday she went to Mother and said she had found out another situation and would be leaving in a week. She wouldn't look at Mother as she spoke—told her some story, though Mother saw through it—and when she was pressed, she broke out in a passion of weeping. She said then that the truth was, the house when she is alone in it has begun to frighten her. She said it has 'turned peculiar' since Pa died, and his empty study, that she must clean, gives her the horrors. She said she cannot sleep at night, for hearing creaks and other sounds she cannot account for—once, she said, she heard a whispering voice, saying her name! She says there have been many times when she has lain awake, frightened to death, too frightened even to creep from her own room to Ellis's; and the result of it is, she is sorry to be leaving us but her nerves are shattered, she has found out a new place in a house at Maida Vale.

Mother said she never heard such nonsense in her life.

'Ghosts!' she said to us. 'To think of ghosts, in this house! To think of your poor father's memory being sullied, like that, by a creature like Boyd.'

Priscilla said she did think it rather queer that, if Pa's ghost should walk anywhere, it should be in the tweeny's attic. She said, 'You sit very late, Margaret. Have you heard nothing?'

I said that I had heard Boyd snoring; and that where I had thought her only sleeping she might, after all, have been snoring in fear . . .

Mother said then, she was glad I found it comical. There was nothing comical about the task she had now, getting another girl and training her up!

Then she sent for Boyd again, to bully her a little more.

The rain having kept us all so close at home, the argument has dragged miserably on. This afternoon I could not bear it any longer and, despite the weather, I drove to Bloomsbury—I went to the reading-room at the British Museum. I called up Mayhew's book on the prisons of London, and the writings on Newgate of Elizabeth Fry, and one or two volumes recommended to me by Mr Shillitoe. A man who stepped to help me carry them said, Why was it that the gentlest readers invariably ordered such brutes of books? He held the volumes up to read their spines, and smiled at them.

It made me ache a little with the loss of Pa, to be there. The reading-room is very unchanged. I saw readers I last saw two years ago, still clutching the same limp folio of papers, still squinting over the same dull books, still fighting the same small, bitter battles with the same disobliging staff. The gentleman who sucks his beard; the gentleman who chuckles; the lady copying Chinese characters, who scowls when her neighbours murmur . . . They were all there still, in their old places beneath the dome—like flies, I thought, in a paperweight of amber.

I wonder, did anyone remember me? Only one librarian gave any sign of it. 'This is Mr George Prior's daughter,' he said to a younger attendant as I stood at his window. 'Miss Prior and her father were readers here for several years—why, I seem to see the old gentleman now, asking after his books. Miss Prior was assistant to her father while he worked on his study of the Renaissance.' The attendant said he had seen the work.

The others, who do not know me, call me 'madam' now, I noticed, instead of 'miss'. I have turned, in two years, from a girl into a spinster.

There were many spinsters there to-day, I think—more, certainly, than I remember. Perhaps, however, it is the same with spinsters as with ghosts; and one has to be of their ranks in order to see them at all.

I didn't stay many hours there, but was restless—and, besides that, the rain made the light very poor. But I did not want to come home, to Mother and to Boyd. I took a cab to Garden Court, on the chance that the weather would have kept Helen there, alone. It had: she had had no visitors since yesterday, but was sitting making toast before the fire, feeding the crusts of it to Georgy. She said to him when I went in, 'Here is your Aunt Margaret, look!' and she held him to me, and he braced his legs against my stomach and kicked. I said, 'Well, what great fat handsome ankles you have,' and then, 'What a great red crimson cheek.' But Helen said his cheek was only crimson because of a new tooth, that hurt him. After a little time in my lap he began to cry, and then she passed him to his nurse, who took him away.

I told her about Boyd and the ghosts; and then we talked of Pris and Arthur. Did she know they mean to honeymoon in Italy?—I think she had known it for longer than I, but would not admit to it. She said only, that anyone might go to Italy if they liked. She said, 'Would you have everyone stop at the Alps, because you were meant to go to Italy once, and were kept from it? Don't make Priscilla miserable over this. Your father was her father too. Do you think it hasn't been hard for her, to have to hold her wedding off?'

I said that I remembered how Priscilla had cried herself into a fit when Pa was first found to be ill—that was because she had had a dozen new gowns made, that must be all returned and sent back black. When I wept, I asked her, what did they do with me?

She answered, not looking at me, that when I had wept it had been different. She said, 'Priscilla was nineteen, and very ordinary. She has had two hard years. We should be glad that Mr Barclay has been so patient.'

I said, rather sourly, that she and Stephen had been luckier; and she answered levelly: 'We were, Margaret—because we were able to marry and have your father see it. Priscilla won't have that, but her wedding will be finer without your poor pa's illness to rush the planning of it. Let her enjoy it, won't you?'

I stood, and went to the fireplace and put my hands before the flames. I said at last, that she was stern to-day; that it was dandling her baby and being a mother that did that to her. 'Indeed, *Mrs Prior*, you sound like my own mother. Or would do, if you were not so sensible . . .'

When she heard me say that she coloured and said I must hush. But she also laughed and put her hand across her mouth, I saw her in the glass above the mantel. I said then, that I had not seen her blush so since she was plain Miss Gibson. Did she remember, how we laughed and blushed? 'Pa used to say your face was like the red heart on a playing card—mine, he said, was like the diamond. Do you remember, Helen, how Pa said that?'

She smiled, but had tilted her head. 'There is Georgy,' she said.—I had not heard him. 'How his poor tooth makes him cry!' And she rang for Burns, her maid, and had the baby brought again; and I did not stay long with her, after that.

6 October 1874

I feel not at all like writing to-night. I have come up, pleading a head-ache, and soon I suppose Mother will follow, to bring my medicine. I have had a dreary day, at Millbank Prison.

They know me there now, and are jolly with me at the gate. 'What, back again Miss Prior?' said the Porter when he saw me come. 'I should've said you might have had enough of us by now—but there, it is remarkable how fascinating the penitentiary is, to those that do not have to work here.'

He likes to call the prison by that older name, I notice; and he sometimes calls the warders *turnkeys*, the matrons *taskmistresses*, on the same principle. He told me once that he has been porter at Millbank for thirty-five years, and so has seen many thousand convicts pass through his gate and knows all the most desperate and terrible histories of the place. To-day being another very wet day, I found him standing at the gate-house window, cursing the rain that made a slurry of the Millbank earth. He said the soil holds the water and makes the men's work in the grounds very miserable. 'This is an evil soil, Miss Prior,' he said. He made me stand with him at the glass, and he showed me where there had once, in the first days of the penitentiary, been a dry trench, that must be crossed like the moat of a castle, with a drawbridge. 'But,' he said, 'the soil would not have it. As fast as they set convicts to drain it, so the Thames could seep; and they would find it, every morning, full of black water. At last they had to earth it in.'

I stayed a little while with him, warming myself before his fire; and when I went in to the women's gaol I was passed on, as usual, to Miss Ridley, that she might take me round some of its sites. To-day she showed me the infirmary.

Like the kitchen, this is situated away from the body of the women's building, in the prison's central hexagon. It is a bitter-smelling room, but warm and large, and it might be pleasant, for it is the only chamber in which the women associate for purposes other than labour or prayer. Even here, however, they must be silent. There is a matron whose role it is to stand and watch them as they lie, and keep them from talking; and there are separate cells, and beds with straps, for the sick when they grow troublesome. On the wall there is a picture of Christ bearing a broken fetter, and a single line of text: *Thy love constraineth us.*

They have beds, I think, for fifty women. We found perhaps twelve or thirteen there, most of whom seemed very ill—too ill to raise their heads to us, they only slept, or shuddered, or turned their faces into their grey pillows as we passed by. Miss Ridley gazed hard at them; and at the bed of one, she stopped. 'Look here,' she said to me, gesturing to a woman who was laid out with her leg exposed, her ankle livid and wrapped with a bandage, and so swollen it was as thick, almost, as the thigh above it. 'Now, this is the kind of patient I have no time for. You tell Miss Prior, Wheeler, how your leg came to be so hurt.'

The woman ducked her head. 'If you please, miss,' she said to me, 'it got cut with a dinner-knife.' I remembered those blunt knives, and how the women had had to saw away at their bits of mutton, and looked at Miss Ridley. 'Tell Miss Prior,' she said, 'how your blood came to be so poisoned.'

'Well,' said Wheeler in a slightly meeker tone, 'the cut got rust worked into it, and turned bad.'

Miss Ridley gave a snort. It was marvellous, she said, what things got worked into cuts and turned them bad, at Millbank. 'The surgeon found a piece of iron from a button, bound to Wheeler's ankle to make the flesh swell. Indeed, so well *had* it swollen, he had to take his own knife to it, to get the button out! As if the surgeon is employed here, for *her* convenience!' She shook her head, and I looked again at the bloated ankle. The foot below the bandage was quite black, the heel white and cracked as the rind of a cheese.

When I spoke to the infirmary matron a little later, she told me that the prisoners will 'try any sort of trick' to get themselves admitted to her ward. 'They will fake fits,' she said. 'They will swallow glass if they can get it, to bring on bleeding. They will try and hang themselves, if they think they will be found in time and taken down.' She said there had been two or three at least, who had attempted that and misjudged it, and so been choked. She said that was a very hard thing. She said a woman would do that out of boredom; or for the sake of joining her pal, if she knew her pal was in the infirmary already; or else she might do it, 'purely to create a little stir with herself at its centre'.

I did not of course tell her that I had once tried a similar 'trick' myself. But, listening to her, my look must have changed, and she saw that and misinterpreted it. 'Oh, they are not like you and me, miss,' she said, 'the sort of women who pass through here! They hold their lives very cheap . . .'

Near us stood a younger matron, making a preparation for disinfecting the room. They do it with plates of chloride of lime, on which they pour vinegar. I watched her tip the bottle, and the air at once turned sharp; then she walked along the line of beds, carrying the plate before her as a priest might bear a censer in a church. At last the scent of it grew so bitter I felt my eyes sting, and turned away. Then Miss Ridley led me from there, and took me to the wards.

These we found not at all as I have come to know them, but filled with movement and murmuring voices. 'What's this?' I said, still wiping at my eyes to take the itch of disinfectant from them. Miss Ridley explained it to me. To-day is a Tuesday—I had not visited on a Tuesday before—and on this day, and on Friday, every week, the women are given lessons in their cells. I met one of their school-mistresses, on Mrs Jelf's ward. She shook my hand when the matron introduced me, and said she had heard of me—I thought she meant, from one of the women; it turned out she knew Pa's book. Her name, I think, is Mrs Bradley. She is employed to teach the women and has three young ladies to assist her. She said it is always young ladies who help her, and a new crop each year, for they no sooner start with her than they find husbands; and then they leave her. I could tell from the way she spoke to me that she thought me older than I am.

When we met her she was wheeling a small trolley down the wards, stacked with books and slates and papers. She told me that the women come to Millbank generally very ignorant, 'even of the Scriptures'; that many prisoners can read but not write, that others can do neither—she believes they are worse, on that score, than the men. 'These,' she said, indicating the books upon her trolley, 'are for the better women.' I bent to look at them. They were very worn, and rather limp; I imagined all the work-roughened fingers that had pinched and twisted them, over their term at Millbank, in idleness or frustration. I thought there might be titles there that we had had at home, Sullivan's *Spelling Book*, a *Catechism of the History of England*, Blair's *Universal Preceptor*—I am sure Miss Pulver made me recite from that when I was a girl. Stephen on his holidays would sometimes seize such books and laugh at them, saying they could teach one nothing.

'Of course,' said Mrs Bradley as she saw me squinting at the ghostly titles, 'it does not do to give the women very new texts. They are so careless with them! We find pages torn out, and put to all manner of uses.' She said the women use the paper for putting curls in their shorn hair, beneath their caps.

I had taken up the *Preceptor*; now, as the matron admitted Mrs Bradley to a cell nearby, I opened it, to pick a little through its crumbling pages. Its questions, in that particular setting, seemed bizarre ones—yet they had, I thought, a curious kind of poetry to them. *What sorts of grain best suit stiff soils? What is that acid which dissolves silver?* From far off down the passage came a dull, unsteady murmur, the crunch of stout-soled shoes on sand, Miss Ridley's cry: 'You stand still and say your letters, like the lady asks you!'

Whence come sugar, oil and India rubber?
What is relief, *and how should shadows fall?*

At last I returned the book to its trolley and moved off down the passage, pausing as I did so to gaze in at the women as they frowned or muttered over their pages of print. I passed kind Ellen Power; and the sad-faced Catholic girl—Mary Ann Cook—who stifled her baby; and Sykes, the discontented prisoner who pesters the matrons for news of her release. And when I reached the archway at the angle of the ward I heard a murmur that I recognised, and walked a little further. It was Selina Dawes. She was reciting some Biblical passage to a lady, who listened and smiled.

I forget which text it was. I was struck by her accent, which sounds so oddly on the wards, and by her pose, which was so meek—for she had been made to stand, at the centre of her cell, with her hands clasped neatly at her apron and her head quite bowed. I have been imagining her—when I have been thinking of her at all—as the Crivelli portrait, lean and stern and sombre. I have thought sometimes of all she said about her spirits, their gifts, that flower—I have remembered her unsettling gaze. But to-day, with her delicate throat working beneath the ribbons of her prison bonnet, her bitten lips moving, her eyes cast down, the smart lady teacher looking on, she seemed only young, and powerless, and sad, and underfed, and I was sorry for her. She did not know I stood and watched until I took another step—then she looked up, and her murmurs ceased. Her cheeks flamed red, and I felt my own face burn. I had remembered what she said to me, about how all the world might gaze at her, it was a part of her punishment.

I made to move away, but the school-mistress had also caught sight of me and now rose and nodded. Did I wish to speak with the prisoner? They wouldn't be a moment. Dawes knew her lesson quite by heart.

'Go on,' she said then, 'you are doing splendidly.'

I might have watched and listened as another woman made her halting recitation, and then was praised for it, then left to silence; but I did not like to look at Dawes do that. I said, 'Well, I shall call on you another day, since you are busy.' And I nodded to the school-mistress, and had Mrs Jelf escort me to the cells of the further ward; and I passed an hour visiting the women there.

But oh! that hour was a miserable one, and the women all seemed dreary to me. The first I went to put her work aside and stood and curtseyed, and nodded and cringed while Mrs Jelf refastened her gate; but as soon as we were alone she drew me to her and said, in a reeking whisper: 'Come close, come closer! They mustn't hear me say it! If they hear me, they'll nip me! Oh, they'll nip me till I scream!'

She meant *rats*. She said that rats come in the night; she

feels their cold paws on her face as she lies sleeping, and wakes with their bites upon her; and she rolled up the sleeve of her gown and showed me marks upon her arm—I am sure the marks were of her own teeth. I asked her, how could the rats get into her cell? She said the matrons bring them. She said, 'They pass them through the eye'—she meant the inspection slit, beside her door—'they pass them through by the tails, I see their white hands passing them. They drop them to the stone floor, one by one . . .'

Would I speak with Miss Haxby, to get the rats taken off?

I said I would, only to pacify her; and then I left her. But the next woman I visited seemed almost as mad, and even the third—a prostitute named Jarvis—I took to be feeble-minded at first, for all the time we spoke she stood and fidgeted, not meeting my gaze, yet sending her lustreless glance slithering over the details of my costume and my hair. At last, as if she couldn't help herself, she burst out, How could I bear to dress so plain? Why, my gown was as dull, almost, as the matrons'! It was bad enough that they must wear what they must; she thought it would kill her to wear a frock like mine if she was only free again and might dress how she pleased!

I asked her then, what would she choose if she were me? and she answered promptly, 'I would have a gown of Chamberry gauze, and a cloak of otter, and a hat of straw, with lilies on it.' And for her feet?—'Silk slippers, with ribbons to the knee!'

But that, I protested gently, was a costume for a party or a ball. She wouldn't wear such a costume there, would she, to Millbank?

Wouldn't she! With Hoy and O'Dowd to see her in it, and Griffiths and Wheeler and Banks, and Mrs Pretty, and Miss Ridley! Oh, just *wouldn't* she!

In the end her enthusiasm grew so wild it began to trouble me. She must lie in her cell every night, I should think, imagining her gown, fretting over the fancy details. But when I made to step to the gate and call for the matron, she jumped forward to join me, and came very close. Her gaze was not at all dull now, but rather sly.

'We have had a nice talk, miss, haven't we?' she said. I nodded—'We have'—and moved to the gate again. Now she came even closer. Where, she asked me quickly, was I visiting next? Was it to be B ward? For if it was, Oh, would I please just pass a message, to her friend Emma White? She advanced her hand towards my pocket, towards my book and pen. Just a page of my book, she said, I might slip it through the bars of White's cell, 'quick as winking'. Only half a page! 'She is my cousin, miss, I swear, you may ask any matron.'

I had drawn away from her at once, and now pushed her pressing hand away. 'A message?' I said in surprise and dismay. Oh, but she knew very well that I mustn't carry messages! What would Miss Haxby think of me if I did that? What would Miss Haxby think of *her*, for asking? The woman drew back a little, but still she kept on with it: it couldn't harm Miss Haxby, for White to know that her friend Jane was thinking of her! She was sorry, she said, that she had asked me to spoil my book; but mightn't I just pass a word on?—mightn't I just do that?—mightn't I just tell White that her friend Jane Jarvis was a-thinking of her, and wished that she might know it?

I shook my head, and rapped at the bars of the gate for Mrs Jelf to come and free me. 'You know you mustn't ask,' I said. 'You know you must not; and I am very sorry that you have.' At that, her sly look became sullen, and she turned away and hugged her arms about herself. 'Damn you then!' she said, quite plain—though not so plain that the matron could catch it, above the rasp of her prison boots upon the sanded passage-way.

It was curious to know how little her curse moved me. I had blinked to hear her say it, but now I only gazed levelly at her; and she saw that, and looked sour. Then the matron came. 'On with your sewing now,' she said gently, as she released me from the cell and locked the gate. Jarvis hesitated, then drew her chair across the floor and took up her work. And then she looked, not sullen or sour but—as Dawes had—she looked only miserable, and ill.

There were still the sounds of Mrs Bradley's young ladies, working their way through the cells of Ward E; but I left that floor now, and went down to the First Class wards, and walked along them with their matron, Miss Manning. Gazing in at the women in their cells I found myself wondering, after all, which one of them it was that Jarvis was so eager to send word to. At last I said, very quietly, 'Have you a prisoner named Emma White here, matron?'—and when Miss Manning said that she had, and should I like to visit her?, I shook my head, and hesitated, then said that it was only that another woman was keen for news of her, on Mrs Jelf's ward. Her cousin, was it?—Jane Jarvis?

Miss Manning gave a snort. 'Her cousin, did she tell you? Why, she is no more cousin to Emma White than I am!'

She said that White and Jarvis are notorious in the gaol as a pair of 'pals', and were 'worse than any sweethearts'. She said I would find the women 'palling up' like that, they did it at every prison she ever worked at. It was the loneliness, she said, that made them do it. She herself had seen hard women there turn quite love-sick, because they had taken a fancy to some girl they had seen, and the girl had turned the shoulder on them, or had a pal already that she liked better. She laughed. 'You must watch that no-one tries to make a pal of *you*, miss,' she said. 'There have been women here who have grown romantic over their matrons, and have had to be removed to other gaols for it. And the row they have raised, when they get taken, has been quite comical!'

She laughed again, then led me a little further down the ward; and I followed, though uneasily—for I have heard them talk of 'pals' before, and have used the word myself, but it disturbed me to find that the term had *that* particular meaning and I hadn't known it. Nor, somehow, do I care to think that I had almost played the medium, innocently, for Jarvis' dark passion . . .

Miss Manning brought me to a gate. 'There's White for you,' she murmured, 'that Jane Jarvis thinks so much of.' I gazed into a cell to see a stout, yellow-faced girl, squinting at a row of crooked stitches in the canvas bag she had been set to sew. When she saw us watching her she rose and made a curtsey. Miss Manning said, 'All right, White. Any news yet of your daughter?'—and then, to me: 'White has a daughter miss, left in the care of an aunt. But we think the aunt a bad one—don't we, White?—and are in fears she will let the little girl go the same way.'

White said she had had no word. When she caught my eye I turned from her, and left Miss Manning at her gate and found another matron to escort me to the men's gaol. I was glad to go, glad even to step into the darkening grounds and feel the rain upon my face; for all that I had seen and heard of there—the sick women and the suicides, and the mad-woman's rats, and the pals, and Miss Manning's laughter—it had all grown horrible to me. I remembered how I had walked from the prison into the clear air after my first visit and imagined my own past being buckled up tight, and forgotten. Now the rain made my coat heavy, and my dark skirts grew darker at the hem, where the wet earth clung to them.

I came home in a cab, and lingered over the paying of the driver, hoping Mother would see it. She didn't: she was in the drawing-room examining our new maid. This is a friend of Boyd's, an older girl, she has no time for ghost stories, and claims to be eager to take up the vacant place—I should say Boyd has been so terrorised by Mother she has bribed her to it, for the friend is presently used to rather better wages. She says, however, that she is ready to forfeit a shilling a month for the sake of a little room of her own and a bedstead all to herself: in her current place she must share her quarters with the cook, who has 'bad habits'; besides that, she has a friend in another situation near to the river and would like to be near her. Mother said, 'I am not sure. My other maid will not like it if you have ideas above your duties. And your friend should know, mind, that she is not to call on you here. Nor will I have you cutting your hours to go and visit her.' The girl said she would never consider it; and Mother has agreed to try her for a month. She is to come to us on Saturday. She is a long-faced girl and her name is *Vigers*. I shall enjoy pronouncing that, I never much liked *Boyd*.

'A shame she is so plain!' said Pris, watching at the curtain as she left the house; and I smiled—then thought a terrible thing. I remembered Mary Ann Cook, at Millbank, being pestered by her master's son; and I thought of Mr Barclay about the house, and Mr Wallace, and Stephen's friends that sometimes come—and I was glad she is not handsome.

And perhaps, indeed, Mother thought something similar, for at Prissy's comment she shook her head. Vigers would be a good girl, she said. The plain ones always were, they were more faithful. A sensible girl, she would know her place all right. There would be no more nonsense, now, over creaks on the staircase!

Pris grew grave, listening to that. She will have many girls to manage, of course, at Marishes.

'It is still the custom in some great houses,' said Mrs Wallace as she sat playing cards with Mother to-night, 'to keep the maids in the kitchens, sleeping on shelves. When I was a child we always had a boy to sleep upon the box that held the plate. The cook was the only servant in the house to possess a pillow.' She said she did not know how I could bear to lie with the tweeny fidgeting about in her room above me. I said I was ready to brave it for the sake of my view of the Thames, which I could not give up; and that anyway, in my experience tweenies—when they weren't frightening themselves into fits—were generally too tired to do anything in their beds but sleep.

'So they should be!' she cried.

Mother said then that Mrs Wallace should pay no mind to anything I might say on the subject of servants. 'Margaret has as much sense of handling a servant,' she said, 'as she has of handling a cow.'

Then, on a different tack, she asked us, Could we explain a curious matter to her? There were supposed to be thirty-thousand distressed needlewomen in the city, and she had yet to find a single girl capable of putting a straight seam, upon a linen cloak, for less than a pound . . . *&c.*

I thought Stephen might come, bringing Helen with him; but he did not—perhaps the rain kept them at home. I waited until ten, then came up here, and now Mother has been, to give me my dose. I was sitting in my night-dress when she came, and had the rug about me, and because I had taken off my gown my locket showed at my throat. She noticed that, of course, and said, 'Really, Margaret! To think of all the handsome pieces of jewellery you have, that I never see on you, and yet you still wear that old thing!' I said, 'But I had this from Pa,'—I didn't tell her about the curl of pale hair that lies inside it, she doesn't know I have that. She said, 'But, such a plain old thing!' She asked me, if I wanted a keepsake of my father, why I never wore the brooches or the rings she had had made up after he died? I didn't answer her, but tucked the locket inside my gown. It was very cold against the bare flesh of my bosom.

And as I drank the chloral for her, I saw her looking at the pictures I have pinned at the side of my desk, and then at this book. I had closed the covers, but had my pen between the pages to keep the place. 'What's that?' she said. 'What are you writing there?' She said it was unhealthy to sit at a journal so long; that it would throw me back upon my own dark thoughts and weary me. I thought, If you don't want me to grow weary, then why do you give me medicine to make me sleep? But I did not say it. I only shut the book away—then took it out again when she had gone.

Two days ago, Priscilla put a novel aside and Mr Barclay picked it up, and turned its pages, and laughed at it. He does not care for lady authors. All women can ever write, he says, are 'journals of the heart'—the phrase has stayed with me. I have been thinking of my last journal, which had so much of my own heart's blood in it; and which certainly took as long to burn as human hearts, they say, do take. I mean this book to be different to that one. I mean this writing not to turn me back upon my own thoughts, but to serve, like the chloral, to keep the thoughts from coming at all.

And oh! it would do, it would do, were it not for the queer reminders Millbank has thrown at me to-day. For I have catalogued my visit, I have traced my path across the female gaol, as I have before; but the work has not soothed me—it has made my brain sharp as a hook, so that all that my thoughts pass over they seem to catch at and set wriggling. 'Think of us,' said Dawes to me last week, 'the next time you are wakeful'—and now, as wakeful as she could wish me, I do. I think of all the women there, upon the dark wards of the prison; but where they should be silent, and still, they are restless and pacing their cells. They are looking for ropes to tie about their own throats. They are sharpening knives to cut their flesh with. Jane Jarvis, the prostitute, is calling to White, two floors below her; and Dawes is murmuring the queer verses of the wards. Now my mind has caught the words up—I think I shall recite them with her, all night long.

What sorts of grain best suit stiff soils?
What is that acid which dissolves silver?
What is *relief*, and how should shadows fall?

12 October 1872

Common Questions and their Answers
on the Matter of the Spheres
by
The Spirit-Medium's Friend

Where does a spirit travel when it leaves the body that has held it?
It travels to the lowest sphere that all new souls must come to.

How does the spirit remove there?
It removes there in the company of one of those guides or guardian spirits whom we call *angels.*

How does the lowest sphere appear to the spirit that is fresh departed from the earth?
It appears to it as a place of great calmness, brightness, colour, joy, *&c.*, any pleasant quality may be substituted here, this sphere has all of them.

By whom in this sphere is the new spirit received & made welcome?
On attaining this sphere, the spirit is taken by the guide that we have spoken of to a place wherein are gathered all those friends & family members who have preceded him there. They will greet him with smiles, then lead him to a pool of shining water & there let him bathe. They will give him garments to cover his limbs; they will have made ready a house for him. The garments & the house will be of gorgeous substances.

What are the spirit's duties, while he resides in this sphere?
His duties are to purify his thoughts in preparation for his elevation to the next sphere.

How many spheres are there, that a departed spirit must pass through in this way?
There are seven, & the highest of them is the home of LOVE that we call GOD!

What expectations of successful promotion through these spheres may be entertained by the spirits of persons not more than averagely religious, benevolent, well-placed &c.?
Persons cultivating a kind & gentle disposition will make an easy progress, whatever their station on the earth-plane. Persons of low, violent or vindictive tempers will find their passage – here the paper has been torn, I think the word must be *hindered*. Persons of especial baseness will not be admitted even into that lowest sphere we have described above. They will be taken instead to a place of darkness, & made to toil there until they have admitted & repented of their wrongs. This process may take many millennia to achieve.

How does the spirit-medium stand in relation to these spheres?
The spirit-medium is not permitted to enter the seven spheres, but he or she may sometimes be taken to the gate of them, & so catch glimpses of their marvels. He or she may also be taken to that dark place where toil the wicked spirits, & invited to gaze at that.

What is the spirit-medium's proper home?
The spirit-medium's proper home is neither this world nor the next, but that vague & debatable land which lies between them. – At this spot Mr Vincy has pasted a notice, *Are you a spirit-medium in search of your proper home? You will find it at* – & he gives the address of this hotel. He has had the book from a gentleman at Hackney, & means to pass it to another on the Farringdon Road. He brought it to me very

quietly, saying 'Mind, I don't show such things to everyone. I won't, for example, be passing this to Miss Sibree. I keep books like this only for those persons about whom I have a *feeling*.'

To keep a flower from fading. – Add a little glycerine to the water in the flower's vase. This will keep the petals from falling or turning brown.

To make an object luminous. – Purchase a quantity of luminous paint, preferably from a shop in a district where you are not known. Thin the paint with a little turpentine, & soak strips of muslin in it. When the muslin is allowed to dry & then shaken, a luminous powder will fall from it, that may be collected & used to cover any object. The odour of the turpentine may be disguised with a little perfume.

15 October 1874

To Millbank. I arrived at the inner gate to find a little knot of warders gathered there, and a pair of matrons—Miss Ridley and Miss Manning—their prison gowns hidden beneath bear-skin cloaks and their hoods pulled high against the cold. Miss Ridley saw me and nodded. They were expecting a delivery of prisoners, she said, from the police cells and other gaols, and she and Miss Manning had come to take off the women. I said, 'Will you mind, if I wait with you?' I had never seen before, how they deal with newcomers. We stood a while, the warders blowing on their hands; then there came a cry from the porter's lodge, and the sound of hooves and iron wheels, and a grim-looking, windowless vehicle—the prison van—swung into Millbank's gravelled courtyard. Miss Ridley and a senior warder stepped up to greet its driver, and then to open its doors. 'They will let the women off first,' said Miss Manning to me. 'Here they come, look.' She moved forward, pulling her cloak a little closer about her. I, however, hung back, to study the prisoners as they emerged.

There were four of them—three girls, quite young, and one middle-aged woman with a bruise upon her cheek. Each had her hands held fast and stiff before her in a pair of hand-cuffs; each stumbled a little as she dropped from the van's high back step, then stood a second and gazed about her, blinking at the pale sky, and at Millbank's ghastly towers and yellow walls. Only the older woman seemed unafraid—but she, it turned out, was used to the sight, for as the matrons stepped up to chivvy the women into a ragged line and lead them off I saw Miss Ridley narrow her eyes. 'You again, then, Williams,' she said; and the woman's bruised face seemed to darken.

I walked at the rear of the little group, behind Miss Manning. The younger women continued to look about them rather fearfully, and one leaned to murmur something to her neighbour, and had to be scolded. Their uncertainty reminded me of my own first visit to the gaol—less than a month ago, still; but how familiar have I grown, since then, with the plain, monotonous routes, that once so baffled me!, and with the warders, the matrons, the very gates and doors of the place, its locks and bolts—each of which has a subtly different *slam* or *click* or *thud* or *creak*, depending on its strength and purpose. It was curious to think this, half satisfying and half alarming. I recalled Miss Ridley saying that she had crossed the prison corridors so often, she could walk them blindfolded; and I remembered how I had once pitied the poor matrons, for being as subject to the grim routines of Millbank as their prisoners.

So I was almost pleased to find us entering the female building by a doorway I did *not* know, and passing through it into a series of rooms that I had never visited before. In the first of these we found the reception-matron, the officer responsible for examining the papers of all new convicts, and entering their details in a thick prison ledger. She too looked hard at the woman with the bruise. 'No need to tell me *your* name,' she said, as she wrote upon the page before her. 'What are the horrible particulars, Miss Ridley?'

Miss Ridley had a paper, and was reading from it. 'Thievery,' she said shortly. 'And assaulting the officer that apprehended her, very viciously. Four years.' The reception-matron shook her head: 'And you were just sent out of here last year, weren't you, Williams? And in high hopes of a situation, I recall, in a Christian lady's household. What happened there then?'

Miss Ridley answered that it was in the Christian lady's household that the theft had taken place; and with a piece of the Christian lady's property that the officer had been assaulted. When all the points had been properly noted, she gestured for Williams to move back, and for one of the other prisoners to step forward. This one was dark-haired—dark as a gipsy. The reception-matron let her stand a moment while she added some fresh detail to her book. 'Now then, Black-Eyed Sue,' she said mildly at last, 'what's your name?'

The girl was named Jane Bonn, was two-and-twenty, and had been sent to Millbank for procuring an abortion.

The next—I forget her name—was four-and-twenty, and was a street-thief.

The third was seventeen, and had broken into the cellar of a shop and set a fire there. She began to weep as the reception-matron questioned her, raising a hand to her face to rub miserably at her streaming eyes and nose, until Miss Manning stepped forward and handed her a napkin. 'There, now,' said Miss Manning. 'You are only crying because it is so strange.' She put her fingers to the girl's pale brow and smoothed her curling hair. 'There, now.'

Miss Ridley looked on, but said nothing. The reception-matron said 'Oh!'—she had found a mistake at the top of her page, and now leaned, frowning, to re-write it.

When all the business in this chamber had been completed the women were taken into the next; and no-one suggesting to me that I ought now to pass on to the wards, I thought I might as well go with them, and see the process to its close. In this room there was a bench, on which the women were instructed to sit; and a single chair. The chair stood, rather ominously, in the centre of the floor, beside a little table. The table had a comb upon it, and a pair of scissors, and when the girls caught sight of these they gave a kind of collective shudder. 'That's right,' said the older woman then with a leer, 'you shake. This is where they has the hair off you.' Miss Ridley silenced her at once; but the words had done their work, and the girls now looked wilder than ever.

'Please, miss,' cried one of them, 'don't cut my hair! Oh please, miss!'

Miss Ridley picked up the scissors and gave a couple of snaps with them, then looked at me. 'You would think I was after their eyes, wouldn't you, Miss Prior?' She pointed with her blades to the first of the trembling girls—the arsonist—and then to the chair. 'Come along, now,' she said—and then, when the girl only hesitated: 'Come *along*!' in a terrible tone that made even me flinch. 'Or shall we fetch some keepers, to hold your legs and arms down? They are fresh off the men's wards, mind, and apt to be rough.'

At that the girl reluctantly rose, and sat shivering in the chair. Miss Ridley plucked her bonnet from her, then worked her fingers over her head, loosening her curls and drawing out the pins that kept them tight; the bonnet was passed to the reception-matron, who made an entry regarding it in her great book, whistling lightly as she did so, and turning a sweet—a white mint—upon her tongue. The girl's hair was a rusty brown, and stiff and dark in places with sweat or hair-oil. When she felt it fall against her neck she began to cry again, and Miss Ridley sighed and said, 'You silly girl, we must only cut it to the jaw. And who will there be to see you, *here*?'—this, of course, made the girl weep harder. But while she shuddered the matron combed the greasy tresses, then gathered them together between the fingers of one fist and prepared to cut. I became suddenly conscious of my own hair, which Ellis had lifted and combed, with a similar gesture, not three hours before. I seemed to feel each single strand start up, and pull against the wires that pinned it. It was horrible, to have to sit and look on while the scissor-blades rasped, and the pale girl wept and shuddered. It was horrible—and yet, I could not turn my gaze. I could only watch along with the three fearful prisoners, fascinated and ashamed, until at last the matron lifted her fist, and the severed hair hung limp; and when a strand or two of it sprang to the girl's damp face, she twitched, and so did I.

Miss Ridley asked her then, did she wish the hair to be kept?—The prisoners, it seems, may have their shorn hair bound and stored with their things, to take with them when they are freed. The girl gazed once at the quivering pony's tail, and shook her head. 'Very well,' said Miss Ridley. She carried the tresses to a wicker basket, and there let them fall. 'We have uses for hair,' she said to me, darkly, 'at Millbank.'

The other women were brought up for their barbering then—the older prisoner submitting to it with a grand display of coolness; the thief as miserable as the first girl; and Black-Eyed Susan, the abortionist—whose hair hung long and dark and heavy, like a hood of tar or treacle—cursing and kicking and ducking her head, so that the reception-matron had to be summoned to come and help Miss Manning hold her wrists, and Miss Ridley, cutting, grew breathless and red. 'There now, you little brute!' she said at last. 'Why, what a great lot of hair you have, I can barely close my hand around it!' She held the black locks high, and the reception-matron stepped to study them, and then to rub a tress or two beneath her fingers. 'Such a fine bit of hair!' she said admiringly. 'Real Spanish hair, they call that. We must have a thread, Miss Manning, to put about it. That will make a handsome hair-piece, that will.' She turned to the girl—'Don't you look so fierce! We'll see how glad you are to have your old hair back, six years from now!' Miss Manning brought a string, the hair was fastened, and the girl returned to her place upon the bench. Her neck showed red where the scissors had caught it.

I sat through all this, feeling increasingly awkward and strange, the women occasionally sending sly, fearful glances my way, as if they wondered what terrible role I was to play in their incarceration—once, when the gipsy girl struggled, Miss Ridley said, 'For shame, with the Lady Visitor watching! She shan't be visiting *you*, now she's seen your temper!' When the hair-cutting was completed and she had stepped aside to wipe her hands upon a cloth, I went to her and asked her, quietly, what was to happen to the women now? She answered in her usual tone that they would undress themselves, then be taken and made to bathe, then passed over to the prison surgeon.

'We shall see, then,' she said, 'that they have nothing about themselves'—she said the women sometimes carry objects into the gaol, like that, about their persons, 'plugs of tobacco, or even knives'. After their examinations they are given their prison costumes, and are addressed by Mr Shillitoe and Miss Haxby; in their cells they are visited by the chaplain, Mr Dabney. 'After that they are visited by no-one, ma'am, for a day and a night. That helps them think the better on their crimes.'

She returned her towel to a hook upon the wall, then looked past me to the miserable women on the bench. 'Now then,' she said, 'let us have the dresses off you. Come along, look sharp!' The women, like so many lambs, grown dumb and meek before their shearers, began at once to rise and fumble with the fastenings of their frocks. Miss Manning produced four shallow wooden trays, and placed them at their feet. I stood a second watching the scene—the little arsonist shrugging off the bodice of her gown to expose the filthy under-clothes beneath; the gipsy girl raising her arms and showing the darkness of her armpit, then turning, with a hopeless modesty, as she worked at the hooks of her stays. Miss Ridley leaned nearer to me to ask, 'Will you go in with them ma'am, and watch them bathe?'—and the movement of her breath against my cheek made me blink, and I looked away. I said no, I would not accompany them there, but would go on to the wards. She straightened, and her mouth twitched, and I thought I caught a flash of something behind her pale, bare gaze—a sour kind of satisfaction, or amusement.

But what she said was: 'As you wish, ma'am.'

I left the women then, and didn't look at them again. Miss Ridley called to a matron she heard passing in the corridor beyond, and had her escort me to the prison proper. As I walked with her I saw, through a half-open door, what must have been the surgeon's chamber: a dismal-looking room with a tall wooden couch, and a table with instruments laid out upon it. There was a gentleman there—the surgeon himself, I suppose—he didn't look up as we passed by. He was standing with his hands held to a lamp, paring his nails.

The woman I walked with now was named Miss Brewer. She is young—I thought her very young for a matron, but it turned out she is not a matron at all, in the ordinary sense, but clerk to the chaplain. She wears a different-coloured mantle to the matrons on the wards, and her manner seemed kinder than theirs, her speech gentler. Her duties include handling the prisoners' post. The women of Millbank, she told me, may send and receive one letter every two months; there being so many cells, however, there is generally post for her to carry every day. She said her job is a pleasant one—the pleasantest one in all the gaol. She never grows weary of seeing the expressions on the faces of the prisoners when she stops at their cell gates and hands them their letters.

I saw something of this, for I had caught her as she was about to make her round, and walked with her on it; the women she beckoned to gave screams of delight, and clutched at the letters she passed to them and sometimes pressed them to their bosoms or their mouths. Only one looked fearful as we approached her gate. Miss Brewer said to her quickly, 'Nothing for you, Banks. Don't be afraid'—and she told me then that that prisoner has a sister in a very poor way, and every day expects a letter bringing news of her. That, she said, was the only unpleasant part of the business. She would be very sorry to have to carry *that* letter—'for, of course, I shall know what is inside it, before Banks does'.

All the letters, to and from the gaol, pass through the chaplain's office, and are inspected before they leave it by Mr Dabney or by her. I said, 'Why, then you know all the women's lives here! All their secrets, all their plans . . .'

She heard that, and coloured—as if she had not thought of it in quite that light before. 'The letters must be read,' she answered. 'Those are the rules. And the messages in them, you know, are very commonplace.'

We climbed the tower staircase then, past the penal wards, and reached the highest floor; and here I thought of something. The packet of letters grew smaller. There was one for Ellen Power, the elderly prisoner; she saw it, and then me, and winked: 'One from my little grand-daughter,' she said. 'She never forgets me.' We passed on like this, drawing nearer to the angle of the ward, and at last I moved closer to Miss Brewer and asked her, had she anything for Selina Dawes? She looked at me, and blinked. For Dawes? Why, nothing! And how odd that I should ask it, for she was just about the only woman in the gaol for whom she *never* had a letter!

Never? I asked her.—Never, she said. She could not say as to whether any letters had come for Dawes when she was first admitted—that was before Miss Brewer's time there. But there had certainly come nothing for her, nor had she sent a single letter out, within the past twelve months.

I said, 'Has she no friends, no family, to remember her?' and Miss Brewer shrugged: 'If she ever had, she has quite cast them off—or they, of course, might have cast off her. I believe that happens.' Now her smile grew stiffer. 'You see, there are some women here,' she said, 'who keep their secrets to themselves . . .'

She said it rather primly, then moved on; and when I caught up with her she was engaged in reading aloud a letter to a woman who—I suppose—was unable to read it for herself. But her words had made me thoughtful. I went past her, then walked the little distance to the second line of cells. I stepped softly, and before Dawes raised her eyes to mine I had a second or two in which to gaze at her, through the bars of her gate.

I hadn't thought much before about who there might be, in the outer world, to miss Selina Dawes, to visit her, to send her letters that were commonplace or kind. To know that there was no-one made the solitude and silence in which she sat seem to grow thicker. I thought then that Miss Brewer's words were truer than she knew: Dawes does keep her own secrets; she keeps them even there, at Millbank. And I remembered, too, something another matron told me once—that, handsome as Dawes was, no prisoner ever sought to make a *pal* of her. I understood that now.

And so I looked at her, and felt a rush of pity. And what I thought was: *You are like me.*

I wish I had only thought that and moved on. I wish I had left her. But as I watched she raised her head, and smiled, and I saw then that she looked expectant. And then I could not leave her. I gestured to Mrs Jelf, who was further down the ward; and by the time she had brought her key and opened the gate, Dawes had put her needles aside and risen to greet me.

Indeed, it was she—once the matron had united us, and fidgeted over us, and hesitantly left us to our business—who spoke first. She said, 'I'm glad you've come!' She said that she was sorry not to see me, last time.

I said, last time? 'Oh yes. But you were busy with your school-mistress.'

She tossed her head. '*Her*,' she said. She said they think her quite a prodigy there, because she is able to remember in the afternoons the lines of Scripture read to them at chapel, in the morning. She said she wonders what else they think she has, to fill her empty hours up.

She said, 'I would far rather have spoken with *you*, Miss Prior. I'm afraid you were kind to me, when we last talked; and I didn't deserve it. I have been wishing, since then—well, you said you came to be my friend. I don't have much cause to remember the ways of friendship, here.'

Her words were satisfying ones for me to hear, and made me like and pity her all the more. We talked a little, about the habits of the gaol. I said, 'I think you might be moved from here, in time, to a kinder prison—perhaps, to Fulham?'—and she only shrugged, saying one prison was as good as any other.

I might have left her then, and gone on to another woman, and been tranquil now; but I was too intrigued by her. At last I could not help myself. I said that one of the matrons had told me—quite in the friendliest fashion, of course—that she received no letters . . .

I asked her, Was that true? Was there really no-one, beyond Millbank, to take an interest in her sufferings there? She studied me for a moment, so that I thought she might grow proud again, and not answer. But then she said, that she had many friends.

Her spirit-friends, yes. She had told me of them. But, there must be others, from her life outside, who missed her?—Again she shrugged, saying nothing.

'Have you no family?'

She had an auntie, she said, 'in spirit', who sometimes visits her.

'Have you no friends,' I said, 'who are *alive*?'

Then I think she did grow a little proud. How many friends, she wondered, would come to visit *me*, if *I* were put in Millbank? The world she moved in before, she said, it wasn't a grand world, but it wasn't a world of 'thieves and bullies', like many of the women's there. Besides, she 'doesn't care to be seen', she said, in such a place. She prefers the spirit-people, who do not judge her, to those people who have only laughed at her in her 'misfortune'.

That word seemed carefully chosen. Hearing it I thought, reluctantly, of those other words, marked on the enamel tablet outside her gate: *Fraud and Assault*. I told her that the other women I visit sometimes find it comforting to talk to me about their crimes.—She said at once, 'And you would have me tell you about mine. Well, and why shouldn't I? Except that there was no crime! There was only—'

Only what?

She shook her head: 'Only a silly girl, who saw a spirit and was frightened by it; and a lady who was frightened by the girl, and died. And I was blamed, for all of it.'

I had had this much already, from Miss Craven. I asked her now, Why was the girl made afraid? She said, after a second's hesitation, that the spirit had turned 'naughty'—that was the word she used. The spirit had turned naughty, and the lady, 'Mrs Brink', saw it all and was so startled—'Well, there was a weakness about her heart that I never knew of. She fell in a faint, and later died. She was a friend to me. No-one ever thought of that, all through my trial. They only must find some cause for it, some thing that they could understand. The mother of the girl was brought to say her daughter had been harmed, as well as poor Mrs Brink; and then the cause of it all was found to lie with me.'

'When all the time it was the—naughty spirit?'

'*Yes.*' But what judge is there, she said, what jury—unless a jury made of spiritualists, and God knows how she longed for that!—what judge is there, that would believe her? 'They only said it couldn't be a spirit, because spirit-people don't exist'—here she pulled a face. 'In the end they made it a case of fraud, as well as assault.'

I asked her then, What had the girl said—the girl who was struck? She answered that the girl had certainly felt the spirit, but had grown confused. 'The mother was rich, and had a lawyer that could make the best of things. My own man was no good, and still cost all my money—all the money I earned, through helping people, all gone—like that!—on nothing.'

But if the girl had seen a spirit?

'She didn't *see* him. She only felt him. They said—they said it must be my hand she had felt . . .'

I remember her now pressing her two slender hands close together, and slowly working the fingers of one across the rough and reddened knuckles of the other. I said, Had she had no friends, to support her? and her mouth gave a tilt. She said she had had many friends, and they had liked to call her a 'martyr to the cause'—but only at first. For she was sorry to say that there were jealous people, 'even in the spiritual movement', and some were very glad to see her brought low. Others were only frightened. In the end, when she was found guilty, there was nobody to speak in her behalf . . .

She looked miserable at that, and terribly delicate and young. I said, 'And you insist it was a *spirit* that should have the blame?'—She nodded. I think I smiled. 'How hard it seems,' I said, 'that you were sent here, while it got off quite free.'

Oh, she said then, I must not think that 'Peter Quick' was free! She gazed past me, at the iron gate that Mrs Jelf had fastened at my back. 'They have their own kind of punishments,' she said, 'in the other world. Peter is in as dark a place as I am. He is only waiting—quite like me—to serve his term out and move on.'

Those were her words; and they seem odder to me as I write them here, than they seemed then, as she stood, gravely and earnestly, answering my questions, point for point, with her own neat logic. Even so, to hear her talk, familiarly, of 'Peter', of 'Peter Quick'—again I smiled. We had moved rather near to one another. Now I stepped away a little, and when she saw that she looked knowing. She said, 'You think me a fool, or an actress. You think me a sharp little actress, like they do—'*No,*' I answered at once. 'No, I don't think that of you'—for I don't, and didn't, even talking with her then—not quite. I shook my head. I said it was only that I was used to thinking very different sorts of things. Ordinary things. My mind, I supposed, must be 'very uninstructed as to the limits of the marvellous'.

Now she smiled, but very faintly. *Her* mind, she said, had known too much of the marvellous. 'And my reward for it was, that they put me here . . .'

And she made one small gesture with her hand as she spoke, that seemed to describe the whole hard colourless gaol, and all her sufferings in it.

'It is very terrible for you here,' I said, after a moment.

She nodded. 'You think spiritualism a kind of fancy,' she said. 'Doesn't it seem to you, now you are here, that *anything* might be real, since Millbank is?'

I looked at the bare white wall, the folded hammock—the slop-box, that had a fly upon it. I said, I was not sure. The prison might be hard—but that did not make spiritualism any truer. The prison was at least a world that I could see, and smell and hear. Her spirits, however—well, they might be real, but they meant nothing to me. I could not talk of them, did not know how.

She said I must talk of them how I pleased, because talking of them would 'give them power'. Better still I ought to listen to them. 'Then, Miss Prior, you might hear them talking of *you*.'

I laughed. Of me? Oh, I said, but it must be a very quiet day indeed in Heaven, if they had only Margaret Prior to discuss there!

She nodded, and tilted her head. She has a way about her—I have noticed it, before to-day—a way of shifting mood, of changing tone, and pose. She does it very subtly—not as an actress might, with a gesture that must be seen across a dark and crowded theatre; she does it as a piece of quiet music does it, when it falls or rises into a slightly different signature.

She did it now, as I stood smiling, still saying, how dull the spirit-world must be, if they had only me to talk of! She began to look patient. She began to look wise. And then she said, gently and quite evenly: 'Why do you say such things? You know there are spirits to whom you are very dear. You know there is *one* spirit, in particular—he is with us now, he is closer to you than I am. And you are dearer to him, Miss Prior, than anyone.'

I stared at her, feeling the breath catch in my throat. This was not at all like hearing her talk of spirit-gifts and flowers: she might have cast water in my face, or pinched me. I thought stupidly of Boyd, hearing Pa's feet upon the attic stairs. I said, 'What do you know, of him?'—She didn't answer. I said, 'You have seen my dark coat, and made a guess—'

'You are clever,' she said. She said that what she is, that has nothing to do with cleverness. She must be what she is, as she must breathe, or dream, or swallow. She must be it—even there, even at Millbank! 'But do you know,' she said, 'it is an odd thing. It is like being a sponge, or a—what are those creatures, that don't care to be seen, and change their skins to suit their settings?' I did not answer. 'Well,' she went on, 'I used to think, in my old life, that I must be a creature just like that. People would come to me sick sometimes and, sitting with them, I would grow sick too. A woman came to me once who was with child, and I felt her baby, inside *me*. Another time a gentleman came, wanting to speak with his son in spirit: when the poor boy came through, I felt the breath pressed out of me, my head crushed as if it would burst! It turned out he had died in a falling building. His last sensation, you see, *I* felt.'

Now she put her hand upon her breast, and drew a little closer to me. She said, 'When *you* come to me, Miss Prior, I feel your—sorrow. I feel your sorrow as a darkness, *here*. Oh, what an ache it is! I thought at first that it had emptied you, that you were hollow, quite hollow, like an egg with the meat blown out of it. I think you think that, too. But you are not empty. You are full—only shut quite tight, and fastened like a box. What do you have here that you must keep locked up like that?' She tapped at her breast. Then she raised her other hand and touched me, lightly, where she had touched herself . . .

I gave a twitch, as if her fingers had some charge to them. Her eyes widened, and then she smiled. She had found—it was the purest chance, the purest, queerest chance—she had found, beneath my gown, my locket; and now she began to trace its outline with her fingertips. I felt the chain tighten. The gesture was so close and so insinuating, as I write it here it seems to me that she must have followed the line of links to my throat, have curled her fingers beneath my collar and drawn the locket free—but she did not do this, her hand remained at my breast, only delicately pressing. She stood very still with her head a little cocked, as if she was listening to my heart where it beat against the gold.

Then her features gave another, stranger kind of shift, and she spoke, in a whisper. 'He is saying, *She has hung her care about her neck, and will not put it aside. Tell her she must lay it aside.*' She nodded. 'He is smiling. Was he clever, like you? He was! But he has learned many new things now, and—oh! how he longs for you to be with him and learn them too! But what is he doing?' Her face changed again. 'He is shaking his head, he is weeping, he is saying, *Not that way! Oh! Peggy, that was not the way! You shall join me, you shall join me—but, not like that!*'

I find I am trembling as I write the words here; I trembled worse, hearing her say them, with her hand upon me and her face so strange. I said quickly, 'That's enough!' I knocked her fingers from me and drew away from her—I think I struck against her iron gate and made it rattle. I placed my own hand where hers had been. 'That's enough,' I said again. 'You are talking nonsense!' Her cheek had grown pale, and when she looked at me now it was with a kind of horror, as if she saw it all—all the weeping and the shrieking, and Dr Ashe and Mother, the bitter reek of morphia, and my tongue swollen from the pressing of the tube. I had come to her, thinking only of her, and she had thrust my own weak self at me again. She looked at me, and *her* eyes had pity in them!

I could not bear her gaze. I turned away from her and put my face to the bars. When I called to Mrs Jelf, my voice was shrill.

As if she had been very near, the matron appeared at once and proceeded, silently, to free me. She sent a single sharp, anxious glance over my shoulder as she did so—perhaps she had caught the strangeness of my cry. Then I was in the passage-way, with the gate refastened. Dawes had picked up a length of wool, and was drawing it mechanically through her fingers. Her face was lifted to mine, and her eyes seemed full, still, of an awful knowledge. I wished I might say something, some ordinary thing. But I was terribly afraid that if I did she would begin again to speak—would speak of Pa, or *for* him or *as* him—would speak of his sorrow or his anger, or his shame.

So I only turned my head, and moved away from her.

On the ground-floor wards I found Miss Ridley, delivering the women whose reception I had witnessed earlier. I should not have known them, but for the older woman's bruised cheek, for they all looked alike now, in their mud-coloured frocks and their bonnets. I stood and watched until the gates and doors were closed on them, then I came home. Helen was here, but I did not want to talk with her now; I only came straight here and made my own door fast. I have had Boyd in here, only—no, not Boyd, Boyd has gone, it was Vigers, the new one—bringing me water for a bath; and lately Mother has come with the phial of chloral. Now I am so cold, the flesh is shivering upon my back. Vigers has not built my fire high enough, she doesn't know how late I like to sit. But I mean to keep here now, until the tiredness comes. I have screwed my lamp down very low, and sometimes set my hands upon the globe of it, to warm them.

My locket hangs in my closet beside the glass, the only shining thing among so many shadows.

16 October 1874

I woke bewildered this morning, after a night of terrible dreams. I dreamt my father was alive—that I glanced from my window to see him leaning on the parapet of Albert Bridge, gazing bitterly at me. I ran out, and called to him: 'Good

God, Pa, we thought you were dead!' 'Dead?' he answered. 'I have been two years at Millbank! They put me on the treadmill and my boots are worn to the flesh beneath—look here.' He lifted his leg, to show me his soleless shoes and his cracked and battered feet; and I thought, How strange, I don't believe I ever saw Pa's feet before . . .

An absurd dream—and certainly very different to the dreams that used to torment me in the weeks after his death, in which I would find myself squatting at the side of his grave, calling to him through the newly-turned earth. I would open my eyes from those and seem to feel the soil still clinging to my fingers. But I woke afraid this morning, and when Ellis brought my water I made her stay and talk with me, until at last she said she must leave me or my water would be cold. I went and dipped my hands in it then. It was not quite chill, but it had misted the looking-glass; and as I wiped that I looked, as I always looked, for my locket.—*My locket was gone!* and I cannot say where. I know I hung it beside the glass last night, and perhaps I later went and turned it in my fingers. I cannot say when quite it was that I at last went to my bed; but that is not a queer thing with me—it is the point, after all, of the chloral!—and I am certain that I didn't take it with me.—Why would I have? So it could not have been broken and lost in the sheets—besides, I have searched for it among the bed-clothes, very carefully.

And now, all day, I have felt dreadfully naked and miserable. I feel the loss of it, above my heart, quite like a pain. I have asked Ellis, and Vigers—even Pris. But I have not mentioned it to Mother. She would think, first, that one of the girls had taken it; and then, when she saw the folly of that—for, as she has said herself, it is such a plain piece, and I am used to keeping it alongside so many far finer items—then she would think I had grown ill again. She would not know, they none of them could know, the strangeness of my losing it, on such a night!—after such a visit, and such a conversation, with Selina Dawes.

And now, *I* begin to fear I have grown ill again. Perhaps it was the chloral, working on me. Perhaps I rose and seized the locket and placed it somewhere—like Franklin Blake in *The Moonstone*. I remember Pa reading that scene, and smiling over it; but I remember, too, a lady who was visiting us shaking her head. She said she had had a grandmother on whom the laudanum had so worked, she had risen from her sleep and taken a kitchen knife and cut her own leg with it, then returned to her bed, and the blood had flowed into the mattress and half killed her.

I don't believe I would do such a thing. I think, after all, one of the girls must have it. Perhaps Ellis took it up and broke its chain, and was afraid to show me? There is a prisoner at Millbank who says she broke a brooch of her mistress's, and took it to be mended, but was caught with it upon her and charged as a thief. Perhaps Ellis fears that. Perhaps she is so afraid, she has simply thrown the broken locket away. Now I suppose a dust-man will find it, and he will give it to his wife. She will put her dirty fingernail to it and find the lock of shining hair inside it, and wonder for a second whose head it was cut from and why it was kept . . .

I do not care if Ellis broke it, or if the dust-man's sweetheart has it—she might keep the locket, though I had it from Pa. There are a thousand things, in this house, to remind me of my father. It is the curl of Helen's hair I am afraid for, that she cut from her own head and said I must keep, while she still loved me. I am only afraid of losing that—for God knows! I've lost so much of her already.

3 November 1872

I thought no-one would come today. The weather keeps so poor, no-one has come to the house at all, not for 3 days, not even for Mr Vincy or Miss Sibree. We have kept only quietly amongst ourselves, making dark circles in the parlour. We have been trying for forms. They say a medium must try for forms now, that in America it is all the sitters ask for. We tried till 9 o'clock last night but, no spirit coming, we finally put up the lights & had Miss Sibree sing. When we tried again to-day, with again no phenomena occurring, Mr Vincy showed us how a medium might seem to make a limb come, that really was only his own. He did it like this –

I held his left wrist, & Miss Sibree seemed to hold his right. *In fact* however, we held the *same arm*, it was only that Mr Vincy had made it so dark we could not see. 'With my free hand,' he said 'I may do anything, for example this', & he put his fingers against my neck, I felt them & screamed. He said 'You see how a person might be cheated by an unscrupulous medium, Miss Dawes. Imagine if my hand had been made first very hot or very cold, or very wet, then how much realer might it not seem?' I said he ought to show Miss Sibree, & I went & took another seat. Still, I was glad to learn about the arm trick.

We sat until 4 or 5 &, the rain falling heavier than ever, we were all finally certain no-one would come. Miss Sibree stood at the window & said 'O, who would envy us our vocations! We must be here for the living & the dead to call on, just as they please. Do you know I was woken at 5 this morning, by a spirit laughing in the corner of my room?' She put her hands to her eyes & rubbed them. I thought 'I heard that spirit, it came out of a bottle last night, you were laughing it into your chamber-pot,' but Miss Sibree has been kind to me over Aunty, I would never think of saying such a thing aloud. Mr Vincy said 'Our calling is indeed a hard one. Don't you think, Miss Dawes?' Then he got up & yawned & said that, since no-one would come now, we might as well put a cloth on the table & have a game of cards. No sooner had he brought the cards out however, than the bell did sound. Then he said 'So much for our game, ladies! That will be for me, I daresay.'

But when Betty came to the room, it was not him she looked at, it was me. She had a lady with her, & a girl that was the lady's own maid. When the lady saw me rise she put a hand to her heart, crying out 'Are you Miss Dawes? O, I know that you are!' I saw Mrs Vincy looking at me then, & Mr Vincy, & Miss Sibree & even Betty. I however, was as surprised as any of them, the only idea coming into my head being, that this was the mother of the lady I saw a month ago, whose children I said would die. I thought 'This is what comes of being too honest. I should be like Mr Vincy after all. I was sure that the lady had done herself some injury in grief, & now her mother had come to charge me with it.'

But when I looked at the lady's face I saw a pain in it but, behind the pain, a happiness. I said 'Well, I suppose you had better come to my room. It is quite at the top of the house though. Shall you mind the stairs?' She only smiled at her maid & then answered 'Mind them? I have been searching for you for 25 years. I shall not be kept from you now, by a staircase!'

Then I thought she might be a little queer in the head. But I brought her here, & she stood & looked about her, then she looked at her maid & then looked hard at me again. I saw then that she was quite a lady, with hands that were very white & neat, & very handsome though old-fashioned rings. I thought she might be 50 or 51. Her dress was black, a better black than mine. She said 'You do not know, do you, why I have come to you? That is strange. I thought you might have guessed.' I said 'You have been brought here by some sorrow.' She answered 'I was brought here, Miss Dawes, *by a dream.*'

She said a dream had made her come to me. She said she dreamed, 3 nights ago, my face & my name, & the address of Mr

Vincy's hotel. She said she dreamed them, but never thought they might be true until she looked this morning in the *Medium & Daybreak* & saw the notice I put there 2 months ago. That made her come to Holborn to find me out, & now that she had seen my face she said she knew what the spirits wanted by it. I thought 'Well, that is more than I know,' & I looked at her & her maid, & waited. The lady said then 'O Ruth, do you see that face? Do you see it? Shall I show her?' & the maid said 'I think you ought to, ma'am.' Then the lady took something from her coat that was wrapped in a length of velvet, & she uncovered it & kissed it, then showed it to me. It was a portrait in a frame, she held it to me, almost weeping. I looked at it & she watched me, & her maid also watched me. Then the lady said '*Now* I think you see, don't you?'

All I really saw however, was the picture's frame, which was of gold, & the lady's white hand, which trembled. But when she put the picture in my fingers at last I cried out 'O!'

Then she nodded, & placed her hand again upon her breast. She said 'There is so much work that we must do. When shall we start it?' I said we ought to start it straight away.

So she sent her maid out to wait on the landing, & she stayed with me for an hour. Her name is Mrs Brink, & she lives at Sydenham. She came all the way to Holborn, only for me.

6 November 1872

To Islington, to Mrs Baker for her sister Jane Gough, that passed into spirit March '68, *brain-fever*. 2/-

To Kings Cross, to Mr & Mrs Martin, for their boy Alec lost from the side of a yacht – *Found Great Truth in the Great Seas*. 2/-

Here, Mrs Brink, for her especial spirit. £1

13 November 1872

Here, Mrs Brink 2 hrs. £1

17 November 1872

When I came out of my trance today I came out shaking, & Mrs Brink made me lie upon my bed & put her hand upon my forehead. She got her maid to fetch a glass of wine from Mr Vincy & then, when the wine came, she said it was very poor stuff, & she made Betty run to a public house to buy a better sort. She said 'I have made you work too hard.' I said it was not that, but that I often fainted or was ill, & then she looked about her & said she was not surprised, she thought it would make any person poorly to have to live in my room. She looked at her maid & said 'Look at that lamp', she meant the lamp that Mr Vincy has put red paint on, that smokes. She said 'Look at this dirty carpet, look at these bed-clothes', she meant the old silk cover that I brought from Bethnal Green, that Aunty sewed. She shook her head, then held my hand. She said I am far too rare a jewel to be kept in a poor box like this.

17 October 1874

A very curious conversation this evening, regarding Millbank, and spiritualism, and Selina Dawes. We had Mr Barclay to dinner; later came Stephen and Helen, and Mrs Wallace, to play at cards with Mother. We are all asked now, with the wedding so close, to call Mr Barclay 'Arthur'; Priscilla, perversely, now calls him simply *Barclay*. They talk a great deal of the house and grounds at Marishes, and how it will be when she is mistress there. She is to learn to ride, and also to drive a carriage. I have a very clear vision of her, perched on the seat of a dog-cart, holding a whip.

She says there will be a great welcome for us, at the house, after the wedding. She says there are so many rooms, they might put us all in them and nobody would know it. Apparently there is an unmarried cousin of the family's there, that I am sure to take to: a very clever lady—she collects moths and beetles, and has exhibited, at entomological societies, 'alongside gentlemen'. Mr Barclay—Arthur—said that he has written to tell her of my work among the prisoners, and that she has said she will be very pleased to know me.

Mrs Wallace asked me then, when was I last at Millbank? 'How is that tyrant, Miss Ridley,' she said, 'and the old lady who is losing her voice?'—she meant Ellen Power. 'Poor creature!'

'Poor creature?' said Pris then. 'She sounds feeble-minded. Indeed, all of the women that Margaret tells us of sound feeble-minded.' She said she wondered how it was that I could bear their company—'I am sure, you never seem able to bear *our* company for any time at all.' She gazed at me, but it was really Arthur she spoke for and he, who was seated on the carpet at her feet, answered at once that that was because I knew that nothing she said was worth listening to. 'It is all a lot of air. Isn't that so, Margaret?'—he calls me that now, of course.

I smiled at him, but looked at Priscilla, who had leaned to catch at his hand and pinch it. I said that she was quite wrong to call the women feeble-minded. It was only that their lives had been so very different from her own. Could she imagine, how different they had been?

She said that she didn't care to imagine it; that I did nothing *but* imagine it, and things like it, and that made the difference between us. Now Arthur held her wrists, her two slim wrists in one of his great hands.

'But really, Margaret,' Mrs Wallace went on, 'are they all of that class? And are their crimes all so miserable? Have you no famous murderesses there?' She smiled and showed her teeth—which have fine, dark, vertical cracks to them, like old piano keys.

I said that the murderesses were usually hanged; but I told them about a girl there, Hamer, who battered her mistress with a skillet, but was let off when it was proved that the mistress had been cruel to her. I said that Pris ought to look out for that sort of thing, when she is at Marishes.—'Ha ha,' she said.

'There is also a woman,' I went on, '—quite a lady, they paint her on the wards—who poisoned her husband—'

Arthur said, that he certainly hoped there would be nothing of *that* sort at Marishes. 'Ha ha,' said everybody, then.

And while they laughed and began to talk of other things I thought, Shall I say, there is also a curious girl, a spiritualist . . .? I decided first, that I would not—then thought, Why shouldn't I? And when I finally did say it, my brother answered at once, quite easily, 'Ah yes, the medium. Now, what is her name? Is it Gates?'

'It is Dawes,' I said, in some surprise. I had never said the name aloud before, outside of Millbank Prison. I had never heard anyone speak of her, who was not a matron on the wards. But now Stephen nodded—of course, he remembered the case. The prosecuting lawyer in it had been, he said, a Mr

Locke—'a very fine man, retired now. I should like to have worked with him.'

'Mr Halford Locke?' said Mother then. 'He came to dinner once. Do you remember, Priscilla? No, you were too young to sit at table with us then. Do you remember, Margaret?'

I don't remember it. I am glad I don't. I looked from Stephen to Mother—and then I turned to Mrs Wallace and stared at her. 'Dawes, the medium?' she was saying. 'Oh, I know *her*! It was she who struck Mrs Silvester's daughter on the head—or throttled her—or, anyway, nearly killed her . . .'

I thought of the Crivelli portrait that I have sometimes liked to look at. Now it was as if I had brought it shyly down and had it snatched from me, and was watching it being passed about the room and growing grubby. I asked Mrs Wallace, did she really know the girl in the case, the girl that was injured? She said she knew the mother; that the mother was American, and 'quite infamous', and the daughter had a fine head of red hair, but also a white face and freckles. 'What a stink Mrs Silvester raised about that medium! Still, the girl, I think, was made very nervous by her.'

I told her what Dawes has said to me: that the girl was only frightened rather than hurt, and that another lady was frightened by that, and then died. The lady was named Mrs Brink. Did Mrs Wallace know her?—No, she did not. I said, 'Dawes is quite firm. She says a spirit did it all.'

Stephen said that he would say a spirit did it all, too, in her place—indeed, he was astonished they don't hear the claim more often in the courts. I told him that Dawes seemed to me quite guileless. He answered that, of course, a spirit-medium *would* seem guileless. He said they school themselves to seem so, for the sake of their trade.

'They are an evil crew, the lot of them,' said Arthur briskly then. 'A lot of clever conjurers. And they make a very handsome living, preying on fools.'

I put a hand to my breast, to the spot at which my locket should have been hanging; though whether I meant to draw attention to the loss of it—or to conceal it—I could not say. I looked at Helen, but she was smiling with Pris. Mrs Wallace said she was not sure that every medium was wicked. Her friend had been once to a spiritualist ring, and a gentleman had told her a very many things he could not possibly have known—about her mother, and about her cousin's boy, who was burned in a fire.

'They have books,' said Arthur then. 'They are famous for it. They keep books of names, like ledgers, which they circulate amongst themselves. Your friend's name, I am afraid, is probably in one. *Your* name is probably in one.'

Mrs Wallace heard that and gave a cry: 'A spiritualist bluebook! Not really, Mr Barclay?' Pris's parrot shook its feathers. Helen said, 'There was a place at the turn of my grandmother's stairs where one was said to be able to see a ghost, of a girl who had fallen there and broken her neck. She had been on her way to a dance, in silken slippers.'

Mother said, ghosts!—It was all anyone in this house seemed capable of talking of. She could not say why we didn't just go down and join the servants in the kitchen . . .

After a time I went to Stephen's side and, while the others still talked, I asked him if he really thought Selina Dawes quite guilty?

He smiled. 'She is at Millbank. She must be guilty.'

I said that that was the sort of answer he had used to make to tease me, when we were children; that he might as well have been a barrister, even then. I saw Helen watching us. There were pearls at her ears—they looked like drops of wax, I remember seeing them upon her in the old days and imagining them melting with the heat of her throat. I sat upon the arm of Stephen's chair and said, To think of Selina Dawes so violent, and so calculating. 'She is so young . . .'

He said that that meant nothing. He said he frequently sees, in court, girls of thirteen and fourteen—little girls, who have to be placed on boxes so that the juries might view them. But he added, that with girls like that there is invariably an older woman or a man at the back of them, and that if Dawes's youth points to anything, it is probably to that—that she 'fell foul of some sort of influence'. I told him how certain she seems, that the only influences there were, were spiritual ones. He said, 'Well, then there may be a person whom she wishes to protect.'

A person for whom she would spend five years of her life in prison? In Millbank Prison?

Such things occur, he said. Was Dawes not young, and rather handsome? 'And was the "spirit" in the case—now I remember it—not supposed to be some sort of fellow? You know that most of the ghosts performing tricks at séances are actors, dressed in muslin.'

I shook my head. I said I was sure he was not right! I was sure of it!

But as I said it I saw him studying me, thinking, What do *you* know, about the passions that might drive a pretty girl to prison for the sake of her young man?

And what *do* I know about such things? I felt my hand move to my breast again, and tugged at the collar of my gown, to hide the gesture. I said, Did he really think spiritualism a nonsense? And all mediums frauds? He raised his hand—'I did not say *all*, I said *most*. It is Barclay who believes them all a pack of crooks.'

I didn't want to talk to Mr Barclay. 'What *do* you think?' I asked again. He answered that he thought what any rational man should think, given all the evidence: that most spirit-mediums undoubtedly were simple conjurors; that some were perhaps the victims of an illness or a mania—and Dawes might well be one of those, and in that case was to be pitied rather than mocked; but that others—'Well, our age is a marvellous one. I may go to a telegraph office and communicate with a man, in a similar office, on the other side of the Atlantic. How is that done? I could not say. Fifty years ago such a thing would have been deemed perfectly impossible, a contradiction of all the laws of nature. But when the man sends me his message I do not suppose, for that reason, that I have been tricked—that there is a fellow secreted in the room next door and it is he that is tapping out the signal. Nor do I assume—as some ministers, I believe, assume of spiritualism—that the gentleman addressing me is really a demon in disguise.'

But the telegraph machines, I said, are connected by a wire. He said that there are already engineers who believe there can be developed similar machines, working *without* the wire. 'Perhaps there are wires in nature—little filaments—' he waggled his fingers, 'so fine and strange that science has no name for them; so fine that science cannot even see them yet. Perhaps it is only delicate girls, like your friend Dawes, who can sense these wires and hear the messages that pass along them.'

I said, 'Messages, Stephen, from the *dead*?' and he answered, that if the dead do live on in another form, then we should certainly need very rare and curious means to hear them speaking . . .

I said if that was true and Dawes was innocent—

But he didn't say that it was true, of course; he only said it might be. 'And even if it were true, it doesn't mean that *she* is to be trusted.'

'But *if* she is really innocent—'

'If she is, then let her spirits prove it! Besides, there is still the question of the nervous girl, the lady frightened to death. I shouldn't like to have to argue against *them*.' Mother had rung for Vigers, and now he leaned to take a biscuit from her plate. 'I think after all,' he said, brushing crumbs from his waistcoat, 'that I was right the first time. I prefer the beau in muslin to the little filaments.'

When I looked up I found Helen still watching us. I suppose she was glad to see me being kind and ordinary with Stephen—I am not always, I know. I might have gone to her then, but Mother called her to the card-table, to join Pris and Arthur and Mrs Wallace. They played at *Vingt-et-un*, for half an hour or so; then Mrs Wallace cried that they would beggar her of all her buttons, and rose to go upstairs. When she came back, I stopped her, and made her talk to me again of Mrs Silvester and her daughter. How had the daughter seemed to her, I asked, when she had seen her last? She said that she had seemed 'as miserable as mud'—that her mother had matched her with a gentleman with a great black beard and red lips, and 'all Miss Silvester would say to those who asked after her was, "I am to be married"—thrusting her hand at them, that had an emerald upon it the size of an egg, and with all that red hair, too. You know, of course, that she is quite an heiress.'

I said then, where did the Silvesters live? and Mrs Wallace looked arch. 'Gone back, my dear, to America,' she said. She had seen them once before the trial was ended, then next anyone knew their house was all sold up, the staff cleared out—she said she never saw a woman in such a haste as Mrs Silvester was then, to take her daughter home and marry her. 'But there, where there's a trial there's always a scandal, I suppose. I dare say they do not feel such things so keenly, in New York.'

At that, Mother—who had been directing Vigers—said 'What's that? Who are you talking of? Not ghosts, still?' Her throat was green as a toad's, from the reflection of the table she sat at.

I shook my head, and let Priscilla speak again. 'At Marishes,' she began, as the cards were dealt to her; and then, a moment later: 'In *Italy* . . .'

There was some broken talk, then, about the wedding-trip. I stood at the fire and watched the flames, and Stephen sat and dozed over a newspaper. At last I heard Mother saying, '. . . never been, sir, and have no wish to! I could not bear the upset of the journey, the heat, the food'—she was talking of Italy, still, with Arthur. She told him of Pa's trips there, when we were small; and of the visit he had planned to make, with Helen and me to help him. Arthur said that he had not known that Helen was such a scholar, and Mother answered, Oh, but it was Mr Prior's work we had to thank, for Helen being among us at all!

'Helen attended Mr Prior's lectures,' she said, 'and, Margaret meeting her there, she was brought to the house. She was always a great guest of ours after that, and always a favourite with Mr Prior. Of course, we did not know—did we, Priscilla—that it was all on Stephen's account that she came here.—You must not blush, Helen dear!'

I stood at the fire, and heard it all. I watched Helen colour, but my own cheek stayed cool. After all, I have heard the story told that way so many times, I am half-way to believing it myself. And besides that, my brother's words had made me very thoughtful. I didn't speak to anyone else; but before I came up here I went again to Stephen and I woke him from his doze and said, 'That fellow in muslin you spoke of—well, I have seen the prison post-mistress, and do you know what she tells me? Selina Dawes has received not a single letter, in all her time at the gaol—nor has she written one. So you tell me this: who would go voluntarily to Millbank Prison to protect a lover *who sent nothing*—not a letter, not a word?'

He could not answer me.

25 November 1872

An awful row tonight! I had Mrs Brink with me all afternoon, & so was late to the dinner-table. Mr Cutler is very often late & no-one minds it. Mr Vincy seeing me slip in now however, said 'Well Miss Dawes, I hope Betty has kept some meat back for you & not given it to the dog. We thought you might be grown too fine to eat with us.' I said I was sure that such a day would never come. – To which he answered 'Well you, with your *rare gifts*, you should be able to look into the future & tell us all that.' He said there was a time 4 months ago when I had been very glad to take a little place in his establishment, now however it seemed I had my eye on better things. He passed me my plate, that had a bit of rabbit on it & a boiled potato. I said 'Well, it certainly would not be hard to find a better thing than Mrs Vincy's dinners', at which everyone put down their forks & looked at me, & Betty laughed, & Mr Vincy slapped her, & Mrs Vincy began to call out 'O! O! I have never been so insulted, at my own table, by one of my own paying guests!' She said 'You little trollop, my husband took you in, on a low rent, out of the hugeness of his heart. Don't think I haven't seen you cutting your eyes at him.' I said 'Your husband is a beastly old medium-farmer!', & I took the boiled potato from my plate & threw it at Mr Vincy's head. I did not see if it hit him. I only ran from the table, I ran up every stair to here & I lay upon my bed & wept, & then laughed, but finally was sick.

And out of all of them, only Miss Sibree has come to see me, to bring me some bread & butter & a taste of port from her own glass. Mr Vincy I heard talking in the hall downstairs. He said he never wanted another girl medium under his roof, not even if she had her own father with her. He said 'I've heard them called powerful, & powerful they might be. But a young woman in the grip of a spiritual passion – by God, Mr Cutler, that is a frightful thing to see!'

21 October 1874

Can one grow used to chloral? It seems to me that Mother must measure me ever larger quantities of it in order for me even to grow weary. And when I do sleep, I sleep fitfully, there seem to come shadows across my eyes, or murmurings at my ear. They wake me, and I rise and look across the empty room, bewildered. Then I lie another hour, hoping to grow tired again.

It is the losing of my locket that has made me like this. It keeps me restless in the night and, in the day, dull. This morning I was so stupid over some little matter to do with Prissy's wedding, Mother said she does not know what has become of me. She says that mixing with the coarse women at Millbank is making me simple. To spite her, I made a visit there—now, because of it, I am very wakeful indeed . . .

They showed me, first, the prison laundry. This is a frightful room, low and hot and damp and stinking. There are huge, cruel-looking mangles in it, and pots of boiling starch, and lines of racks suspended from the ceiling, from which various nameless shapeless yellow-white items—sheets, under-vests, petticoats, I could not tell—dangle and drip. I could only bear to stay a minute there before I felt the heat begin to draw upon my face and scalp. And yet, the matrons say that the women prefer laundry work over any other kind. For the launderers are allowed a better diet than the regulars, and have eggs, and new milk, and meat above the ration, to keep them strong. And of course, they work together, and I suppose must sometimes talk.

The ordinary wards seemed very chill and miserable, after the heat and bustle of that room. I did not make many visits, but went to two prisoners I had not seen before. The first of these was one of their 'lady' prisoners, a woman named Tully, who is there on a charge of jewel-swindling. She took my hand when I went to her and said, 'Oh, for some sensible conversation at last!' All she would ask for, however, were stories from the newspapers—and those, of course, I am forbidden to repeat there.

She said, 'But is the dear Queen well?—you may tell me that, at least.'

She told me that she had been twice as a guest to parties at Osborne, and she mentioned the names of one or two grand ladies. Did I know them?—I did not. She wondered then 'who my people were'; her manner seemed to cool, I thought, when I told her Pa had only been a scholar. She asked me, finally, if I might have any influence with Miss Haxby over the issue of fitting stays, and tooth-paste.

I did not stay long with her. The second woman I saw, however, I liked much better. She is named Agnes Nash, and was sent to Millbank three years ago for passing bad coins. She is a stout girl, dark-faced and whiskery, but with very blue and handsome eyes. She rose when I entered her cell, did not curtsey, but offered me her chair and leaned, for the rest of the interview, against her folded hammock. Her hands were pale, and very clean. One finger ended at the second knuckle—she said the tip of it had been 'bitten clean off, by a butcher's dog, while she was quite a baby'.

She was quite bold about her crime, and talked about it curiously. 'I come from a neighbourhood of thieves,' she said, 'and ordinary people think us very bad sorts, but we are kind to our own. I was raised to steal when I had to—and did so, many times, I don't mind telling you; but I never needed to much, for my brother was quite top-sawyer in the trade, and he kept us comfortable.' She said that it was bad coining that proved her downfall. She had taken to it—she said many girls take to it, for the same reason—because the work is light and pleasant. She said: 'They have me in here as a passer, but I never passed, I only worked the moulds at home and left the pitching to others.'

I have heard many such fine distinctions made, upon the wards, between grades or kinds or qualities of crimes.

Hearing this one I said, Was hers the lesser offence, then?—At which she replied, that she was not claiming it was lesser, but was only stating it for what it was. 'It is,' she said, 'a business that is little understood. And it is on account of that that I am here at all.'

I said then, What did she mean? It could never be right, could it, to be a counterfeiter? It was not fair, for one thing, on the person who received the bad coins.

'It ain't fair, no. But, bless you, did you think all our queer goes into *your* purse? Some of it does, I don't doubt—and worse luck to you, when you gets a bit! But most of it we keep quietly, between ourselves. I might slip a coin to a chum of mine, for a tin of tobacco. My chum might pass it on to a chum of his own, and that fellow will give it to Susie or Jim—perhaps, for a bit of mutton off the barges. Susie or Jim will only hand it back to me. It is quite a family business, and no harm done to no-one. But the magistrates hear "bad coiner" and think they hear "thief"; and I am to pay for it, with five years . . .'

I said I had not thought, before, that there might be such a thing as a thieves' economy; and that her defence of it was terribly persuasive. She nodded at that. She said I must be sure and bring the subject up, next time I was having supper with a judge. 'I aim to have my go at things, you see, bit by bit,' she said, 'through ladies like yourself.'

She did not smile. I couldn't tell if she was serious, or teased. I said that I would certainly study my shillings rather carefully, in future—now she did smile. 'Do that,' she said. 'Who can say? Perhaps you have one in your purse, even now, as was moulded and trimmed by me.'

But when I asked her how I should know such a coin from all the others, she grew modest—said, there *was* a little sign, but—'Well, I must, you know, preserve my craft—even in here.'

She held my gaze. I said I hoped she didn't mean by that, that she planned to take to the work again when she was freed? She shrugged—said, what else should she hope to do? For hadn't she told me, that she was bred to the trade? Her people would not think much of her, were she to go back to them saved!

I said then that I thought it a very great shame, that she had nothing better to think about than the crimes she would commit in two years' time. She answered: 'It is a shame. But, what else is there for me to do?—except, to count the bricks that make my cell, or the stitches in my sewing—I have done that. Or to wonder how my children do, without a mother—I have done that, too. That is very hard thinking.'

I said she might think about why her children are motherless. She might think about all her old bad ways and where they have put her.

She laughed. 'I did that,' she said. 'I did that, for a year. We all do—you might ask any of us. Your first year at Millbank, you see, is a frightful thing. You will swear to anything, then—you will swear to starve and take your family with you, rather than do another wicked deed and get sent back here. You will promise anything to anyone, you are that sorry. But only for the first year. After that, you ain't sorry. You think of your crimes—you don't think, "If I had not done that, I wouldn't be here", you think, "If I had only done that *better* . . ." You think of all the tremendous swindles and snatches you shall pull off, when you are out. You think, "They have put me here because they think me wicked. Well, damn me if I don't show them wickedness, four years from now!"'

She gave me a wink. I stared at her. At last I said, 'You cannot hope that I will say I'm pleased to hear you talk like that'—and she answered at once, still smiling, that of course she wouldn't think of hoping such a thing . . .

When I got up to leave her she rose too, and walked with me the three or four steps to the gate of her cell, as if showing me out of it. She said, 'Well miss, I am glad to have spoke with you. You remember, now, about them coins!' I said I would, then looked along the passage for the matron. Nash nodded. 'Who are you visiting next?' she asked me—and, since she seemed to mean no harm by it, I answered, guardedly, 'Perhaps your neighbour, Selina Dawes.'

'Her!' she said at once. 'The spooky girl . . .' And she rolled her fine blue eyes, and laughed again.

I did not like her quite so well, then. I called through the bars, and Mrs Jelf came and released me; and then I did go to Dawes. Her face, I thought, seemed paler than before, and her hands were certainly redder and rougher. I had a heavy coat upon me, folded close at the breast; I didn't mention my locket to her, or refer to anything that she had said, last time. But I did say, that I had been thinking of her. I said I had been thinking of the things that she had told me, about herself. I asked her, Would she tell me more, to-day?

She said, What should she tell me?

I said she might tell me more about how her life had been, before they sent her to Millbank. 'How long,' I asked, 'have you been—what you are?'

'What I am?'—She tilted her head.

'What you are. How long have you been seeing spirits?'

'Ah.' She smiled. 'For as long, I think, as I have been seeing anything at all . . .'

And she told me then how it had been for her, when she was young—that she had lived with an aunt, and been many times ill; and that once, when she was iller than at any other time, a lady had come to her. The lady, it turned out, was her own dead mother.

'So my Auntie told me,' she said.

'And weren't you afraid?'

'Auntie said I shouldn't be afraid, because my mother loved me. That was why she came . . .'

And so, the visits had continued, until at last her aunt had thought they ought to 'make the best of the power in her', and began to take her to a spirit-circle. Now there came raps, and shrieks, and more spirits. 'Now I *was* a little frightened,' she said. 'These spirits weren't all so kind as my mother!' And how old was she now?—'Perhaps, thirteen . . .'

I imagine her slender and terribly pale, calling 'Auntie!' when the table tilts. I do wonder at the older woman, exposing her to things like that; when I said as much, however, she shook her head, saying it was good for her that her aunt had done it. She said it would have been worse to have had to meet such spirits all alone—as some lonely mediums, she assured me, have to. And then, the things she saw, they grew familiar to her. 'Auntie kept me very close,' she said. 'Other girls seemed dull, they talked about such ordinary things; and of course, they thought me queer. I might meet someone, sometimes, and I would know they were like me. But that was no good of course, if the person did not know it too—or, worse, if she guessed at it and was afraid . . .'

She held my gaze, until I flinched from it and looked away. 'Well,' she said, more briskly, 'the circle helped my powers grow better.' Soon she knew when to turn 'low' spirits back and reach for the good ones; soon they began to give her messages, 'for their dear friends on earth'. And then, that was a happy thing for people, wasn't it? To have kind messages brought to them when they were grieving and sad?

I thought of my absent locket, and of the message she once brought to *me*—still we had made no reference to it. I said only, 'And so, you were established as a spirit-medium. And people came to you, and paid you money?'

She said very firmly that she had 'never taken a penny' for her own sake; that sometimes people gave her gifts—which was quite a different thing; and that anyway the spirits were known to say that there was never any shame for a person in receiving coins, if it let her or him do spiritual work.

When she spoke about this time in her life, she smiled. 'They were pleasant months for me,' she said, 'though I think I hardly knew that as I lived them. My aunt had left me—gone over, as we would say, to the spirit-side. I missed her, but she was more content there than she had ever been on earth, I could not long for her. I lived for a time in a hotel at Holborn: that was with a spiritualist family, who were kind to me—though they turned against me later, I am sorry to say. I did my work, that made people so glad. I met many interesting people—clever people—people like yourself, Miss Prior! I was several times, indeed, in houses at Chelsea.'

I thought of the jewel-swindler, talking boastfully of her visits to Osborne. Dawes's pride seemed terrible, with the close cell walls about her. I said, 'And was it in one of those houses, that the girl and lady that you are charged with hurting, were made ill?'

She looked away from me. No, she said quietly, that was in a different house, a house at Sydenham.

Then she said, What did I think? There had been such a great stir at morning prayers! Jane Pettit, from Miss Manning's ward, had thrown her prayer-book at the chaplain . . .

Her mood had changed. I knew she wouldn't tell me any more, and I was sorry—I had wanted to hear more about that 'naughty' spirit, 'Peter Quick'.

I had been sitting very still to listen to her. Now, becoming more aware of myself, I found that I was cold, and I drew my coat a little closer about me. The action made my note-book show at my pocket, and I saw her looking at it. All the time we talked, then, her gaze kept returning to that edge of book; until at last, when I rose to leave her, she said, Why did I always carry a book with me? Did I mean to write about the women of the gaol?

I told her then that I take my note-book with me wherever I go—that it was a habit I had fallen into when helping my father with his work. I said I should feel very strange without it, and that what I wrote in it I sometimes later put into another book, that was my diary. I said that *that* book was like my dearest friend. I told it all my closest thoughts, and it kept them secret.

She nodded. My book was like her, she said—it had no-one to tell. I might as well say my closest thoughts there, in her cell. Who did she have, to pass them on to?

She spoke not sulkily, but almost playfully. I said that she might tell her spirits—'Ah,' she said, and she tilted her head. '*They*, you know, see everything. Even the pages of your secret book. Even should you write it'—here she paused, to pass a finger, very lightly, across her lips—'in the darkness of your own room, with your door made fast, and your lamp turned very low.'

I blinked. Now, I said, that was very odd, for that was just how I *did* write my journal; and she held my gaze for a second, then smiled. She said that that was just how everybody wrote. She said she used to keep a diary herself, when she was free, and she always wrote in it at night, in the darkness, and writing it would make her yawn and want to sleep. She said she thought it very hard that now, when she kept wakeful and had all the hours of the night to write in, she must write nothing.

I thought of the wretched sleepless nights I passed, when Helen first told me she was to marry Stephen.—I don't believe I slept three nights together, in all the weeks that passed between that day and the day of Pa's death, when I first took morphia. I thought of Dawes lying open-eyed in her dark cell; I imagined taking morphia or chloral to her, and watching her drink . . .

Then I looked at her again, and saw that she still had her eyes upon the book at my pocket—that made me put my hand to it. And when she saw the gesture, her look grew a little bitter.

She said I was right to keep it so close—that they were all wild for paper there, paper and ink. 'When they bring you to the gaol,' she said, 'they make you put your name upon the page of a great black book'—that was the last time she held a pen and wrote her own name with it. That was the last time she heard her own name spoken—'They call me *Dawes* here, like a servant. If anyone were to say *Selina* to me now, I think I should hardly turn my head to answer. *Selina—Selina*—I have forgotten who that girl is! She might be dead.'

Her voice shook a little. I remembered the prostitute, Jane Jarvis, who had asked me once for a page of my book, to send a message to her pal White—I never called on her again, after that day. But to want a sheet of paper, only to write one's name upon it, so that one might feel oneself conjured through it into life and substance—

It seemed a very little thing to want.

I think I listened once, to make sure that Mrs Jelf was still busy further down the ward. Then I took the note-book from my pocket, opened it to a blank page and placed it flat upon the table; and then I offered her my pen. She gazed at it, and then at me; she held it in her hand, and clumsily unscrewed it—the weight and shape of it, I suppose, were unfamiliar. Then she held it, trembling, above the page, until a glistening bead of ink welled at its nib; and then she wrote: *Selina*. And then she wrote her name in full—*Selina Ann Dawes*. And then the christian name alone again: *Selina*.

She had come to the table to write, her head was very near my own, and her voice, when she spoke, was little more than a whisper. She said, 'I wonder, Miss Prior, if you ever, when you are writing in your diary, write this name there?'

I couldn't answer her for a moment; for, hearing her murmur, feeling the warmth of her in that chill cell, I was struck with the thought of how often I *have* written of her. But then, why *shouldn't* I write of her, since I write of the other women there? And it is surely better to write of her, than of Helen.

So what I said was only, 'Should you mind it, if I did write of you?'

Mind it? She smiled. She said she would be glad to think of anyone—but especially of me, seated at my desk—writing of her, writing, *Selina said this* or *Selina did that*. She laughed: '*Selina told me a lot of nonsense about the spirits* . . .'

She shook her head. But then, as swiftly as it had risen in her, her laughter died and, as I watched, her smile faded. 'Of course,' she said in a lower tone, 'you would not say that. You would say only *Dawes*, like they do.'

I told her, that I would say any name she liked.

'Would you?' she asked me then. 'Oh,' she added, 'you mustn't think that I would ever ask to call you anything but "Miss Prior", in return . . .'

I hesitated. I said, that I supposed the matrons would not think it very proper.

'They would not! And yet,' she looked away from me, 'I would not *say* the name upon the wards. But I find, when I think of you—for I do think of you, at night, when the gaol is quiet—and it is not "Miss Prior" that I say then. It is—well, you were kind enough to tell it to me, once, the time you said you came to be my friend . . .'

A little awkwardly, she placed the pen upon the page again and wrote, beneath her own name: *Margaret.*

Margaret. I saw it, and flinched: she might have put some oath there, or drawn my features in a caricature. She said at once, Oh! She shouldn't have written it, it was too familiar of her! I said, No, no, it was not that, 'It is only—well, it is a name I never cared for. It is a name that seems to have all the worst of me in it—my sister, you know, has a handsome name. When I hear it, I hear my mother's voice. My father called me "Peggy" . . .'

'Then let me say that,' she said. But I remembered then that she had said it once to me already—and I still cannot think of that, without shuddering. I shook my head. She murmured at last, 'Give me another name, then, to call you by. Give me any name but "Miss Prior"—which might be the name of a matron, or of any common visitor; which might as well be nothing to me. Give me a name that will be something—give me a secret name, a name that has, not the worst of you, but the best . . .'

She went on like this—until at last, in the same quick, queer spirit in which I had handed her the book, and then the pen, I said: 'Aurora! You may say then, Aurora! For that is a name—it is a name that—'

I did not of course say it was a name that Helen gave me, before she married my brother. I said it was a name I used to like to call myself, 'when I was young'. And then I blushed, to hear the foolish thing spoken aloud.

She, however, only looked solemn. She gripped the pen again, wrote a line through *Margaret*, and put *Aurora* in its stead.

And then she said, 'Selina, and Aurora. How well they look! They look like angels' names—don't they?'

The ward seemed all at once terribly quiet. I heard the slam of a gate in some distant passage, and the shrieking of a bolt, and then I thought I caught the sound of sand crunched beneath a prison heel, much nearer. Awkwardly, feeling her fingers hard against my own, I took the pen from her. I said, 'I'm afraid I have wearied you.'

'Oh, no.'

'Yes, I think so.' I rose, and went fearfully to the gate. The corridor beyond was empty. I called, 'Mrs Jelf!', and heard an answering cry—'One moment, miss!'—from some far cell. Then I turned and—since there was no-one, after all, to overhear or to see—I held out my hand. 'Good-bye then, Selina.'

Again came her fingers in mine, and she smiled. 'Good-bye, *Aurora*'—she whispered it into the cold air of the cell, so that for one long second the word hung white as gauze before her lips. I drew away my hand and made to turn towards the gate; and then it seemed to me that her look again lost a little of its artlessness.

I said, Why did she do that?

'Do what, Aurora?'

Why did she smile, in that secret way?

'Do I smile, in a secret way?'

'You know you do. What is it?'

She seemed to hesitate. Then she said, 'It is only that you are so very proud. All our talk of spirits, and—'

And what?

But she had grown suddenly playful again. She would only shake her head and laugh at me.

At last, 'Give me the pen again,' she said; and before I could reply she had seized it from me and stepped again to the book, and begun to write upon it very rapidly. Now I did hear Mrs Jelf's boot upon the passage-way. 'Quickly!' I said—for my heart had begun to beat so fast in my breast, I saw the cloth above it give a quiver, like a drum-skin. But she smiled, and wrote on. Still the boot came closer, still my heart thumped!—and then the book was closed at last, the pen screwed up and returned to my hand, and Mrs Jelf made her appearance at the bars. I saw her dark eyes searching, in their usual fretful way; but there was nothing now to see, except my fluttering breast—and that I covered with my coat while she still turned the key and pushed the gate. Dawes had taken a step away from me. Now she put her arms across her apron and bowed her head, not smiling at all. She said only: 'Good-bye, Miss Prior.'

I nodded to her once, then let myself be escorted from her cell, and across the wards, without a word.

But all the time I walked I felt my note-book swing against my hip: she had made a strange and terrible burden of it. At the junction of the gaols I took my glove off, and placed my naked palm upon the binding, and the leather seemed warm, still, from the grip of her rough fingers. But I did not dare to draw it from my pocket. Only when they had shut me into a cab, and the driver had put the whip to his horse, did I pull the book free again; then it took me a moment to find the page, and then another to tilt it so that the street-light fell upon what she had written. I saw it, then closed the book at once and placed it back inside my pocket, but kept my hand upon it, still, through all that jolting ride—at last the leather grew damp.

Now I have it before me. There are the blots of ink, the names she wrote—her own, and my old, secret one. And there, beneath them, is this:

All our talk of spirits & not a mention of your locket.
Did you think they wouldn't tell me, when they took it?
How they smiled Aurora, to see you search!

I am writing by candle-light, and the flame is very low, and dipping. The night is a harsh one, the wind slithers beneath the doors and lifts the carpet from the floor. Mother and Pris are asleep in their beds. The whole of Cheyne Walk might be asleep, the whole of Chelsea. Only I sit awake—only I, and Vigers, for I hear her stir above me, in Boyd's old room—what has she heard, that makes her so restless? I used to think the house grew still at night; now I seem to catch the beating of every clock and watch in it, the creaking of every board and stair. I look at my own face, that is reflected in my bulging window: it seems strange to me, I am afraid to gaze too hard at it. But I am afraid, too, to look beyond it, to the night which presses at it. For the night has Millbank in it, with its thick, thick shadows; and in one of those shadows *Selina* is lying—*Selina*—she is making me write the name here, she is growing more real, more solid and quick, with every stroking of the nib across the page—*Selina*. In one of those shadows *Selina* is lying. Her eyes are open, and she is looking at me.

26 November 1872

I wish my aunty might see me where I am now. – For I am at Sydenham, at Mrs Brink's house! She has brought me here, all in the space of a single day, saying she would rather have me perish than have me pass another hour at Mr Vincy's. Mr Vincy said 'You may have her, ma'am! & much trouble I hope she will bring you', though Miss Sibree wept to see me pass her door, saying she knows I will be very great. Mrs Brink drove with me in her own carriage, & when we arrived at her house I thought I should faint, for it is the grandest place you ever saw, with a garden all about it & a path of gravel leading up to the front door. Mrs Brink saw me looking & said 'My child, you are white as chalk! Of course, this will be queer for you.' Then she took my hand to lead me through the porch, then took me quietly from room to room, saying 'Now, how does this seem to you? Do you know this – & this?' I said I was not sure, because my thoughts were cloudy, & she answered 'Well I daresay it will come, in time.'

Then she brought me to this room, that was once her mother's & is now to be mine. It is so large, I thought at first it must be another parlour. Then I saw the bed in it, & I went & touched the post of it, & I must have turned white again for Mrs Brink said then 'O! This has been too great a shock for you after all! Shall I take you back, to Holborn?'

I said she must not think of doing that. I said we must expect that I should grow weak, but the weakness was nothing & would certainly pass. She said 'Well, I shall leave you for an hour, to grow used to your new home.' Then she kissed me. She did it, saying 'I suppose I may do this, now?' I thought of all the weeping ladies whose hands I have taken in the past half-year, & besides them of Mr Vincy, putting his fingers on me & waiting at my door. Yet no-one has kissed me, no-one at all, since Aunty died.

I had not thought of it before today, I only felt it now, feeling her lips come upon my cheek.

When she left me I went to look at the view from the window, which is all of trees & the Crystal Palace. The Crystal Palace however, I do not think is quite so marvellous as people say. Still, it is a better view than I had at Holborn! When I had looked at it, I walked about this room a little &, the floor being so wide, I tried a polka step upon it, the polka being a dance I have always longed to dance in a large room. I danced very quietly for a quarter of an hour, first taking care to remove my shoes so that Mrs Brink might not hear me in the rooms below. Then I looked about me, at the things that are here.

This is, after all, quite a queer sort of room, for there are a great many cabinets & drawers here, with things in all of them, such as, pieces of lace, papers, drawings, handkerchiefs, buttons, &c. There is a vast closet, & this is filled with gowns, & has rows & rows of little shoes, & shelves with folded stockings & bags of lavender. There is a dressing-table, with brushes & half-used bottles of scent upon it, & a box of brooches & rings & an emerald necklace. And though all these things are extremely old, they are all kept dusted & polished & smelling fresh, so that anyone seeing them, not knowing Mrs Brink, would think what a neat lady her mother must be. They would think 'I'm sure I ought not to be here handling her things, she is sure to be back in a moment' – when in fact of course, she has been dead for 40 years, they might stand & handle them for ever. I knew this, but even I felt I ought not to touch those things. I thought that if I did, then I would turn & see her standing at the door, looking at me.

And as I thought that I *did* turn, & *did* look at the door, & there *was* a woman standing looking at me! And I saw her, & my heart went into my mouth –

But it was only Mrs Brink's maid, Ruth. She had come quietly, not like Betty used to come but like a real lady's maid, like a ghost. She saw me jump & she said 'O, miss, I do beg your pardon! Mrs Brink said you would be resting.' She had brought water for me to wash my face in, & when she had come & poured it into Mrs Brink's mother's china bowl she said 'Where is the gown you will be changing into, for dinner? If you like, I shall take it & have our girl press it up for you.' She kept her eyes on the floor, not looking at me, though I think she might have noticed that my feet were bare, & I wonder if she could have guessed I had been dancing. She stood waiting for my gown, though of course I only have one dress that is finer than the one I was wearing then. I said 'Do you really suppose that Mrs Brink will expect me to change?' & she said 'I think she will, miss.' So I gave her my velvet dress & she brought it to me later, they had steamed it & it was very warm.

I sat in that dress until I heard a bell struck at 8, which is the astonishing hour at which they serve the dinner here. Ruth came for me then, & she unfastened the bow at my waist & retied it, saying 'There, don't you look handsome?' & when she took me into the dining-room Mrs Brink saw me & said 'O, but how handsome you look!' so that I saw Ruth smile. They put me at one side of a great polished table, Mrs Brink sitting at the other, watching me eat & saying all the time 'Ruth, will you give Miss Dawes a little more potato? – Miss Dawes, will you let Ruth cut you some cheese?' She asked me if I cared for the food, & what sorts of food I liked best. The meal was an egg, a pork chop & a kidney, cheese & some figs. Once I thought of Mrs Vincy's rabbit, & laughed. When Mrs Brink asked me why I was laughing I said it was because I was happy.

After dinner Mrs Brink said 'Now, shall we see what influence this house might have upon your powers?' & I sat entranced for an hour, & she I think was very satisfied. She says that tomorrow she will take me shopping for some gowns, & that on the next day or the day after that she will have me lead a circle for her friends, who want very much to have me work for them. She brought me to this room again, & again she kissed me, & Ruth brought more hot water & took my pot, which was not at all like Betty taking it, & made me blush. Now it is 11 o'clock & I am wide awake as anything, which I always am after a trance, though I did not like to tell them that here. There is not a sound in all this vast house. There is only Mrs Brink & Ruth, & the cook &

another servant, & me, in all of it. We might just be a lot of nuns in a nunnery.

The great high bed has Mrs Brink's mother's white lace gown laid out upon it, which Mrs Brink says she hopes I will wear. But I should not be surprised if I do not close my eyes at all tonight. I have been standing at the window, looking at the lights of the town. I have been thinking of the very great & marvellous change that has come so suddenly upon me, & all because of Mrs Brink's dream!

The Crystal Palace I will admit looks something now, with all its lamps lit.

Part Two

23 October 1874

It has grown colder this week. The winter has come early, as it came early in the year that Pa died, and I've begun to see the city change again, as I watched it changing in the miserable weeks when he lay ill. The hawkers on the Walk now stand and stamp their ragged-booted feet, cursing the cold; and where horses wait you see knots of children, huddling at the side of the beasts' great wet flanks for the sake of their heat. There was a mother and her three sons found starved and frozen to death, Ellis told me, in a street across the river from here, two nights ago. And Arthur says that when he drives along the Strand in the hours before dawn, he sees beggars crouched in doorways with their blankets rimed with frost.

There have come fogs, too—yellow fogs and brown fogs, and fogs so black they might be liquid soot—fogs that seem to rise from the pavements as if brewed in the sewers in diabolical engines. They stain our clothes, they fill our lungs and make us cough, they press against our windows—if you watch, in a certain light, you may see them seeping into the house through the ill-fitting sashes. We are driven into evening darkness now, at three or four o'clock, and when Vigers lights the lamps the flames are choked, and burn quite dim.

My own lamp is burning very dimly now. It is as dim, almost, as the rush-lamps that used to be lit for us at night, when we were children. I remember very clearly lying, counting the bright spaces in the rush-lamp's chimney, knowing I was the only wakeful person in all the house, hearing my nurse breathe in her bed, and Stephen and Pris sometimes snore, sometimes whimper, in theirs.

I still recognise this room as the one we slept in then. There are still marks on the ceiling where a swing once hung, and still some of our nursery books upon my shelves. There is one there—I see the spine of it now—that was a favourite of Stephen's. It has pictures of devils and phantoms in it, painted vividly, and the object of it is that you must gaze at each figure very hard, then look quickly at a blank wall or a ceiling—when you do that, you see the phantom floating there, very clearly, but in quite a different colour to the original.

How my mind runs to ghosts, these days!

It has been dull, at home. I went back this morning to read at the British Museum—but it was darker than ever there, because of the fogs, and at two o'clock the murmur was sent out that the reading-room was to be closed. There are always complaints when that happens, and calls for lights to be brought; but I—who was taking notes from a prison history, as much for idleness' sake as for any more serious purpose—I didn't mind it. I thought it even rather marvellous, to emerge from the museum and find the day become so grey and thick, and so unreal. I never saw a street so robbed of depth and colour as Great Russell Street was then. I almost hesitated to step into it, in fear that I would grow as pale and insubstantial as the pavements and the roofs.

Of course, it is the nature of fog to appear denser from a distance. I did not grow vaguer, but stayed sharp as ever. There might have been a dome about me then, that moved when I did—a dome of gauze, I saw it very clearly, it was the kind that servants set on plates of summer cakes to keep the wasps from them.

I wondered if every other person who walked along that street saw the dome of gauze that moved when they did, as clearly as I saw mine.

Then the thought of those domes began to oppress me; I thought I ought to walk and find a cab-rank, and take a carriage home, and keep the blinds down till I got there. I started to walk towards Tottenham Court Road; and, as I went, I gazed at the names upon the door-plates and the windows that I passed—taking a sad kind of comfort from the thought of how little that parade of shops and businesses had changed, since I walked there with my arm in Pa's . . .

And even as I thought it, I saw a square of brass beside a door that seemed to shine a little brighter than the plates on either side of it; and then I drew close, and I saw the plate's dark legend. It said: *British National Association of Spiritualists—Meeting-Room, Reading-Room and Library.*

That name-plate was never there, I am sure, two years ago; or perhaps I only never saw it then, when spiritualism was nothing to me. Seeing it now I stopped, then went a little nearer to it. I couldn't help but think, of course, of *Selina*—it is still a novelty to me, to write her name. I thought, *She* might have come here, when she was free; she might have passed me on this very street. I remembered waiting at that corner once for Helen, in the days when I first knew her. Perhaps Selina passed me then.

The thought was a curious one. I looked again at the brass name-plate, and then at the handle of the door; and then I grasped the handle and turned it, and went inside.

There was nothing to see, at first, but a narrow staircase—for the rooms there are all on the first and second floors, above a shop, and you must climb to them. The stairs take you to a little office. It is panelled with wood, quite handsomely, and has wooden blinds that, to-day, were turned flat against the fogs beyond the windows; between the windows there is a very large picture—done badly, I thought—of *Saul at the House of the Witch of Endor.* There is a carpet of crimson, and a desk; and seated at the desk I found a lady with a paper and, beside her, a gentleman. The lady had a brooch of silver at her breast, cast in that device of clasping hands one sees sometimes on grave-stones. The gentleman wore slippers, worked in silk. They saw me and smiled, then looked sorry. The man said he was afraid the stairs were very steep ones; and then: 'What a shame, you have had a wasted climb! Did you want the demonstration? It has been cancelled, because of the fog.'

He was very ordinary and kind. I said I hadn't come for the demonstration, but—what was perfectly true—that I had stumbled on their doorstep quite by chance, and crossed it out of curiosity. And at that they looked, not sorry, but horribly *sage*. The lady nodded and said, 'Chance, and curiosity. What a marvellous conjunction!' The gentleman reached to shake my hand; he was the daintiest man, with the slenderest feet and hands, I think I ever remember seeing. He said, 'I'm afraid we have little enough to interest you, in this sort of weather, which keeps all our visitors away.' I mentioned their reading-room. Was it open? Might I use it? It was, I might—but they would charge me a shilling. It didn't seem like a very great sum. They had me sign my name in a book upon the desk—'*Miss Pri-or*,' said the man, tilting his head to read it. The lady, he told me then, was named Miss Kislingbury. She is the secretary of the place. He is its curator, and his name is Mr Hither.

Then he showed me to the reading-room. It seemed modest enough to me—the kind of library, I suppose, that might be kept in clubs or little colleges. It had three or four book-cases, all of them very full, and a rack of wands, with newspapers and magazines hung out upon them like dripping laundry. It had a table and leather chairs, and a variety of pictures on the walls, and a glass-fronted cabinet—the cabinet is the really curious or I should say horrible thing, though I didn't know that until later. I went only, at first, to the books. They reassured me. For the fact is, I had begun to wonder why, after all, I had gone in there, and what it was that I was looking for. At a book-case, however—well, a book may be on any queer subject, but one can at least always be certain how to turn a page and read it.

And so, I stood and looked across the shelves, and Mr Hither bent to whisper with a lady who was seated at the table. She was the only other reader there, and quite elderly, and she had one soiled white-gloved hand upon the pages of a pamphlet, keeping it open. When she had first caught sight of Mr Hither she had made an urgent, beckoning gesture. Now she said, 'Such a wonderful text! So inspiring!'

She lifted her hand, and her pamphlet sprang shut. I saw its title—it was *Odic Power*.

The shelves before me, I saw now, were filled with books bearing such titles; and yet, when I drew one or two of them forth, the advice they gave seemed of the very plainest—such as, 'On Chairs', which cautioned against the influences which gathered in stuffed or cushioned chairs used promiscuously by many persons, and advised spirit-mediums to seat themselves on cane-bottomed or wooden-seated chairs only. When I read this I had to turn my head, for fear that Mr Hither would look and catch me smiling. Then I left the book-shelves, and wandered towards the rack of newspapers, and at last I turned my eyes to the pictures on the wall above it. These were of 'Spirits Manifested Through the Mediumship of Mrs Murray, October 1873', and showed a lady looking placid in a chair beside a photographer's palm while, behind her, loomed three misty white-robed figures—'Sancho', 'Annabel' and 'Kip', said the label on the frame. They were more comical even than the books, and I thought suddenly and painfully, Oh, how I wish Pa might have seen these!

As I thought it I felt a movement at my elbow, and I started. It was Mr Hither.

'We are rather proud of those,' he said, nodding to the photographs. 'Mrs Murray has such a powerful control. Do you note the detail, look, on Annabel's gown? We had a piece of that collar framed beside the pictures once, but within a week or two of our having obtained it, it had—after the manner of spirit-stuff, alas for us!—quite melted away. We were left with nothing but an empty frame.' I stared at him. He said, 'Yes, oh yes.' Then he moved beyond me to the glass-fronted cabinet, and he waved for me to follow, saying, Now, these were the real pride of their collection; and here, at least, they had evidence a little more permanent . . .

His voice and manner were intriguing. From a distance it had seemed to me as if the cabinet might be filled with broken statuary, or with pale rocks. When I drew near, however, I saw that the display behind the glass was not of marble, but of plaster and of *wax*—plaster casts, and waxen moulds, of faces and fingers, feet and arms. Many were distorted, rather strangely. Some were cracked, or yellowing with age and with exposure. Each had a label on it, as the spirit-photographs had.

I looked again at Mr Hither. 'You are familiar, of course,' he said, 'with the process? Ah, well, it is as simple and as clever as can be! One materialises one's spirit, and provides two pails—one of water and the other of melted paraffin-wax. The spirit obliges with a hand or a foot, or whatever; the limb is plunged first into the wax, and then, very swiftly, into the water. When the spirit departs, it leaves a mould behind. Few, of course,' he added apologetically, 'are perfect. And not all are so robust that we can venture making casts from them in plaster.'

It seemed to me that most of the objects before us were quite horribly *im*perfect—identifiable by some small, grotesque detail, a toe-nail or a wrinkle or a prick of lashes at a bulging eye; yet incomplete, or bent, or strangely blurred, as if the participating spirits had begun the journey back to their own realm with the wax still warm about their limbs. 'See this little cast here,' said Mr Hither. 'This was made by an infant spirit—do you see the dear little fingers, the dimpling arm?' I saw it, and felt queasy. It looked, to me, like nothing so much as a baby born, grotesque and incomplete, before its time. I remember my mother's sister being delivered of such a thing when I was young, and how the adults whispered over it, and how the whispers haunted me and brought me dreams. I looked away, into the lowest, dimmest corner of the cabinet. Here, however, was the grossest thing of all. It was the mould of a hand, the hand of a man—a hand of wax, yet hardly a hand as the word has meaning, more some awful tumescence—five bloated fingers and a swollen, vein-ridged wrist, that glistened, where the gas-light caught it, as if moist. The infant cast had made me queasy. This made me almost tremble, I cannot say why.

And then I saw the label upon it—and then I did shake.

'Hand of Spirit-Control "Peter Quick",' it said. 'Materialised by Miss Selina Dawes.'

I looked once at Mr Hither—who was still nodding over

the dimpled baby's arm—and then, trembling as I was, I couldn't help but move a little closer to the glass. I gazed at the bulging wax, and remembered Selina's own slender fingers, the delicate bones that move in her wrists as they arch and dip above the putty-coloured wool of prison stockings. The comparison was horrible. I became aware of myself suddenly, stooped low before the cabinet, misting the dull glass with my quick breaths. I straightened—but must have done so too swiftly, for what I felt next was the grip of Mr Hither's fingers upon my arm. 'My dear, are you quite well?' he said. The lady at the table looked up and put one grimy white hand before her mouth. Her pamphlet sprang closed again and tumbled to the floor.

I said the stooping had made me dizzy, and that the room was very warm. Mr Hither brought a chair and made me sit in it—that brought my face close to the cabinet, and again I shuddered; but when the lady reader half-rose and asked, Should she fetch a glass of water and Miss Kislingbury? I told her that I was quite all right now, that she was very kind and must not trouble. Mr Hither, I thought, studied me, but quite evenly; and I saw him looking at my coat and gown. It occurs to me now, of course, that perhaps many ladies go to those rooms in the colours of mourning, claiming chance, and curiosity, have sent them over the threshold and up the stairs; perhaps some of them even swoon, at the cabinet of wax. For when I looked again at the moulds upon the shelves, Mr Hither's gaze and voice grew gentle. He said, 'They *are* a little queer, aren't they? But rather marvellous, for all that?'

I didn't answer him, but let him think what he liked. He told me again then about the wax, the water, the dipping limbs; and at last I grew calm. I said, that I supposed the mediums who brought the ghosts that made the moulds were very clever ones?—and at that, he looked thoughtful.

'I should say *powerful* rather than clever,' he said, '—no cleverer than you or I, perhaps, in matters of the brain. These are matters of the spirit, and that is rather different.' He said it is that that can make the spiritualist faith sometimes seem such a 'rag-tag affair' to non-believers. The spirits have no time, he said, for age, or station, 'or any mortal distinction like that', but find the gift of mediumship scattered amongst the people, like so much grain in a field. I might visit with some great gentleman, he said, that might be sensitive; in the gentleman's kitchen there will be a girl, blackening her master's boots—it might be *she* who is the sensitive one. 'Look here'—he gestured again to the cabinet. 'Miss Gifford, who made this mould—she was a parlour-maid, she never knew her powers until her mistress fell ill with a tumour; then she was guided to place her hands upon the lady's flesh and the tumour was healed. And here, Mr Severn. He is a boy of sixteen, has been bringing spirits since he was ten. I have seen mediums of three and four. I have known babies gesture from their cradles—take up pens and write, that the spirits love them . . .'

I looked back to the shelves. After all, I knew very well why I had gone into those rooms, and what it was I had been looking for there. I put my hand to my breast and nodded to the waxen hands of 'Peter Quick'. I said, What of that medium, Selina Dawes? Did Mr Hither know anything, at all, of her?

Oh, he said at once—and as he said it the lady at the table again lifted her eyes to us. Oh, but of course! Had I never heard, of poor Miss Dawes's misfortune? 'Why, they have her in a prison cell, locked up!'

He shook his head, and looked very grave. I said then that after all I believed I *had* heard something of that. But I had not thought to find Selina Dawes so celebrated . . .

Celebrated? he said. Ah, not in the larger world perhaps. But amongst spiritualists—why, every spiritualist in the country must have trembled, when he heard of poor Miss Dawes's apprehension! Every spiritualist in England had his eyes upon the details of her trial—and wept, too, when he heard the outcome of it; wept—or should have wept—for her sake and for his own. 'The law has us as "rogues and vagabonds",' he said. 'We are meant to practise "palmistry and other subtle crafts". What was Miss Dawes charged with? Assault, was it?—and fraud? What *calumny*!'

His cheek had grown quite pink. His passion astonished me. He asked me, was I familiar with all the details of Miss Dawes's arrest and imprisonment?—and when I answered that I knew only a little, but should certainly like to know more, he took a step towards the shelves of books, ran his eyes and fingers along a set of leather volumes, then drew one forth. 'See here,' he said, lifting the cover. 'This is *The Spiritualist*, one of our newspapers. Here are last year's numbers, from July until December. Miss Dawes was taken by the police—when was it?'

'I believe it was August,' said the lady with the soiled gloves. She had overheard all our talk, and still looked on. Mr Hither nodded, then turned the pages of the magazine. 'Here it is,' he said after a moment. 'Look here, my dear.'

I gazed at the line of print to which he gestured. 'SPIRITUALIST PETITIONS URGED FOR MISS DAWES,' it said. '*Materialising Medium Detained by Police. Spiritualist Testimonies Discounted.*' Beneath this was a brief report. It described the apprehension and detainment of the materialising medium Miss Dawes, following the death of her patron, Mrs Brink, during a private development sitting at Mrs Brink's residence at Sydenham. The subject of the sitting, Miss Madeleine Silvester, was also understood to have been injured. The disturbance was thought to have originated with Miss Dawes's spirit-control 'Peter Quick', or with a low and violent spirit masquerading as that control . . .

This was the same account that I had had, from the matron Miss Craven, and from Stephen, and Mrs Wallace, and Selina herself—though it was the first, of course, to chime with hers and paint the spirit as the guilty one. I looked at Mr Hither. I said, 'I hardly know what to make of this. Really, I know nothing of spiritualism. You think Selina Dawes has been abused—'

Grossly abused, he said. He was quite certain of it. I answered, '*You* are certain of it'—for I had remembered something from Selina's own story. 'But was every spiritualist as confident as you? Were there not some, who were less convinced?'

He bowed his head a little. There were, he said, some doubts, 'in certain circles'.

Doubts? Did he mean, as to her honesty?

He blinked, and then he lowered his voice, in surprise and a kind of reproach. 'Doubts,' he said, 'as to Miss Dawes's *wisdom*. Miss Dawes was a powerful medium, but also a rather young one. Miss Silvester was even younger—just fifteen, I think. It is often to just such mediums as that, that boisterous spirits attach themselves; and Miss Dawes's control—Peter Quick—was sometimes very boisterous indeed . . .'

He said it was perhaps not quite prudent of Miss Dawes to have exposed her sitter, alone and unsupervised, to such a spirit's attentions—for all that she had done it before, with other ladies. There was the question of Miss Silvester's own undeveloped gifts. Who knew how they might not have worked on Peter Quick? Who knew but that the sitting was invaded by some base power? Such powers, as he had said, made special objects of the inexperienced—used them, to make their mischief with. 'And it is mischief,' he said, '—not the marvels of our movement! no, never those!—that the papers seize on. There were many spiritualists, I am afraid—and some of them the very people who had most celebrated her successes!—who turned their backs to poor Miss Dawes, when she stood most in need of their good wishes. And now, I hear, the experience has quite embittered her. She has turned her back to *us*—even to those of us who would be still her friends.'

I gazed at him in silence. To hear him celebrate Selina; to hear her called, respectfully, 'Miss Dawes', 'Miss Selina Dawes', instead of 'Dawes' or 'prisoner', or 'woman'—well, I cannot say how disconcerting that was. It was one thing to have had her story from her own lips, in that dim half-world of the wards, so different, I realise now, to all the worlds that I am used, that no-one in it—not the women, not the matrons, not even myself when I am there—seem quite substantial or quite real. It was very different to hear it here, told by a gentleman. I said at last, 'And was she really so successful then, before her trial?'—and at that he clasped his hands together as if in rapture and said, My goodness me, but yes, her séances were things of wonder! 'She was never so famous, of course, as the best of the London mediums—as Mrs Guppy, Mr Home, Miss Cook, of Hackney . . .'

Them I had heard of. Mr Home, I knew, was said to be able to float through windows, and to handle coals from an open fire. Mrs Guppy was once transported, from Highbury to Holborn—'Transported,' I said, 'whilst writing "onions" on her shopping-list?'

'Now you smile,' said Mr Hither. 'You are like everybody else. The more extravagant our powers are, the more you care for them, for then you may disclaim them as a nonsense.'

His gaze was still kind. I said, Well, perhaps he was right. But Selina Dawes: *her* powers were not usually so startling as Mr Home's and Mrs Guppy's—were they?

He gave a shrug, and said that his definition of the startling, and mine, might be quite different. As he spoke he stepped again to the shelves and drew another volume from them—it was *The Spiritualist* again, but an earlier number. He took a moment to find the piece he wanted, then passed it to me, saying, Was that what I would term 'startling'?

The report told of Selina leading a séance at Holborn, where there were bells brought in the darkness and shaken by spirits, and a voice that whispered through a paper tube. He handed me a second book—a different paper, I forget the title of it, it described a private meeting at Clerkenwell, at which invisible hands dropped flowers, and chalked names upon a slate. An earlier number of the same newspaper told of a grieving gentleman, amazed to find a message from the spirit-world stand out, in words of crimson, on Selina's naked arm . . .

This, I suppose, was the time she had told me of. She had spoken of it proudly, as a 'happy time' for her; but her pride had made me sad even then—now the memory of it made me sadder. The flowers and the paper tubes, the words marked out upon her flesh—it seemed a tawdry sort of show, even if put on by spirits. She had held herself at Millbank as an actress might, surveying a marvellous career. Behind the newspaper reports now I thought I saw that career for what it really was—the career of a butterfly or a moth, a career passed in the homes of strangers, a career spent lurching from one dreary district to the next, performing garish tricks for petty payments, like a music-hall turn.

I thought of the aunt, who had set her upon it. I thought of the lady who died—Mrs Brink. I had not realised until Mr Hither told me of it now, that Selina had lived *with* Mrs Brink, in her own house—'Oh yes,' he said. He said it was that which made the charges that were levelled against Selina—charges of deception, as well as of violence—so very gross; for Mrs Brink had so admired her, she had given a home to her—'was quite a mother to her'. It was through her care that Selina's gifts were nurtured, and grew. It was at the house at Sydenham that she first acquired her spirit-control, 'Peter Quick'.

I said, And yet, it was Peter Quick that so frightened Mrs Brink—so frightened her, she died?

He shook his head. 'It seems a curious business to us, a thing that no-one could explain except the spirits. Alas, *they* were not called, to speak in Miss Dawes's defence.'

His words intrigued me. I looked at the first paper he had shown me, that was dated for the week of her arrest. I asked, had he the later numbers? Did they report the trial, the verdict, the taking of her to Millbank? He said, Of course, and after a moment's search he found them for me, and fastidiously tidied the earlier volumes away. I brought a chair up to the table, setting it far from the white-gloved woman, and placing it at an angle which put the cabinet of moulds out of my gaze. Then, when Mr Hither had smiled, and bowed, and left me, I sat and read. I had my note-book with me, there were phrases in it I had copied from the prison histories at the British Museum. Now I folded those pages away and began to take notes instead on Selina's trial.

First they question Mrs Silvester, the American woman, the mother of the nervous girl, Mrs Wallace's friend. She is asked, 'When did you first make the acquaintance of Selina Dawes?'—and she answers: 'It was at a séance at the house of

Mrs Brink, in July. I had heard her spoken of, in London, as a very clever medium, and I wanted to see her for myself.'

'And what was your opinion of her?'—'I saw at once that she was very clever indeed. She also seemed modest. There were two rather wild young gentlemen at the meeting, who I thought she might try to flirt with. She did not, and I was glad of it. She seemed quite the girl of quality that everybody painted her. Of course, I should not on any other terms have allowed the intimacy between her and my daughter to develop.'

'And what was your purpose in encouraging this intimacy?'—'It was a professional one, a medical one. I had hopes that Miss Dawes might be able to assist in restoring my daughter to a proper state of health. My daughter has been ill for several years. Miss Dawes persuaded me that the condition had its origins as a spiritual ailment, rather than a physical one.'

'And Miss Dawes attended your daughter at the house at Sydenham?'—'Yes.'

'Over what period of time?'—'Over a period of two weeks. My daughter sat in a darkened room with Miss Dawes for an hour a day, and for two days in each week.'

'Did she sit alone with Miss Dawes on these occasions?'—'No. My daughter was fearful, and I sat with her.'

'And what was your daughter's state of health over this two-week period of attendance by Miss Dawes?'—'It struck me as improved. I believe now, however, that the improvement was the product of an unhealthy excitement on my daughter's part, encouraged in her by Miss Dawes's treatment.'

'Why do you believe that?'—'Because of the condition in which I found my daughter, on the night on which Miss Dawes finally abused her.'

'This was the night on which Mrs Brink suffered her fatal seizure? That is, the night of the third of August, 1873?'—'Yes.'

'And on this night, contrary to your usual practice, you allowed your daughter to visit Miss Dawes alone. Why was that?'—'Miss Dawes persuaded me that my presence at her sittings was hindering Madeleine's progress. She claimed there must be certain channels opened between my daughter and herself, that my presence was obstructing. She was an artful speaker, and I was taken in.'

'Well, that of course is for the gentlemen here to decide. The fact is, you allowed Miss Silvester to travel alone to Sydenham.'—'Quite alone. She was accompanied only by her maid, and of course by our driver.'

'And how did Miss Silvester appear to you on setting out for her appointment with Miss Dawes?'—'She appeared nervous to me. I now believe her, as I have said, to have been unhealthily excited by the attentions of Miss Dawes.'

'In what way "excited"?'—'Flattered. My daughter is a simple girl. Miss Dawes encouraged her to believe that she had the powers of a spirit-medium. She said her good health would be attained once these had begun to be developed.'

'Did you believe your daughter might be the possessor of such gifts?'—'I was ready to believe anything, sir, that would explain my daughter's illness to me.'

'Well, and then your faith on this issue will be seen to do you credit.'—'I hope it will.'

'I am certain it will. Now, you have told us of your daughter's state of health as she left you to visit Miss Dawes. When, Mrs Silvester, did you see your daughter next?'—'Not until several hours later. I had expected her return at nine o'clock, and by half-past ten had had no word of her.'

'What did you make of that delay?'—'I was beside myself with fear for her! I sent our footman in a cab, to enquire after her safety. He returned having seen my daughter's maid; he told me my daughter was injured and that I must go to her at once. I did that.'

'And how did the house seem to you, when you reached it?'—'It was upset, with servants running from floor to floor and all the lights turned high.'

'And in what condition did you find your daughter?'—'I found her—oh! I found her in a waking swoon, with her clothes very dishevelled, and marks of violence upon her face and throat.'

'And what was her response on seeing you come to her?'—'She was not in her senses. She thrust me from her, and spoke to me foully. She was infected, by that little charlatan Miss Dawes!'

'Did you see Miss Dawes?'—'I did.'

'What was her condition?'—'She seemed distracted. I cannot say, I am sure she was acting. She told me that my daughter had been roughly handled by a male spirit; I had never heard of anything more grotesque. And when I told her as much, she grew abusive. She told me to be silent, and then she wept. She said that my daughter was a silly girl, and thanks to her, she had lost everything. It was then I learned that Mrs Brink had had a seizure and lay ill upstairs. I believe she died about that time, while I was attending to my daughter.'

'And you are certain of Miss Dawes's words? Are you certain that is what she said: "I have lost everything"?'—'Yes.'

'And what did you understand her to mean by that?'—'Why nothing, then. I was too anxious for the health of my daughter. Now, however, I understand very well. She meant that Madeleine had thwarted her ambitions. She meant to make my daughter her particular friend, and squeeze her for every cent. And how could she do that, with my daughter having fallen into such a state, and with Mrs Brink dead, besides . . .?'

There is a little more, but I did not copy it. This comes in one edition of the newspaper; in the next week's number there is a report of the examination of the girl herself, Miss Madeleine Silvester. There are three attempts to question her, and she breaks down weeping at every one. Mrs Silvester I don't much care for—she reminds me of my mother. Her daughter, however, I hate: she reminds me of myself.

They ask her, 'What, Miss Silvester, can you remember of the events of that night?'—'I am not sure. I am not certain.'

'Do you remember leaving your own house?'—'Yes, sir.'

'Do you remember arriving at Mrs Brink's?'—'Yes, sir.'

'What was the first thing that happened to you there?'—'I took tea, in a room with Mrs Brink and Miss Dawes.'

'And how did Mrs Brink seem to you? Did she seem healthy?'—'Oh yes!'

'Did you observe her manner towards Miss Dawes? Did it strike you as being at all cool or unfriendly, or in any way remarkable?'—'It was only friendly. She and Miss Dawes sat very near one another, and sometimes Mrs Brink held Miss Dawes's hand and touched her hair or her face.'

'And can you remember anything that was said by Mrs Brink or Miss Dawes?'—'Mrs Brink said to me that she thought I must be excited; I said that I was. She said I was a lucky girl, to have Miss Dawes to teach me. Then Miss Dawes said that she guessed it was time for Mrs Brink to go and leave us. Then Mrs Brink went.'

'Mrs Brink left you alone with Miss Dawes? What happened then?'—'Miss Dawes took me to the room in which we usually sat, that had the cabinet in it.'

'This is the room in which Miss Dawes conducted her séances, her so-called "dark circles"?'—'Yes.'

'And the cabinet is the covered space in which Miss Dawes would sit when she became entranced?'—'Yes.'

'What happened next, Miss Silvester?'—[*Witness hesitates.*] 'Miss Dawes sat with me and held my hands, and then she said she must prepare herself. She went into her cabinet and when she came out she had removed her gown and was dressed only in her petticoat. Then she said that I must do the same—only, I mean, not in the cabinet, but before her.'

'She asked you to remove your gown? Why do you think she did that?'—'She said that I must do it for the development to work properly.'

'Did you remove your gown? You must only tell us the truth, and not mind these gentlemen.'—'Yes, I did. That is, Miss Dawes did, because my maid was in another room.'

'Did Miss Dawes also ask you to remove any item of jewellery?'—'She told me to take off my brooch, because it had been pinned right through the clothing beneath my gown and I shouldn't have been able to get the gown off without ripping it.'

'What did she do with the brooch?'—'I don't remember. My maid Lupin got it back for me later.'

'Very well. Now, tell me. After Miss Dawes had induced you to remove your gown, how did you feel?'—'I felt strange at first, but then I found I did not mind. The night was such a hot one, and Miss Dawes had locked the door.'

'Was the room brightly lit, or rather dark?'—'It was not dark, but not very bright either.'

'You could see Miss Dawes quite clearly?'—'Oh yes.'

'And what happened next?'—'Miss Dawes took my hands again, and then began to say there was a spirit coming.'

'How did that make you feel?'—'It made me feel afraid. Miss Dawes said I mustn't be afraid, because the spirit was only Peter.'

'That is, the spirit allegedly named "Peter Quick"?'—'Yes. She said it was only Peter, and I had seen him before at the dark circle and now he only wanted to come and help in the development.'

'Did you feel less afraid then?'—'No, I began to be more afraid. I closed my eyes. Miss Dawes said, "Look Madeleine, he is here", and I heard a sound as if there were someone in the room, but I didn't look, I was too afraid.'

'You are sure you heard another person there?'—'I think so.'

'What happened then?'—'I am not sure. I was so frightened I began to cry. Then I heard Peter Quick say "Why are you crying?"'

'Are you sure that it was another voice that said that, and not Miss Dawes's?'—'I think so.'

'Was there ever a moment at which Miss Dawes and this other person spoke at once, together?'—'I can't say. I am sorry, sir.'

'You need not be sorry, Miss Silvester, you are very brave. Tell us, what happened now, can you remember that?'—'I remember, sir, that a hand was put upon me and the hand was very rough and cold.' [*Witness weeps.*]

'Very well, Miss Silvester, you are doing very well indeed. I have just a few more questions. Can you answer them?'—'I will try.'

'Good. You felt a hand upon you. Where was the hand placed?'—'On my arm, sir, above the elbow.'

'Miss Dawes claims that at this point you began to cry out. Do you remember that?'—'No, sir.'

'Miss Dawes says that you fell into a kind of fit, that she attempted to calm you and, in the attempt, was obliged to grip you rather hard. Do you remember that?'—'No, sir.'

'What do you remember of this time?'—'I don't remember anything, sir, until Mrs Brink came and opened the door.'

'Mrs Brink came. How did you know it was she? Did you now have your eyes open?'—'No, I still had my eyes closed, because I was still afraid. But I knew it was Mrs Brink because I heard her calling at the door, then I heard the door unlocked and opened, then Mrs Brink's voice again, very near me.'

'Your maid has told us already that at this point she heard you calling out to the house. That you cried out, "Mrs Brink, oh Mrs Brink, they mean to murder me!" Do you remember calling that?'—'No, sir.'

'You are certain that you don't remember calling or saying those words?'—'I am not sure, sir.'

'Can you think of why you might have said such a thing?'—'No, sir. Except, that I was very frightened of Peter Quick.'

'Frightened, because you thought he meant to do you harm?'—'No, sir, only frightened because he was a ghost.'

'I see. Well, can you tell us now what happened when you heard Mrs Brink open the door? Can you tell us what she said?'—'She said, "Oh Miss Dawes", and then she cried out "Oh!" again. And then I heard her call out for her mother, and her voice seemed peculiar.'

'In what way "peculiar"?'—'Very thin and high. Then I heard her fall.'

'What happened then?'—'Then I think Miss Dawes's servant came, and I heard Miss Dawes tell her to help her with Mrs Brink.'

'And were your eyes open now, or still shut?'—'Now I opened them.'

'Was there any sign of any kind of spirit in the room?'—'No.'

'Was there anything in the room, that had not been there before you closed your eyes—for example, any item of clothing?'—'I don't think so.'

'And what happened next?'—'I tried to put my gown on, and after a minute Lupin, my maid, came. When she saw me she began to cry, and that made me cry again. Then Miss Dawes said that we must be quiet, and that we should help her with Mrs Brink.'

'Mrs Brink had fallen upon the floor?'—'Yes, and Miss Dawes and her servant were trying to lift her.'

'Did you help her, as she had asked you?'—'No, sir, Lupin wouldn't let me. She took me downstairs to the parlour, and went to fetch me a glass of water. Then I don't remember any other thing until after my mother came.'

'Do you remember speaking to your mother when she arrived?'—'No, sir.'

'You don't remember saying anything indelicate to your mother? You don't recall being encouraged to say anything indelicate, by Miss Dawes?'—'No, sir.'

'Did you see Miss Dawes again, before you left?'—'I saw her speaking to my mother.'

'How did she seem to you then?'—'She was crying.'

There are other witnesses—servants, the policeman who was summoned by Mrs Silvester, the doctor who attended Mrs Brink, friends of the house; but the paper does not have space for all their testimonies, and the next it gives is that of Selina herself. I hesitated a little before I read her speeches, and imagined her being led across the gloomy court. Her hair, I think, would be very splendid and bright, for all the gentlemen around her would be in suits of black; and I think her cheek would be pale. She 'bore herself bravely'—so *The Spiritualist* says. It says the court was filled with people come to see her examined; and that her voice was rather low, and sometimes shook.

She was questioned first by her own lawyer, Cedric Williams, and then by her prosecutor, Mr Locke—Mr

Halford Locke, that is, who came to dinner once at Cheyne Walk, and whom my brother knows to be a very fine man.

Mr Locke said: 'Miss Dawes, you resided with Mrs Brink in her own house for a period of a little less than a year. Is that right?'—'Yes.'

'On what terms did you reside there?'—'I was Mrs Brink's guest.'

'You did not pay a rent to Mrs Brink?'—'No.'

'Where did you reside, before taking up a place in Mrs Brink's household?'—'I lived in rooms in a hotel at Holborn, at Lamb's Conduit Street.'

'How long did you intend to remain the guest of Mrs Brink?'—'I did not think about it.'

'You had no thoughts at all, for your future?'—'I knew the spirits would guide me.'

'I see. Was it spiritual guidance that led you to Mrs Brink?'—'Yes. Mrs Brink came to see me at the hotel at Holborn that I have spoken of, and was moved to ask me to attend her at her own house.'

'You conducted spiritual sittings with Mrs Brink, in private?'—'Yes.'

'And you continued to offer private séances, to paying customers, at Mrs Brink's house?'—'At first I did not. Later it was impressed upon me by the spirits that I ought to. But I never obliged my sitters to pay me anything.'

'You did indeed hold séances, however; and it was the custom, I believe, for your visitors to leave you gifts of money, at the conclusion of your services to them?'—'Yes, if they liked.'

'What was the nature of your services to them?'—'I would consult the spirits in their behalf.'

'How would you do this? Would you put yourself into a trance in order to do this?'—'Usually.'

'And what would happen then?'—'Well, I would have to rely on my sitters to tell me, afterwards. But usually a spirit would speak through me.'

'And often a "spirit" would appear?'—'Yes.'

'Is it true that most of your customers—pardon me, your

"sitters"—were ladies and girls?'—'I was visited by gentlemen, as well as by ladies.'

'Did you receive gentlemen in private?'—'No, never. I only ever received gentlemen as sitters at dark circles, when there were always also ladies present.'

'But you received ladies individually, for private consultation with the spirits and for spiritual tuition?'—'Yes.'

'These private sittings placed you in a position, I should say, to exercise considerable influence over your lady sitters?'—'Well, it was in order to receive my influence that they came to me.'

'And what, Miss Dawes, was the nature of this influence?'—'What do you mean?'

'Would you say it was of a healthy, or an unhealthy nature?'—'It was healthy, and very spiritual.'

'And some ladies found this influence beneficial in the alleviation of certain indispositions and complaints. Miss Silvester, in fact, was one such lady.'—'Yes. Many ladies came to me with symptoms such as hers.'

'Symptoms such as . . .?'—'Such as weakness, nervousness, and aches.'

'And your treatment—what was it? [*Witness hesitates.*] Was it homeopathic? Mesmeric? Galvanic?'—'It was spiritual. I have often found that ladies with symptoms such as Miss Silvester's were spiritually sensitive—that they were clairvoyante, but their powers needed developing.'

'And this was the particular service you offered?'—'Yes.'

'And it involved—what? Rubbing? Shampooing?'—'There was a certain amount of laying on of hands.'

'Rubbing and shampooing.'—'Yes.'

'For which your visitors were required to remove certain articles of clothing?'—'Sometimes. Ladies' gowns are often cumbersome. I think, any doctor of medicine would ask his patients to do the same.'

'He would not, I hope, also remove his own clothes.' [*Laughter.*]—'Spiritual and ordinary medicine require different conditions.'

'I am glad of it. Let me ask you, Miss Dawes: were many of

your lady callers—I mean the kind, now, who came to you for spiritual shampoos—were many of them wealthy?'—'Well, some were.'

'I should say they all were, were they not? You would not, would you, ever have introduced a woman into Mrs Brink's house, who was anything other than a lady?'—'Well, no, I should not have done that.'

'And Madeleine Silvester, of course, you knew to be a very wealthy girl. It was for that very reason, was it not, that you sought to make her your particular friend?'—'No, not at all. I was only sorry for her, and hoped to make her better.'

'You have made many ladies better, I suppose?'—'Yes.'

'Will you give us their names?'—[*Witness hesitates.*] 'I would not think it very proper to do that. It is a private thing.'

'I think you are right, Miss Dawes. It is a very private thing. So private, indeed, that my friend Mr Williams can find not a single lady willing to stand before this court and testify to the efficacy of your powers. Do you find that curious?'—[*Witness does not reply.*]

'How large, Miss Dawes, is Mrs Brink's house at Sydenham? How many rooms has it?'—'It has, I suppose, nine or ten.'

'It has thirteen, I believe. How many rooms had you the tenancy of, in your hotel at Holborn?'—'One, sir.'

'And what was the nature of your relationship with Mrs Brink?'—'What do you mean?'

'Was it professional? Affectionate?'—'It was affectionate. Mrs Brink was a widow, and had no children of her own. I am an orphan. There was a sympathy between us.'

'She regarded you, perhaps, as a kind of daughter?'—'Well, perhaps.'

'Did you know she suffered from a weakness of the heart?'—'No.'

'She never discussed that with you?'—'No.'

'Did she ever discuss with you how she planned to settle her goods and property, after her death?'—'No, never.'

'You spent many hours alone with Mrs Brink, I believe?'—'Some hours.'

'Her maid Jennifer Wilson has testified that it was your custom to spend an hour or more alone with Mrs Brink, each night, in her own chamber.'—'That was when I would consult the spirits in her behalf.'

'You and Mrs Brink would spend an hour at the close of each night, consulting spirits?'—'Yes.'

'Consulting one spirit in particular, perhaps?'—[*Witness hesitates.*] 'Yes.'

'On what matters did you consult it?'—'I cannot say. It was a private matter of Mrs Brink's.'

'The spirit said nothing to you about weak hearts, or wills?' [*Laughter.*]—'Nothing at all.'

'What did you mean when you said to Mrs Silvester, on the night of Mrs Brink's death, that Madeleine Silvester was "a silly girl, and thanks to her you had lost everything"?'—'I don't remember saying that.'

'Do you mean to imply by that, that Mrs Silvester has lied to the court?'—'No, only that I don't remember saying it. I was very upset, because I thought that Mrs Brink might die; and I think it is rather hard of you to tease me about it now.'

'It was a terrible thought to you, that Mrs Brink might die?'—'Of course.'

'Why did she die?'—'Her heart was weak.'

'But Miss Silvester has testified to us that Mrs Brink appeared very healthy and calm, only two or three hours before she died. It was on opening the door to your chamber, it seems, that she became ill. What was it that so frightened her then?'—'She saw Miss Silvester in a fit. She saw a spirit handling Miss Silvester rather roughly.'

'She did not see you, garbed as a spirit?'—'No. She saw Peter Quick, and the sight upset her.'

'She saw Mr Quick—Mr Quick-tempered, perhaps we should call him. This is the Mr Quick whom you were in the habit of "materialising", at séances?'—'Yes.'

'Whom you "materialised", in fact, on Monday, Wednesday and Friday evenings—and at other times, for single ladies at private sittings—throughout the whole of a six-month period, from February this year until the night of Mrs Brink's death?'—'Yes.'

'Will you "materialise" Mr Quick for us now, Miss Dawes?'—[*Witness hesitates.*] 'I don't have any of the proper equipment.'

'What do you need?'—'I would need a cabinet. The room would have to be made dark—no, it cannot be done.'

'It cannot be done?'—'No.'

'Mr Quick is rather shy, then. Or is Mr Quick afraid he will be charged in your place?'—'He could not appear in any place where the atmosphere is so unspiritual and repellent. No spirit could.'

'That is a pity, Miss Dawes. For the fact remains that, with no Mr Quick to speak on your behalf, the evidence is rather pointed. A mother entrusts a delicate girl into your care, and that girl is distressed and queerly handled—so queerly, that the sight of you with your hands upon her is enough to send your patron, Mrs Brink, into a fit that soon proves fatal.'—'You have it absolutely wrong. Miss Silvester was only made afraid, by Peter Quick. She has told you as much, herself!'

'She has told us what she fancied she believed, under your influence. I think she was certainly made very afraid—so afraid, indeed, that she called out that you meant to murder her! Now, that was rather troublesome, wasn't it? I should think you would try any kind of rough handling, to silence cries like those, that would bring Mrs Brink; that would bring Mrs Brink and expose you to her, dressed as the spirit you had cheated her with. But Mrs Brink came anyway. And what a vision she had then, poor lady! A vision hard enough to break her heart—to make her call, in her distress, on her own dead mother! Then she remembered, perhaps, how "Peter Quick" had come to her, night after night; then she remembered, perhaps, how he had spoken of you—how he had praised you and flattered you, called you the daughter she had never had, made her give you gifts, and give you money.'—'No! It isn't true! I never took Peter Quick to her. And what she gave me, she gave me for my own sake, because she loved me.'

'Then she thought, perhaps, of all the ladies that had come to you. Of how you had made them your particular friends, and flattered them, had raised in them—in Mrs Silvester's words—an "unhealthy excitement". Of how you had extracted from them gifts, and money, and favours.'—'No, no, that is perfectly untrue!'

'I say it is not untrue. How otherwise can you explain to me your interest in a girl such as Madeleine Silvester—a girl your junior in years, and very much your superior in social standing; a girl of evident fortune, and uncertain health; a frail and vulnerable girl? What *was* your interest, if not a mercenary one?'—'It was of the highest and the purest and the most spiritual kind: a desire to assist Miss Silvester in knowing her own clairvoyant powers.'

'And that was all?'—'Yes! What else could there have been?'

There are shouts from the public gallery at this, and also hisses. It is quite true, what Selina told me at Millbank: the paper makes a kind of champion of her at first, yet, as the trial proceeds, its sympathies wane. 'Why are there no ladies willing to advertise their experiences of Miss Dawes's methods?' it asks, early on, in a kind of outrage; the question sounds rather different, however, when repeated after Mr Locke's examination. Then there comes the testimony of a Mr Vincy, proprietor of the hotel at which Selina lodged, at Holborn. 'I always found Miss Dawes a very designing sort of girl,' he says. He calls her 'artful', a 'provoker of jealousies', and 'prone to fits of temper . . .'

Finally there is a cartoon, reprinted from the pages of *Punch*. It shows a sharp-faced medium drawing a necklace of pearls from the throat of a timid young lady. 'Must the pearls come off, too?' asks the timid girl. The cartoon is entitled 'Un-Magnetic Influences'. It was drawn, perhaps, while Selina stood pale and received her verdict, or was led, handcuffed, into the prison van—or sat shivering while Miss Ridley put the scissors to her head.

I found I did not like to gaze at it. Instead, I looked up—and when I did that, I at once caught the eye of the lady who was seated at the far end of the table.

She had been there, with her head bowed over *Odic Power*, while I had written out my notes. I think that we had sat there together for two hours and a half, and I had not thought of her once. Now, seeing me raise my eyes, she smiled. She said she never saw a lady so industrious! She believed there was an aura to that room, that inspired one to marvellous feats of learning. 'But then'—she nodded to the book before me—'I think you have been reading about poor Miss Dawes. What a story hers is! Do you mean to act in her behalf? I went very frequently, you know, to her dark circles.'

I gazed at her, and almost laughed. It seemed to me suddenly that if I were to go into the street and touch any person on the shoulder and say 'Selina Dawes' to them, they would have some queer fact or article of knowledge for me, some piece of the history that had been shut off by the closing of the Millbank gates.

Oh yes, said the lady, seeing my face. Yes, she had been to the séances at Sydenham. She had many times seen Miss Dawes entranced, she had seen 'Peter Quick'—she had even felt his hand grip hers, felt him place a kiss upon her fingers!

'Miss Dawes was such a gentle girl,' she said. 'You could not look at her and not admire her. Mrs Brink would bring her into us and she would be dressed in a simple gown, with all her golden hair let down. She would sit with us, and have us pray a little; and even before the prayer was said, she would have slipped into a trance. She would do it so neatly, you would hardly know that she was gone. You would only know when she began to speak, for then of course the voice would be not her voice, but a spirit's . . .'

She said she had heard her own grandmother speak to her, through Selina' s mouth. She had told her not to grieve; and that she loved her.

I said, Would she bring messages like that, to all the people in the room?

'She would bring messages until the voices proved too feeble or, perhaps, too loud. Sometimes the spirits would crowd about her—spirits, you know, are not always polite!—and that would make her tired. Then Peter Quick would come, to chase the spirits away—only he, of course, was sometimes as rowdy as they. Miss Dawes would say, that we must take her to the cabinet, very quickly; that Peter was coming, and would pluck the life from her, if we did not place her in her cabinet at once!'

She said 'her cabinet' as if she might be saying 'her foot', 'her face', 'her finger'. When I asked about it, she answered in surprise, 'Oh! but every medium has their cabinet, their place from which they make the spirits come!' She said the spirits will not come in the light, because it hurts them. She said she had seen cabinets specially made, of wood, with locks upon them, but that Selina's was only a pair of heavy curtains, that they hung before a screen, across a hollow in the wall. Selina would be placed between the curtains and the screen; and it was as she sat in that darkness that Peter Quick would come.

'He would come,' I asked her, 'how?'

They would know when he arrived, she said, for Selina would cry out. 'That was the not quite pleasant part of it, for she of course must give her spirit-matter up, for him to use, and it was painful to her; and I think, in his eagerness, he was rough with her. He was always a rough spirit, you see, even before the death of poor Mrs Brink . . .'

She said that he would come, and Selina would cry out; then he would appear before the curtain—no bigger, at first, than a ball of ether. But the ball of ether would *grow*, it would shake and lengthen until it was as tall as the curtain itself; and slowly it would take on the appearance of a man—at last, it *was* a man, a man with whiskers, bowing to you, and gesturing. 'It was the queerest, quaintest sight you ever saw,' she said; 'and I saw it, I can tell you, many times. He would always begin, then, to speak of spiritualism. He would tell us of the new time that is coming, when so many people will know spiritualism to be true, spirits will walk the pavements of the city, in the day-light—that is what he said. But, well, he was mischievous. He would start to say this, but then he would grow tired of it. You would see him look about the room—there was a little light, a little phosphorised light, a spirit can bear that. You would see him look about him. Do you know what he was looking for? He was looking for the handsomest lady! When he found her, he would step very close to her and say, How would she like to walk with him, upon a London street? And then he would take her up, and have her walk with him about the room; and then he would kiss her.' She said he was 'always one for kissing ladies or bringing them gifts, or teasing them'. The gentlemen he never cared for. She had known him pinch a gentleman, or pull his beard. She once saw him strike a man upon the nose—so hard, the nose was bloodied.

She laughed, and coloured. She said that Peter Quick would go among them like this, perhaps for half-an-hour; but then he would grow weary. He would return to the cabinet curtains and then, just as before he had grown, so now he would *shrink*. At last there would be nothing left of him but a pool of shining stuff upon the floor—then even that would dwindle and grow dim. 'Then,' she said, 'Miss Dawes would cry again. Then there would be silence. There would come knocks, to tell us to draw back the cabinet curtain; then one of us would go to Miss Dawes and untie her, and bring her out—'

I said, *untie* her?—again her cheeks grew flushed. She said: 'Miss Dawes would have it. I think we should never have minded had she been kept quite at her liberty—or, perhaps, with a simple ribbon about her waist, to fix her to her chair. But she said it was her task to show proofs to the faithful and the doubting both alike, and would have herself perfectly tied at the start of each showing. Mind, she never had a gentleman do it: it was always a lady that tightened the ropes—always a lady that took her and searched her, and always a lady that tied her . . .'

She said that Selina's wrists and ankles would be bound to her chair, and the knots then sealed with wax; or else, her arms would be folded behind her, and her sleeves sewn to her gown. A band of silk would be placed across her eyes and another put over her mouth, and sometimes a length of cotton might be threaded through the hole in her ear and fixed to the floor outside the curtain—more usually, though, she would have them put ‘a little velvet collar’ about her throat, and a rope would be attached to the buckle of that and held by a lady that was seated in the circle. ‘When Peter came the rope might be tugged a little; when we went to her later, however, those bonds would be all tied fast, and the wax unbroken. She would be only then so weary and so weak. We would have to place her upon a sofa and give her wine, and Mrs Brink would come and chafe her hands. She would sometimes have a girl or two to sit with her then—but I would never stay. It seemed to me, you know, that we had tired her enough.’

All the time she spoke, she made small gestures with her grubby white hands—showing me where Selina would have the ropes tightened and fixed, how she would sit, how Mrs Brink would rub her. In the end I had to turn in my chair and look away from her, her words and gestures made me queasy. I thought of my locket, and of Stephen and Mrs Wallace, and of how I had come across that reading-room—by chance, it *was* by chance, and yet it had so much of Selina in it . . . It didn’t seem comical to me now. It seemed only queer. I heard the woman stand and draw on her coat, and still I kept my eyes from her. But she stepped to replace her book upon the shelves, and that brought her closer to me; and then she gazed at the page before me and shook her head.

‘They mean it for Miss Dawes,’ she said, indicating the caricature of the sharp-faced medium, ‘but no-one could see her and draw her like that. Did you ever know her? She had the face of an angel.’ She bent, and turned the pages of the book until she found another picture—or, rather, two pictures, that had been published in the month before Selina’s arrest. ‘Look here,’ she said. Then she stood a moment and watched me gaze at them; and then she went.

The pictures were portraits, set side-by-side upon the page. The first was an engraving taken from a photograph, dated June 1872 and showing Selina herself, aged seventeen. It showed her rather plump, and with brows that are dark and shapely: she is clad in a high-necked gown, perhaps of taffeta, and there are jewelled pendants at her neck and her ears. Her hair is rather fussily dressed—a shop-girl's Sunday *coiffure*, I thought it; but one can see, for all that, that it is thick and fair and very handsome. She looks not at all like the Crivelli *Veritas*. I should say that she was never stern, before they sent her to Millbank.

The other portrait might be comical, if it were not so queer. It is a pencil drawing by a spiritual artist, and shows a bust of Peter Quick as he appeared for the dark circles at Mrs Brink's house. There is a cloth of white about his shoulders and a cap of white upon his head. His cheek seems pale, his whiskers full and very dark; dark, too, are his brows and lashes, and his eyes. He is set upon the paper in a three-quarter profile, facing the picture of Selina—and so appears to gaze at her, as if compelling her to turn her eyes to his.

So, anyway, it seemed to me this afternoon; for I sat and studied those portraits, after the lady had left, until the ink upon the page appeared to waver and the flesh upon the faces to give a twitch. And as I sat and stared, I remembered the cabinet, and the yellow wax mould of Peter Quick's hand. I thought, 'Suppose that is quivering, too?' I imagined I might turn and see the hand jerk, might see it pressed to the glass of the cabinet with one gross finger crooked and *beckoning* to me!

I didn't turn; but still I sat, a little longer. I sat, and looked at Peter Quick's dark eyes. They seemed—how odd it sounds!—they seemed *familiar* to me, as if I might have gazed at them already—perhaps, in my dreams.

9 December 1872

Mrs Brink says I must never think of rising in the mornings before 10. She says we must do everything we can to preserve my powers & make them stronger. She has given her own maid Ruth entirely over to the care of me & has taken another girl, named Jenny, for herself. She says her own comforts mean nothing to her compared with mine. Now Ruth brings me my breakfast & handles my gowns, & if I let my napkin or my stocking or any slight thing fall she picks it up, & if I say 'Thank you' she smiles & says 'I'm sure, miss, you don't have to thank me.' She is older than me. She says she came to the house when Mrs Brink's husband died 6 years ago. I said to her this morning 'I think Mrs Brink might have had many spirit-mediums come here, since then?' & she answered 'She has had just about a thousand, miss! All trying for the one poor spirit. They all proved crooks however. We soon saw through them. We saw all their tricks. You will understand, how a maid feels about her mistress. I would sooner break my heart 10 times, than have a hair upon my mistress's head hurt once, by a person like that.' She said this, fastening my gown about me, looking at me in the glass. All my new gowns close at the back, & need her hand to fasten them.

When I am dressed I generally go down to Mrs Brink & we sit for an hour, or she will take me to a shop or to the gardens at the Crystal Palace. Sometimes her friends will come, to make dark circles with us. They see me & say 'O, but you are quite a young girl! You are younger even than my own daughter.' But after we have sat they take my hand & shake their heads. Mrs Brink has told everyone she knows that she has me with her, & that I am something out of the way special – I think however, that there must be many media she has said that about. They say 'Will you see if there is any spirit near me now, Miss Dawes? Will you ask it, has it any little message for me?' I have been doing those things for 5 years, I could do them on my head. But they see me doing them in my nice dress, in Mrs Brink's fine parlour, & are astonished. I hear them saying quietly to Mrs Brink 'O, Margery, what a talent she has! Will you bring her to my house? Will you let her lead a circle, at a party of mine?'

But Mrs Brink says she would not dream of letting me water my gifts by attending gatherings like that. I have said she must let me use my powers to help other people as well as her, since that is what I was given powers for, & she always answers 'Of course, I know that. I will do that, in time. It is only that, now I have you, I want to keep you to myself. Will you think me so very selfish if I do that, just a little while longer?' And so her friends come in the afternoon, but never at night. The nights she keeps for us to sit in. She only has Ruth come sometimes, bringing wine & biscuits if I grow faint.

28 October 1874

To Millbank. It is only a week since my last visit, but the mood of the prison has shifted, as if with the season, and it is a darker and more bitter place now, than ever. The towers seemed to have grown higher and broader, and the windows to have shrunk; the very scents of the place seemed to have changed, since I last went there—the grounds smelling of fog and of chimney smoke as well as of sedge, and the wards reeking of nuisance-buckets still, of cramped and unwashed hair and flesh and mouths, but also of gas, and rust, and sickness. There are great black, blistering radiators at the angle of the passages, and these make the corridors very airless and close. The cells, however, remain so chill that the walls are wet with condensation, the lime upon them turned to a kind of bubbling curd, that marks the women's skirts with streaks of white. There is, in consequence, much coughing on the wards, and many pinched and sorrowful faces and trembling limbs.

There is a darkness to the building, too, that I am not used to. They are lighting lamps there now at four o'clock, and with their high, narrow windows black against the sky, their sanded flags lit by pools of flaring gas-light, their cells dim, the women in them hunched, like goblins, over their sewing or their coir, the wards seem more terrible and more antique. Even the matrons seem touched by the new darkness. They move about the passage-ways with softer treads, their hands and faces yellow in the gas-light, their mantles black against their gowns like cloaks of shadow.

They took me, to-day, to the prisoners' visiting-room, the place in which the women receive their friends and husbands and children—I think it is the dreariest place that I have seen there. They call it a room, but it is hardly that; it more closely resembles some sort of shed, for cattle, for it is made up of a series of narrow stalls or niches, which are arranged in a row, on either side of one long passage. When a prisoner receives a visitor at Millbank, her matron escorts her to one of these stalls and places her in it; above her head is fixed an hour-glass, and the salt in this is now set running. Before the prisoner's face is an aperture, with bars upon it. Exactly opposite to her, on the other side of the passage-way, is another aperture—this one with mesh across it only, rather than bars. This is where the prisoner's visitor is permitted to stand. There is another little hour-glass fixed here, which is turned to keep time with the first.

The passage-way between the stalls is, perhaps, seven feet wide, and a watchful matron continually patrols it, to ensure that nothing is passed across the space. The prisoner and visitor are obliged to raise their voices a little, in order to be heard—the din, therefore, is sometimes fierce. At other times a woman must call to her friends, and have her business overheard by all about her. The salt in the hour-glasses runs for fifteen minutes, and when it has done so the visitor must leave, the woman return to her cell.

A prisoner at Millbank may receive her friends and family, in this manner, *four times a year.*

'And they may come no nearer to one another than this?' I asked the matron who had escorted me, as I walked with her along the corridor in which the prisoners' stalls are set. 'May a woman not even embrace her husband—not even touch her own child?'

The matron—not Miss Ridley, to-day, but a fair-haired, younger woman named Miss Godfrey—shook her head. 'Those are the rules,' she said. How many times have I heard that phrase, there? '*Those are the rules.* They seem harsh to you, Miss Prior, I know. But once we let prisoner and visitor together, there come all manner of things into the gaol. Keys, tobacco . . . Infants may be taught to pass on blades, in their very kisses.'

I studied the prisoners she led me by, gazing at their friends across the passage, across the patrolling matron's shadow. They didn't look as if they longed to be embraced only to have a knife or a key smuggled to them. They looked more wretched than I had seen any of the women look before. One, a woman with a scar upon her cheek straight as a razor's cut, put her head to the bars, the better to hear her calling husband; and when he asked her was she well? she answered, 'As well, John, as they will let me be—which is to say, not much . . .' Another—it was Laura Sykes from Mrs Jelf's ward, the woman who presses the matrons to petition for her with Miss Haxby—was visited by her mother, a shabby-looking lady who could do nothing but flinch from the iron mesh before her face and weep. Sykes said, 'Come now, Ma, this won't do. Will you tell me what you know? Have you spoke yet, with Mr Cross?' But when the mother heard her daughter's voice, saw the passing matron, she only shuddered the more. And at that Sykes gave a cry—Oh! There were half her minutes gone, her mother had wept them clean away! 'You must send Patrick next time. Why isn't Patrick here? I won't have you come, only to weep at me . . .'

Miss Godfrey saw me looking, and nodded. 'It *is* hard on the women,' she conceded. 'Some, indeed, cannot bear it at all. They sit waiting for their friends to come, marking off the days and fretting; but we bring them here and, after all, the upset proves too much for them. They tell their friends not to come at all, then.'

We began the walk back to the wards. I asked her, were there any women who received no visits, from anyone?—and she nodded: 'Some. They have no friends or family, I suppose. They come in here and seem to be forgotten. I cannot say what they must do when they are sent out. Collins is like that, and Barnes, and Jennings. And—' she struggled to twist a key inside an awkward lock '—and Dawes, I believe, on E ward.'

I think I had known she was about to say the name, before she said it.

I asked her no more questions then, and she took me up to Mrs Jelf. I made my way, as usual, from one woman to another—I did it in a flinching sort of way at first, for it seemed terrible, after what I had just seen, that I, who am nothing to them, should be able to call on them just as I please, and they must speak with me. And yet of course, they must speak with me or stay silent, I couldn't forget that; and I saw at last that they were grateful to see me at their gates, and glad to come and tell me how they did. Many, as I have said, did badly. Perhaps because of this—and perhaps because, even through the thickness of the prison walls and windows, they have sensed the subtle shifting of the season and the year—there was much talk of 'times' and when they were due, such as: 'It is seventeen months to-day, mum, to my time!' And: 'A year and a week, Miss Prior, off my time!' And: 'Three months, miss, to my time. What do you think of that?'

This last was Ellen Power, imprisoned—as she says—for letting boys and girls kiss in her parlour. I have thought much of her since the weather turned colder. I found her looking frail and slightly trembling, but not as ill as I had feared. I had Mrs Jelf shut me in with her and we talked together for half an hour; and when I took her hand at last I said that I was pleased to feel her grip so strong, and to see her so healthy.

I said it, and she grew crafty. She answered, 'Well, you are not to say a word, miss, to Miss Haxby or Miss Ridley—indeed, you must pardon me for asking, for I know you would not. But the truth is, it is all thanks to my matron, Mrs Jelf. She brings me meat from her own plate, and she has given me a length of red flannel to wear about my throat at night. And when the air is extra chill, she has a bit of rubbing stuff she puts upon me here'—she touched her chest and shoulders—'with her own hand; and that makes all the difference. She is as good to me as my own girl—in truth, she calls me "Mother". "We must have you quite ready, Mother," she says, "for your ticket-of-leave" . . .'

Her eyes gleamed as she spoke the words, and then she took her coarse blue kerchief and pressed it for a moment to her face. I said that I was glad that Mrs Jelf, at least, was kind to her.

'She is kind to us all,' she said. 'She is the kindest matron in the gaol.' She shook her head. 'Poor lady! She ain't been here long enough to learn proper Millbank ways.'

I was surprised at that: for Mrs Jelf is so grey and careworn, I should never have guessed her to have had a life, so recently, beyond the prison walls. But Power nodded. Yes, Mrs Jelf had been there—well, not quite a year, she thought. She did not know why a lady like Mrs Jelf should ever have come to Millbank, at all. She never saw a matron suited less to Millbank duties, than her!

The exclamation might have conjured her up. We heard footsteps in the corridor and raised our heads to see Mrs Jelf herself, making her patrol past Power's gate. She saw our faces turned her way and slowed her step, and smiled.

Power grew pink. 'You have caught me a-telling Miss Prior about your kindnesses, Mrs Jelf,' she said. 'I hope you won't mind it.'

At once, the matron's smile grew stiff, and she put her hand to her breast and turned to look, a little nervously, along the corridor. I understood she was afraid Miss Ridley might be near, so I said nothing about the flannel and the extra meat, only nodded to Power, then gestured to the gate. Mrs Jelf unlocked it—still, however, she wouldn't catch my eye, nor acknowledge the smile I turned on her. At last, to put her at her ease, I said I had not known that she had come so recently to Millbank. What was it that she worked at, I asked her, before the gaol?

She took a moment to secure the chain of keys upon her belt, and to brush a streak of lime-dust from her cuff. Then she made me a kind of curtsey. She had been in service, she said; but the lady she maided for having been sent abroad, she had not cared to find out a place with another.

We had begun to walk along the passage-way. I asked if her work suited her?—She said she would be sorry to leave Millbank, now. I said, 'And you don't find the duties rather hard? And the hours? And haven't you a family? The hours must be very hard on *them*, I should have thought.'

She told me then that, of course, none of the wardresses

there have husbands, but are all spinsters, or else widows like herself. 'You must not be a matron,' she said, 'and also married.' She said that some matrons had children, who must be put to nurse with other mothers; but that she herself was childless. She kept her eyes lowered all this time. I said, Well, perhaps she was a better matron for it. She had a hundred women on her wards, all helpless as infants, all looking to her for care and guidance; and I thought she must be a kind mother to them all.

Now she did gaze at me, but with eyes made dark and mournful by the shadow of her bonnet. She said, 'I hope I am, miss,' and brushed again at the dust upon her sleeve. Her hands are large, like my own—the hands of a woman rendered lean and angular, through labour or through loss.

I didn't like to question her further then, but went back to the women. I went to Mary Ann Cook, and to Agnes Nash, the coiner; and finally, as usual, to Selina.

I had crossed the mouth of her cell already, in order to move into the second passage; but I had kept back the visiting of her—just as I have kept back the writing of her, here—and when I passed her gate I turned my face to the wall and wouldn't look at her. It was, I suppose, a kind of superstition. I remembered the visiting-room: now it was as if there was an hour-glass that would be turned upon *our* visit—I didn't want a single grain to slither through the glass before the salt was properly set running. Even while I stood before her gate with Mrs Jelf, I would not gaze at her. Only when the matron had turned her key, then fussed another moment with her belt and chain, then fastened us into the cell and gone on her way, did I raise my eyes at last to hers. And when I did—well, then I found that after all there was scarcely a feature to her upon which my glances could settle and be quite calm. I saw, at the edges of her bonnet, her hair, which had once been handsome and now was blunt. I saw her throat, that had had velvet collars buckled to it; and her wrists, that had been fastened; and her little crooked mouth, that spoke in voices not her own. I saw all these things, all these tokens of her queer career, they seemed to hang about her poor pale flesh and blur it, they were like the signs of the stigmata on a saint. But she was not changed—it was I who was changed, by my new knowledge. It had worked upon me, secretly and subtly—as a drop of wine will work upon a cup of plain water, or as yeast will leaven simple dough.

It made a little *quickening* within me, as I stood gazing at her. I felt it—and with it came a prickle of fright. I put a hand to my heart, and turned away from her.

Then she spoke, and her voice—I was glad of it!—was quite familiar and quite ordinary. She said, 'I thought you might not come. I saw you pass the cell and go to the next ward.'

I had moved to her table and touched the wool that lay upon it. I must visit other women, as well as her, I said. Then, because I felt her look away and seem to grow sad, I added, that I would always, if she wished it, come to her at the last.

'Thank you,' she said.

Of course, she is like the other women, and would rather talk to me than be confined to silence. So when we spoke, it was of prison things. The damp weather has brought great black beetles into the cells—they call them 'blackjacks', she said she thinks they come there every year; and she showed me the smudges upon her limewashed wall where she had crushed a dozen of them with the heel of her boot. She said that some simple women are rumoured to catch the beetles and make pets of them. Others, she said, have been driven by hunger to eat them. She said she doesn't know if that is true, but has heard the matrons say it . . .

I listened as she spoke, nodding and grimacing—I didn't ask her, as I might have, how she had known about my locket. I didn't tell her that I had gone to the offices at the Association of Spiritualists, and sat there two and half hours, talking of her and taking notes upon her. But still I could not look at her without remembering all I had read. I looked at her face, and thought of the portraits in the newspaper. I studied her hands and remembered the wax moulds on the shelves.

Then I knew I could not go from her and leave those things unmentioned. I said that I hoped she would tell me more about her old life. I said, 'You spoke, last time, about how it was for you before you went to Sydenham. Will you tell me now, about what happened to you there?'

She frowned. She said, why did I want to know it?—I said I was curious. I said that I was curious about all the women's stories, but that hers—'Well, you know yourself, it is a little rarer than the others . . .'

It seemed rare to me, she said after a moment; but if I was a spiritualist—if I had moved all my life among spiritualist people, as she had—well, it wouldn't seem so curious then. 'You ought to buy a spiritualist newspaper and look at the notices in it—that will show you, how common I am! You would think, looking at those, that there were more spirit-mediums in this world than there are spirits, in the other.'

No, she said, she had never been *rare*, in the days with her aunt, and then at the spiritualist house at Holborn . . .

'It was when I met Mrs Brink, and she took me to live with her: *that* was when I became rare, Aurora.'

Her voice had fallen, and I had leaned to catch it. Now, hearing her say that foolish name, I felt myself blush. I said, 'What was it about Mrs Brink that changed you? What did she do?'

Mrs Brink had gone to her, she said, while she was still at Holborn. 'She came to me, I thought she had come only as an ordinary sitter—but the fact is, she had been guided to me. She had come to me for a special purpose, that only I could answer.'

And the purpose was?

She closed her eyes, and when she opened them again they seemed a little larger, and green as a cat's. She spoke, and it was as if she spoke of something wonderful. 'She required a spirit bringing to her,' she said. 'She required me to give up my own flesh, for the spirit-world to use it for itself.'

She held my gaze, and from the corner of my eye I saw a quick, dark movement upon the floor of her cell. I had a very vivid vision, then, of a hungry prisoner, prising the shell from the back of a beetle, sucking the meat from it and biting at the wriggling legs.

I shook my head. 'She kept you there,' I said, 'this Mrs Brink. She had you there, performing spirit-tricks.'

'She brought me to my fate,' she answered—I remember her saying this, quite clearly. 'She brought me to myself, that waited for me at her house. She brought me to where I could be found, by the spirits that searched for me. She brought me to—'

To *Peter Quick*!—I said the name for her, and she paused, then nodded. I thought of how the lawyers had spoken at her trial; I thought of all they had implied about her friendship with Mrs Brink. I said slowly, 'She brought you to her, to where *he* might find you. She brought you there, so you might take him to her, quietly, at night . . .?'

But as I spoke, her look changed, and she seemed almost shocked. 'I never took him to *her*,' she said. 'I never took Peter Quick to Mrs Brink. It wasn't for *his* sake that she had me there.'

Not for his sake? Then, for whose sake was it?—She wouldn't answer me at first, she only looked away, shaking her head. 'Who was it you took to her,' I said again, 'if not Peter Quick? Who was it? Was it her husband? Her sister? Her child?'

She put her hand to her lips, then said quietly at last: 'It was her mother, Aurora. Her mother, who had died while Mrs Brink was still a little girl. She had said she would not leave, that she would come back. But she had not; for Mrs Brink had not found any medium to bring her, not in twenty years of looking. Then she found me. She found me through a dream. There was a likeness between her mother and myself; there was a—a sympathy. Mrs Brink saw that, she took me to Sydenham, she let me have her mother's things; then her mother would come to her through me, to visit her in her own room. She would come in the darkness, she would come and—comfort her.'

She did not, I know, admit to any of this in court; and it cost her some sort of effort to admit it now, to me. She seemed reluctant to speak further—and yet I think there was more, and she half-wished that I might guess it. I could not. I could not think what there might be. It seems only a curious and not quite pleasant thing, that the lady I have imagined Mrs Brink to be should ever have looked at Selina Dawes, at seventeen, and seen the shadow of her own dead mother in her, and persuaded her to visit her at night, to make that shadow grow thick.

But we did not talk of it. I only asked her more about Peter Quick. I said, *He*, then, had come only for her?—Only for her, she said. And why had he come?—Why? He was her guardian, her familiar-spirit. He was her *control*. 'He came for me,' she said simply, 'and—what could I do then? I was his.'

Now her face had grown pale, with spots of colour at the cheeks. Now I began to feel an excitement in her, I felt it rising in her, it was like a quality upon the sour air of the cell.—I almost envied it. I said quietly, 'What was it like, when he came to you?' and she shook her head—Oh! How could she say? It was like losing her self, like having her own self pulled from her, as if a self could be a gown, or gloves, or stockings . . .

I said, 'It sounds terrible!'—'It was terrible!' she said. 'But it was also marvellous. It was everything to me, it was my life changed. I might have moved, then, like a spirit, from one dull sphere into a higher, better one.'

I frowned, not understanding. She said, how could she explain it to me? Oh, she could not find the words . . . She began to look about her, for a way to show me; and at last she gazed at something that lay upon her shelf, and she smiled. 'You spoke to me of spirit-tricks,' she said. 'Well . . .'

She came close to me, and held her arm to me as if she wanted me to take her hand. I flinched, thinking of my locket, her message in my book. But she only smiled, still, and then said softly: 'Put back my sleeve.'

I could not guess what she was about to do. I looked once into her face, then, cautiously, pushed at her sleeve until her arm was bare to the elbow. She turned it, and showed me the inner flesh of it—it was white, and very smooth, and warm from her gown. 'Now,' she said as I gazed at it, 'you must close your eyes.'

I hesitated a moment, then did as she asked; and then I took a breath, to nerve myself for whatever queer thing she might do next. But all she did was reach beyond me, and seem to take up something from the pile of wool upon the table; and after that I heard her step to her shelf and take something from there. Then there was a silence. I kept my eyes tight shut, but felt the lids upon them quiver, then begin to jerk. The longer the silence lasted, the more uncertain I grew. 'Just a moment,' she said, seeing me twitch—and then, after another second: 'Now you may look.'

I unclosed my eyes, but warily. I could only imagine that she had taken her blunt-edged knife to her arm and made it bleed. But the arm seemed smooth, still, and unhurt. She held it close to me—though not as close as she had before; and she kept the shadow of her gown upon it, where before she had turned it to the light. I think that, if I had looked hard at it, I might have seen a little roughness or redness there. But she would not let me look harder. While I still blinked and stared, she raised her other arm and passed her hand, very firmly, over the flesh that she had bared. She did this once, then twice, and then a third time and a fourth and, with the movement of the fingers I saw, upon that flesh, a *word* emerge, marked there in crimson—marked roughly, and rather faintly, but perfectly legibly.

The word was: TRUTH.

When it was fully-formed she took her hand away, and watched me, saying, Did I think that clever? I could not answer. She brought the arm closer and said I must touch it—and then, when I had done that, that I must put my fingers to my mouth, and taste them.

Hesitantly, I raised my hand and gazed at my finger ends. There seemed a whitish substance upon them—I thought of ether, spirit-stuff. I couldn't bear to put it to my tongue, but felt almost queasy. She saw that, and laughed. Then she showed me what she had taken up, while I sat with my eyes closed.

It was a wooden knitting needle, and her box of dinner-salt. She had used the needle to mark the word out; and the working of the salt into the letters had turned them crimson.

I took hold of her arm again. Already the marks upon it were growing less livid. I thought of what I had read, in the spiritualist newspapers. They had announced this trick there as a proof of her powers, and people had believed it—Mr Hither had believed it—I think that I had believed it. I said to her now, 'Did you do this, to the poor, sad people who came to you for help?'

She pulled back her arm, and slowly covered it with her prison sleeve, and shrugged. They shouldn't have been made happy, she answered, if they had not seen signs like that, from the spirits. Did it make the spirits less true, if she sometimes passed a piece of salt across her flesh—or let a flower fall, in the darkness, into a lady's lap? 'Those mediums I told you of,' she said, 'the ones that advertise: there's not a one of them that would shrink from pulling a stunt like that—no, not a one.' She said she knew ladies who kept darning-needles in their hair, for writing spirit-messages upon themselves. She knew gentlemen who carried paper cones, to make their voices sound queer in the darkness. It was a commonplace of the profession, she said: some days the spirits come to one; on other days, they must be helped . . .

And that was how it had been for her, before she went to Mrs Brink's house. Afterwards—well, the tricks meant nothing to her then. All her gifts might have been tricks, before she went to Sydenham! 'I might never have had powers—do you see what I am saying? They were nothing to the power I found in myself, through Peter Quick.'

I looked at her, saying nothing. I know that what she told and showed to me to-day she has told and shown perhaps to no-one. As to the larger power that she was talking of now—her rareness—well, I have felt a little of that, haven't I? I cannot dismiss it, I know that it is *something*. But still there is a mystery to her, a shadow in the design, a gap . . .

I said—what I had said to Mr Hither—that I did not understand. Her power, that was so marvellous, had brought her *there*, to Millbank Prison. Peter Quick she said was her own guardian, and yet, it was through him that the girl was hurt, through him that Mrs Brink herself was frightened—frightened to death! How had he helped her, by bringing her there? What use were all her powers to her, now?

She looked away from me, and she said—just what Mr Hither had said. That 'the spirits had their purposes, that we could not hope to fathom'.

What the spirits could possibly mean by sending her to Millbank, I answered, *I* certainly could not fathom! 'Unless they are jealous of you, and mean to kill you, and make you one of them.'

But she only frowned, not understanding me. There were spirits who envied the living, she said slowly. But even they wouldn't envy her, as she was now.

As she spoke she put a hand to her throat, and rubbed at the white flesh of it. I thought again of the collars that used to be fastened there, and of the bindings that were put about her wrists.

Her cell was cold, and I shivered. I could not say how long we had spoken for—I think we must have said much more than I have written here—and when I looked at her window I found the day behind it was very dark. She still had her hand at her throat; now she coughed, and swallowed. She said that I had made her speak too much. She went to her shelf and took down her jug, and drank a little water from the lip of it, then coughed again.

And while she did that, Mrs Jelf came to her gate and seemed to study us, and I grew conscious again of the time I might have spent there. I rose, reluctantly, and nodded for the matron to free me. I looked at Selina. I said we would talk more, next time—she nodded. She still chafed at her throat, and when Mrs Jelf saw her doing that her kind eyes clouded, she ushered me past her into the passage, then went to Selina's side. She said, 'What is it? Are you ill? Shall I fetch the surgeon to you?'

I stood and watched her move Selina so that the dim light from the gas-jet fell upon her face; and as I did that, I heard my name spoken, and looked to the gate of the neighbouring cell to see Nash, the coiner, there.

'You are still with us then, miss?' she said. Then she jerked her head towards Selina's cell and said, in a soft, exaggerated sort of way: 'I thought she might have magicked you off—had them spooks of hers take you, or make you a frog or a mouse.' She gave a shudder. 'Oh, them spooks! Did you know she has them visiting her in there, at night? I hear them come to her cell. I hear her talking to them, and sometimes laughing—sometimes, weeping. I tell you, miss, I would for all the world then that I was in any cell but this, hearing them ghosts' voices in the quiet of the night.' She shuddered again, and grimaced. She might I suppose have been teasing, as she had teased me once over her counterfeit coins; but she did not laugh. And when, remembering something Miss Craven told me once, I said that I supposed the quiet wards made the women fanciful?, she snorted. Fanciful? She said she hoped she knew a fancy from a spook! Fanciful? I ought to try sleeping in her cell, she said, with Dawes as a neighbour, before I told her *fanciful*!

She returned to her sewing, grumbling and shaking her head, and I moved back along the passage. Selina and Mrs Jelf still stood beside the gas-jet: the matron had lifted her hands to make the kerchief more secure about Selina's throat, and now patted it. They did not look at me. Perhaps they thought me gone. But I saw Selina put her own hand once to the arm that had that fading red word—TRUTH—upon it, that was covered now by the linsey gown; and then I remembered my finger-ends, and tasted the salt upon them at last.

I was still doing that when the matron came to me, to walk with me along the ward. We were pestered then by Laura Sykes, who put her face to her gate to cry, Oh, would we take a word for her to Miss Haxby? If Miss Haxby would only let her brother come, if she might only be allowed to get a letter to her brother, her case was sure to be heard a second time. She only needed Miss Haxby's word, she said, and she would be free within a month!

17 December 1872

This morning Mrs Brink came to me when I was dressed. She said 'Now Miss Dawes, I have something to settle with you. Are you quite sure you will not let me pay you a fee?' I have not let her give me money since she brought me here, & hearing her now I said again what I have said before, that all she had given me in the way of gowns & dinners was fee enough, & that anyway I could never accept money for the spirits' work. She said 'You dear child, I guessed you would say that.' She took my hand & led me to her mother's box that is on my dressing-table still, & she opened it. She said 'You will not take a fee but you won't, I'm sure, refuse an old lady's gift, & there is a thing here that I should so like you to have.' The gift she meant was the necklace of emeralds. She took it up & put it about my neck, standing very close to me to fasten it. She said 'I thought I should never give anything of my mother's away. But I feel that this is yours now more than anybody's, & O! how it becomes you! The emeralds set off your eyes, they used to set off *her* eyes too.'

I went to the glass to see how they suited me, & they do suit me amazingly, though they are so old. I said, which was the plain truth, that no-one had ever given me such a handsome thing before, & I was sure I did not deserve it for only doing what the spirits asked of me. She said that if I didn't deserve it, she would like to know who did.

Then she came close to me again & put her hand upon the clasp of the necklace. She said 'You know I am only trying to make your powers greater. I would do anything for that. *You* know how long I have waited. To have had the messages you have brought, O! I thought I should never hear words like that! But Miss Dawes, Margery is growing greedy. If she thought that, as well as words, she might see a shape or feel a hand. Well! She knows there are media in the world who have begun to bring such things. She would give a whole box of jewels to a medium who could do that for her, & consider it no loss at all.'

She stroked the necklace, & my bare skin with it. Of course, every time I tried for forms with Mr Vincy & Miss Sibree I got nothing. I said 'You know a medium must have a cabinet for work like that? You know it is a very serious thing, & not properly understood yet?' She said she did know it. I saw her face in the glass, she had her eyes upon me, & my own eyes, that had been made so green by the shine of the jewels, seemed not my eyes at all but another person's altogether. And when I closed them I might still have had them open. I saw Mrs Brink looking at me, & my own neck with the necklace on it, but the setting of the necklace was not gold then but grey, it seemed made of lead.

19 December 1872

Tonight when I went down to Mrs Brink's parlour I found Ruth there, she had sewn a length of dark cloth to a rod & she was hanging it across the alcove. I had said only that it ought to be black cloth, but when I went to look at it I saw that it was velvet. She saw me touch it & she said 'It is a fine piece, isn't it? It was me that chose it. I chose it for you, miss. You ought to have velvet now, I think. This is a great day for you, & for Mrs Brink, & for all of us here. And you are not, after all, at Holborn any more.' I looked at her & said nothing, & she smiled & held the cloth for me to put my cheek to. When I stood against it in my own old black velvet dress she said 'Why, it is like you are being eaten up by a shadow! I can only see your face & your bright hair.'

Mrs Brink came then, & sent her away. She asked me if I was ready, & I said that I supposed I was, I would not know until we had begun. We sat for a while with the lamps turned very low, then I said 'I think if it will happen, it will happen now.' I went behind the curtain & Mrs Brink put out the light entirely, & for a moment then I was afraid. I had not thought the dark would be so deep or so hot, & the space I sat in being so shallow, it seemed to me I would soon breathe all the air that was in it & then choke. I called out 'Mrs Brink, I am not sure!' but she answered only 'Please *try*, Miss Dawes. Please try, for Margery's sake! Have you any little sign, or hint, anything at all?' Her voice, coming through the velvet curtain, was high & changed, & seemed to have a hook upon it. I felt it begin to draw at me, finally it seemed to draw the very dress from off my back. Then all at once the dark seemed full of colours. A voice cried 'O! I *am here*!' & Mrs Brink said 'I see you! O, I see you!'

When I went out to her afterwards she was crying. I said 'You must not cry. Aren't you glad?' She said it was the gladness that made her cry. Then she rang for Ruth. She said 'Ruth, I have seen impossible things done in this room tonight. I have seen my mother stand & gesture to me, I saw her dressed in a shining robe.' Ruth said she believed it, since the parlour looked strange to her, & smelled strange, full of queer perfume. She said 'That means angels have been near us for sure. It's well known that, when angels visit a circle, they carry perfume to it.' I said that I had never heard that said before, & she looked at me & nodded. She said 'O yes, it's true', & she put her finger to her lip. She said the spirits carry the perfume in their mouths.

8 January 1873

We have kept very close to the house for a fortnight, doing nothing but waiting for the day to end so that the parlour might be dark enough for a spirit's limbs to bear it. I have said to Mrs Brink that she must not expect her mother to come every night, that sometimes she might see only her white hand or her face. She says she knows this & yet, each night, she grows fiercer, she draws me nearer to her, saying 'Will you come, O! Won't you come a little nearer? Do you know me? Will you kiss me?'

Three nights ago however, when she finally was kissed, she screamed, putting a hand against her breast, & frightening me so hard I thought I should die. When I went out to her Ruth was beside her, she had come running & lit a lamp. Ruth said 'I have seen this coming. She has waited so long & now, it has proved too much for her to bear.' Mrs Brink took salts from her, & then was a little calmer. She said 'I shall not mind it next time. Next time I will be ready. But Ruth, you must sit with me. You must sit with me, you must give me your strong hand to hold, & then I shan't be frightened.' Ruth said she would. We did not try again that night but now, when I go out to Mrs Brink, Ruth sits at her side & watches. Mrs Brink says 'Do you see her Ruth? Do you see my mamma?' & she answers 'I see her ma'am. I see her.'

But then it seems to me that Mrs Brink forgets her. She takes her mother's 2 hands in hers & holds them. She says 'Is Margery good?' & her mother answers 'She is very, very good. That is why I have come to her.' Then she says 'How good is she? Is she 10 kisses worth of good, or 20?' Her mother says 'She is 30 kisses worth', & when she closes her eyes I bend & kiss them – only her eyes & cheeks, never her mouth. When she has had her 30 kisses she sighs, then puts her arms about me, her head against her mother's bosom. She will keep like that for half an hour, until finally the gauze about the bosom will grow wet & she will say 'Now Margery is happy' or 'Now Margery is full!'

And all the time Ruth sits & watches. But she does not touch me. I have said no-one must touch the spirit but Mrs Brink, since it is her spirit, & her that it comes for. Ruth only watches, with her black eyes.

And when I am entirely myself again, she will walk with me to my room & take my dress from me. She says I must not think of handling my own garments, that a lady would never do that. She takes my dress & smooths it, she takes the shoes from my feet, & then she makes me sit upon my chair & she brushes my hair. She says 'I know how handsome ladies like to have their hair brushed. Look at my great arm. I can brush a lady's hair from crown to waist until it lies smooth as water or silk.' Her own hair, which is very black, she keeps close beneath her cap, but I have sometimes seen the parting of it, it is white & straight as a knife. Tonight she made me sit, but when she brushed my hair I began to cry. She said then 'Why are you crying?' I said the brush was pulling at my hair. She said 'Fancy crying over a brush!' She stood & laughed, & then she brushed again a little harder. She said she would give me a 100 strokes, she made me count them.

Then she put the brush aside & she took me to the glass. She held her hand above my head, & my hair gave a crackle & flew to her palm. I stopped crying then, & she stood & gazed at me. She said 'Now, Miss Dawes, don't you look handsome? Don't you look like a proper young lady, & awfully fit for a gentleman's eye?'

2 November 1874

I have come to my room, for the stir downstairs is frightful. With every day that takes us nearer to Pris's wedding, they find some new thing to add to the frenzy of ordering and planning—seamstresses yesterday, cooks and hair-dressers the day before. I cannot bear to see any of them. I have said I shall have Ellis dress my hair as she has always dressed it, and—though I have consented to narrower skirts—that I shall keep my gowns grey, and my coats all black. This, of course, makes Mother scold. She scolds so hard, she might be spitting pins. If I am not handy she will scold Ellis or Vigers—she will even scold Gulliver, Prissy's parrot. She will scold until he whistles and beats his poor clipped wings, in sheer frustration.

And Pris sits at the centre of it all, calm as a skiff at the eye of a storm. She has resolved to keep her features very steady until her portrait is complete. Mr Cornwallis, she says, is a very faithful painter. She is afraid of making shadows and wrinkles that he will be obliged to add to the canvas.

I would rather sit with the prisoners at Millbank than sit with Priscilla now. I would rather talk with Ellen Power, than be chided by Mother. I would rather visit Selina, than go to Garden Court to visit Helen—for Helen is as full of wedding talk as any of them, but Selina they have so removed from ordinary rules and habits, she might be living, cold and graceful, on the surface of the moon.

So, anyway, it has seemed to me before to-day; this afternoon, however, when I arrived at the gaol, I found it upset, and Selina and the women very distracted. 'You have picked a sad time to come, miss,' said the matron at the gate. 'A prisoner has broken out, and caused all sorts of bother on the wards.' I stared at her—of course, I thought she meant a woman had escaped. But when she heard that, she laughed. What they term *breaking out* there is a mad sort of fit that they say takes the women sometimes, sending them smashing up their cells in fury. Miss Haxby explained it to me. I met her on one of the tower staircases. She was climbing it rather wearily, with Miss Ridley at her side.

'It is an odd thing, the breaking-out,' she said, 'and quite peculiar to female gaols.' She said there is a thought that prison women have an instinct for it; she knows only that, at some point in their terms at Millbank, her girls will nearly all of them submit. 'And when they are young and strong and determined—well, then they are like savages. They shriek and crash about—we cannot get near them, but have to send for the men. The entire gaol hears the racket, and it takes all my power to calm the wards. For when one woman has broken out, another is sure to follow. The urge, that has been slumbering, is woken in her; and then she almost cannot help herself.'

She passed a hand across her face. The woman that had broken out this time, she said, was Phœbe Jacobs, the thief, on D ward. She and Miss Ridley had been called to inspect the damage.

'Will you come with us,' she said, 'to see the broken cell?'

I remembered D Ward, with its cell doors all shut fast, and its sullen inmates, and its fetid, coir-choked air, as the ghastliest passage in the prison; now it seemed more grim than ever, and peculiarly still. We were met at the end of it by Mrs Pretty, rolling her sleeves down and dabbing at her wet top lip—she might have come fresh from a wrestling-ring. When she saw me she gave an approving nod. 'You have come to view the smash-up, ma'am? Well—ha, ha—it's a rare one!' She made a gesture, and we followed her a little way along the ward, to where a cell gate stood unfastened. 'Watch your skirts there, ladies,' she said, as Miss Haxby and I drew near to the doorway. 'The devil has overturned her nuisance-bucket . . .'

I tried to describe the chaos of Jacobs' cell, to-night, to Helen and Stephen; they sat, shaking their heads, but I could tell they didn't think it much. 'If the cells are so bleak already,' asked Helen once, 'how can the women spoil them or make them bleaker?' They could not imagine the scene I saw today. It was like some little room in hell—or more, like a chamber in some madman's epileptic brain, after a fit.

'It is astonishing, their ingenuity,' said Miss Haxby quietly, as she and I stood in the cell and gazed about us. 'The window—look, the iron guard pulled free, to expose the glass for smashing. The gas pipe torn away—we have had to stop that up with a piece of rag—do you see?—to save the other prisoners a gassing. The blankets not just ripped but *shredded.* They do that with their mouths. We have found teeth, in the past, that they have lost in their great fury . . .'

She was like a house agent, but with an inventory of violence: tick, tick, tick she seemed to go, drawing my eye to every wretched detail. The hardwood bed smashed up to splinters; the great wooden door, dented by the blows of a prison heel, and gouged at; the prison rules torn down and trampled; the Bible—most terrible of all, Helen blanched when I told her of it—mashed to a bilious gruel at the bottom of the overturned slop-box. The fastidious reckoning went on and on, and all in the same dull murmur; and when I asked a question in an ordinary tone Miss Haxby put a finger to her lips. 'We mustn't speak too loudly,' she said. She feared the other women would find a pattern in her words, and copy it.

Eventually she stood aside with Mrs Pretty, to talk with her about the tidying of the cell. Then she took out her watch. She said, 'Jacobs has been in the darks for—how long, Miss Ridley?'—For almost an hour, the matron said.

'Then we had better visit her.' She hesitated, then turned to me. Should I like to see that, too? she asked. Should I like to go with them, to the dark cell?

'The dark cell?' It seemed to me I had been round and round the pentagon a dozen times; and I had never heard them mention such a place before. The dark cell? I said again—what was that?

I had arrived at the prison a little after four, and in the time it had taken us to climb to the broken cell and study it, its corridors had grown gloomy. I am still not accustomed to the thickness of the Millbank night, the lurid glare of the gas-jets; now the silent cells and towers seemed all at once quite unfamiliar. We took a passage, too—Miss Ridley, Miss Haxby and I—that I did not recognise; a passage which, to my surprise, led away from the wards, towards the heart of Millbank—a passage which wound downwards, via spiralling staircases and sloping corridors, until the air grew even chiller and more rank, and vaguely saline, and I was sure we must be below the level of the ground—perhaps, below the level of the Thames itself. At last we passed into a slightly wider corridor where there were several antique wooden doors, all rather low. Miss Haxby paused before the first of these and, at her nod, Miss Ridley unfastened it and stepped to light the room that lay beyond.

'You may as well also see this,' Miss Haxby said to me as we moved inside, 'since we are here. It is our chain-room, where we keep our shackles, jackets and the like.'

She gestured to the walls, and I gazed at them with her, but in a kind of horror. They were not whitewashed, like the walls above, but rough, unfinished, and quite glistening with damp. Each was densely hung with iron—with rings and chains and fetters, and with other, nameless, complicated instruments whose purposes I could only, shuddering, guess at.

Miss Haxby saw my expression, I think, and gave a mirthless smile.

'These items mostly date from Millbank's earliest days,' she said, 'and hang here as a kind of exhibition, merely. You'll see that they are clean and kept well-oiled, however: we can never be sure that a woman won't arrive within our walls, so vicious as to require us to fetch them out again! Here we have handcuffs—some for girls, look—look how dainty these are, like a lady's bracelets! Here we have gags,'—these are strips of leather, with holes punched in them to let the prisoner breathe 'but not cry out'—'and here, hobbles'. She said the hobbles are used on women only, never on men. She said, 'We use them to restrain a prisoner when she has a mind—as they often do!—to lie upon the floor of her cell and kick her feet against its door. Can you see how, when the hobble is fitted, it would grip? This strap fastens the ankle to the thigh; this fixes the hands. A woman in this must rest quite upon her knees, and a matron must feed her her supper from a spoon. They soon tire of that and grow meek again.'

I fingered the strap of the hobble she had caught up. It was marked quite clearly, with a ridge and a polished, blackened groove where the buckle had been tightened on it. I asked, did they use such things often? and Miss Haxby replied that they resort to them as often as they must—she thought, perhaps five or six times in the year. 'Would you say, Miss Ridley?' Miss Ridley nodded.

'Our main form of restraint, however—and that a pretty adequate one,' she went on then, '—is the jacket. See, here.' She stepped to a closet and drew out two heavy, canvas items, so rough and shapeless I thought at first they must be sacks. She passed one to Miss Ridley, and held the other one up against herself, as if trying out a gown before a glass. Then I saw that the thing was indeed a crude kind of over-dress—only, with straps about the sleeves and waist instead of braid or bows. 'We place these over the women's prison frocks, to stop them tearing at them,' she said. 'Look at the fastenings'—these were not buckles but stout brass screws. 'We have keys for them, and can make them very fast indeed. Miss Ridley there, has a strait-waistcoat.' The matron now shook *her* jacket out, and I saw that its sleeves were of tar-coloured leather, unnaturally long, closed at the cuff, and tapering to straps. Like the straps upon the hobbles, these had marks upon them where they had been repeatedly drawn against a buckle. I gazed at them, and felt my hands, inside their gloves, begin to sweat. They begin to sweat as I remember now, for all that the night is such a chill one.

The matrons made all neat again then, and we left that ghastly chamber to proceed further along the passage until we reached a low, stone archway. Beyond this point the walls were barely wider than our skirts. There were no gas-jets, only a single lighted candle in a sconce, which Miss Haxby seized and held before us as we walked, her hand about it to shield its leaping flame from some salt, subterranean breeze. I looked about me. I had not known there was a place like this, at Millbank. I had not known there was a place like this in all the world, and for a second I felt a rush of terror. I thought, They mean to murder me! They mean to take the candle and leave me here, to find my own, blind, groping way to light, or madness!

Then we reached a set of four doors and Miss Haxby stopped before the first of them. Miss Ridley fumbled, in the uncertain candle-light, at the chain at her waist.

When she turned her key and seized the door, she did not swing it to as I expected, but rather slid it: I saw then that it was thick, and padded like a mattress—they have it there to drown the curses and the weeping of the prisoner in the room beyond. She, of course, now caught the movement of it. There came, suddenly—and horribly, in that dim, small, silent space—a single great *thud* upon the door, and then another *thud*, and then a cry—'You bitch! Have you come to watch me rotting! Damn you, if I don't choke myself the next time you are gone!' The padded door being now put back, Miss Ridley unfastened a wicket panel in the second wooden door that lay behind it. Beyond the panel there were bars. Beyond the bars there was a darkness—a darkness so unbroken, so intense, I found my eyes could make no purchase on it. I stared, and became aware that my head was aching. The shouting had ceased, the cell seemed quite still—then all at once, looming out of that unfathomable dark to press itself against the bars, there came a face. A terrible face—white and streaming and bruised, with blood and spittle at its lips and its eyes wild, yet also squinting against the feeble light of our candle. At the sight of it Miss Haxby flinched, and I stepped back; and the face was turned on me then—'Damn you for gazing at me!' the woman began. Miss Ridley slapped with the heel of her hand upon the wood, to silence her.

'You watch your filthy manners, Jacobs, or we'll have you down here for a month, do you hear?'

The woman placed her head against the bars, kept her white lips fastened, but continued to fix us all with her wild and terrible gaze. Miss Haxby moved a little way towards her. 'You have been very foolish, prisoner,' she said, 'and Mrs Pretty, Miss Ridley and I are very disappointed in you. You have spoiled a cell. You have hurt your own head. Is that what you wanted, to hurt your own head?'

The woman took a ragged breath. 'I must hurt something,' she said. 'As for Mrs Pretty—that bitch! I shall shake her to pieces, and not care how many days in the dark you make me serve for it!'

'That's enough!' said Miss Haxby. 'That's enough. I shall call on you again tomorrow. We shall see how sorry you are after a night in the dark. Miss Ridley.' Miss Ridley moved forward with her key, and Jacobs looked wilder than ever.

'Don't you fasten that lock on me, you cat! Don't you take that candle from me! Oh!' She ground her face against the grate, and before Miss Ridley closed the wooden flap I caught a glimpse of her jacket where it showed at the neck—the strait-waistcoat, I think it was, with its blunt black sleeves and its buckles. Once the key was turned there came another *thud*—she must have used her head to butt the wood with—and then a muffled cry, in a different, higher tone: 'Don't leave me here, Miss Haxby! Oh! Miss Haxby, I'll be good as anything!'

This cry was worse than the curses. I turned to the matrons, saying, They surely could not mean to leave her there? They could not really mean to leave her there alone, and in such darkness? Miss Haxby stood very stiff. She said there would be officers sent, to watch her; and in another hour they would bring her bread.—'But such darkness, Miss Haxby!' I said again.

'The darkness is the punishment,' she answered simply. She moved away from me, taking the candle with her, her white hair showing pale in the shadows. Miss Ridley had closed the padded door. The woman's cries had grown very muffled, but were still clear enough—'You bitches!' she cried. 'God-damn you—*and the lady too*!' I stood for a second and watched the light grow dimmer; then the cries grew even higher and I stepped after that dancing flame so hastily I almost stumbled. 'You bitches, you bitches!' the woman still cried—she might be crying it still. 'I shall die in the dark—do you hear me, lady? I shall die in the dark, like a stinking rat!'

'So they all say,' said Miss Ridley sourly. 'A pity none of them do.'

I thought Miss Haxby would check her. She did not. She only walked on, past the door of the chain-room, back into the sloping passage that led upwards to the cells; and there she left us, to return to her bright office. Miss Ridley took me higher. We crossed the penal wards, and saw Mrs Pretty leaning with another matron at the gate of Jacobs's cell, while two prisoners laboured with pails of water and brooms, wiping the slops. I was handed to Mrs Jelf. I looked at her and then, when Miss Ridley had gone, I put my hands to my eyes. She murmured, 'You have been to the darks,' and I nodded. I said, Could it be right, to treat the women like that? She could not answer me, she only looked away and shook her head.

I found her wards as strangely silent as the others, the women in them stiff and watchful. All spoke at once of the breaking-out when I went in to them; each wanted to know what had been smashed and who had smashed it, what had been done with her. 'Sent to the darks, was she?' they would ask with a shudder.

'Has she gone to the darks, Miss Prior? Was it Morris?'

'Was it Burns?'

'Is she very much hurt?'

'I should say she's sorry for it, now!'

'I was put in the darks one time, ma'am,' Mary Ann Cook told me. 'It was the fearfullest place I ever was in. Some girls only laugh at the blackness—but not me, ma'am. Not me.'

'Not me, Cook, either,' I said.

Even Selina seemed touched by the mood of the wards. I found her pacing her cell, her knitting lying idle. When she saw me come she blinked, and crossed her arms, and continued to move agitatedly from foot to foot, so that I wished that I might go to her and place my hands on her and make her calm.

'There's been a breaking-out,' she said, while Mrs Jelf still shut the gate on us. 'Who was it—was it Hoy? Or Francis?'

'You know I cannot tell you,' I said, a little dismayed. She looked away. She said that she had only asked to test me—that she knew very well, it was Phœbe Jacobs. They had taken her to the dark cell, in a jacket with a screw. Did I think that was kind?

I hesitated, then asked, Did she think it was kind, to be as troublesome as Jacobs?

'I think that we have all forgotten kindness here,' she answered, '—and wouldn't miss it, if it weren't for ladies like you, come to stir us all up with your manners!'

Her voice was harsh—as harsh as Jacobs's, as harsh as Miss Ridley's. I sat upon her chair and placed my hands upon her table, and when I straightened my fingers I saw them tremble. I said I hoped she did not mean what she had said.—She answered at once, that she did mean it! Did I know how terrible it was, to have to sit and hear a woman breaking up her cell, with the bars and bricks about one? It was like having sand cast in one's face, and being forbidden to blink. It was like an itch, an ache—'you must cry out, or die! But when you do cry out, you know yourself a—a beast! Miss Haxby comes, the chaplain comes, *you* come—we cannot be beasts then, we must be women. I wish you wouldn't come at all!'

I never saw her so nervous and distracted. I said, that if she could only know herself a woman through my visits, then I would go more often to her, not less.—'Oh!' she cried then, gripping at the sleeves of her gown until her flaming knuckles were mottled with white. 'Oh! That is just what *they* say!'

She had begun to pace again, back and forth from the gate to the window, the star on her sleeve showing unnaturally vivid where the gas-light struck it, like a flashing beam of warning. I remembered what Miss Haxby had said, about how the women sometimes caught the fit of breaking-out from one another. I could think of nothing more terrible than Selina being cast in that dark cell, Selina in a strait-coat with a mad and bleeding face. I made my voice very level. I said,

'Who says that, Selina? Miss Haxby, do you mean? Miss Haxby, and the chaplain?'

'Ha! If they would only say anything so sensible!'

I answered: 'Hush.'—I feared Mrs Jelf might hear her. I looked at her. I knew very well who it was that she spoke of. I said, 'You mean your spirit-friends.'—'Yes,' she said, '*them*.'

Them. They have seemed real to me, here, at night, in the darkness. But to-day at Millbank, that had grown suddenly so violent and so hard, they seemed flimsy, a kind of nonsense. I think I put my hand before my eyes. I said, 'I am too weary for your spirits to-day, Selina—'

'*You* are weary!' she cried then. '*You*, who never had a spirit press at you—whisper or shriek at you—pluck at you, with a pinching hand—' Now her lashes were dark with tears. She had stopped her pacing, but still gripped herself, and still shook.

I said I had not known her friends were such a burden to her, but had thought them only a comfort. She replied miserably that they were a comfort—'It is only that, they come, as you come; and then, like you, they leave me. And then I am more bound, more wretched, more *like them*'—she nodded towards the other cells—'than ever.'

She let out her breath, and closed her eyes. And while she had them shut I went to her at last, and took her hands—meaning to make some ordinary gesture, that would calm her. I think it did calm her. She opened her eyes, her fingers moved in mine; and I found myself flinching, to feel them so stiff and so cold. I didn't think any more then about what I should or should not do. I drew off my gloves and placed them on her, then held her hands again. '*You mustn't*,' she said. But she didn't pull her hands away, and after a moment I felt her flexing her fingers a little, as if to savour the unfamiliar sensation of the gloves against her palm.

We stood like that for, perhaps, a minute. 'I wish you might keep these,' I said. She shook her head. 'You must ask your spirits to bring you mittens then. Wouldn't that be more sensible, than flowers?'

She turned away from me. She said quietly that she would be ashamed for me to know the things that she has asked the spirits to bring her. That she has asked for food, for water and soap—even for a glass, to see her own face in. She said they brought them to her, when they were able. 'Other things, however . . .'

She said she asked once for keys, to all the locks of Millbank; and for a suit of ordinary clothes, and money.

'Do you think that a terrible thing?' she asked.

I said I did not think it terrible; but that I was glad her spirits had not helped her, for to escape from Millbank would certainly be very wrong.

She nodded. 'That is what my friends said.'

'Your friends are wise then.'

'They are very wise. It is only hard, sometimes, when I know that they might take me, yet still keep me here, day after day.'—I must have stiffened, hearing her say that. She went on: 'Oh yes, it is they who keep me here! They might free me, in an instant. They might take me now, as you stand holding me. They shouldn't even have to trouble over the locks.'

She had grown too earnest. I took my hands from her. I said that she might think such things, if they made her hours there rather lighter; but that she oughtn't to think about them so that other things—real things—grew strange to her. I said, 'It is Miss Haxby that keeps you here, Selina. Miss Haxby, and Mr Shillitoe, and all the matrons.'

'It is the spirits,' she said steadily. 'They have me here, and they will keep me here, until—'

Until what?

'Until their purpose is fulfilled.'

I shook my head, and asked her, What purpose was that? Did she mean her punishment? and if she did, then what of Peter Quick? I thought that it was he who should be punished? She said, almost impatiently, 'Not *that*, I don't mean *that* reason, Miss *Haxby's* reason! I mean—'

She meant, some *spiritual* purpose. I said, 'You told me of this, before. I didn't understand it then, and don't now. And nor, I think, do you.'

She had turned away a little; now she gazed at me again, and I saw that her look had changed, and become very grave. When she spoke, it was in a whisper. And what she said was: 'I think I do begin to understand it. And I am—afraid.'

The words, her face, the gathering gloom—I had grown stern with her, and uneasy, but now I pressed her hands again, and then I took the gloves from her and warmed her naked fingers for a moment in my own. I said, What was it? What was she frightened of? She wouldn't answer, only turned away. And as she did so her hands twisted in mine and my gloves fell from me, and I stooped to retrieve them.

They fell upon the cold, clean flags. And when I picked them up I saw, beside them on the floor, a smear of white. The white smear glistened, and when I pressed it, it cracked. It was not lime, from the streaming walls.

It was wax.

Wax. I gazed at it and began to shake. I stood, and looked at Selina. She saw that my face was pale, but not what I had looked at. 'What's the matter?' she said. 'What's the matter, Aurora?' The words made me flinch, for I caught, behind them, the voice of Helen—of Helen, who had once named me for a figure in a book; and who I had said could never take a better name, since her own suited her so well . . .

'What's the matter?'

I put my hands upon her. I thought of Agnes Nash, the coiner, saying that she hears, from Selina's cell, the voices of ghosts. I said, 'What you're afraid of—what is it? Is it *him*? Does he come to you, still? Does he come to you at night, even now, even *here*?'

I felt, beneath the sleeves of her prison gown, the slender flesh upon her arms and, beneath the flesh, her bones. She drew in her breath, as if I hurt her, and when I heard that I let my grip grow slack, and stepped from her, and was ashamed. For it was Peter Quick's waxen hand that I had thought of. And that was shut in a cabinet, a mile from Millbank; and was only a hollow mould, and could not harm her.

And yet, and yet—oh, there was a ghastly kind of logic to it, that impressed itself upon me now and made me shudder.

That hand *was* a waxen one—but I thought of the reading-room. How would it be there, at night? It would be silent, dark and very still; the shelves of moulds, however, might not lie still. The wax might ripple. The lips upon the spirit-face might twitch, and the eyelids roll; the dimple upon the baby's arm would grow deeper as the arm unfolded—so I saw it now, in Selina's cell, as I stepped from her and shuddered. The swollen fingers of Peter Quick's fist—I saw them, I saw them!—were uncurling, and flexing. Now the hand was inching its way across the shelf, the fingers drawing the palm over the wood. Now they were parting the cabinet doors—they left smears upon the glass.

Now I saw all the moulds begin to creep, across the silent reading-room; and as they crept they softened, and blended, the one into the other. They formed a stream of wax, I saw it ooze into the streets, it oozed to Millbank, to the quiet prison—it oozed across the tongue of gravel, across the gaols, it seeped through the cracks in the hinges of the doors, the gaps in the gates, the wickets, the *key-holes*. The wax was pale beneath the gas-light, but no-one looked for it; and when it crept, it crept quite soundlessly. There was only Selina, in all the sleeping prison, to catch the subtle slither of the stream of wax upon the sanded passage of her ward. I saw the wax inch its way up the limewashed bricks beside her door, I saw it nudge at the flap of iron, then ooze into her shadowy cell, then collect upon the chill stone floor. I saw it grow, sharp as a stalagmite at first, and hardening.

Then it was Peter Quick, and then he embraced her.

I saw it in a second—so vividly, the force of it made me sick. Selina came close to me again, and I moved from her; and when I looked at her I laughed—the laughter sounded terrible to me. I said, 'I'm no help to you to-day, Selina. I meant to comfort you. I've finished by frightening myself, with nothing.'

But it was not nothing. I knew it was not nothing.

Beside her heel the splash of wax stood out upon the stone floor, very white—how *could* it have got there? Then she took another step, and the smear was shadowed by the hem of her gown, then hidden.

I stayed with her a little longer, but was queasy and distracted; at last I began to think how it would be if a matron should come past her cell and see me there, so pale and awkward. I thought she would see some sign about me, something dishevelled or illuminated.—I remembered then fearing the same thing of Mother, when I went back to her from visiting Helen. I called for Mrs Jelf. She looked at Selina, however, rather than at me, and when we walked along the passage together, we walked in silence. Only at the gate at the end of the ward did she put her hand to her throat and speak. She said, 'I daresay you found the women rather nervous, to-day? They always are, poor things, at a breaking-out.'

And it seemed then a wretched thing for me to have done, after all Selina had said to me—to have left her alone, afraid, and all because of a single crust of glistening wax! But, I could not go back to her. I only stood hesitating at the bars, Mrs Jelf watching me all the time with her dark, kind, patient eyes. I said, that the women *had* been nervous; and that I thought that Dawes—Selina Dawes—might be the most nervous of them all.

I said, 'I'm glad it's you, Mrs Jelf, that, out of all the matrons, has the care of *her*.'

She lowered her eyes, as if in modesty, and answered that she liked to think she was a friend to all the women. 'As for Selina Dawes, however—well, Miss Prior, you mustn't fear that any piece of harm will come to her, while *I* am here to guard her.'

Then she put her key to the gate and I saw her large hand, pale against the shadows. I thought again of the streaming wax, and again felt queasy.

Outside, the day was dark, the street made vague by a thickening fog. The Porter's man was slow to find a cab for me; when I climbed in one at last I seemed to take a skein of mist in with me, that settled upon the surface of my skirts and made them heavy. Now the fog still rises. It rises so high, it has begun to seep beneath the curtains. When Ellis came this evening, sent by Mother to fetch me to supper, she found me upon the floor, beside the glass, making the sashes tight with wads of paper. She said, what was I doing there?—that I would take a chill, that I would hurt my hands.

I said I was afraid the fog would creep into my room, in the darkness, and stifle me.

25 January 1873

This morning I went to Mrs Brink & said there was something I must tell her. She asked me 'Is it about spirits?' & when I said it was, she took me to her own room & I sat with my hands in hers. I said 'Mrs Brink, I have been visited.' She heard that & her look changed, I saw who she thought it was but I said 'No, it was not *her*, it was rather a spirit entirely new.' I said 'It was my *guide*, Mrs Brink. It was my own *control*, that every medium waits for. He has come, & shown himself to me at last!' She said at once 'He has come to you' & I shook my head, saying 'H*e*, *she*, you ought to know that in the spheres there are no differences like that. But this spirit was a gentleman on earth & is now obliged to visit me in that form. He has come, meaning to demonstrate the truths of spiritualism. He wants to do it, Mrs Brink, in your house!'

I thought she would be glad, but she was not. She took her hands from me & turned away, saying 'O, Miss Dawes, I know what this means! It means an end to our own sittings! I knew I should not keep you, that I should lose you at the last. I never thought a gentleman would come, like this!'

Then I knew why she had kept me so close, with only her own lady-friends to look at me. I laughed & took her hands again. I said 'Now, how could it mean that? Do you think I don't have power for all the world & you besides?' I said 'Does Margery think her mamma would go from her again, & not come back? Why, I think Margery's mamma might come through better, if my own guide is there to take her arm & help her! But if we do not let the guide come, then my powers might be harmed. And I can't say what that might not mean, then.'

She looked at me, & her face grew white. She said in a whisper 'What ought I to do?' & I told her what I had promised – that she ought to send out to 6 or 7 of her friends, to ask them to come for a dark circle tomorrow night. That she ought to move the cabinet to the second alcove, because it had been impressed upon me that the magnetism was better in that spot than in the other. That she ought to prepare a jar of phosphorised oil, which would make a light to see a spirit by, & that she should give me nothing but a little white meat & some red wine. I said 'This will be a very great & astonishing event, I know it.'

I didn't know it however, but was awfully afraid. But she rang for Ruth & repeated my words over to her, & Ruth went herself to the houses of Mrs Brink's friends. And when she came back she said that there were 7 people who said they will certainly come, & also that Mrs Morris had asked might she bring her nieces the 2 Miss Adairs, since they were holidaying with her & liked a dark circle as much as anyone? So altogether there will be a crowd of 9, which is more than I used to care for even in the days before forms. Mrs Brink saw my face & said 'What, are you nervous? After all you told me?' & Ruth said 'Why are you frightened? This will be marvellous.'

26 January 1873

It being a Sunday, I went as usual to church with Mrs Brink this morning. After that however I kept to my room, only going down to take a little cold chicken & a piece of fish, that Ruth had been to the kitchen & made especially for me. When they gave me a glass of warm wine I grew calmer, but I sat then listening to the voices of the people as they went into the parlour, & when Mrs Brink finally took me in to them, & I saw the chairs all set before the alcove & the ladies looking, I began to shake. I said 'I cannot say what will happen tonight, more especially since there are strangers here. But my guide has spoken to me & told me to sit for you, & I must obey.' Someone said then 'Why have you moved the cabinet to the alcove with the door in it?' Mrs Brink told them about the magnetism being better there, & said that they must not mind about the door, that it was never opened since the housemaid lost the key to it, & besides that she had put a screen before it.

Then they all fell silent & looked at me. I said we should sit in the dark & await a message &, after we had sat for 10 minutes, there came a few raps, & then I said it had been communicated to me that I should take my place inside the cabinet & they should uncover the jar of oil. They did that, I saw the bluish light of it upon the ceiling, at the top of the alcove where the curtain does not reach. Then I said they ought to sing. They sang 2 hymns with all the verses, & I began to wonder whether after all it would work or not, & I hardly knew whether I was sorry, or glad. But just at that moment when I began to wonder it, there came a great stir beside me & I called out 'O, the spirit has come!'

Then it was not at all as I had thought it would be, there was *a man* there, I must write *his great arms, his black whiskers, his red lips*. I looked at him & I trembled, & I said in a whisper 'O God, are you real?' He heard my shaking voice & then his brow went smooth as water, & he smiled & nodded. Mrs Brink called 'What is it Miss Dawes, who is there?' I said 'I don't know what I should say' & he bent & put his mouth very close to my ear, saying 'Say it is your master.' So I said it, & he went from me into the room & I heard them all cry 'O!' & 'Mercy!' & 'It is a spirit!' Mrs Morris called 'Who are you, spirit?' & he answered in a great voice 'My spirit-name is I*rresistible*, but my earth-name was P*eter* Q*uick*. You mortals must call me by my earth-name, since it is as a man that I shall come to you!' I heard someone then say 'Peter Quick', & as she said the words I said them with her, for I had not known until that moment what the name would be myself.

Then I heard Mrs Brink say 'Will you pass among us, Peter?' But he would not do that, he only stood & took their questions – they all the time making sounds of astonishment, to hear him giving so many true answers. Then he smoked a cigarette that we had put out for him, then he took a glass of lemonade, he tasted it & laughed & said 'Well, you might at least have put a drop of *spirits* in it.' When someone asked him where would the lemonade be when he had gone? he thought a moment then said 'It will be in Miss Dawes's stomach.' Then Mrs Reynolds, seeing him hold the glass, said 'Will you let me take your hand Peter, so I might know how solid it is?' Then I felt him grow doubtful, but finally he told her to come close. He said 'There, how does it feel to you?' & she answered 'It is warm & hard!' He laughed. Then he said 'O, I do wish you would hold it a little longer. I am from the Borderland, where there are no ladies handsome as you.' He said it however with his mouth turned to the curtain, not to tease me, rather as if to say 'Do you hear me? What does she know about who I think is handsome?' But he said it, & Mrs Reynolds gave a wriggling sort of laugh, & when he came back behind the curtain he put his hand upon my face & I seemed to smell her wriggling on his palm. Then I shouted that they must all sing hard again. Someone said 'Can she be well?' & Mrs Brink answered that I was taking the spirit-matter back into myself, & that they must not disturb me until the exchange was quite complete.

Then I was alone again. I called for the gas to be lit & then went out to them, but I shook so hard I could hardly walk. They saw that, & laid me flat upon the sofa. Mrs Brink rang the servant's bell & first Jenny came, then Ruth, Ruth saying 'O, what has happened? Was it marvellous? Why does Miss Dawes look so pale?' When I heard her voice I shook worse than ever &, Mrs Brink noticing that, she took my hands & rubbed them, saying 'You are not too weakened?' & Ruth drew the slippers from me & put her hands about my feet, then bent & breathed on them. Finally however, the elder Miss Adair said to her 'That will do, let me see to her now.' Then she sat beside me & another lady held my hand. Miss Adair said quietly 'O Miss Dawes, I never saw anything to match that spirit! What was it like, when he came to you in the darkness?'

When they went, 2 or 3 of them left money for me with Ruth, I heard them putting the coins into her hand. I was so tired however, I could not have cared if they had been pennies or pounds, I should only have been glad to be able to creep into some dark place & lay my head there. I kept upon the sofa, hearing Ruth putting the bolt across, & Mrs Brink stepping about the floor of her room, then getting into her bed & waiting. Then I knew who she was waiting for. I went to the stairs & put my hand to my face, & Ruth looked at me once & nodded. 'Good girl,' she said.

Part Three

5 November 1874

It was two years, yesterday, since my own dear father died; and to-day my sister Priscilla was married at last, at Chelsea church, to Arthur Barclay. She has gone from London until at least the start of next year's season. They are to have ten weeks upon the honeymoon then travel straight from Italy to Warwickshire, and there is talk of us holidaying with them there, from January until the spring—though I don't care to think of that, just yet. I sat in the church with Mother and Helen, and Pris came with Stephen, one of the Barclay children carrying her flowers in a basket. She wore a white lace veil, and when she walked from the vestry and Arthur had turned it back—well, the straight face she has been maintaining for the past six weeks clearly had its effect, for I don't believe I ever saw her so handsome. Mother put her handkerchief to her eyes, and I heard Ellis weeping at the door of the church. Pris has a girl of her own now, of course, sent to her by the housekeeper at Marishes.

I had thought it might be hard, to see my sister pass me in the church. It was not; I was only a little moodish when it came time to kiss them both farewell, and I saw their boxes tied and labelled, Priscilla brilliant in a mustard-coloured cloak—the family's first piece of colour, of course, in twenty-four months—and promising us parcels from Milan. I thought that there were one or two curious or pitying glances cast my way—but not so many, I am sure, as there were at Stephen's wedding. Then, I suppose, I was my mother's burden. Now I am become her *consolation*. I heard people say it, at the breakfast: 'You must be thankful you have Margaret, Mrs Prior. So like her father! She will be a comfort to you now.'

I am not a comfort to her. She doesn't want to see her husband's face and habits, on her *daughter*! When all the wedding guests had gone I found her wandering about the house, shaking her head and sighing—'How quiet it seems!'—as if my sister had been a child, and she missed the sound of her shrieks upon the staircase. I followed her to the door of Priscilla's bedroom, and gazed with her at the empty shelves. It has all been boxed and sent to Marishes, even the little girlish things—which I suppose Pris will want for her own daughters. I said, 'We are becoming a house of empty rooms,' and Mother sighed again.

Then she stepped to the bed and pulled one of the curtains from it, and then the counterpane, saying they must not be left to grow damp and moulder. She rang for Vigers and had her strip the mattress, then take the rugs and beat them, and scour the grate. We heard the unfamiliar bustle as we sat together in the drawing-room—Mother exclaiming peevishly that Vigers was 'clumsy as a calf'; or glancing at the mantel clock to sigh again and say, 'Priscilla will be at Southampton now' or 'Now they will be upon the Channel . . .'

'How loud the clock sounds!' she said, another time; and then, turning to gaze at the spot where the parrot had used to sit: 'How quiet it is, now Gulliver has gone.'

She said that that was the disadvantage of bringing creatures into the house: one grew used to them, and then, one had the upset of their loss.

The clock beat on. We spoke of the wedding and the guests, and of the rooms at Marishes, and of Arthur's handsome sisters and their gowns; and in time Mother took out a piece of sewing and began to work at it. Then at nine or so I rose, as usual, to bid her good-night—and when I did that she gave me a sharp, odd look. She said, 'You won't leave me alone, I hope, to grow stupid. Go on and fetch your book, and bring it here. You can read it to me, I have had no-one read to me since your father died.' I said, in a rising kind of miserable panic, that she knew she would not care for any book of mine. She answered, that I must fetch her something she *would* care for, a novel or a book of letters;

and, while I still stood staring at her, she rose and went to the case beside the fireplace, and took a book from that, quite randomly. It turned out to be the first volume of *Little Dorrit*.

And so I read to her, and she sat and pricked at her sewing, and threw more glances at the clock, and rang for cake and tea, and tutted when Vigers tipped the cup; and from Cremorne there came the fitful cracking of fireworks, and from the street occasional shouts and bursts of laughter. I read—she didn't seem to listen very hard, she didn't smile or frown or tilt her head—yet when I paused she would nod and say, 'Go on, Margaret. Go on, to the next chapter.' I read, and watched her from beneath my lashes—and I had a clear and terrible vision.

I saw her ageing. I saw her growing old and stooped and querulous—perhaps, a little deaf. I saw her growing bitter, because her son and her favourite daughter had homes elsewhere—had gayer homes, with children and footsteps and young men and new gowns in them; homes which, were it not for the presence of her spinster daughter—her *consolation*, who preferred prisons and poetry to fashion-plates and dinners, and was therefore no consolation at all—she would certainly be invited to share. Why hadn't I guessed it would be like this when Pris left? I had thought only of my own envy. Now I sat and watched my mother, and felt fearful, and ashamed of my own fear.

And when once she rose and went to her room I walked to the window and stood at the glass. They were still sending up rockets, behind the trees at Cremorne, even when it rained.

That was to-night. To-morrow night Helen is to come with her friend Miss Palmer. Miss Palmer is soon to be married.

I am twenty-nine. In three months' time I shall be thirty. While Mother grows stooped and querulous, how shall I grow?

I shall grow dry and pale and paper-thin—like a leaf, pressed tight inside the pages of a dreary black book and then forgotten. I came across just such a leaf yesterday—it was a piece of ivy—amongst the books upon the shelves behind

Pa's desk. I went there, telling Mother I meant to begin to look through his letters; but I went only to think of him. The room is kept just as he left it, with his pen upon the blotter, his seal, the knife for his cigars, the looking-glass . . .

I remember him standing before that, two weeks after they first found the cancer in him, and turning his face from it with a ghastly smile. His nurse had told him, when he was a boy, that invalids should not gaze at their own reflections, for fear their souls would fly into the glass and kill them.

Now I stood a long time before that mirror, looking for him in it—looking for anything in it from the days before he died. There was only myself.

10 November 1874

I went down this morning to find three of Pa's hats upon the hat-stand, and his cane in its old place against the wall. For a moment I stood quite ill with fear, remembering my locket. I thought, '*Selina* has done this, and now, how am I to account for it to the house?' Then Ellis appeared, looked queerly at me, and explained. Mother said for the things to be put there: she believes it will frighten off burglars, if they think we have a gentleman with us! She has asked for a policeman, too, to patrol the Walk, and now, when I go out, I see him looking and he touches his cap to me—'Good afternoon, Miss Prior.' Next I suppose she will be making Cook sleep with loaded pistols beneath her pillow, like the Carlyles. And then Cook will roll over in the night and get shot in the head, and Mother will say, what a shame, there never was a cook could turn out cutlets and ragout like Mrs Vincent . . .

But, I have grown cynical. Helen told me so. She was here this evening, with Stephen. I left them both talking with Mother, but Helen came tapping at my door a little later—she often does that, she comes to wish me good-night, I am quite used to it. This time when she came, however, I saw that she had something in her hand, that she held awkwardly. It was my phial of chloral. She said, not looking at me, 'Your mother saw that I was coming to you and asked me would I bring your medicine? I said I thought you wouldn't like it. But she complains about the extra stairs—that they make her legs ache. She said that she would rather trust the task to me than to a servant.'

I think I would rather Vigers brought it than Helen. I said, 'She will have me standing in the drawing-room next, taking it from a spoon, before company. And did she let you fetch it from her room, alone? You are honoured, to know where she keeps it. She won't tell me.'

I watched her taking pains over the mixing of the powder in the glass. When she brought it to me I put it on my desk and let it sit there, and she said, 'I must stay until you drink it.' I told her I would take it in a moment. I said she must not worry: I would not keep it there, only to make her stay. At that she blushed, and turned her head from me.

We had a letter from Pris and Arthur this morning, posted at Paris, and now we spoke a little of that. I said, 'Do you know how stifled I have felt here, since the wedding? Do you think me selfish for it?' She hesitated. Then she said, that this would of course be a difficult time for me, with my sister married . . .

I gazed at her, and shook my head. Oh, I said, I had heard words like that, so many times! When Stephen went to school when I was ten: they said that that would be 'a difficult time', because of course I was so clever, and would not understand why I must keep my governess. When he went to Cambridge it was the same; and then, when he came home and was called to the bar. When Pris turned out so handsome they said that would be difficult, we must expect it to be difficult, because of course I was so plain. And then, when Stephen was married, when Pa died, when Georgy was born—it had been one thing leading to another, and they had said only, always, that it was natural, it was to be expected that I should feel the sting of things like that; that older, unmarried sisters always did. 'But Helen, Helen,' I said, 'if they expect it to be hard, why don't they change things, to allow it to be easier? I feel, if I might only have a little liberty—'

Liberty, she asked me then, to do what? And when I could not answer her, she only said, that I must go more to Garden Court.

'To look at you and Stephen,' I said flatly. 'To look at Georgy.' She said, that when Pris returned, then there was sure to be an invitation to Marishes, and that would make a change to my routines.—'Marishes!' I cried. 'And they will put me, at supper, beside the curate's son; and I shall spend my days with Arthur's spinster cousin—helping her fix black beetles to a green baize board.'

She studied me. It was then she said I had grown cynical. I said, that I had always been cynical—she had only never called it that. She had said rather that I was *brave*. She had called me an *original*. She had seemed to admire me for it.

That made her colour again; but it also made her sigh. She walked from me and stood at the bed—and I said at once, 'Don't go too near the bed! Don't you know it's haunted, by our old kisses? They'll come and frighten you.'

'Oh!' she cried then, and she beat her fist against the bed-post, then sat upon the bed and put her hands before her face. She said, would I torment her for ever? She *had* thought me brave—she thinks me brave, even now. But I, she said, had thought her brave, too—'And I was never that, Margaret, not enough, not for what you wanted. And now, when you might still be my dear friend—oh! I want so much to be your friend! But you make it like a battle! I am so weary of it.'

She shook her head, and closed her eyes. I felt her weariness then, and with it, my own. I felt it dark and heavy upon me, darker and heavier than any drug they ever gave me—it seemed heavy as death. I looked at the bed. I *have* seemed to see our kisses there sometimes, I've seen them hanging in the curtains, like bats, ready to swoop. Now, I thought, I might jolt the post and they would only fall, and shatter, and turn to powder.

I said, 'I am sorry.' I said—though I did not feel it, have never felt it, will never be glad of it—I said, 'I am glad that Stephen has you, of any man. I think he must be kind.'

She answered, that he was the kindest man she ever knew.

Then she hesitated, then said that she wished—she thought, if I might move a little more in company—that, there were other kind men . . .

They might be kind, I thought. They might be sensible and good. They will not be like you.

But I did not say it. I knew it would mean nothing to her. I said something—something ordinary and mild, I cannot think what. And after a time she came and kissed my cheek, and then she left me.

She took the phial of chloral with her—but she had forgotten, after all, to stand and watch me take my drink. It still sat upon my desk, the water clear and thin and weak as tears, the chloral muddy at the bottom of the tumbler. A moment ago I rose and poured the water off, then I took the drug with a spoon—the grounds I could not reach with that I put my finger to, and then I sucked my finger. Now my mouth is very bitter, but its flesh quite numb. I believe I could bite my tongue until it bled, and scarcely feel it.

14 November 1874

Well, Mother and I are twenty chapters into *Little Dorrit*, and I have been marvellously good and patient, all week long. We have been to tea at the Wallaces', and to Garden Court for supper with Miss Palmer and her beau; we have even been to the dress shops of Hanover Street together. And oh! what a hateful business it is, watching the small-chinned, prim-faced, plump-throated girls walk simpering before one, while the lady lifts the folds of skirt to show the *faille*, the *groseille* or the *foulard* detail underneath. I said, Had they nothing in grey?—the lady looked doubtful. Had they anything slim and plain and neat?—They showed me a girl in a cuirass gown. She was small, and shapely—she looked like an ankle in a well-shaped boot. I knew I would put the same gown on and look like a sword in a scabbard.

I bought a pair of buff kid gloves—and wished I might buy a dozen more of them, to take to Selina in her cold cell.

Still, I think Mother believed we were making great strides forward. This morning, as I took my breakfast, she presented me with a gift, in a silver case. It was a set of calling-cards she has had printed up. They are edged with a curving border of black, and bear our two names—hers printed first, and mine, beneath it, in a less ambitious script.

I looked at them and felt my stomach close, like a fist.

I have not mentioned the prison to her, and I have kept away from there, for almost a fortnight—all for the sake of making trips with her. I thought she must have guessed that and been grateful to me. But when she brought the cards to me this morning and said she planned to pay a call, and would I go with her or stay and read? I answered at once that I believed, after all, that I would go to Millbank—and she looked sharply at me, in real surprise. 'Millbank?' she said. 'I thought you had finished with all of that.'

'Finished? Mother, how could you think it?'

She gave a snap to the clasp of her purse. 'You must do as you please, I suppose,' she said.

I said I would do just as I had before Priscilla left. I said, 'Nothing has changed, has it, apart from that?'—She would not answer.

Her new nervousness, the week of patient visits and *Little Dorrit*, that awful, foolish supposition that I had somehow 'finished' with my visiting, all had their effect on me and made me dreary. Millbank itself—as is usual when I keep away from it a little—seemed wretched, and the women in it sorrier than ever. Ellen Power has a fever and a cough. She coughs so hard the cough convulses her, and leaves threads of blood upon the cloth she wipes her lips with—so much for the extra meat, the scarlet flannel, from kind Mrs Jelf. The gipsy-girl, the abortionist they named 'Black-Eyed Sue', now wears a dirty bandage upon her face, and must eat her mutton with her fingers. She had not been in her cell three weeks before she tried, in her despair or madness, to put out one of her dark eyes with her dinner-knife; her matron said the eye was pierced and she is blind in it. The cells are still as cold as larders. I asked Miss Ridley, as she led me between the wards, how it could help the women to be kept so cold and hopeless?—to be made ill? She said: 'We are not here to help them, ma'am. We are here to punish them. There are too many good women who are poor or ill or hungry, for us to bother with the bad ones.' She said they would all stay warm enough, if they would only *sew briskly*.

I went to Power, as I have said; and then to Cook and to another woman, Hamer; and then to Selina. She raised her head when she heard my step, and her gaze met my own, over the matron's dipping shoulder, and her eyes grew bright. I knew then how hard it had been to keep, not just from Millbank, but from her. I felt that little *quickening*. It was just as I imagine a woman must feel, when the baby within her gives its first kick.

Does it matter if I feel that, that is so small, and silent, and secret?

It didn't seem to matter, at that moment, in Selina's cell.

For she was so grateful to have me go to her! She said, 'You were patient with me, last time, when I was so distracted. And then, when you didn't come for so long—I know it isn't long, but it seems terribly long to me, here at Millbank. And when you didn't come, I thought, perhaps you had changed your mind and meant never to visit again . . .'

I remembered that visit, and how queer and fanciful it had made me. I said she mustn't think such things as that; and I looked, as I spoke, at the stone cell floor—there were no marks of white upon it now, no trace of wax or grease or even limewash. I said that I had only been obliged to keep away a little. I had been rather occupied, with duties at home.

She nodded, but looked sad. She said that she supposed I had many friends? She could see how I would rather spend my days with them, than go to Millbank.

If she could only know how slow and dull and empty my days are!—as slow as hers. I went to her chair, and sat in it, and put my arm upon her table. I told her that Priscilla had married, and that my mother needed me more at home now she was gone. She looked, and nodded: 'Your sister married. Is it a good marriage?'—I said it was very good. She said,

'Then you must be happy for her'—and when I only smiled and wouldn't answer, she drew a little nearer.

She said, 'I think, Aurora, that perhaps you envy your sister a little.'

I smiled. I said she was right, that I did envy her. 'Not,' I added, 'because she has a husband, not for that, oh no! But because she has—how can I say it? She has *evolved*, like one of your spirits. She has moved on. And I am left, more firmly *un*evolved than ever.'

'You are like me, then,' she said. 'Indeed, you are like all of us at Millbank.'

I said I was. And yet, they had their terms, that would expire . . .

I lowered my eyes, but felt her keep her gaze upon me. She asked me, would I tell her more about my sister? I said she would think me selfish—'Oh!' she said at once, 'I could never think that.'

'You will. Do you know, I couldn't bear to look upon my sister as she set off upon her honeymoon. I couldn't bear to kiss her, or to wish her farewell. *That* is when I was envious! Oh, I might as well have had vinegar in my veins, then, as blood!'

I hesitated. Still she studied me. And at last she said quietly, that I must not be ashamed to tell my true thoughts there, at Millbank. That there, there were only the stones in the walls to hear me—and herself, who they kept dumb as a stone, and so could tell no-one.

She has said as much to me, before; I never felt the force of it, however, as I did to-day, and when I spoke at last, it was as if the words were pulled from me, that had been tight, inside my breast, upon a thread. I said, 'My sister has gone, Selina, to Italy; and I was to have travelled there, with my father and—with a friend.' I have never of course mentioned Helen at Millbank. I said now only that we had planned to go, to Florence and to Rome; that Pa had meant to study in the archives and the galleries there, and that my friend and I had meant to help him. I told her that Italy had become a kind of mania with me, a kind of emblem. 'We meant to make the trip before Priscilla married, so that my mother might not be left alone. Now Priscilla *is* married. She has gone there, with not a thought for all my careful plans. And I—'

I have not wept in many months but, to my horror and my shame, I found myself near weeping now, and I twisted away from her, towards the bubbling limewashed wall. When I turned to her again I found her closer than ever. She had lowered herself at the side of the table and rested with her arms upon it, her chin upon her wrists.

She said that I was very brave—the same thing Helen said, a week ago. Hearing it again, I almost laughed. Brave! I said. Brave, to bear my own complaining self! When I would rather lose that self—but cannot, could not, was forbidden even that—

'Brave,' she said again, shaking her head, 'to have brought yourself here, to Millbank, to all of us that wait for you . . .'

She was close to me, and the cell was chill. I felt the warmth of her, the life of her. But now, keeping her eyes upon me, she rose and stretched. 'Your sister,' she said, 'that you're so envious of. What do you have to envy, really? What has she done, that is so marvellous? You think she has *evolved*—but is it that? To have done what everyone does? She has only moved to more of the same. How clever is that?'

I thought of Pris—who has always, like Stephen, favoured Mother, while I resemble Pa. I imagined her in twenty years, scolding her daughters.

But people, I said, do not want cleverness—not in women, at least. I said, 'Women are *bred* to do more of the same—that is their function. It is only ladies like me that throw the system out, make it stagger—'

She said then that, it was doing the same thing always that kept us 'bound to the earth'; that we were made to rise from it, but would never do that until we *changed*. As for *women* and *men*, she said—well, that was the first thing that must be cast off.

I did not understand her. She smiled. 'When we rise,' she said, 'do you think we take our earth-features with us? It is only new, bewildered spirits that look about them for the things of the flesh. When guides come to them, the spirits gaze at them and don't know how to talk to them—they say "Are you a man, or a lady?" But the guides are neither, and both; and the spirits are neither, and both. It is only when they have understood that, that they are ready to be taken higher.'

I tried to imagine the world she spoke of—the world she says has Pa in it. I imagined Pa, unclothed and sexless, and with myself beside him.—It was a terrible vision, that made me sweat.

No, I said. It meant nothing, what she was saying. It could not be true. How could it be? It would be chaos!

'It would be freedom.'

It would be a world without distinction. It would be a world without love.

'It is a world that is *made* of love. Did you think there is only the kind of love your sister knows for her husband? Did you think there must be here, a man with whiskers, and over here, a lady in a gown? Haven't I said, there are no whiskers and gowns where spirits are? And what will your sister do if her husband should die, and she should take another? Who will she fly to then, when she has crossed the spheres? For she will fly to someone, we will all fly to someone, we will all return to that piece of shining matter from which our souls were torn with another, two halves of the same. It may be that the husband your sister has now has that other soul, that has the affinity with her soul—I hope it is. But it may be the next man she takes, or it may be neither. It may be someone she would never think to look to on the earth, someone kept from her by some false boundary . . .'

It strikes me now, what an extraordinary conversation this was for us to be having—with the gate fastened on us and Mrs Jelf patrolling by it, and the coughs and grumbles and sighs of three hundred women all about us, and the rattling of bolts and keys. But with Selina's green eyes upon me, I did not think of it. I looked only at her, heard her voice only; and when I spoke at last, it was to ask her this: 'How will a person know, Selina, when the soul that has the affinity with hers is near it?'

She answered, 'She will know. Does she look for air, before she breathes it? This love will be guided to her; and when it comes, she will know. And she will do anything to keep that love about her, then. Because to lose it will be like a death to her.'

She still kept her eyes upon me—now, however, I saw her gaze grow strange. She looked at me, as if she did not know me. Then she turned from me, as if she had shown me too much of herself, and was ashamed.

I looked again at the floor of her cell, for that smear of wax.—There was nothing.

20 November 1874

Another letter to-day from Priscilla and Arthur—this one from Italy, from Piacenza. When I told Selina, she made me repeat the name to her three or four times: '*Piacenza, Piacenza* . . .'—and she smiled to hear me say it. She said, 'It might be a word from a piece of poetry.'

I told her then that I had often used to think the same. I told her how, when Pa was alive, I would lie awake and, instead of saying prayers or verses, I would count off all the towns of Italy—*Verona*, *Reggio*, *Rimini*, *Como*, *Parma*, *Piacenza*, *Cosenza*, *Milan* . . . I said I had spent many hours, thinking of how it would be when I saw those places.

She said, that I might of course see them still.

I smiled. 'I should think—not.'

'But you have years and years,' she said, 'to go to Italy in!'

I said, 'Perhaps. But not, you know, as I was then.'

'As you are *now*, Aurora,' she said. 'Or as you might be, soon.'

And she held my gaze, until I looked away.

Then she asked me, what was it anyway about Italy that I admired so very much? and I said at once, 'Oh, Italy! I think Italy must be the most perfect place on earth . . .' I said she must imagine how it has been for me, to have spent so many years helping my father with his work; to have seen all the marvellous paintings and statues of Italy, in books, and prints—in blacks and whites and greys, and muddy crimsons. 'But to visit the Uffizi, and the Vatican,' I said, 'to step into any simple country church with a fresco in it—I think that would be, to step into colour and light!' I told her about the house in Florence, on the Via Ghibellina, where one may visit the rooms of Michelangelo, and see his slippers and his cane, the cabinet he wrote in. Imagine, I said, seeing such a thing as that! Imagine seeing the tomb of Dante, in Ravenna. Imagine the days, that were long and warm all the year round. Imagine every corner with a fountain at it, and boughs of orange-blossom—imagine the streets, filled with the scent of orange-blossom, where ours were filled with fogs! 'The people there, they are easy and frank. Englishwomen may walk freely, I think, about the streets there—quite freely. Imagine how the seas must sparkle! Why, imagine Venice: a city so much a part of the sea you must hire a boat to take you across it . . .'

I spoke on—until I became conscious all at once of my own voice, and of how she stood listening, smiling at my pleasure. Her face was half-turned to the window, and the light that fell upon it made its sharp, asymmetrical lines seem very fine. I remembered the sensation with which I had studied her first, and how she had reminded me of the Crivelli *Veritas*—and the memory I suppose made my expression change, for now she asked me, Why had I fallen silent? What was I thinking of?

I said that I was thinking of a gallery at Florence, and a painting that hangs in it.

A painting I hoped to study, she asked me, with my father and my friend?

I said, no, it was a painting that meant nothing to me when I made those plans . . .

She frowned, not understanding; and when I would say no more she shook her head, and then she laughed.

She must be careful not to laugh, next time. When Mrs Jelf had released me, and I had gone down through the wards and reached the gate that leads from the women's prison to the men's, I heard my name called; and I looked round to see Miss Haxby approaching, her face rather stiff. I had not seen her since my visit with her to the punishment cell; I remembered how I had clutched at her in the darkness then, and I felt myself colour. She asked me, Did I have a moment I might spare her?—and when I nodded, she dismissed the matron who had escorted me, and led me through the gate, and corridors beyond, herself.

'How are you, Miss Prior?' she began. 'We were brought together so unfortunately last time, I did not have the opportunity to discuss your progress with you. You must think me very slack.' She said that the fact was, she had trusted her matrons with the care of me, and had had reports from them—'and in particular, from my deputy Miss Ridley'—which suggested that I had managed well enough without her help.

It had never occurred to me before that I might be the subject of 'reports', or of any kind of exchange, between Miss Haxby and her staff. I thought of the great dark Character Book that she keeps upon her desk. I wonder if she has a special section there, marked 'Lady Visitors'.

What I said, however, was that her matrons had all been most helpful to me, and most kind. We paused, while a warden unfastened a gate for us—of course, her ring of keys is useless there, on the men's wards.

Then she asked me, How did I find the women? She said that one or two of them—Ellen Power, Mary Ann Cook—always spoke kindly of me to her. She said, 'You have made friends of them, I think! They will feel the worth of that. For if a lady takes an interest in them then it will encourage them, of course, to take an interest in themselves.'

I said I hoped so. She glanced at me, then looked away. Of course, she said, there was always a danger that such a friendship would mislead a prisoner—would cause her to take *too much* interest in herself. 'Our women are required to spend many solitary hours, and this sometimes makes their fancies rather keen. A lady comes, she calls a woman "friend", she returns to her own world—the woman sees nothing of that, of course.' She hoped I could appreciate the dangers of it. I thought I could. She said that such things were sometimes easier to know than to act on . . .

'I do wonder,' she said at last, 'whether your interest in some of our prisoners mightn't be a little more—specific—than it ought to be.'

I think I slowed my step for a second; and then I walked on, a little faster than before. Of course, I knew who she meant—I knew it at once. But I asked, 'In which prisoners, Miss Haxby?'

She answered: 'In one prisoner, Miss Prior, in particular.'

I did not look at her. I said, 'You mean, I suppose, Selina Dawes?'

She nodded. She said the matrons had told her I spend the main part of my visits in Dawes's cell.

Miss Ridley has told you, I thought bitterly. I thought, *Of course* they will do this to her. They have taken her hair from her, and her ordinary clothes. They make her sweat into a filthy prison gown, they make her fine hands rough with useless labour—*of course* they will seek to take from her the scraps of comfort and relief she has grown used to having now from me. And again I remembered her as I had seen her first, holding a violet in her hands. I had understood—even then, I had understood—that, had they found that flower about her, they would have taken it and crushed it. Just so did they want to crush our friendship, now. It was *against the rules*.

I knew better, of course, than to let my bitterness show. I said the truth was, I had taken a special interest in Dawes's case; and I thought it was a common practice, for Lady Visitors to take notice of certain prisoners, individually. Miss Haxby said it was. She said that ladies had helped many of her girls—had helped them at last to places suited to their station, had led them to new lives, away from their shame, away from their old influences, away from England itself sometimes, to marriage, in the Colonies.

She fixed her sharp eyes on me and asked, Did I perhaps have a plan like this, for Selina Dawes?

I told her that I have no plans at all for Selina. That I seek only to bring her the little comfort that she needs. 'You must have seen this,' I said, 'you, who know her history. You must have guessed, how particular her circumstances are.' I said that she was not a girl that might be set up as a lady's maid. She was thoughtful and feeling—almost a lady, indeed, herself. 'I think the rigours of prison life tell on her,' I said, 'more than on the other women.'

'You have brought your own ideas with you into the gaol,' Miss Haxby said, after a moment. 'But our ways at Millbank—as you can see—are rather narrow ones.' She smiled, for we had now entered a passage-way that obliged us to draw in our skirts a little and step one before the other. She said that there were no distinctions to be made there, save those they thought it best to make, as officers, and Dawes had all the benefits of those already. She said that, if I continued in marking one girl out for special attention, I would make her less contented with her lot, not more so; and I would finish by discontenting the other prisoners with theirs.

She said, in short, that it would oblige her and her staff if, in the future, I would visit Dawes less, and keep my visits rather briefer.

I turned my gaze from her. The bitterness I had felt at first had begun to turn now to a kind of fear. I remembered how Selina had laughed: she had never smiled, when I first went to her, she had only been sullen and sad. I remembered how she said that she looked forward to my visits, and was sorry when I did not come, because the Millbank hours were so slow. I thought, If they stop me seeing her now, they might as well take her to the darks, and leave her!

There was a part of me, too, that thought, They might as well take *me* there.

I did not want Miss Haxby to know that I thought that. But she still seemed to study me, and now—we had reached the gate of Pentagon One—now I saw the warder, also eyeing me a little curiously, and I felt my cheek burn redder. I put my hands before me and clasped them tight; and then I heard a footstep in the passage-way behind us, and turned to look at it. It was Mr Shillitoe. He called my name. How lucky it was, he said, that he had met me! He nodded to Miss Haxby, then took my hand. He said, How were the visits progressing?

I said, 'The visits are progressing just as well as I could wish'—my voice, after all, was very steady. 'Miss Haxby has been cautioning me, however.'—'Ah,' he said.

Miss Haxby said that she had been advising me against marking women out for special privileges. That I had made a 'protégée'—she pronounced it queerly—of one particular prisoner, and she thought the prisoner less steady than she seemed. The girl was Dawes, the 'Spiritist'.

Mr Shillitoe said 'Ah' in a slightly different tone, when he heard that. He said he often thinks of Selina Dawes, and wonders how her new habits suit her.

I told him they suit her very ill. I said she was weak—he answered at once, that that did not surprise him. All people of her type were weak, he said, it was that quality that made them a vehicle for the unnatural influences they termed *spiritual.* Spiritual they might be, but there was 'nothing of God in them'—nothing holy, nothing good—and they must all, at the last, reveal themselves as wicked. Why, Dawes was a proof of it! He would like to see every Spiritualist in England in a prison cell, locked up beside her!

I stared at him. Beside me, Miss Haxby draw her mantle a little higher about her shoulders. I said, slowly, that he was right. That Dawes, I thought, had been used—impressed—by some queer power. But she was a gentle girl, and the loneliness of prison life told on her. When a fancy came to her, she could not shake it off. She needed guidance.

'She has the guidance of her matrons,' said Miss Haxby, 'as all the women have.'

I said that she needed the guidance of a Visitor—of a friend, from beyond the prison walls. She needed an object upon which to fasten her thoughts, while she worked, or while she lay still and silent—at night, when the wards were quiet. 'For then, I think she feels those morbid influences come upon her. And she is weak, as I have said. I think they—baffle her.'

The matron said then that, if they were to indulge the women every time they thought themselves *baffled*, they should have to bring in a troop of ladies to do the work!

But Mr Shillitoe had narrowed his eyes a little, and now tapped with his foot upon the flags of the passage, considering. I watched his face, and Miss Haxby watched it: we stood before him like the two fierce mothers—one true, one false—who stood before Solomon, arguing over a child . . .

And then at last he turned to his matron and said he thought, after all, that 'Miss Prior might be right'. They had a duty to their prisoners—a duty to protect them, as well as to punish. Perhaps that protection, in Dawes's case, could be applied a little more—thoughtfully. A troop of ladies was what they needed, indeed! 'We should be grateful that Miss Prior is willing to devote *her* labour to the task.'

Miss Haxby said then that she was grateful for it. She made him a curtsey, and her ring of keys let out a muffled ring.

When she had gone, Mr Shillitoe took my hand again. 'How proud your father would be,' he said, 'if he could only see you now!'

10 March 1873

So many people come for the dark circles now, we have to put Jenny at the door when the room is full, to take their cards & tell them to come back another evening. It is mostly ladies that come, though some bring gentlemen. Peter prefers the ladies. He goes among them & lets them hold his hand & feel his whiskers. He has them light his cigarettes. He says 'My eye, but you're a beauty! You're the best beauty I saw, this side of Paradise!' He says things like that & they laugh & answer 'O, you naughty thing!' They think that kisses from Peter Quick don't count.

The gentlemen he teases. He says 'I saw you last week, visiting a pretty girl. Didn't she like the flowers you took her!' Then he looks at the gentlemen's wives & he whistles & says 'Well, I can see which way the wind is blowing here, & shall say no more.' He says 'I am a chap that knows how to keep a secret, all right!' Tonight there was a gentleman in the circle, a Mr Harvey, that had a silk hat with him. Peter took the hat & put it on his own head, & walked about the parlour. He said 'Now I am a regular swell. You may call me Peter Quick of Savile Row. I should like my spirit-chums to see me in this.' Mr Harvey said then 'Well, you may keep it' & Peter answered 'May I?' in a tone of wonder. When he came back into the cabinet however, he showed me the hat & whispered 'Now, what shall I do with this? Shall I put it in the chamber-pot in Mrs Brink's room?' I heard that & laughed, they heard me laughing in the circle & I called out 'O! Peter is teasing me!'

When they searched the cabinet later of course, it was perfectly empty, & then everybody shook their heads to think of Peter walking in the spirit-world in Mr Harvey's hat. Then afterwards they found the hat. It had been put upon the picture-rail in the hall, & its brim was broken & its crown struck clean through. Mr Harvey said that after all, it was too solid a thing to make the journey through the spheres, but that Peter was very brave to try to take it. He held it as if it might be made of glass. He says he will have it put in a frame as a spiritual trophy.

Ruth told me later however, that the hat was not from Savile Row, but only from some cheap tailor's at Bayswater. She said Mr Harvey might hold himself like a rich man, but she didn't think much of his taste in toppers.

21 November 1874

It is not quite midnight, and bitterly cold and bleak, and I am tired, and dull with chloral—but the house is quiet, and I must write this. I have had another of those visits or signs, from Selina's spirits. And where can I say it, except here?

It came while I was at Garden Court. I went there this morning and stayed until three, and when I came home I came straight, as I always do, to this room; and then I knew at once that something had been touched or taken, or tampered with. The room was dark, I couldn't see that anything was changed, I only felt it. My first terrible thought was, that perhaps Mother had gone to my desk and found this book, and sat and read it.

But it was not the book; and when I took another step, I saw. There were flowers here, in a vase from the mantel. The vase was placed upon my desk, and there were orange-blossoms in it—orange-blossoms, in an English winter!

I couldn't go to them at once. I could only stand, with my cloak still upon me and my gloves tight in my fist. There was a fire lit, and the air was warm and had the flowers' scent upon it—it was that, I suppose, that I had caught before. Now it made me tremble. I thought, She has done this to please me, and it has made me afraid.—They made me frightened of her!

Then I thought, What a fool you are! This is like seeing Pa's hats upon the stand. They must be from Priscilla. Priscilla has sent us flowers, from Italy . . . And then I did go to them, and held them to my face. Only from Pris, I thought, only from Pris.—And sharp as the fear, there came a stab of disappointment.

But still, I was not sure. I thought I ought to be certain. I put the vase down, then rang for Ellis, then walked about the room until I heard her hand upon the door. But it wasn't Ellis—it was Vigers, with her long face leaner and paler than ever and her sleeves rolled to her elbows. Ellis, she said, was setting the table in the dining-room: there had been only her and Cook to answer my bell. I said, Never mind, she would do. I said, 'These flowers—who brought them?'

She looked stupidly at the desk, the vase, and then at me again—'Please miss?'

The flowers! They hadn't been there when I went out. Someone had brought them to the house, someone had placed them in the majolica vase. Was it her?—It was not her. Had she been at home all day?—she said she had. Then a boy must have called, I said, with parcels. Who were the parcels from? Was it my sister, Miss Priscilla—Mrs Barclay—in Italy?

She did not know.

I said, did she know anything? I said, she must go and get Ellis. She went quickly, then brought Ellis to the door, and then they both stood blinking at me while I paced and gestured and said, The flowers! The flowers! Who had brought the flowers to my room, and placed them in the vase there? Who had taken the parcel, that my sister had sent?

'Parcel, miss?'—There had been no parcels.

No parcels from Priscilla?—No parcels from anyone.

Now I was afraid again. I raised my hand to my lip, and I think Ellis saw it tremble. She said, Should she take the flowers away?—and I did not know, I did not know what I should tell her, what I should do. She waited, and Vigers waited; and as I stood, uncertain, there came the sound of a door, and the rustle of Mother's skirts—'Ellis? Ellis, are you there?' She had been ringing.

Now I said quickly, 'That will do, that will do! Leave the flowers and go, both of you!'

But Mother was quicker than I. She had stepped into the hall, looked up, and seen the servants at my door.

'What is it, Ellis? Margaret, is that you?' Her footstep sounded on the stair. I heard Ellis turn and say that Miss

Margaret, ma'am, was asking after some flowers.—And then Mother's voice again: flowers? What flowers?

'It's nothing, Mother!' I called. Ellis and Vigers still hesitated at the door. 'Go on,' I said. 'Go.' But now Mother was behind them, blocking their path. She looked at me, then at the desk—Why, she said, what lovely blossoms! Then she looked at me again. What was the matter? she said. Why did I look so pale? Why was it so dark here? She made Vigers take a taper to the fire and light the lamp.

I said that nothing was the matter. I had made a mistake, and was very sorry to have troubled the girls.

Mistake? she said. What sort of a mistake? 'Ellis?'

'Miss Prior said she didn't know who brought the flowers, ma'am.'

'Not know? Margaret, how can you not have known?'

I said then that I did know, and had only been confused. I said—I said that I had brought the flowers myself. I looked away from her, but felt her gaze grow sharper. At last she murmured to the girls, and they left at once, and she stepped into the room and shut the door behind her. I flinched to have her here—she comes only at night, usually. Now she said, What was this nonsense? I answered, still not catching her eye, that it was not nonsense, only a silly mistake. That she need not stay. That I must take off my shoes and change my gown. I moved about her, hung up my cloak, let my gloves fall—picked them up—let them fall a second time.

She said, What did I mean, *mistake*? How could I have bought such flowers, and then forgotten? What was I thinking of? And then, to grow so nervous before the maids . . .

I said that I had not been nervous; but even as I spoke I heard my voice, and how it trembled. She came a little closer. I made a gesture—put my hand upon my arm, I think, before she could close her own fingers on the flesh of it—and turned aside. But then I saw the blossoms before me, and caught their scent again, stronger than before, and I turned again, away from them. If she doesn't leave me, I thought, I shall weep, or strike her!

But still she came on. She said, 'Are you well?'—and, when I made no answer—'You are not well . . .'

She had seen this coming, she said. I had been too much from the house, I was not fit for it. It was inviting my old illness back.

'But I am perfectly well,' I said.

Perfectly well? Would I only listen to the sound of my own voice? Would I think of how I had sounded, to the girls? They would be downstairs now, their heads together, whispering—

'I am not ill!' I cried then. 'I am very fit and well, and quite cured of my old nervousness! Everyone has said it. Mrs Wallace has said it.'

Mrs Wallace, she replied, did not see me when I was like this. Mrs Wallace did not see me after my trips to Millbank, pale as a spectre. She did not see me sitting at my desk, wakeful and nervous, until all hours of the night . . .

She said that; and I knew then that, careful as I have been—still and secret and silent as I have been, in my high room—she has been watching me, as Miss Ridley watches, and Miss Haxby. I said that I had always been wakeful, even before Pa died, even as a girl. That the wakefulness meant nothing—and that anyway, the medicine always cured it, and made me rest. She said, seizing on the one narrow point, that as a girl I had been indulged. She had left me too much to the care of my father and he had spoiled me; and it was the recklessness of the spoiling that led to the intemperance of my grief—'I have always said it! And now, to see you picking your own wilful way again towards illness—'

I cried then that, if she did not let me alone, I really should be ill! and I took a few determined steps away from her and stood with my face near to the window. I cannot remember what she said then: I wouldn't listen, or answer—at last she said I must go down and sit with her, and if I had not come to her in twenty minutes she would send Ellis. Then she left.

I stood and gazed from the window. There was a boat upon the river, with a man bringing a hammer down upon a sheet of steel. I watched his arm as it lifted and fell, lifted and fell. I saw sparks leap from the metal, but the blow, each time, took a second to sound—the hammer was always raised again before the thud of the steel could catch it.

I counted thirty blows, then went down to Mother.

She said nothing more to me, but I saw her studying my face and hands for signs of weakness, and I gave her none. Later I read *Little Dorrit* to her, very steadily, and now I have screwed my lamp down very low, and I move my pen across the page so carefully—it is possible to be careful, even with the chloral in me—that she might come and press her ear to the panels of my door, she would not hear me. She might kneel and put her eye to the key-hole. I have stopped it up with cloth.

The orange-blossoms I have before me now. Their scent is so heavy upon the close air of my room, it makes me giddy.

23 November 1874

I went back to-day to the reading-room at the Association of Spiritualists. I went to look again for Selina's story, and to study that troubling portrait of Peter Quick, and to stand before the cabinet of moulds. I found it just, of course, as I left it last time, with the shelves and the wax and plaster limbs with a layer of dust upon them, quite undisturbed.

As I stood gazing at them, Mr Hither came to me. He was shod, this time, in a pair of Turkish sandals, and at his lapel there was a flower. He said that he and Miss Kislingbury had been sure I would return to them—'and here you are, and I am very pleased to see it'. Then he peered at me. 'But what is this? Your look is such a dark one! Our exhibits have made you thoughtful, I can see. That is good. But they shouldn't make you frown, Miss Prior. They should make you smile.'

I did smile then; and then he smiled, and his eyes grew clearer and kinder than ever. No other reader coming to the room, we stood and talked, for almost an hour. I asked him, amongst other things, how long it was that he had called himself a spiritualist?—and why he had become one.

He said, 'It was my brother who first joined the Movement. I thought him a terribly believing sort of chap, to follow such nonsense. He said he could see our mother and father in Heaven, watching all the things we did. I could imagine nothing more terrible!'

I asked, what was it then, that made the change in him? and he hesitated, then answered, that his brother had died. I said at once that I was sorry; but he shook his head, and almost laughed—'No, you must never say that, not *here*. For within a month of his passing, my brother came back to me. He came and embraced me, he was as real to me as you are—fitter than he was in life, and with all the marks of his illness quite gone from him. He came, and told me to believe. Still, however, I refused the truth of it. I explained his visit away as a kind of fancy; and when more signs came, I explained *them* away, too. It is amazing what one *will* explain away, when one is stubborn! At last, however, I saw. Now my brother is my dearest friend.'

I said, 'And you are aware of spirits, all about you?'—Ah, he said then, he is aware of them when they *come* to him. He has not the powers of a great medium. 'I catch glimpses, only—"a little flash, a mystic hint", as Mr Tennyson has it—rather than seeing vistas. I hear notes—a simple tune, if I am fortunate. Others, Miss Prior, hear symphonies.'

I said, To be aware of spirits . . .

'One cannot *but* be aware of them, when one has seen them once! And yet'—he smiled—'to gaze at them, too, may be frightening.' He folded his arms; then gave me this curious example. He said I must imagine that nine-tenths of the people of England had a condition of the eye, a condition which prevented them from appreciating, say, the colour red. He said I must imagine myself afflicted with such a condition. I would drive through London, I would see a blue sky, a yellow flower—I would think the world a very fine place. I would not know I had a condition that quite prevented me from seeing part of it; and when some special people told me that I had—told me of another, marvellous colour—I would think that they were fools. My friends, he said, would agree with me. The newspapers would agree with me. Everything I read, indeed, would confirm me in my belief that those people were fools; *Punch* would even print cartoons to demonstrate how foolish they were! I would smile at those cartoons, and be very content.

'Then,' he went on, 'a morning comes and you awaken—and your eye has corrected itself. Now you can see pillar-boxes and lips, poppies and cherries and guardsmen's jackets. You can see all the glorious shades of red—crimson, scarlet, ruby, vermilion, carnation, rose . . . You will want to hide your eyes, at first, in wonder and fear. Then you will look, and you will tell your friends, your family—and they will laugh at you, they will frown at you, they will send you to a surgeon or a doctor of the brain. It will be very hard, to become aware of all those marvellous scarlet things. And yet—tell me, Miss Prior—having seen them once, could you bear ever to look again, and see only blue, and yellow, and green?'

I did not answer him for a moment, for his words made me terribly thoughtful. When I did speak at last, what I said was, 'Suppose a person were to be what you have described'—I was thinking, of course, of Selina. I said, 'Suppose she sees the scarlet. What ought she to do?'

'She must seek others out,' he answered at once, 'who are like her! They will guide her, and keep her from the dangers of herself . . .'

The emergence of spirit-mediumship, he said, is a very grave thing, still imperfectly understood. The person I was thinking of would know herself prey to all manner of changes of the body and the mind. She was being led to the threshold of another world and invited to look across it; but while there would be 'wise guides' there, ready to counsel her, there would also be 'base, obsessing spirits'. Such spirits might appear to her charming and good—but they would seek only to use her, for their own gain. They would want her to lead them to the earthly treasures they had lost, and pined for . . .

I asked, How could she guard herself, from spirits like

that?—He said she must take care, in the choosing of her earth-friends. He said, 'How many young women have there been, driven to despair—driven to madness!—by the improper application of their powers? They might be invited to call on the spirits for sport—they must not do that. They might be persuaded to sit too frequently, in carelessly got-together circles—that will tire and corrupt them. They might be encouraged to sit alone—that is the very worst way, Miss Prior, that they could apply their powers. I knew a man once—a young man, quite a gentleman, I knew him because I was taken to him by a hospital chaplain, a friend of mine. The gentleman was admitted to the chaplain's ward after being found almost dead from a badly cut throat; and he made my friend a curious confession. He was a passive writer—do you know the term? He had been encouraged by a thoughtless friend to sit with pen and paper, and after a time there had come spirit-messages to him, through the independent motion of his arm . . .'

That, said Mr Hither, is a fine spiritualist trick; he said I would find many mediums doing that, to a sensible degree. The young man he spoke of now, however, was not sensible. He began to sit at night, alone—after that, he found that the messages came faster than ever. He began to be roused from sleep. His hand would wake him, twitching upon the coverlet. It would twitch until he put a pen in it and permitted it to write—then he would write upon paper, upon the walls of his room, upon his own bare flesh! He would write until his fingers blistered. The messages he believed at first to come from his own dead relatives—'But you can be sure, no good soul would torment a medium like that. The writings were the work of a single base spirit.'

This spirit finally revealed itself to the gentleman in the most horrible way. It appeared to him, Mr Hither said, in the shape of a toad, 'and it entered his own body, here'—he touched his shoulder, lightly—'at the joint of the neck. Now that low spirit was inside him, and had him in his power. It proceeded to prompt him, Miss Prior, to commit a host of filthy deeds; and the man could do nothing . . .'

This, he said, was a torture. At last the spirit had whispered to the man that he should take a razor, and cut off one of his own fingers with it. And the man did take the razor; but instead of his hand, he put it to his throat—'He was trying, you see, to get the spirit out, and it was that, that had led to him being admitted to the hospital. They saved his life there; but the obsessing spirit had him in his power still. His old base habits returned, and he was declared deranged. They have him now, I think, on the ward of an asylum. Poor man! How differently his story would have turned out—do you see?—if he had only sought out those of his own kind, who could have counselled him wisely . . .'

I remember him lowering his tone as he spoke these last few words, and seeming to gaze at me very meaningfully—I thought then that he might have guessed I had Selina Dawes in mind, since I had shown such interest in her last time. We stood a moment in silence. He seemed to hope that I would speak. But I could not, there was not time—for we were disturbed now by Miss Kislingbury, who pushed at the reading-room door and called Mr Hither to her. He said, 'Just a moment, Miss Kislingbury!', and he put his hand upon my arm, murmuring, 'I wish we might talk further. Should you like that? You must be sure to come another time—will you? And find me out, when I have less to occupy me here?'

I, too, was sorry that he must leave me. After all, I should like to know more of what he thinks about Selina. I should like to know how it must have been for her, to have been obliged to see those scarlet things he spoke of. I know she was afraid—but she was fortunate, she told me once: she did have wise friends, to guide her, to take her gifts and shape them and make them *rare*.

So I think she believes. But who did she have, really? She had her aunt—who made a turn of her. She had Mrs Brink, of Sydenham—who brought strangers to her, and had a curtain hung, that she might sit behind it and be tied with a velvet collar and a rope; who kept her safe, for her own mother's sake—and for Peter Quick to find her.

What did *he* do to her, or prompt her to do, that led her to Millbank?

And who has she now to guard her there? She has Miss Haxby, Miss Ridley, Miss Craven. In all the gaol, there is no-one to be kind to her, no-one at all, save mild Mrs Jelf.

I heard Mr Hither's voice, and Miss Kislingbury's, and another visitor's; but the reading-room door stayed shut, no-one came. I was still standing before the cabinet of spirit-moulds; now I stooped to study them again. The hand of Peter Quick's sat in its old place upon the lowest shelf, its blunt fingers and its swollen thumb close to the glass. It seemed solid to me, last time I looked at it; to-day, however, I did what I had not done then, and moved to the side of the cabinet to study it from there. I saw then how the wax ended, neatly, at the bone of the wrist. I saw how absolutely hollow it was. Inside it, marked out very clearly upon the yellowing surface of the wax, are the creases and whorls of a palm, the dents of knuckles.

I have been used to thinking of it as a hand, and very solid; more properly, however, it is a kind of *glove*. It might have been cast there a moment before, and still be cooling from the closeness of the fingers that had dropped it.—The idea made me nervous, suddenly, of the empty room. I left it, and came home.

Now Stephen is here, I can hear him talking to Mother, his voice is raised and rather peevish. He has a case that was due to come before the courts to-morrow, but the client has fled to France, and now the police cannot pursue him. Stephen must give the matter up, and lose his fee.—There comes his voice again, louder than before.

Why do gentlemen's voices carry so clearly, when women's are so easily stifled?

24 November 1874

To Millbank, to Selina. I went to her—I went to one or two other women first, and made a show of putting down the details of their talk inside my book—but I went to her at last, and when I did she asked me at once, How had I liked my flowers? She said she had sent them to remind me of Italy, to make me think of the warm days there. She said, 'The spirits carried them. You may keep them for a month, they won't wither.'

I said they frightened me.

I stayed with her for half an hour. At the end of that time there came the slamming of the ward gate and the sound of footsteps—Selina said quietly then: 'Miss Ridley,' and I moved to the bars, and when the matron passed the cell I signalled to her that she might release me. I stood very stiffly, saying only, 'Good-bye, Dawes.' Selina had placed her hands before her, and her face was meek; now she curtseyed to me and answered: 'Good-bye, Miss Prior.' I know she did it for the matron's sake.

I stood and watched Miss Ridley then, as she drew closed the gate to Selina's cell. I watched the turning of the key in the stiff prison lock. I wished the key were mine.

2 April 1873

Peter says I must be fastened in my cabinet. He came to the circle tonight & put his hand upon me very hard, & when he went beyond the curtain he said 'I cannot come among you until I have fulfilled a task I have been given. You know I am sent to you to show the truths of Spiritualism. Well, there are disbelievers in this city, people that doubt the existence of spirits. They mock the powers of our media, they think our media leave their places & walk about the circles in disguise. We cannot appear where there are doubts & unbeliefs like that.' I heard Mrs Brink say then 'There are no doubters here Peter, you may come among us as you always have', & he answered 'No, there is something that must be done. Look here, & you will see my medium, & you will tell & write of this & then perhaps the unbelieving will believe.' Then he caught hold of the curtain & drew it slowly back –

He had never done such a thing before. I sat in my dark trance, but felt the circle gazing at me. A lady asked 'Do you see her?' & another answered 'I see the shape of her in her chair.' Peter said 'It hurts my medium to have you look at her while I am here. The doubting makes me do this, but there is another thing that I can do, it will make a test. You must open the drawer in the table & bring me what you find there.' I heard the drawer open & then a voice say 'There are ropes here' & Peter said 'Yes, bring them to me.' Then he bound me to my seat saying 'You must do this now at each dark circle. If you do not do this I will not come'. He tied me at the wrists & at the ankles & he put a band across my eyes. Then he went into the room again & I heard a chair scrape & he said 'Come with me.' He brought a lady to me, it was a lady named Miss d'Esterre. He said 'Do you see Miss d'Esterre, how my medium is fastened? Put your hand upon her & tell me if those bonds are tight. Take off your glove.' I heard her glove drawn off & then her fingers came upon me, with Peter's fingers pressing them & making them hot. She said 'She is trembling!' & Peter said 'It is for her sake I do this.' Then he sent Miss d'Esterre back to her seat & he leaned to me, whispering 'It is for you I do this' & I answered 'Yes, Peter.' He said 'I am all your power' & I said I knew it.

Then he put a band of silk across my mouth & then drew the curtain closed & went among them. I heard a gentleman say then 'I don't know Peter, I can't be quite easy about this. Won't it harm Miss Dawes's powers for her to be fastened like that?' Peter laughed. He said 'Well, she would be a very poor medium if all it took to weaken her were 3 or 4 silk cords!' He said that the cords held my mortal parts but as for my spirit, that could never be bound or locked. He said 'Don't you know that it is the same for locksmiths with spirits as with love? Spirits laugh at them.'

When they came & unfastened me however, they found that the ropes had chafed my wrists & ankles & made them bleed. Ruth saw that & said 'O, what a brute that spirit is, to do this to my poor mistress.' She said 'Miss d'Esterre, will you help me take Miss Dawes to her own room?' Then they led me here & Ruth put ointment upon me, Miss d'Esterre holding the jar. Miss d'Esterre said she was never so surprised as when Peter came to take her to the cabinet. Ruth said he must have seen a little sign about her, something to lead him straight to her, some sort of specialness that none of the other ladies have. Miss d'Esterre looked at her, & then at me. She said 'Do you think so?' She said 'I do feel, sometimes,' then she looked at the floor.

I saw Ruth's eyes, looking at her, & then Peter Quick's voice might have come whispering the words in my own head. I said 'Ruth is right, Peter certainly seems to have picked you out for something. Perhaps you ought to come & see him a second time, more quietly. Should you like that? Shall you come another day? & then, shall I see if I can't call him back, for just the 2 of us?' Miss d'Esterre said nothing, only sat looking at the pot of ointment. Ruth waited, then said 'Well, think of him to-night, when you are alone & your room is quiet. He did like you.

It may be, you know, that he shall try & visit you without his medium to help him. But I think you had better meet him here, with Miss Dawes, than on your own in your dark bedroom.' Miss d'Esterre said then 'I shall sleep in my sister's bed.' Ruth said 'Well, but he shall still find you there.' Then she took the ointment & put its lid on it, saying to me 'There miss, you are made all better now.' Miss d'Esterre went back downstairs, saying nothing.

I thought of her then, when I went in to Mrs Brink.

28 November 1874

To Millbank to-day—a horrible visit, I am ashamed to write of it.

I was met at the gate of the women's gaol by the coarse-faced matron Miss Craven: they had sent her to me as a chaperon in place of Miss Ridley, who had business elsewhere. I was glad to see her. I thought: That is good. I shall have her take me to Selina's cell, and Miss Ridley and Miss Haxby need never know of it . . .

Even so, we did not go immediately to the wards, for as we walked she asked me, Was there not another part of the gaol I should like to be shown first? 'Or are you keen,' she said dubiously, 'to go only to the cells?' Probably it was a novelty to her to lead me about, and she hoped to make the most of it. But as she spoke, she seemed to me a little knowing—and then I thought that, after all, she might have been charged with the watching of me and I ought to take care. So I said that she should lead me where she pleased; that I imagined that the women on the wards would not mind waiting for me, a little longer. She answered, 'I am sure they won't, miss.'

Where she took me, then, was to the bathroom, and the prison clothes stores.

There is not much to say about them. The bathroom is a chamber with one large trough in it, in which the women are obliged, on their arrival, to sit and soap themselves, communally; to-day, there being no new prisoners, the bath was empty save for half a dozen blackjack beetles, that were nosing at the lines of grime. In the clothes store there are shelves of brown prison gowns and white bonnets, in every size, and boxes of boots. The boots are kept tied at the laces, in pairs.

Miss Craven held up a pair she thought would fit me—monstrous great things they were, of course, and I thought she smiled as she held them. She said that prison shoes were the stoutest of all, stouter even than soldiers' boots. She said that she heard of a Millbank woman once who beat her matron and stole her cloak and keys, then made her way quite to the gate, and would have escaped, except that a warder who looked at her there saw the shoes on her, and knew her by them for a convict—then the woman was taken again, and put in the darks.

She told me this, then cast the boots she held back into their box, and laughed. Then she led me to another storeroom, that they call there the 'Own-Clothes Room'. This is the place—I hadn't thought before, that there must of course be such a place there—where are kept all the dresses and hats and shoes, and bits of stuff, which the women carry with them into Millbank when they arrive.

There is something wonderful and terrible about this room and all that it contains. Its walls are arranged—after the Millbank passion for queer geometry—in the shape of a hexagon; and they are lined entirely, from floor to ceiling, with shelves, that are filled with boxes. The boxes are made of a buff kind of card, studded with brass and with brass corners: they are long and narrow, and bear plates with the prisoners' names upon them. They resemble nothing so much as little coffins; and so the room itself, when I first stepped into it, made me shudder—it looked like a children's mausoleum, or a morgue.

Miss Craven saw me flinch, and put her hands upon her hips. 'Rum, ain't it?' she said as she looked about her. She said, 'Do you know what I think, miss, when I come in here? I think: *buzz, buzz*. I think, Now I know just how a bee or a wasp feels, when it comes back home to its own little nest.'

We stood together, gazing at the walls. I asked her, Was there really a box there for every woman in the gaol? and she nodded: 'Every one, and some to spare.' She stepped to the shelves, pulled out a box quite randomly, and set it down before her—there was a desk there, with a chair at it. When she drew off the lid of the box there rose a vaguely sulphurous scent. She said they must bake all the clothes they store, for most come in verminous, but that 'some frocks, of course, can bear that better than others'.

She lifted out the garment that lay within the box she held. It was a thin print gown, that had clearly not been much improved by its fumigation, for its collar hung in tatters and its cuffs seemed singed. Beneath it there was a set of yellowing undergarments, a pair of scuffed red leather shoes, a hat, with a pin of flaking pearl, and a wedding ring, grown black. I looked at the plate on the box—*Mary Breen*, it said. She is the woman I visited once, who had the marks of her own teeth upon her arm, that she said were rats' bites.

When Miss Craven had closed this box and returned it to its place upon the shelf I moved closer to the wall, and began to look, quite carelessly, across the names; and she continued to finger the boxes, lifting the lids of them and gazing inside. 'You would think it wonderful,' she said, peering into one, 'what few sad little bits some women come to us with.'

I stepped to her side and looked at what she showed me: a rusty black dress, a pair of canvas slippers, and a key on a length of twine—I wondered what the key unfastened. She closed the box and gave a low *tut-tut*: 'Not so much as a hankie for her head.' Then she worked her way along the row, and I moved with her, peeping in at all the boxes. One held a very handsome dress, and a velvet hat with a stiff, stuffed bird upon it, complete with beak and glittering eye; yet the set of underthings beneath were so blackened and torn they might have been trampled by horses. Another contained a petticoat splattered with grim brown stains that I saw, with a shudder, must be blood; another made me start—it held a frock and petticoats and shoes and stockings, but also a length of reddish-brown hair, bound like the tail of a pony or like a queer little whip. It was the hair that had been cut from its owner's head when she first came to the prison. 'She will be keeping it for a hair-piece,' said Miss Craven, 'for when she is let out. Much good, however, it will do *her*! It is Chaplin—do you know her? A poisoner, she was, and went almost to the rope. Why, her fine red head will have turned quite grey, before she gets *this* back again!'

She closed the box and thrust it back, with a practised, peevish gesture; her own hair, where it showed beneath her bonnet, was plain as mouse-fur. I remembered then how I had seen the reception matron rubbing at the shorn locks of Black-Eyed Sue the gipsy girl—and I had a sudden, unpleasant vision, of her and Miss Craven whispering together over the severed tresses, or over a frock, or the hat with the bird upon it: '*Try it on—why, who is to see you? How your young man would admire you in that! And who will know who wore it last, four years from now?*'

The vision and the whispers were so vivid I found I had to turn and press my fingers to my face to chase them away, and when I next looked at Miss Craven she had moved on to another box, and was giving a snort of laughter at what she saw within it. I watched her. It seemed all at once a shameful thing to do, to look upon the sad and slumbering remnants of the women's ordinary lives. It was as if the boxes were coffins after all, and we were peeping, the matron and I, at their little occupants, while their mothers mourned, all unawares, above us. But what made it shameful also made it fascinating; and when Miss Craven moved on idly to another shelf, for all my squeamishness I couldn't help but follow. Here there was the box of Agnes Nash, the coiner; and that of poor Ellen Power, with a portrait in it of a little girl—her grand-daughter, I suppose. Perhaps she had thought they would let her keep the picture in her cell.

And then, how could I help but think of it? I began to look about me, for *Selina's* box. I began to wonder how it would be, to gaze at what it held. I thought, If I could only do that I should see something—I didn't know what—something of hers, something of her—some thing, anything, that would explain her to me, bring her nearer . . . Miss Craven went on plucking at the boxes, exclaiming over the sad or handsome costumes they contained, sometimes laughing at an antique fashion. I stood near her, but did not look to where she gestured. Instead I raised my eyes and gazed about me, searching. At last I said, 'What is the sequence here, matron? How are the boxes placed?'

Even while she explained and pointed, however, I found the plate I sought. It was above her reach; there was a ladder against the shelves, but she had not climbed it. Already, indeed, she had begun to wipe at her fingers, in readiness to escort me back to the wards. Now she rested her hands at her hips and lifted her eyes, and I caught her murmuring idly, beneath her breath: '*Buzz buzz, buzz buzz . . .*'

I must get rid of her; and could think of only one way to do it. I said, 'Oh!'—I put my hand to my head. I said, Oh, I believed that all the gazing had made me faint!—and of course I did feel dizzy now—with apprehension—and I must have paled, for Miss Craven saw my face and gave a cry, and took a step towards me. I kept my hand at my brow. I said I would not swoon, but, could she—might she just—a cup of water—?

She led me to the chair and made me sit. She said, 'Now, dare I leave you? There are salts in the surgeon's office, I think; but the surgeon is at the infirmary, it will take me a minute or two to fetch the keys—Miss Ridley has them. If you was to fall—'

I said I would not fall. She put her hands together—oh, here was a piece of drama she had not bargained for! Then she hurried from me. I heard the ring of her chain, and her footsteps, and the banging of a gate.

And then I rose, and seized the ladder, and brought it to where I knew I must climb; and then I lifted my skirts and climbed it, then pulled Selina's box to me and knocked back its lid.

There came, at once, the bitter smell of sulphur, that made me turn my head aside and narrow my eyes. Then I found that, with the light behind me, I was casting my own shadow into the box—I could make out nothing of what lay inside it, but must lean awkwardly from the ladder, placing my cheek against the hard edge of a shelf. Then I began to distinguish the garments that lay there—the coat, and the hat, and the dress, of black velvet; and the shoes, and the petticoats, and the white silk stockings . . .

I touched and lifted and turned them all—looking, still looking, though I did not know for what. But, after all, they might have been any girl's clothes. The gown and coat seemed new, almost unworn. The shoes were stiff and polished, with unmarked soles. Even the plain jet earrings I found, knotted into a corner of a handkerchief, were neat, their wires untarnished—the handkerchief itself was very crisp, with a black silk edging, quite uncreased. There was nothing there, nothing. She might have been dressed, by a shop clerk, in a house of mourning. I could find no trace of the life I think she must have led—no hint, from any of those garments, of how her slender limbs had held them. There was nothing.

Or so I thought—until I turned the velvet and the silk a final time, and saw what else lay in that box, coiled in its shadows like a slumbering serpent—

Her hair. Her hair, bound tight and plaited into one thick rope, and fastened, where it had been cut from her, with coarse prison twine. I put my fingers to it. It felt heavy, and dry—as snakes are, I believe, for all their glossiness, said to feel dry to the touch. Where the light caught it it gleamed a dull gold; but the gold was shot through with other colours—with some that were silver, some that were almost green.

I remembered studying Selina's picture, and seeing the fancy twists and coils of her hair then. It had made her vivid to me; it had made her real. The coffinlike box, the airless room—it seemed suddenly a dark and terrible place for her hair to be confined in now. I thought, *If it might only have a little light upon it, a little air* . . . And I had again that vision of the whispering matrons. Suppose they should come and laugh over her tresses, or stroke and finger them with their own blunt hands?

It seemed to me then that, if I did not take it, they would certainly come and spoil it. I grasped it, and folded it—I meant, I think, to thrust it in the pocket of my coat or behind the buttons at my breast. But as I held it, fumbling, still reaching awkwardly from the ladder, still feeling my cheek ground hard against the shelf—as I did that, I heard the door at the end of the passage-way slam, and then the sound of voices. It was Miss Craven, and with her, Miss Ridley! The fright of it made me almost fall. The plait of hair might really have been a snake, then: I flung it from me as if it had suddenly woken and shown me its fangs, then I pulled at the lid of the box, and stepped heavily to the floor—the voices of the matrons coming closer, closer, all the time I worked.

They found me with my hand upon the chair-back, trembling with fear and shame, the mark of the shelf I suppose at my cheek, my coat dusty. Miss Craven came close to me with the bottle of salts, but Miss Ridley's eyes were narrow. Once I thought I saw her gazing at the ladder, and at the shelf, and at the boxes upon it—which, in my haste and nervousness, I may have left disordered, I cannot say. I did not turn to see. I looked only, once, at her; then turned away and shuddered harder. For it was those bare eyes, that gaze, which made me as ill at last as Miss Craven, with her salts, could have supposed me. For I knew at once what Miss Ridley would have seen, had she come sooner. I saw it all—I see it now, still, with a crisp and dreadful certainty.

It was myself, a spinster, pale and plain and sweating and wild, and groping from a swaying prison ladder after the severed yellow tresses of a handsome girl . . .

I let Miss Craven stand and hold a glass of water to my mouth. I knew that Selina sat, sad and expectant, in her cold cell; but I couldn't bring myself to go to her—I should have hated myself, if I had gone to her now. I said I would not visit the wards to-day. Miss Ridley agreed that that was wise. She led me to the Porter's lodge herself.

This evening as I read to Mother she said, What was that mark upon my face? and I looked in the glass to find a bruise there—the shelf had bruised me. After that my voice was unsteady, and I put the book aside. I said I should like to bathe, and had Vigers fill me a bath before my fire, and I bent my legs and lay in it, and studied my own flesh, then put my face beneath the cooling water. When I opened my eyes

Vigers was there with the towel, and her gaze seemed dark, her face pale as my own. She said, as Mother had, 'You have hurt your cheek, miss.' She said she would put vinegar on it. I sat and let her hold the cloth to my face, meek as a child.

Then she said, What a shame it was that I had been from home to-day, since Mrs Prior—that is, Mrs Helen Prior, that was married to my brother—had come to the house, bringing her baby with her, and was sorry to have missed me. She said, 'What a pretty lady she is, isn't she, miss?'

I heard that, and thrust her from me, saying the vinegar made me sick. I said she must take away my bath, then tell my mother to bring my medicine: I wanted my medicine at once. When Mother came she said, 'What is the matter with you?' and I said, 'Nothing, Mother.' But my hand trembled so much she wouldn't let me take the glass, but held it for me—just as Miss Craven had.

She said, Had I seen some hard thing at the prison, that had upset me? She said I mustn't make the visits, if they left me like this.

After she went I paced my room, twisting my hands, thinking, *You fool, you fool* . . . Then I took up this diary, and began to turn the pages of it. I remembered that comment of Arthur's, that women's books could only ever be *journals of the heart*. I think I thought that, in making my trips to Millbank, in writing of them here, I would somehow disprove or spite him. I thought that I could make my life into a book that had no life or love in it—a book that was only a catalogue, a kind of list. Now I can see that my heart has crept across these pages, after all. I can see the crooked passage of it, it grows firmer as the paper turns. It grows so firm at last, it spells a name—

Selina.

I almost burned this book to-night, as I burned the last one. I could not do it. But when I looked up from it I saw the vase upon my desk, that held the orange-blossoms: they have kept white and fragrant all this time, just as she promised. I went to them and pulled them dripping from the vase; and it was them I burned, I held them hissing on the coals, watching them twist and blacken. One bloom only I kept. I have pressed it here, and now shall keep these pages shut. For if I turn them again, then the scent of it will come, to warn me. It will come quick and sharp and dangerous, like the blade of a knife.

2 December 1874

I hardly know how to write of what has happened. I hardly know how to sit or stand or walk or speak, or do any ordinary thing. I have been out of my head for a day and a half, they have brought the doctor to me, and Helen has come to me—even Stephen has come, he stood at the foot of the bed and gazed at me in my night-dress, I heard him whispering when they thought I was asleep. And all the time I knew I should be well, if they would only leave me to myself and let me think, and write. Now they have set Vigers in a chair outside the door, and left the door ajar in case I should cry out; but I have come quietly to my desk, and have my book before me, at last. It is the only place I can be honest in—and I can hardly see, to fix the words upon the line.

They have put Selina in the darks!—and I am the cause of it. And I should go to her, but am afraid.

I made a bitter kind of resolution to keep from her, after my last visit to the gaol. I knew my trips to her had made me strange, not like myself—or worse, that they had made me *too much like* myself, like my old self, my naked *Aurora* self. Now, when I tried to be *Margaret* again, I couldn't. It seemed to me that she had dwindled, like a suit of clothes. I couldn't say what she had done, how she had moved and spoken. I sat with Mother—it might have been a doll that sat there, a paper-doll, nodding its head. And when Helen came, I found I could not look at her. When she kissed me I would shudder, feeling the dryness of my cheek against her lips.

So my days passed, since my last trip to Millbank. And then yesterday I went, alone, to the National Gallery, hoping the pictures would distract me. It was the students' day, and there was a girl there, she had set her easel before Crivelli's *Annunciation*, and she was marking on her canvas, with a stick of lead, the face and hands of the Virgin—the face was Selina's, and seemed realer to me than my own. And then I didn't know why I had kept away from her. It was half-past five, and Mother had invited guests, for dinner.—I didn't think of any of this. I only went at once to Millbank and had a matron take me to the cells. I found the women finishing their suppers, wiping their trenchers with crusts of bread; and when I arrived at the gate of Selina's ward, I caught the voice of Mrs Jelf. She was standing at the angle of the passages, calling out an evening prayer, and the acoustics of the wards made her voice tremble.

When she came and found me waiting for her she gave a start. She took me to two or three of the women—the last of these was Ellen Power, and she was so changed and so ill and so grateful to have me go to her that I couldn't hurry my visit, but sat with her and held her hand, passing my fingers over her swollen knuckles, to calm her. She cannot speak, now, without coughing. The surgeon has given her medicine to take, but they cannot put her in the infirmary, she said, because the beds are filled with younger women. Beside her was a tray of wool and a pair of half-finished stockings—they still make her sit and sew, ill as she is, and she said she prefers to work than to lie idle. I said, 'It cannot be right. I shall speak to Miss Haxby.' But she said at once that it would do no good; and that anyway she would rather I did not.

'My time is up in seven weeks,' she said. 'If they should find me out as a trouble-maker they might put back the date.' I said it would be I that was making the trouble, not her—and even as I said it, I felt the pricking of a shameful fear, that if I *did* interfere in her case, then Miss Haxby might use it in some sly way against me—perhaps, to have my visits stopped . . .

Then Power said, 'You mustn't think of doing it, miss, indeed you mustn't.' She said that she saw twenty women, at exercise, as poorly as herself; and if they changed the rules for her, they must be changed for all of them. 'And why would they do that?' She patted her chest. 'I have my bit of flannel,' she said, with an attempt at a wink. 'I still have that, thank God!'

I asked Mrs Jelf, when she released me, was it true that they would not give Power a bed in the infirmary? She said that when she had attempted to speak to the surgeon on Power's behalf he had answered her frankly, that he thought he knew his own business better. She said he calls Power '*the bawd*'.

'Miss Ridley,' she went on, 'might have some weight with him; but Miss Ridley has strong opinions on the matter of punishments. And it is to her that I must answer, not—' here she looked away '—not to Ellen Power, nor to any of the women.'

I thought then, *You are as snared by Millbank as they are.*

Then she took me to Selina; and I forgot Ellen Power. I stood at her gate and shook—Mrs Jelf watching me, saying, 'You are cold, miss!' I had not known it, until that moment. I might have been, until then, quite frozen, quite numb; but Selina's gaze sent the life trickling back into me, and it was marvellous, but achingly painful and hard. I understood then that I had been a fool to keep away from her—that my feelings had grown, in my absence, not dulled and ordinary, but more desperate and more quick. She looked fearfully at me. 'I am sorry,' she said. I asked her, What was she sorry for? She answered, Perhaps, the flowers? She had meant them as a gift. Then, when I kept away, she remembered how I had said, last time, that they had frightened me. She had thought perhaps I meant to *punish* her.

I said, 'Oh, Selina, how could you think that? I have only kept away because, because I feared—'

Feared my own passion, I might have said. But I didn't say it. For I was visited again by that gross vision, of the spinster, grasping after the switch of hair . . .

I only took her hand in mine, once, very briefly; and then I let the fingers fall. 'Feared nothing,' I said, and turned from her. I said that I had many things to do at home, now that Priscilla was married.

We talked on like this—she watchful, still half-fearful; me distracted, afraid to go too close to her, afraid even to look too hard at her. And then there were footsteps, and Mrs Jelf appeared at the gate, with another matron beside her. I didn't know this matron until I saw her leather satchel, and then I recognised her as Miss Brewer, the chaplain's clerk, who brings the women their letters. She smiled at me, and at Selina, and there was a kind of knowledge behind the smile. She was like a person with a gift, keeping the gift half-hidden. I thought—I knew it at once! and I think Selina knew it too—I thought: She has something with her that will disturb us. She has *trouble*.

Now I hear Vigers, shifting in her seat beyond the door and sighing. I must write quietly, quietly, or she may come and take the book from me, to make me sleep. How can I sleep, knowing what I know? Miss Brewer came into the cell. Mrs Jelf drew closed the gate but did not lock it, and I heard her walk a little way along the ward, then halt—perhaps, to look in upon another prisoner. Miss Brewer said that she was glad to find me there; that she had news for Dawes, that she knew I should be pleased to hear. Selina's hand moved to her throat. She said, What news was that? and Miss Brewer coloured, with the pleasure of her task. 'You are to be moved!' she said to her. 'You are to be moved, in three days' time, to the prison at Fulham.'

Moved? said Selina. Moved, to Fulham? Miss Brewer nodded. She said the order had been brought, that all the Star-class prisoners were to be transferred. Miss Haxby had wanted the women told of it at once.

'Only think of it,' she said to me. 'The habits at Fulham are kind ones: the women work together there, and even talk together. The food, I think, is a little richer. Why, they have chocolate at Fulham, instead of tea! What will you make of that, Dawes?'

Selina said nothing. She had grown very stiff, and her hand was still at her throat; only her eyes seemed to move a little, like the tilting eyes of a doll. My own heart had given a terrible kind of twist at Miss Brewer's words, but I knew I must speak and not betray myself. I said, 'To Fulham, Selina'—thinking, How, oh how, shall I visit you there?

My tone, my face, must have betrayed me anyway. The matron looked puzzled.

Now Selina spoke. She said: 'I won't go. I won't go from Millbank.' Miss Brewer glanced at me. Not go? she said. What did Dawes mean? She hadn't understood. It wasn't a punishment, what they meant to do for her.—'I don't want to go,' said Selina.

'But you must go!'—'You must go,' I echoed bleakly, 'if they say you must.'—'*No.*' Her eyes still moved, but she had not looked at me. She said now, Why should they send her there? Hadn't she been good and done her work? Hadn't she done all the things they wanted, and not complained? Her voice sounded odd, not like itself.

'Haven't I said all my prayers, at chapel? And learned my lessons, for the school-mistresses? And taken my soup? And kept my cell neat?'

Miss Brewer smiled, and shook her head. She said, it was because Dawes had been good that they were moving her. Didn't Dawes want that—to be rewarded? Her voice grew gentle. She said that Dawes was only startled. She said she knew that it was hard for the women at Millbank to understand that there were other, kinder places in the world.

She took a step towards the gate. 'I shall leave you with Miss Prior now,' she said, 'and let her help you grow used to the idea.' She said that Miss Haxby would come later, to tell Selina more.

Perhaps she waited for a reply and, hearing none, looked puzzled again. I am not sure. I know she turned to the gate—perhaps she put her hand to it, I cannot say. I saw Selina move—she moved so sharply, I thought she had swooned, and I took a step to catch her. But she had not swooned. She had darted for the shelf behind the table, she had reached for something that lay upon it. There was a clatter, as her tin mug and her spoon and book went tumbling—at that, of course, Miss Brewer heard, and turned. Then her face gave a twist. Selina had lifted her arm, and now swung it; and what she held in her hand was her wooden trencher. Miss Brewer raised her own arm, but not quickly enough. The trencher struck her—edge-on, I think, upon the eyes, for she put her fingers to them, and then her arms, to protect her face from further blows.

Then she fell, and lay dazed and sprawled and wretched, her skirts kicked high and showing her coarse wool stockings, her garters, the pink flesh of her thighs.

It happened more swiftly than it has taken me to write it; and it happened more quietly than I could have thought possible, the only sounds after the clatter of the mug and spoon being the terrible crack of the trencher and then, Miss Brewer's breath coming in a rush out of her bosom, the scraping of the buckle of her bag against the wall. I had placed my hands upon my face. I think I said, 'My God'—I felt the words upon my fingers—and I made to move, at last, to Miss Brewer's side. Then I saw the trencher still gripped tight in Selina's hand. I saw her face, that was white and sweating and strange.

And I thought—for a moment I thought—I remembered the girl, Miss Silvester, who was hurt—I thought: You *did* strike her! And I am shut in a cell with you! And I stepped back, in horror, and placed my hands upon the chair.

And then she dropped the trencher and sagged against the folded hammock, and I saw that she was trembling worse than I.

Miss Brewer began to murmur and to clutch about her at the wall and table, and then I did go to her, and kneel and place my shaking hands upon her head. I said, 'Lie still. Lie still, Miss Brewer'—she had begun to weep. And then I called into the passage-way: 'Mrs Jelf! Oh, Mrs Jelf, you must come quickly!'

She came at once, came running up the ward, then grasped the bars of the gate to steady herself. And when she saw, she gave a cry. I said, 'Miss Brewer is hurt'—then, in a lower voice: 'She has been struck, in the face.' Mrs Jelf grew white, looked wildly at Selina, then stood for a moment with her hand upon her heart; then she pushed at the gate. It caught on Miss Brewer's skirts and legs: we spent a miserable moment, pulling at her gown, turning her limbs—Selina still and mute and trembling all the while, and watching us. Miss Brewer's eyes had begun to swell and close, and there were bruises already starting out against the pallor of her cheek and brow; her gown and bonnet were thick with lime, from the cell wall. Mrs Jelf said, 'You must help me bring her to my room, Miss Prior, between the wards. Then one of us must go for the surgeon, and—and for Miss Ridley.' Here she held my gaze for a second, then looked again towards Selina. She had now drawn her knees against her chest, and placed her arms about them, and lowered her head. The crooked star upon her sleeve showed very bright in the shadows. It seemed terrible, suddenly, to hasten from her, shuddering—to leave her trembling, with no word of comfort, knowing whose hands would be upon her next. I said, 'Selina'—not caring if the matron heard me—and she moved her head. Her gaze was bleak, and seemed unfocused: I couldn't tell if it was turned on me, on Mrs Jelf, or on the bruised and weeping girl who sagged between us—I think, upon myself. But she said nothing, and at last the matron drew me from her. She fastened the gate, then hesitated, then reached for the second, wooden door and bolted it closed.

We made the journey to the matron's chamber, then—what a journey it was! For the women had heard my shout, the matron's cry, Miss Brewer's weeping, and they were at their gates, their faces pressed to the bars, their eyes upon us as we made our graceless, halting passage. One called, oh, who had hurt Miss Brewer? and was answered: 'Dawes! Selina Dawes has busted up her cell! Selina Dawes has cracked Miss Brewer in the face!' *Selina Dawes!* The name was passed from woman to woman, cell to cell, as if upon a ripple of filthy water. Mrs Jelf cried out that they must be quiet; but her cry was querulous and the shouts went on. And at length one voice broke free of all the others—not to tell or wonder, this time, but to laugh: 'Selina Dawes broke out at last! *Selina Dawes, for the jacket and the darks!*'

I said, 'Oh, God! will they never be silent?' I thought they might drive her to madness. But as I thought it there came the slam of a gate, and another cry I couldn't catch; and the voices faded at once—it was Miss Ridley and Mrs Pretty, the shouting had brought them from the ward below. We had reached the matron's chamber. Mrs Jelf unlocked the door, led Miss Brewer to a chair, and dampened a handkerchief for her to place against her eyes. I said quickly, 'Will they really take Selina to the darks?'—'Yes,' she answered, in the same low tone. Then she bent again to Miss Brewer. By the time Miss Ridley had arrived to say, 'Well, Mrs Jelf, Miss Prior, what is this sorry business?', her hand was steady, her face quite smooth.

'Selina Dawes,' she said, 'has struck Miss Brewer with her trencher.'

Miss Ridley drew in her head, then moved to Miss Brewer to ask, How was she hurt? Miss Brewer said, 'I cannot see.'—Mrs Pretty heard that, and came nearer for a better view. Miss Ridley removed the handkerchief. 'Your eyes have swollen shut,' she said. 'I don't think you are hurt worse than that. But Mrs Jelf shall run and fetch the surgeon'—Mrs Jelf went, at once. Miss Ridley replaced the cloth, and kept one hand upon it; the other she placed upon Miss Brewer's neck. She did not look at me, but turned to Mrs Pretty. '*Dawes*,' she said. And, as the matron moved off into the passage, she added: 'Call me, if she kicks.'

I could only stand, then, and listen. I heard Mrs Pretty's rapid, heavy tread upon the sanded flags, then the sliding of the bolt on the wooden door at Selina's cell, the rattle of the key in the gate. I heard a murmur; I may have heard a cry. This was followed by a silence, then by the quick and heavy tread again with, less distinctly, the sound of lighter feet, that stumbled or were dragged. Then came the slam of a further door. After that, there was nothing.

I felt Miss Ridley's eyes upon me. She said, 'You were with the prisoner, when the trouble started?' I nodded. She asked me, what had provoked it?—I said, I was not sure. 'Why,' she asked then, 'did she hurt Miss Brewer, and not you?' I said again, I wasn't sure, did not know why she had hurt anyone.

I said, 'Miss Brewer came with news.'—'And it was the news that set her off?'—'Yes.'

'What news was this, Miss Brewer?'

'She is to be moved,' said Miss Brewer miserably. She put a hand upon the table at her side: there was a deck of playing-cards upon it, set out by Mrs Jelf for a game of Patience, and now the deck grew muddled. 'She is to be moved, to the gaol at Fulham.'

Miss Ridley gave a snort. '*Was* to be moved,' she said, with a bitter satisfaction.

Then her face gave a twitch—as the face of a clock will sometimes twitch, with the tumbling of the cogs and gears behind it—and her eyes came back to mine.

And then I guessed what she guessed, and then I thought: *My God.*

I turned my back to her. She said nothing more, and after another minute Mrs Jelf returned, with the prison surgeon. He saw me and bowed, then took Miss Ridley's place at Miss Brewer's side, tut-tutting at what he saw behind the handkerchief, producing a powder for Mrs Jelf to mix with water in a glass. I knew the smell of it. I stood and watched Miss Brewer sipping at it, and once, when she spilled a little, I felt myself twitch with the impulse to step and catch the fluid she had wasted.

'You will be bruised,' the surgeon told her. But he said the bruises would fade: she was lucky the blow had not caught the nose or the bone of the cheek. When he had bound her eyes, he turned to me. 'You saw it all?' he said. 'The prisoner did not strike at you?' I said I was quite unhurt. He replied that he doubted that: that this was a bad business for a lady to be mixed up in. He advised me to send for my maid and have her drive home with me at once; and when Miss Ridley protested that I had not yet given my account of the incident to Miss Haxby, he answered that he did not think Miss Haxby would mind the delay, 'in Miss Prior's case'. This was the man, I recollect now, who refused poor Ellen Power her bed in the infirmary. I didn't think of that then, however. I was only grateful to him, for to have had to suffer Miss Haxby's questions and surmises at that moment would, I think, have killed me. I walked with him across the ward and we passed Selina's cell, and I slowed my step and shuddered to see the shrieking, small disorder of it—the doors thrown wide, the trencher, mug and spoon upon the floor, the hammock disarranged out of its Millbank folds, the book—*The Prisoner's Companion*—ripped, and lime trodden into its bindings. I looked, and the surgeon's eyes followed mine, and he shook his head.

'A quiet girl, from all I hear,' he said. 'But there, the quietest bitch will turn sometimes, upon its mistress.'

He had told me to send for a servant and take a cab; I did not think that I could bear the closeness of it, imagining Selina in her own closer place. I walked home, quickly, through the darkness, without a thought for my own safety. Only at the end of Tite Street did I slow my step, to turn my face into the breeze, to cool it. Mother might ask, How had my visit gone? and I knew I must be steady with my answer. I couldn't say, 'A girl broke out to-day, Mother, and struck a matron. A girl went wild, and caused a stir.' I couldn't have said such a thing, to her. Not just because she must still think the women meek, and safe, and sorry—not just because of that. But because I couldn't have said it without weeping or shuddering, or crying out the truth—

That Selina Dawes had struck a matron upon the eyes; had made them thrust her, in a jacket, into a darkened cell, because she could not bear to go from Millbank, and from me.

And so I meant to be calm, and say nothing, and come quietly to my room. I meant to say I was unwell, and they must only let me sleep. But when Ellis opened the door to me, I saw her look; and when she moved to let me pass her I saw, in the dining-room, the table, that was filled with flowers and candles and china plates. Then Mother came to the stairs, white-faced with worry and vexation: 'Oh! How dare you be so thoughtless! How can you thwart and unsettle me so!'

It was our first supper-party since Prissy's wedding, and the guests were due, and I had forgotten it. She came to me and lifted her hand—I thought she meant to strike me, and I flinched.

But she did not strike me. She pulled the coat from me, then put her fingers to my collar. 'Take the gown from her here, Ellis!' she cried. 'We cannot have the filth carried upstairs, trodden into the carpets.' I saw then that I was streaked with lime, that must have come upon me as I helped Miss Brewer. I stood, bewildered, while Mother caught at one of my sleeves, and Ellis seized the other. They pulled the bodice from me, and I stumbled out of the skirts; then they took my hat, and my gloves, and then my shoes, which were thick with street-dirt. Then Ellis bore the clothes away, and Mother caught me by my pimpling arm and drew me into the dining-room and closed the door.

I said, as I had planned, that I was not quite well; but when she heard me say it she gave a bitter laugh. 'Not well?' she said. 'No, no, Margaret. You keep that card to play as you choose. You are ill when it suits.'

'I am ill now,' I said, 'and you are making me iller—'

'You are well enough, I think, for the women of Millbank!' I put a hand to my head. She hit it aside. 'You are selfish,' she said, 'and wilful. I won't have it.'

'*Please*,' I said. '*Please*. If I might only go to my own room and lie upon my bed—'

She said I must go to my room and dress—I must dress myself, since the girls were too busy to help me. I said I could not, was too distracted—had had to endure a most miserable scene, on the wards of the prison.

'Your place is here!' she answered, '—not at the prison. And it is time you showed that you know it. Now Priscilla is married, you must take up your proper duties in the house. Your place is here, your place is here. You shall be here, beside your mother, to greet our guests when they arrive . . .'

So she went on. I said she would have Stephen, Helen—that made her voice grow even sharper. *No!* She could not bear it! She could not bear to have our friends believe me weak, or *eccentric*—she almost spat the word at me. 'You are not Mrs Browning, Margaret—as much as you would like to be. You are not, in fact, Mrs Anybody. You are only *Miss Prior*. And your place—how often must I say it?—your place is here, at your mother's side.'

My head, which had begun to ache at Millbank, now felt as though it might split in two. But when I told her that she said only, waving her hand, that I must take a dose of chloral. She had not the time to fetch it for me, I must take it myself.—And she told me where she keeps it. She has it in the drawer inside her bureau.

I came here then. I passed Vigers in the hall, and turned my face from her, to see her gazing in amazement at my bare arms, my petticoats and stockings. I found my gown spread out upon the bed, and the brooch that I must pin to it; and even as I stood fumbling with the fastenings I heard the first of the carriages drawing up outside—it was a cab, with Stephen and Helen in it. I was clumsy, dressing without Ellis: a piece of wire worked loose at the waist of my gown and I could not see how it might be smoothed. I could not see anything, above the beating in my head. I brushed the lime from my hair, and the brush seemed made of needles. I saw my face in the glass, and my eyes were dark as bruises, the bones at my throat standing out like wires. I heard Stephen's voice, two floors below, and when I was sure the drawing-room door was closed, I went down to Mother's room and found the chloral. I took twenty scruples of it—then, when I had sat, waiting for the tug of it and feeling nothing, I took another ten.

Then I felt my blood begin to treacle and the flesh upon my face seem to grow thick, and the pain behind my brow grew less, and I knew the medicine was working. I put the chloral back inside the drawer, very neatly, just as Mother would like. Then I went downstairs to stand beside her and smile at the guests. She looked at me once when I appeared, to see that I was tidy; after that, she didn't look at me again. Helen, however, came to kiss me. 'You have been arguing, I know,' she whispered. I said, 'Oh Helen, how I wish Priscilla had not gone!' Then I began to fear that she would smell the medicine on my mouth. I took a glass of wine from Vigers' tray, to take the scent away.

Vigers looked at me, as I did that, and said quietly, 'The pins of your hair, miss, are working loose.' She held her tray against her hip a moment, and put her hand to my head—and it seemed the kindest gesture, suddenly, that anyone had ever shown me, anyone at all.

Then Ellis struck the dinner-bell. Stephen took Mother, and Helen went with Mr Wallace. I was taken down by Miss Palmer's beau, Mr Dance. Mr Dance has whiskers, and a very broad brow. I said—but I remember the words now as if another woman said them—I said, 'Mr Dance, your face is very curious! My father used to draw faces like yours for me, when I was a girl. When the paper is turned upside-down there is another face there. Stephen, do you remember those drawings?' Mr Dance laughed. Helen gave me a puzzled look. I said, 'You must stand on your head, Mr Dance, and let us see the other face that you have hidden there!'

Mr Dance laughed again. I remember him laughing very hard, indeed, all through the dinner, until at last the laughter made me tired, and I put my fingers to my eyes. Mrs Wallace said then, 'Margaret is weary to-night. Are you weary, Margaret? You have been too attentive to those women of yours.' I opened my eyes, and the lights upon the table seemed very bright. Mr Dance asked, What women were those, Miss Prior? and Mrs Wallace answered for me, that I went visiting at Millbank Prison and had made friends with all the women. Mr Dance wiped his mouth and said, How curious. I felt the wire in my gown again, it pricked me worse than ever. 'From all that Margaret tells us,' I heard Mrs Wallace say, 'the habits there are very hard. But the women are used, of course, to vicious living.' I gazed at her, and then at Mr Dance. 'And Miss Prior goes,' he asked, 'to study them? To tutor them?'—'To comfort and inspire them,' said Mrs Wallace. 'To offer them her guidance, as a *lady*.'—'Ah, as a *lady* . . .'

Now *I* laughed, and Mr Dance turned his head to me and blinked. He said, 'You must I suppose have seen many very wretched scenes there.'

I remember now looking at his plate, seeing the biscuit

that was on it, the piece of blue-veined cheese, the ivory-handled knife with the curl of butter upon its blade, that was beaded with water, as if sweating. I said slowly that, yes, I had seen wretched things there. I said I had seen women unable to speak, because the matrons kept them silent. I had seen women harm themselves, for the variety of it. I had seen women driven mad. There was a woman dying there, I said, because she was kept so cold and badly fed. There was another who had put out her own eye—

Mr Dance had taken up the ivory-handled knife; now he set it down again. Miss Palmer gave a cry. Mother said, 'Margaret!' and I saw Helen glance at Stephen. But the words came from me, I seemed to feel the shape and taste of them as they left my mouth. I might have sat there and been sick upon the table—they could not have silenced me.

I said, 'I have seen the chain-room, and the dark cell. The chain-room has shackles in it, and strait-coats, and hobbles. The hobbles fasten a woman's wrists and ankles to her thighs, and when she is put in them she must be fed from a spoon, like a baby, and if she soils herself, she must remain in her own slops—' Mother's voice came again, sharper than before, and Stephen's joined it. I said, 'The *dark cell* has a gate across it, and a door, and then another door, padded with straw. The women are put in it with their arms fastened, and the darkness smothers them. There is a girl in it now, and—do you know, Mr Dance, the most curious thing?' I leaned to him, and whispered: 'It is really I who should have been put there!—not her, not her at all.'

He looked away from me, to Mrs Wallace, who had exclaimed when I had whispered. Someone said nervously, What could I mean? What could I mean by saying that?

'But didn't you know,' I answered, 'that they send suicides to gaol?'

Now Mother spoke quickly. 'Margaret was ill, Mr Dance, when her poor father died. And in her illness—such an accident!—she muddled the dosing of her medicine—'

'I took morphia, Mr Dance!' I cried, 'and should have died, if they had not found me. It was careless of me to be found, I suppose. But it was nothing to me—do you see?—if they saved me and knew. Don't you think that queer? That a common coarse-featured woman might drink morphia and be sent to gaol for it, while I am saved and sent to visit her—and all because I am a *lady*?'

I was, perhaps, as mad as I had ever been; and yet, I spoke out of a fearful kind of clarity that might have sounded, I suppose, like a show of temper. I looked about the table and now no-one would gaze at me, no-one save Mother—and she looked at me as if she did not know me. She only said very quietly at last, 'Helen, will you take Margaret to her room?' And she rose, and then all the ladies rose, and then the gentlemen rose to bow them out. The chairs made a wretched sound upon the floor, and the plates and glasses all rocked upon the table. Helen came to me. I said, '*You* needn't put your hand on me!' and she flinched—in fear, I suppose, of what I might say next. But she put her arm about my waist and led me from my seat, past Stephen and Mr Wallace and Mr Dance, and Vigers at the door. Mother took the ladies up to the drawing-room and we followed a little way behind them, then went past them. Helen said, 'What is it, Margaret? I never saw you like this—so unlike yourself.'

I was a little calmer now. I said she must not mind it, that I was only weary, and my head hurt, and my gown pinched. I wouldn't let her into the room with me, but said she must go back and help Mother. I would sleep, I said, and be better by morning. She looked doubtful, but once I put my hand against her face—only in kindness, and to reassure her!—and I felt her flinch from me again, and knew she was afraid of me, and of what I might do or say that might be overheard. Then I laughed; and then she did go down—gazing back at me all the time she walked, her face growing smaller and paler and vaguer in the stairwell shadows.

I found this room quite dark and still, the only light in it the dull glow of the ashy fire, a piece of street-light at the edge of the blind. I was glad of the darkness, I didn't think of taking a taper to the lamp. I only stepped from the door to the window, from the window to the door; and I put my fingers to the hooks of my tight bodice, meaning to loosen it. But my fingers were clumsy—the gown only slid a little way along my arms, and so seemed to grip me tighter. And still I paced. I thought, *It isn't dark enough!* I wanted it darker. *Where is it dark?* I saw the half-open door of my closet; even in there, however, there was a corner that seemed darker than the rest. I went to it, and crouched in it, and placed my head upon my knees. Now my gown had me gripped like a fist, so that the more I wriggled to undo it, the tighter it grew—at last, *There is a screw at my back*, I thought, *& they are tightening it!*

Then I knew where I was. I was with *her*, and close to her, so close—what did she say once? *closer than wax*. I felt the cell about me, the jacket upon me—

And yet, I seemed to feel my eyes bound, too, with bands of silk. And at my throat there was a velvet collar.

I cannot say how long I crouched there. Once there were footsteps on the stairs, a gentle knocking, and a whisper—'*Are you awake?*' It might have been Helen, it might have been one of the girls, I don't think it was Mother. Whoever it was I did not answer her, and she didn't come, but must have thought me sleeping—I wondered vaguely, Why would she think that, seeing an empty bed? Then I heard voices in the hall, Stephen whistling for a cab. I heard Mr Dance's laughter in the street beneath my window, the front door closed and bolted, Mother calling something sharp as she walked from room to room, seeing the fires out. I covered my ears. When I listened next there was only the sound of Vigers moving in the room above my own, and then the sawing and the sighing of the springs of her bed.

When I tried to rise, I staggered: my legs were bent with cold and cramp and wouldn't straighten, and the gown still pinned me at the elbows. But when I did stand, the dress fell easily. I cannot say if I was still in the grip of the medicine, or out of it, but I believed for a moment that I might be sick. I made my way through the darkness and washed my face and mouth, and then I stood bent above my bowl until the surge of sickness had passed. There were two or three coals still faintly glowing in the grate, and I went and held my hands to them, then lit a candle. My lips, my tongue, my eyes felt quite unlike my own, and I think I meant to go to the glass, to see how I was changed. But when I turned I saw the bed, and that there was something at its pillow; and then my fingers shook so violently the candle fell.

I thought I saw a head there. I thought I saw *my own head* there, above the sheet. Now I stood frozen in fright, certain that I lay inside the bed—had perhaps been asleep through all the crouching in the closet, and would now wake, and rise, and come to where I stood, and *embrace myself*. I thought: You must have light! You must have light! You cannot let her come at you in the darkness! I stooped and found the candle—got it lit, held it with both hands, so that it wouldn't gutter and go out—and I went to the pillow, and gazed at what was there.

It was not a head. It was a curling rope of yellow hair, as thick as my two fists. It was the hair that I had tried to steal from Millbank Prison—it was Selina's hair. She had sent it to me, from her dark place, across the city, across the night. I put my face to it. It smelt of sulphur.

I woke, at six this morning, believing I could hear the Millbank bell. I woke as one might wake from death, still gripped by darkness, still sucked at by the soil. I found Selina's hair beside me, its gloss a little marred where the plait had loosened—I had taken it with me into my bed. Seeing it, and remembering the night, I trembled; but I was clever enough to rise with it and put a scarf about it and place it out of sight, in the drawer where I keep this. The carpet seemed to tilt like the deck of a ship as I ran across it; it seemed to tilt even as I lay still and quiet. When Ellis came, she went at once for Mother, and though Mother came frowning, ready to scold, she saw me pale and shivering and wretched, and gave a cry. She sent Vigers for Dr Ashe, and when he came I found I couldn't keep from weeping. I told him it was my monthly time, only that. He said I must take not chloral now but laudanum, and that I must keep to the house.

When he was gone Mother had Vigers heat a plate for me

to press to my stomach, for I told her it ached. Then she brought the laudanum. It tastes pleasanter, at least, than my last medicine.

'Of course,' she said, 'I would not have had you sit with us last night, if I had known how ill you were.' She said they must be more careful, in the future, as to how they let me pass my days. Then she brought Helen, and Stephen, and I heard them whispering. Once I think I slept, and then woke weeping and crying out, and couldn't shake the confusion from me for half an hour. After that I began to be afraid of what I should say if a fever came on me while they stood and watched. At last I said that they must only leave me, and I would be well again. They answered: 'Leave you? What nonsense! Leave you, to be ill alone?'—I think Mother meant to sit with me all night. In the end I made myself lie still and calm, and they agreed I should do well enough with one of the girls to watch me. Now Vigers is to keep beyond the door till dawn. I heard Mother tell her to be sure I do not stir and tire myself—but, if she has caught the turning of these pages, she hasn't come. Once, to-day, she came quietly to the room, bringing a cup of milk that she had boiled, then made sweet and thick with molasses and an egg. She said that if I took a cup of that a day, then I would soon grow better. But I could not drink it. After an hour she took the cup away, her plain face grown sad. I have eaten nothing but water and a little bread; and I have lain, with the shutters still drawn, in candle-light. When Mother lit a brighter lamp, I shrank from it. It made my eyes smart.

26 May 1873

This afternoon, as I sat very quietly in my own room, I heard the door-bell sound, & Ruth brought someone to me. It was a lady named Miss Isherwood, that came to a dark circle last Weds. She looked at me & she burst out weeping, saying she had not slept a single night since that night, & it was all because of Peter Quick. She said he touched her upon her face & hands & she can still feel his fingers there, they left invisible marks that weep a fluid or a rheum, that she feels flowing from her like water. I said 'Give me your hand. Can you feel this rheum upon your hand now?' She said she could. I watched her for a moment, then said '*So can* I.' Then she stared at me & I laughed. Of course, I knew what her trouble was. I said 'You are like me, Miss Isherwood, & don't know it. You have powers! You are so full of spirit-matter it is seeping from you, that is the fluid you feel, it wants to rise. We must help it do so, & then your powers will grow strong as they were meant to. They only want what we call *development*. If we neglect this thing, then your powers will wither, or else they will twist inside you & make you sick.' I looked at her face, which was awfully pale. I said 'I think you have felt those powers begin to twist a little already, haven't you?' She said she had. I said 'Well, they shall not harm you any more. Don't you feel a little better, now I have touched you? Think how I shall help you, with Peter Quick's hand to guide my own.' I told Ruth she must prepare the parlour, & I rang for Jenny & said she must be sure to keep from that room & the rooms about it for an hour.

Then I waited, then took Miss Isherwood downstairs. We passed Mrs Brink. I said Miss Isherwood had come for a private sitting, & when she heard that she said 'O, Miss Isherwood, how fortunate you are! But you won't, I hope, let my angel grow too weary?' Miss Isherwood said she wouldn't. When we went to the parlour we found that Ruth had hung the curtain but, there having been no time to make up a jar of phosphorised oil, she had only left a lamp burning very low. I said 'Now, we shall keep this lamp lit, & you must tell me when you think Peter Quick has come. He will come you see if you have powers, it is only for the dark circles that I must sit behind a curtain, to protect me from the emanations that come from ordinary eyes.' We sat for I should say 20 minutes, Miss Isherwood keeping very nervous all that time, until finally there came a knocking at the wall & she whispered 'What is that?' I said 'I am not sure.' Then the knocking grew louder & she said 'I think he is here!' & Peter came out of the cabinet shaking his head & groaning, saying 'Why have you brought me at this queer time?' I said 'There is a lady here who needs your help. I believe she has the power to bring spirits but that power is weak & needs developing. I believe you have called her to this work.' Peter said 'Is it Miss Isherwood? Yes, I can see the signs I put upon her. Well Miss Isherwood, this is a very great task, it is not a thing to be undertaken lightly. What you have you know is sometimes called a *fatal gift*. The things that happen in this room will sound queer to the ears of unsensitive people. You must keep the spirits' secrets or risk their boundless wrath. Can you do that?' Miss Isherwood said 'I think I can sir. I think that what Miss Dawes says must be true. I think I have a nature that is very like hers, or could be made like it.'

I looked at Peter then, & saw him smile. He said 'My medium's nature is very special. You believe that to be a medium you must hold your spirit aside to let another spirit come. That however, is not how it is. You must rather be a servant of the spirits, you must become a plastic instrument for the spirits' own hands. You must let your spirit be *used*, your prayer must be always *May I be used*. Say that, Selina.' I said it, then he said to Miss Isherwood 'Tell her to say it.' She said 'Say it Miss Dawes' & I said again 'May I be used.' He said 'Do you see? my medium must do as she is bid. You think she is awake but she is entranced. Tell her to do another thing.' I heard Miss Isherwood swallow, then she said 'Will you stand up Miss

Dawes?' but Peter said at once 'You must not ask Will you, you must command her.' Miss Isherwood said then '*Stand up Miss Dawes!*' & I stood, & Peter said 'Say another thing.' She said 'Join your hands, open & shut your eyes, say Amen' & I did all these things & Peter laughed, his voice growing higher. He said 'Tell her to kiss you.' She said 'Kiss me Miss Dawes!' He said 'Tell her to kiss me!' & she said 'Miss Dawes, kiss Peter!' Then he said 'Tell her to take off her gown!' Miss Isherwood said 'O, I cannot do that!' He said '*Tell her!*' & then she told me. Peter said 'Help her with the buttons', & when she did she said 'How fast her heart beats!'

Then Peter said 'Now you see my medium unclothed. That is how the spirit appears when the body has been taken from it. Put your hand upon her, Miss Isherwood. Is she hot?' Miss Isherwood said I was very hot. Peter said 'That is because her spirit is very near the surface of her flesh. You must also become hot.' She said 'Indeed I feel very hot.' He said 'That is good, but you are not hot enough for development to happen, you must let my medium make you hotter. You must take off your gown now & you must grasp Miss Dawes.' I felt her do all this, my eyes being still shut tight, because Peter had not said that I might open them. I felt her arms come about me & her face come close to mine. Peter said 'How do you feel now Miss Isherwood?' & she answered 'I am not sure, sir.' He said 'Tell me again, what must your prayer be?' & she said 'May I be used.' He said 'Say it then.' She said it, & then he said she must say it faster, which she then did. Then he came & put his hand upon her neck & she gave a jog. He said 'O, but your spirit is still not hot enough! It must grow so hot you will feel it melting, you will feel mine come & take its place!' He put his arms about her & I felt his hands on me, now we had her hard between us & she began to shake. He said 'What is the medium's prayer Miss Isherwood? What is the medium's prayer?' & she said it, over & over & over until her voice grew faint, & then Peter whispered to me 'Open your eyes.'

11 December 1874

I have continued to wake all week to that impossible sound, the sound of the Millbank bell ringing the women to their labour. I have imagined them rising, pulling on their woollen stockings and their linsey gowns. I have imagined them standing at their gates with their knives and trenchers, warming their hands against their mugs of tea, then settling to their work and feeling their hands grow cold. Selina, I think, is among them again, for I have felt the darkness lift a little from that portion of me that has shared her cell. But I know she is wretched; and I have not been to her.

At first it was fear, and shame, that kept me from her. Now it is Mother. She has grown querulous again, as I have grown well. The day after the doctor's visit she came to sit with me, saw Vigers bring another plate, and shook her head—'You wouldn't be ill like this,' she said, 'if you were married.' Yesterday she stood and watched while I was bathed, but would not let me dress. She says I must keep to my room, in a bed-gown. Then Vigers came from the closet carrying the walking-suit I have had made for Millbank: it had been put there and forgotten on the night of the supper, and she meant I suppose to tidy it. I saw it, saw the lime upon it, and remembered Miss Brewer staggering against the wall. Mother looked once at me, then nodded to Vigers. She told her to take the gown and clean it, then put it away. And when I said that she must wait—that I would need the gown for Millbank—Mother said, I surely did not mean to continue with my visits, now that *this* had happened?

Then she said to Vigers, more quietly: 'Take the gown and go.' And Vigers looked once at me, then went. I heard her footsteps, fast, upon the staircase.

And so, we had the same dreary argument. 'I won't let you go to Millbank,' said Mother, 'since going there makes you so ill.' I said she could not stop me from going if I still chose to. She answered, 'Your own sense of propriety should prevent you. Your own sense of loyalty, to your mother!'

I said that there was nothing improper about my visits, nor anything disloyal, how could she think it? She said, was it not disloyalty, to shame her as I had at the supper-party before Mr Dance and Miss Palmer? She said she had known it all along, and now Dr Ashe had said as much: the visits to Millbank had made me ill again, just as I had been growing well. I had had too much freedom, my temperament did not suit it. I was too susceptible, visiting the rough women of the gaol made me forget the proper way of things. I had too many blank hours and grew fanciful—*&c. &c.*

'Mr Shillitoe,' she said at last, 'has sent a note, enquiring after you.' It turned out that a letter came the day after my visit. She said she would write an answer to it, saying I was too ill to return.

I had argued and grown weak. Now I saw how it was with her and felt a surge of temper. I thought: *Damn you, you bitch!*—I heard the words hissed very plainly in my head, as by a second, secret mouth. They were so plain I flinched, thinking that Mother must hear them too. But she had only crossed to the door and not looked back; and when I saw how firm her step was, then I knew how I must be. I took my handkerchief and wiped my lips. I called, that she need not write the letter. I would send a note to Mr Shillitoe myself.

I said she was right. I would give Millbank up. I said it, and wouldn't catch her eye, I suppose she read it as shame, for she came to me again and put her hand upon my cheek. 'It is only your own health,' she said, 'that I am thinking of.'

Her rings were cold upon my face. I remembered then how she had come when they had saved me from the morphia. She had come in her gown of black, and with all her hair unfastened. She had put her head upon my breast until my night-gown was wet with her tears.

Now she handed me paper and a pen, and stood at the foot of the bed and watched me write. I wrote:

Selina Dawes
Selina Dawes
Selina Dawes
Selina Dawes

and, seeing the pen move across the page, she left me. Then I burned the paper in the grate.

Then I rang for Vigers and said there had been a mistake, she must clean my gown but return it to me, later, when my mother had gone out; and Mrs Prior need know nothing of it, nor Ellis.

Then I asked, Had she any letters that must be posted?—and, when she nodded and said she had one, I told her she might run with it now to the letter-box, and that, if anyone asked, she was to say it was for me. She kept her eyes well lowered as she made me her curtsey. That was yesterday. Later Mother came, and put her hand to my face again. This time, however, I pretended sleep, and didn't look at her.

Now there is the sound of a carriage in the Walk. Mrs Wallace is coming, to take Mother to a concert. Mother will be here in a moment, I think, to give me my medicine before she leaves.

I have been to Millbank, and seen Selina; and now, everything is changed.

They were ready for me there, of course. I think the Porter was keeping watch for me, for he seemed knowing when I went to him; and when I reached the women's gaol I found a matron waiting, and she took me at once to Miss Haxby's room, and Mr Shillitoe was there, and Miss Ridley. It was like my first interview—that seems in a different life to me now, though it did not this afternoon. Even so, I felt the change between that time and this, for Miss Haxby didn't smile at all, and even Mr Shillitoe looked grave.

He said he was very glad to see me there again. He had

begun to fear, after his letter to me went unanswered, that the business upon the wards last week might have frightened me from them for ever. I said that I had only been a little unwell, and that the letter had been put aside by a careless servant. I saw Miss Haxby studying the shadows about my cheeks and eyes as I spoke—I think my eyes were dark, from that draught of laudanum. I think I should have been worse, however, without it, for I had not been out of my room, before to-day, for more than a week, and the medicine did lend me a kind of strength.

She said she hoped that I was quite recovered; then, that she was sorry not to have been able to talk to me, after the breaking-out. 'There was no-one to tell us what happened, apart from poor Miss Brewer. Dawes, I'm afraid, has been very stubborn.'

I heard the scuff of Miss Ridley's shoes, as she shifted to a more comfortable pose. Mr Shillitoe said nothing. I asked how long it was that they had kept Selina in the darks?—'Three days,' they told me. Which is as long as they are allowed to keep a woman there, 'without a legal order'.

I said, 'Three days seems very hard.'

For assaulting a matron? Miss Haxby did not think so. She said Miss Brewer was so badly hurt and shocked that she has gone from Millbank—gone from prison service altogether. Mr Shillitoe shook his head. 'A very bad affair,' he said.

I nodded, then asked, 'And how is Dawes?'—'She is quite,' said Miss Haxby, 'as wretched as she should be.' They had her now picking coir on Mrs Pretty's ward, she said; and all plans of sending her to Fulham were, of course, forgotten. Here she held my gaze. She said, 'I imagine you, at least, will be glad of that.'

I had thought of this. I said, very steadily, that I was glad of it. For it was now more than ever that Dawes would need a friend, to counsel her. It was now, much more than before, that she would need a Visitor's sympathies—

'*No*,' said Miss Haxby. 'No, Miss Prior.' How could I argue that, she asked, when it was my sympathies that had so worked on Dawes already, they had made her harm a matron and upset her cell? When it was my attentions to her that had led directly to this crisis? She said, 'You call yourself her friend. Before your visits, she was the quietest prisoner in Millbank! What kind of friendship is it, that can provoke such passions in a girl like that?'

I said, 'You mean to stop my visits to her.'

'I mean to keep her calm, for her own sake. She will not be calm, with you about her.'

'She will not be calm, without me!'

'Then she will have to learn it.'

I said, 'Miss Haxby'—but I stumbled over the words, for I had almost said *Mother*! I put a hand to my throat, and looked at Mr Shillitoe. He said, 'The breaking-out was very serious. Suppose, Miss Prior, she should strike *you* next time?'

'She won't strike *me*!' I said. I said, Couldn't they see, how terrible her plight was, and how my visits eased it? They must only think of her: an intelligent girl, a gentle girl—the quietest girl, as Miss Haxby had said, in all of Millbank! They must think of what the prison had done to her—how it had made her, not sorry, not good, but only so miserable, so incapable of imagining the other world beyond her cell, that she had struck the matron who had come to tell her she must leave it! 'Keep her silent, keep her unvisited,' I said, 'I think you will drive her mad—or else, you'll kill her . . .'

I went on like this, and couldn't have been more eloquent had I been arguing for my own life—I know now, it *was* my life I argued for; and I think the voice I spoke with came from another. I saw Mr Shillitoe grow thoughtful, as he had before. I am not sure what was said between us then. I only know he agreed, at last, that I might see her, and they would watch to see how well she did. 'Her matron,' he said, 'Mrs Jelf, has also spoken in your behalf'—that seemed to influence him.

When I looked at Miss Haxby I found her gaze quite lowered; only after Mr Shillitoe had left us, and I rose to make my way to the wards, did she lift her eyes to me again. I was surprised, then, by her expression, for it was not angry so much as awkward, self-conscious. I thought, She has been shamed before me, and of course feels the sting of it. I said, 'Let us not quarrel, Miss Haxby,' and she answered at once that she had no wish to quarrel with me. But I had come into her gaol, knowing nothing about it—Here she hesitated, and glanced quickly at Miss Ridley. She said, 'I must answer of course to Mr Shillitoe; yet, Mr Shillitoe cannot govern here, because this is a gaol for women. Mr Shillitoe doesn't understand its tempers and its moods. I once joked with you that I had spent many terms in prison—so I have, Miss Prior, and I know all the twisting ways that prison habits can turn. I think that, like Mr Shillitoe, you do not know, you cannot guess, the nature of the—' she seemed to grasp after a word, and then repeated, 'of the *temper*—of the queerness of the temper—of a girl such as Dawes, when she is shut up—'

Still she seemed to grope for words: she might have been one of her own women, seeking a term out of the prison ordinary and being unable to find it. I knew, however, what she meant. But the temper she was talking of, it is gross, it is commonplace, it is what Jane Jarvis has, or Emma White—it is not Selina's, it is not mine. I said, before she could speak again, that I would keep her cautions in mind. Then she studied me a little longer, then let Miss Ridley take me to the cells.

I felt the drug upon me, as we walked the white prison passages; I felt it more than ever when we reached the wards, for there were breezes there that made the gas-jets flicker, so that all the solid surfaces seemed to shift and bulge and shiver. I was struck, as always, by the grimness of the penal ward, its fetid air and silence; and when Mrs Pretty saw me come she gave a leer, and her face seemed wide and strange to me, as if reflected in a sheet of buckling metal. 'Well, well, Miss Prior,' she said—I am sure she said this. 'And are you back again, to see your own wicked lamb?' She took me to a door, then put her eye to its inspection slit, very slyly. Then she worked at the lock, and at the bolt of the gate behind it. 'Go on, ma'am,' she said at last. 'She has been meek as anything since her spell in the darks.'

The cell that they have put her in is smaller than those on the ordinary wards, and the iron louvres at its little window, together with the mesh they put about the gas-jets, to keep the women from the flames, make it desperately gloomy. There was no table and no chair: I found her seated on the hardwood bed, hunched awkwardly over a tray of coir. She put this aside when they opened the door to me, and attempted to rise to her feet; then she swayed, and had to reach for the wall to steady herself. They have taken the star from her sleeve and given her a gown that seemed too large for her. Her cheeks were white, her temples and her lips shadowed with blue, and on her forehead there was a yellow bruise. Her fingernails are split down to the quick, from picking coir. Coir fibres dust her cap, her apron, her wrists, and all her bedding.

When Mrs Pretty had closed the door and locked it, I took a step towards her. We had said nothing yet, only gazed at one another in a kind of mutual fright; but now I think I whispered, 'What have they done to you? What have they done?'—and at that her head gave a jerk, and she smiled and, as I watched, the smile sagged and dissolved, like a smile of wax, and she put a hand to her face and wept. I could do nothing then but go to her, and put my arm about her, and sit her back upon the bed and stroke her poor, bruised face till she was calm. She kept her head against the collar of my coat, and gripped me. When she spoke it was to say, in a whisper: 'How weak you must think me.'

'How weak, Selina?'

'It is only that I have wished so much that you might come.'

She shuddered, but at last grew still. I took her hand, to exclaim over her broken fingernails, and she told me then that they must pick four pounds of coir each day, 'or else Mrs Pretty brings us more the next day. The coir flies about—you feel you will choke with it.' She said they have only water and dark bread to eat; and that when she is taken to chapel, she is taken in *shackles*.—I could not bear to hear it. But when I took her hand again, she stiffened, and drew her fingers away. 'Mrs Pretty,' she murmured. 'Mrs Pretty comes and looks at us . . .'

I heard, then, a movement at the door, and after a moment I saw the inspection slit quiver, and it was slowly unclosed by blunt, white fingers. I called, 'You need not watch us, Mrs Pretty!' and the matron laughed, saying, that they must always watch, on *that* ward. But the flap did spring shut again; and I heard her move away, then call at the door of another cell.

We sat in silence. I looked at the bruise on Selina's head—she said that she had stumbled, when they put her in the dark cell. She gave a shiver, remembering it. I said, 'It was very terrible there', and she nodded. She said, '*You* will know, how terrible it was'—and then: 'I should not have been able to bear it, if you had not been there to take a little of the darkness to yourself.'

I stared at her. She went on, '*Then* I knew how good you were, to come to me, after all you had seen. The first hour they had me there, do you know what frightened me the most? Oh, it was a torment to me!—far worse than any punishment of *theirs*. It was the thought that you might stay from me; the thought that I might have driven you away, and with the very thing I meant to keep you near me!'

I knew it—but the knowledge had made me ill, I couldn't bear to have her say it. I said, 'You mustn't, you mustn't'—she answered, in a fierce kind of whisper, that *she must*! Oh, to think of that poor lady, Miss Brewer! She never meant her any harm. But to be moved—to be what they call free, to talk with other prisoners! 'Why should I want to talk with convicts, when I couldn't talk with *you*?'

Now I think I placed my hand upon her mouth. I said again, she *must* not say such things, she *must* not.—At last she pulled my fingers free and said, that it was to say such things that she had hurt Miss Brewer, that it was to say such things that she had suffered the jacket and the darks. Would I make her still be silent, after *that*?

Then I put my hands upon her arms and gripped her, and almost hissed. I said, And what had she gained by it? All she had done was, made them study us the closer! Didn't she know that Miss Haxby wanted to keep me from her? That

Miss Ridley would look, to see how long we were together? That Mrs Pretty would look?—that even Mr Shillitoe would look? 'Do you know how careful we shall have to be now, how sly?'

I had drawn her to me, to say these things. Now I grew conscious of her eyes, her mouth, her breath that was warm and sour. I heard my voice, and what I had admitted.

I opened my hands, and turned from her. She said, 'Aurora.'

I said at once, 'Don't say that.'

But she said it again. *Aurora. Aurora.*

'You mustn't say it.'

'Why mustn't I? I said it in the dark to you, and you were glad to hear it, and answered me! Why do you step from me now?'

I had risen from the bed. I said, 'I must.'

'Why must you?'

I said it wasn't right that we should be so near. That it was against the rules, it was forbidden by the rules of Millbank. But now she stood and, the cell being so close, there was nowhere I could step that she could not reach me. My skirts caught her tray of coir and set the dust of it swirling, but she only stepped through it, and came close, and put her hand upon my arm. She said: 'You want me near.' And when I answered at once that *No, I did not*—'Yes, you want me,' she said. 'Or—why do you have my name, upon the pages of your journal? Why do you have my flowers? *Why, Aurora, do you have my hair?*'

'You sent me those things!' I said. 'I never asked for them!'

'I could not have sent them,' she answered simply, 'if you had not longed for them to come.'

Then I could say nothing; and when she saw my face she stepped away from me and her expression changed. She said I must stand carefully, and be calm, for Mrs Pretty might look. She said I must stand, and listen to what she had to tell me. For she had been in darkness, and knew everything. And now I must know it . . .

She bowed her head a little but kept her eyes upon me, and

they seemed larger than ever and dark as a magician's. She said, Hadn't she told me once, that there was a purpose to her time there? Hadn't she said, that the spirits would come and reveal it to her? 'They came, Aurora, as I lay in that cell. They came and they told me. Can't you guess it? I think I guessed it. It was that that made me frightened.'

She passed her tongue across her lips, and swallowed. I watched her, not moving. I said, What? What was it? Why did they have her there?

She said: '*For you.* So that we might meet and, meeting, know—and knowing, join . . .'

She might have put a knife to me and twisted it: I felt my heart beat hard and, behind the beat, caught another, sharper movement—that *quickening*, grown fiercer than ever. I felt it, and felt an answering twisting in her . . .

It was a kind of agony.

For what she had said seemed only terrible to me. 'You mustn't talk like this,' I said. 'Why are you saying such things? What use is it, what the spirits have told you? All their wild words—we mustn't be wild now, we must be calm, we must be sober. If I am still to come to you, until you are released—'

'Four years,' she said. Did I think they would go on letting me come there, for all that time? Did I think Miss Haxby would let me? Would my own mother let me? And if they did, if I could come, once every week, once every month, for half an hour a time—well, did I think that I could bear it?

I said, that I had borne it until now. I said we might appeal, against her sentence. I said, If we might only take a little care—

'Could you bear it,' she said flatly, 'after to-day? Could you go on being only *careful*, only *cool*? No—' for I had made to step towards her. 'No, don't move! Be steady, keep from me. Mrs Pretty might see . . .'

I put my hands together, and twisted them until the gloves made my flesh burn. What choice did we have? I cried. She was tormenting me! To say that we must *join*—that we must join, *there*, at Millbank! I said again, Why had the spirits said such things to her? Why was she saying them now, to me?

'I am saying them,' she answered, in a whisper so thin I had to lean into the twisting dust to catch it, 'because there is a choice, and you must make it. *I can escape.*'

I believe I laughed. I think I placed my hand across my mouth, and laughed. She watched, and waited. Her face was grave—I thought then, for the first time, that perhaps her days in the dark cell had clouded her reason. I looked at her dead-white cheek, her brow with the bruise upon it, and I grew sober. I said, very quietly: 'You have said too much.'

'I can do it,' she answered levelly.

No, I said. It would be terribly wrong.

'It would be wrong, by their laws only.'

No. Besides, how could she do such a thing, from Millbank?—where there were gates with locks at every passage, and matrons, and warders . . . I gazed about me, at the wooden door, the iron louvres on the windows. 'You would need keys,' I said. 'You would need—unimaginable things. And what would you do, even if you could escape? Where would you go?'

Still she watched me. Still her eyes seemed very dark. Then, 'I would need no key,' she said, 'while I had spirit-help. And I would come to you, Aurora. And we would go away, together.'

Just like that, she said it. Just like that. Now I did not laugh. I said, Did she think that I would go with her?

She said she thought that I would have to.

Did she think that I would leave—

'Leave what? Leave who?'

Leave Mother. Leave Helen and Stephen, and Georgy, and the children still to come. Leave my father's grave. Leave my ticket to the reading-room at the British Museum.—'Leave my life,' I said at last.

She answered, that she would give me a better one.

I said, 'We would have nothing.'

'We would have your money.'

'It is my mother's money!'

'You must have money of your own. There must be things that you might sell . . .'

This was foolish, I said. It was worse than foolish—it was idiotic, insane! How could we live, together, alone? Where would we go?

But even as I asked it, I saw her eyes, and knew . . .

'Think of it!' she said. 'Think of living there, with the sun always upon us. Think of those bright places you long to visit—Reggio and Parma and Milan, and Venice. We could live in any of those places. We should be free.'

I gazed at her—and there came the sound of Mrs Pretty's tread beyond the door, the crunch of grit beneath her heel. I said then, in a whisper, 'We are mad, Selina. To *escape*, from Millbank! You couldn't do it. You should be captured at once.' She said that her spirit-friends would keep her safe; and then, when I cried that, No, I could not believe it, she said, Why not? She said I must think of all the things she had sent me. Why shouldn't she also send *herself*?

Still I said, No, it couldn't be true. 'If it were true, you would have gone from here a year ago.'—She said that she was waiting, that she needed *me*, to go for. She needed me, to take her to myself.

'And if you don't take me,' she said, '—well, when they put an end to your visits, what will you do then? Will you go on envying your sister's life? Will you go on being a prisoner, in your own dark cell, forever?'

And I had again that dreary vision, of Mother growing querulous and aged—scolding when I read too softly or too fast. I saw myself beside her in a mud-brown dress.

But we should be found, I said. The police would take us.

'They could not seize us, once we had left England.'

People would learn what we had done. I would be seen, and recognised. We would be cast off, by society!

She said, When had I ever cared for being a part of that sort of society? Why should I trouble over what it thinks? We would find a place, away from all that. We would find the place that we were meant for. She would have done the work that she was made to do . . .

She shook her head. 'All through my life,' she said, 'all through the weeks and months and years of it, I thought I understood. But I knew nothing. I thought I was in light, when all the time, my eyes were closed! Every poor lady that came to me, that touched my hand, that drew a small part of my spirit from me to her—they were only shadows. Aurora, they were shadows of you! I was only seeking you out, as you were seeking me. You were seeking me, your own *affinity*. And if you let them keep me from you now, I think we shall die!'

My own affinity. Have I known it? She says that I have. She said, 'You guessed it, you felt it. Why, I think you felt it, even before I did! The very first time you saw me, I think you felt it then.'

I remembered, then, watching her in her bright cell—her face tilted to catch the sun, the violet flower in her hands. Hadn't there been a kind of purpose to my gazing, just as she said?

I put my hand to my mouth. 'I am not sure,' I said. 'I am not sure.'

'Not sure? Look at your own fingers. Are you not sure, if they are yours? Look at any part of you—it might be me that you are looking at! We are the same, you and I. We have been cut, two halves, from the same piece of shining matter. Oh, I could say, *I love you*—that is a simple thing to say, the sort of thing your sister might say to her husband. I could say that in a prison letter, four times a year. But my spirit does not love yours—it is *entwined* with it. Our flesh does not love: our flesh is the same, and longs to leap to itself. It must do that, or wither! *You are like me.* You have felt what it's like, to leave your life, to leave your self—to shrug it from you, like a gown. They caught you, didn't they, before the self was quite cast off? They caught you, and they pulled you back—you didn't want to come . . .'

She said, Did I think the spirits would have let them do that, if there had not been a purpose to it? Didn't I know my father would have taken me, if he had known that I should go? 'He sent you back,' she said, 'and now I have you. You were careless with your life; but now I have it. Will you fight that, still?'

Now my heart beat terribly hard at my breast. It beat at the place my locket used to hang. It beat like a pain, like a hammer blow. I said, 'You say I am like you. You say my limbs might be your limbs, that I have been made from shining matter. I think you must never have looked at me—'

'I have looked at you,' she said quietly then. 'But do you think I look at you, with *their* eyes? Do you think I haven't seen you, when you have put your strait grey gowns aside?—when you have taken down your hair, and lain, white as milk, in the darkness . . .?

'Do you think,' she said finally, 'that I will be like *her*—like *her*, that chose your brother over you?'

Then I knew. I knew that all she said, all she had ever said, was true. I stood, and wept. I stood and wept and shivered, and she made no move to comfort me. She only watched, and nodded, saying, 'Now you understand. Now you know, why we cannot be only careful, only sly. Now you know, why you are drawn to me—why your flesh comes creeping to mine, and what it comes for. Let it creep, Aurora. Let it come to me, let it creep . . .'

She had made her voice into a fierce, slow whisper. It sent the drug, that had been heavy in me, pulsing about my veins. I felt the tug of her, then. I felt the lure of her, the grasp of her, I felt myself drawn across the coir-thick air to her whispering mouth. I clutched at her cell wall—but the wall was smooth, and slippery with limewash—I stood against it, but felt it slide from me. I began to think I must be stretching, bulging—I thought my face was bulging from its collar, my fingers swelling in their gloves . . .

I looked at my hands. She had said that they were her hands, but they were large and strange. I felt the surface of them, I felt the creases and the whorls upon the flesh of them.

I felt them harden and grow brittle.

I felt them soften and begin to drip.

And then I knew whose hands they were. They were not her hands, they were *his*—they had made those waxen moulds, they had come to her cell in the night and left smears in it. They were my hands, and they were Peter Quick's! The thought was frightful.

I said, '*No*, it cannot be done. No, *I will not do it*!'—and the bulging and the quickening ceased at once, and I stepped away, and placed my hand upon the door—and it was my own hand, in a glove of black silk. She said, 'Aurora.'—I said, 'Don't call me that, it isn't true! It was never true, never at all!' I put my fist to the door and I shouted: 'Mrs Pretty! Mrs Pretty!' And when I turned to look at her, I found her face mottled red, as if from a slap. She stood, stiff and shocked and wretched. Then she began to weep.

'We will find another way,' I told her. But she shook her head and whispered, 'Don't you see? Don't you see, how there is no other way than this?' A single tear brimmed at the corner of her eye, then quivered and ran, and was muddied by coir dust.

Then Mrs Pretty came and nodded me past her, and I went, not turning—for I knew that if I turned, then Selina's tears, her bruises and my own fierce longing would send me back to her, and then I would be lost. The door was closed and fastened, and *I walked from it*—as one might walk, in a terrible torture, gagged and goaded and feeling the flesh ripped from one's bones.

I walked until I reached the tower staircase. Mrs Pretty left me there, thinking I suppose that I would make my way downstairs. But I did not go. I stood in the shadows, and put my face against the chill white wall; and I did not move again until I heard feet upon the steps above me. I thought it might be Miss Ridley there, and I turned, and brushed at my cheek, for fear that there were tears or lime upon it. The feet came nearer.

It was not Miss Ridley. It was Mrs Jelf.

She saw me, and blinked. She had heard a movement on the stairs, she said, that made her wonder . . . I shook my head. When I told her that I had just come from seeing Selina Dawes, she shivered; she seemed as miserable, almost, as myself. She said, 'My ward is very changed, now they have taken her from it. All the Star-class women have gone, and I have new prisoners in their cells, and some are strangers to me. And Ellen Power—Ellen Power is also gone.'

'Power gone?' I said dully. 'I am glad for her, at least. They will be gentler with her, perhaps, at Fulham.'

When she heard me say that, however, she looked more miserable than ever. 'Not gone to Fulham, miss,' she said. She said she was sorry that I didn't know it, but they had moved Power to the infirmary at last, five days before, and she had died there—her grand-daughter had come, to take the body. All Mrs Jelf's kindness had gone for nothing after all, for they had found the bit of scarlet flannel beneath Power's gown, and were harsh with her over it; and Mrs Jelf was to lose wages, as a punishment.

I listened to this in a numb kind of horror. 'My God,' I said at last, 'how have we borne it? How shall we go on bearing it?'—*for four more years*, was what I meant.

She shook her head, then put her hand to her face and turned from me. I heard the slithering of her feet upon the steps, fading to silence.

I went down, then, to Miss Manning's wards, and walked the length of them, and gazed in at the women as they sat in their cells—every one of them hunched and shivering, every one wretched, every one ill or nearly ill, hungry or nauseous, and with fingers cracked with prison work and with cold. At the end of the ward I found another matron to take me to the gate of Pentagon Two, and then a warder to escort me through the men's gaol—I didn't speak to them. At the tip of the tongue of gravel that leads down to the Porter's lodge I found the day grown dark, the river breezes harsh with hail. I tipped my hat, and staggered against the wind. All about me Millbank reared, bleak as a tomb, and silent, yet filled with wretched men and women. I had never, in all my visits, felt the weight of their combined despair as I felt it press upon me now. I thought of Power, who had once blessed me and now was dead. I thought of Selina, bruised and weeping, calling me her *affinity*—saying, we had been seeking one another out and if we lost each other now, then we would die. I thought of my own room above the Thames, and Vigers in her chair beyond the door—there was the Porter swinging his keys, he had sent a man to fetch a cab for me. I thought, What time is it? It might have been six o'clock, it might have been midnight. I thought, Suppose Mother is at home—what shall I say? I have lime upon me, and the scent of the wards. Suppose she writes to Mr Shillitoe, or sends for Dr Ashe?

Now I hesitated. I was at the Porter's door. Above me was the filthy, fog-choked London sky, beneath my feet the reeking Millbank soil, that no flowers will grow in. Against my face beat hailstones, sharp as needles. The Porter stood ready to guide me into his lodge—still, however, I hesitated. He said, 'Miss Prior? What is it, miss?' and he put his hand across his face, to wipe the water from it.

I said, 'Wait'—I said it quietly at first, he had to lean and frown, not hearing me. Then I said, 'Wait,' again—I said it louder; I said, '*Wait*, you must *wait*, I must go back, I must go back!' I said there was something I had not done, that I must go back for!

Perhaps he spoke again—I didn't hear him. I only turned and headed back into the shadows of the gaol—almost running, and turning my heels upon the gravel. To every warder I met I said the same thing—that I must go back! I must go back into the women's wards!—and though they looked at me in wonder, they let me pass. At the female gaol I found Miss Craven, just come upon her duties at the gate. She knew me well enough to let me through, and when I said I didn't need a guide—had only left some small business undone—she nodded me by and didn't look at me again. I told the same story, then, upon the ground-floor wards; and then I climbed the tower staircase. I listened for Mrs Pretty's step and, when she had passed into the further ward, I ran to the door of Selina's cell and put my face to the eye of it, and pressed it, and gazed at her. She sat slumped beside her tray of coir, feebly pulling at it with her bleeding fingers. Her eyes were still wet and rimmed with crimson, and her shoulders shook. I didn't call her; but as I watched she looked up, and gave a jerk of fright. I whispered, 'Come quick, come quick to the door!' She ran, and leaned to the wall, until her face was close to mine and her breath came on me.

I said, 'I'll do it. I'll go with you. I love you, and I cannot give you up. Only tell me what I must do and I will do it!'

Then I saw her eye, and it was black, and my own face swam in it, pale as a pearl. And then, it was like Pa and the looking-glass. My soul left me—I felt it fly from me and lodge in her.

30 May 1873

Last night I had an awful dream. I dreamed that I woke up & all my limbs were stiff & I could not move them, & my eyes had a paste on them that kept them shut & it had run into my mouth & kept my lips shut too. I longed to call out to Ruth or to Mrs Brink but, because of the paste, I could not, I heard the sound I was making & it was only a groan. I began to be afraid then that I should have to lie like that until I choked or starved, & when I thought that I began to cry. Then my tears began to wash away the paste from over my eyes until finally there was a little space that I might just peep through, & thought, 'Now I shall look & see my own room, at least.' The room, however, that I expected to see, was not my room at Sydenham, it was my room at Mr Vincy's hotel.

But when I did look, I saw only that the place I lay in was entirely dark, & then I knew that I was buried in my own coffin, that they had put me in it thinking I was dead. I lay crying in my coffin until the tears melted the paste from my mouth, & then I did call out, thinking 'If I only call hard enough someone is sure to hear me & let me out.' But no-one came, & when I lifted my head it knocked upon the wood that was above me & by the sound of that knock I knew that there was earth above the coffin, & that I was already in my grave. Then I knew that no-one would hear me however loudly I called.

I lay very still then, wondering what I should do, & as I did that there came a whispering voice beside me, it came against my ear & made me shiver. The voice said 'Did you think you were alone? Didn't you know that I was here?' I looked for the person that spoke, but it was too dark for me to see them, there was only the feeling of the mouth close to my ear. I couldn't tell if it was Ruth's mouth, or Mrs Brink's, or Aunty's, or someone else entirely. I only knew, from the sound of the words, that the mouth was smiling.

Part Four

21 December 1874

They come every day now, the tokens from Selina. They come as flowers, or as scents; sometimes they come only as a subtle alteration to the details of my room—I return to it and find an ornament taken up and set down crooked, the door to my closet ajar and my dresses with marks of fingers on the velvet and the silk, a cushion with a dent in it, as if a head has lain there. They never come when I am here and watching. I wish they would. They would not frighten me. I should be frightened, now, if they ceased! For while they come, I know they come to make the space between us thick. They make a quivering cord of dark matter, it stretches from Millbank to Cheyne Walk, it is the cord through which she will send me herself.

The cord grows thickest at night, as I lie sleeping with the laudanum on me. Why didn't I guess that? I take the medicine gladly, now. And sometimes, when Mother is out—for the rope must be made in the day-time, too—sometimes I go to her drawer and steal an extra draught of it.

I shall no longer need my medicine, of course, when I am in Italy.

Mother is patient with me now. 'Margaret has been three weeks away from Millbank,' she says, to Helen and the Wallaces, 'and look at the change in her!' She says she has not seen me look so well in all the time since Pa died. She doesn't know about the trips I make to the prison, secretly, while she is out. She doesn't know that my grey visiting gown lies in the press—Vigers, good girl, has never told her, and I have Vigers to dress me now, instead of Ellis. She doesn't know about the promise I have made, my bold and terrible intention to abandon and disgrace her.

Sometimes I do tremble a little, when I think of that.

And yet, I *must* think of it. The cord of darkness will fashion itself, but if we are truly to go, if she is truly to *escape*—and oh! how quaint the word sounds! as if we were a pair of footpads from the penny presses—if she is to come it must be soon, it must be planned, I must prepare, it will be perilous. I shall have to lose one life, to gain another. It will be like death.

I thought dying was simple, once; but it was very hard. And this—surely this will be harder?

I went to her to-day, while Mother was out. They have her still on Mrs Pretty's ward, she is still wretched, her fingers bleed worse than ever, but she does not weep. She is like me. She said, 'I could bear anything, now I know why I am bearing it.' Her fierceness is there, but it is all contained, it is like the flame behind the chimney of a lamp. I am frightened the matrons will see it, and guess. I was frightened, to-day, when they looked at me. I seemed to walk flinching through the gaol, it might have been my first trip there; I was conscious again of the great size, the crushing weight of it—of its walls, its bolts and bars and locks, its watchful keepers in their suits of wool and leather, its odours, its clamour, that seemed cut from lead. I thought then, as I walked, that we had been fools, ever to think she could escape from it! It was only when I felt her fierceness, that I was sure again.

We talked of the preparations I must make. She said we shall need money, all the money I can find; and we shall need clothes, and shoes, and boxes to put them in. She said we must not wait until we arrive at France before we buy these things, for we mustn't seem strange in any way upon the train, we must seem like a lady and her companion and have the luggage to show for it. I had not thought of it as she had. It sometimes seems a little foolish, thinking such things in my own room. It didn't seem foolish, hearing her plan and order, fiercely, with glittering eyes.

'We shall need tickets,' she whispered, 'for the train and for the boat. We shall need passport papers.' I said I could get those, for I remember Arthur speaking of them. I know everything that one must do, indeed, for travelling to Italy, from listening to my sister tell the details of her wedding-trip, over and over.

Then she said, 'You must be ready when I come to you'—and because she had not spoken yet of how that would be, I found myself shaking. I said, 'I am afraid of it! Is it to be something odd? Am I to sit in darkness, or say magic words?'

She smiled. 'Do you think it works like that? It works through—love; and through wanting. You need only want me, and I will come.'

She said I must only do the things that she has told me.

To-night, when Mother asked me to read to her, I took her *Aurora Leigh*. I should never have done such a thing, a month ago. She saw the book and said, 'Read me the part where Romney returns—poor man—so scarred and blinded'—but I wouldn't read that. I think I shall never read that part again. I read her Book Seven, that has Aurora's speeches to Marian Erle. I read for an hour, and when I had finished Mother smiled and said, 'How sweet your voice sounds to-night, Margaret!'

I did not take Selina's hand to-day. She will not let me take her hand now, in case a matron passes and sees. But I sat as we talked, and she stood very near me, and I placed my foot against her own—my own stern shoe against her sterner prison boot. And our skirts of linsey and of silk we raised a little then—just a little, just enough so that the leather might kiss.

23 December 1874

We received a package to-day from Pris and Arthur, with a letter containing definite news of their return upon the 6th of January, and an invitation, to all of us—to Mother, myself, Stephen, Helen and Georgy—to holiday with them at Marishes until the Spring. There has been talk of such a thing for months; I didn't know, however, that Mother meant for us to go so soon. She speaks of leaving in the second week of the New Year, on the 9th—less than three weeks from now. The news threw me into a panic. I asked her, would they really want us with them, so soon after their return? I said Pris would be mistress now of a great house and a staff. Oughtn't we to leave her to grow used to her new duties? She said that it is at just such a time as this that a new wife requires her mother's advice. She said, 'We cannot rely on Arthur's sisters to be kind.'

Then she said she hoped that *I* would be a little kinder to Priscilla than I was upon her wedding-day.

She thinks she sees into all my weaknesses. She does not, of course, see the greatest one. The truth is, I haven't thought of Pris and her ordinary triumphs for a month and more. I have left them quite behind me. I am separating myself, indeed, from all the things in my old life, and all the people—Mother, Stephen, Georgy . . .

Even from Helen I feel distant now. She was here last night. She said, 'Is it true what your mother tells me, that you are calmer in yourself and growing stronger?' She said she couldn't help but think that I was only quieter—that I only kept my troubles to myself, more than ever.

I gazed at her, at her kind, regular face. I thought, Shall I tell you? What would you think? And for a moment I thought I *would* tell her, that it would be the easiest and the slightest thing imaginable—that after all, if anyone would understand it, *she* would. That I need only say, 'I am in love, Helen! I am in love! There is a girl so rare and marvellous and strange, and—Helen, she has all my life in her!'

I imagined saying it—so vividly, the passion of the words stirred me, almost to tears; and then I thought I *had* said it. But I had not—Helen still gazed at me, anxious and kind, waiting for me to speak. So then I turned and nodded to the Crivelli print that is pinned above my desk, and passed my fingers over it. I said—to test her—'Do you think this handsome?'

She blinked. She said she thought it handsome in its way.

Then she leaned closer to it. She said, 'But, I can hardly make out the features of the girl in it. Her face, poor thing, seems to have been rubbed quite from the paper.'

And then I knew that I should never tell her about Selina. That if I did, she wouldn't hear me. That if I brought Selina to her now, she would not see her—just as she could not see the sharp, dark lines upon the *Veritas*. They are too subtle for her.

I, also, am growing subtle, insubstantial. I am *evolving*. They do not notice it. They look at me and see me flushed and smiling—Mother says that I am thickening at the waist! They do not know that, when I sit with them, I keep myself amongst them through the sheer force of my will. It is very tiring. When I am alone, as I am now, it is quite different. Then—now—I gaze at my own flesh and see the bones show pale beneath it. They grow paler each day.

My flesh is streaming from me. I am becoming my own ghost!

I think I will haunt this room, when I have started my new life.

I must remain a little longer in the old one, however. This afternoon, at Garden Court, while Mother and Helen sat laughing with Georgy, I went to Stephen and said that there was something I should like to ask of him. I said, 'I should like you to explain to me the business of Mother's money, and of mine. It's something of which I know nothing.' He answered—as he has answered me before—that it was something of which I *need* know nothing, since he is there to act as my trustee; but this time I pressed him. I said that he had been generous, to take on all the burdens of our affairs after Pa's death, but that I should like to know a little, too. I said, 'I think that Mother worries, about the security of our home—about the income I should have, were she to die.' I said that if I were to know these things, I might discuss them with her.

He hesitated for a second, then placed his hand upon my wrist. He said quietly, that he guessed that *I* might be a little anxious, too. He said he hoped I knew that there would always be a place for me—whatever should happen with Mother—with Helen and him, at their home.

The kindest man I ever knew, Helen called him once. Now his kindness seemed ghastly to me. I thought suddenly, How will it hurt him—how will it hurt him, as a barrister—when I have done what I am planning? For when we have gone they will think, of course, that it was I, not the spirits, that helped Selina from the gaol. They might discover about the tickets, and the passports . . .

Then I remembered how the barristers had hurt *her*; and I thanked him and said nothing. He went on: 'As for the security of Mother's house, you needn't waste your hours worrying over that!' He said that Pa was very thoughtful. He wished half the fathers whose affairs he must argue over were as thoughtful as ours! He said that Mother is a wealthy woman, and will remain so. He said, 'You too, Margaret, are wealthy, quite in your own right.'

I have known this, of course; but it has always been, for me, an empty kind of knowledge—a useless knowledge, so long as my wealth has had no purpose. I looked at Mother. She had a little black doll upon a wire that she was making dance for Georgy, and its china feet were clattering upon the table-top. I leaned closer to Stephen. I said I should like to know *how* wealthy I was. I should like to know how my wealth was made up, and how it might be realised.

'It is only the theory of the thing that I want,' I added quickly, and he laughed. He said he knew it. I wanted the theory, he said, of everything, and always had.

But he could not help me to the figures at once, since most of the papers he would need are here, in Pa's study. We have arranged to spend an hour together, tomorrow night. He said, 'You won't mind it, on Christmas Eve?' I had forgotten for the moment that it *was* Christmas, and that made him smile again.

Then Mother called, that we must come and see how Georgy giggled at the doll. And when she saw how thoughtful I had grown she said, 'Stephen, what have you been saying to your sister? You mustn't encourage her to be so grave! You know there shall be none of this, in a month or two?'

She says she has many great schemes in mind for filling up my days, in the new year.

24 December 1874

Well, I have just come from my lesson with Stephen. He set the figures down for me upon a sheet, and when I looked at them I trembled. 'You are surprised,' he said; but it was not that. I trembled because it seemed curious to me, that Pa took care to secure my wealth. It is as if he saw, through the veil of his own illness, all the plans that I should make at the close of mine, and sought to help me with them. Selina says she sees him gazing at me even now, and smiling; but I am not sure. How could he gaze at all my quickenings and queer longings—and my desperate scheme, and my falseness—and only *smile*? She says he sees with spirit-eyes, and the world is changed through them.

Now I sat at the desk in his study and Stephen said, 'You are surprised. You hadn't guessed the measure of your affairs.' Much of my wealth is of course of a rather notional kind—tied up in property and in stock. But it forms an income, together with the money which Pa left me, independently, that is securely mine.—'Unless, of course,' said Stephen, 'you marry.'

Here we smiled at one another—though I think that privately we smiled at different things. I asked, could my income be drawn upon, wherever I lived? He said it is not bound to be received at Cheyne Walk.—But that is not what I meant. I said, How would it be if I were to go abroad? He stared at me. I said he must not be surprised—that I had begun to think, if Mother could be brought to countenance it, that I might make a tour, 'with some companion'.

Perhaps he thinks I have made some earnest spinster friend, at Millbank or at the British Museum. He said he thought it an excellent plan. As to the income—it is my own, he says, I may spend it how I please, receive it anywhere. It cannot be tampered with.

Could it not be tampered with, I asked him—and here I trembled again—if I were to displease our mother, in some serious way?

He said again, the money was my own, not hers; and, so long as he had the trusteeship of it, quite secure from interference.

'And if I were to displease *you*, Stephen?'

He gazed at me. From some room in the house there came the sound of Helen, calling Georgy's name. We had left them both with Mother: I had told them we were discussing some aspect of Pa's estate, some literary thing—Mother had grumbled at it, though Helen had smiled. Now Stephen touched the papers before him and said that, as far as the income was concerned, he stood with it in relation to me as Pa had. He said: 'While you are sound in mind, and unless you fall foul of curious influences—unless you are persuaded to apply your income to the pursuit of some scheme harmful to yourself!—well, then your receipt of it, I promise you, shall never be contested by me.'

Those were his words; and as he said them, he gave a laugh—so that I wondered for a moment if all his kindness was not a form of show, and he had guessed my secret and spoke cruelly. I could not be sure. So what I next asked him was, If I should need money now, in London—that is, more money than I am given by Mother—how should I get it?

He said that I need only go to my bank and withdraw it, by presenting them with an order that has been countersigned by him. He took such an order from amongst his papers as he spoke, then unscrewed his pen and wrote on it. I must only place my name beside his own, and complete the details.

I studied his signature, and wondered if it was his true one—I think it was. He watched me. He said, 'You might ask me for such an order, you know, at any time.'

I held the paper before me. There was a place upon it—blank—where I must write the figure, and I sat and gazed at that space while Stephen folded his documents away, until the space seemed to grow large—as large as my hand. Perhaps he saw how strangely I looked at it, for at last he placed the tips of his own fingers upon it and lowered his voice. 'I needn't say, of course,' he said, 'how careful you must be with this. It's not something, for example, that the maids should see. And you won't—' he smiled '—you won't carry it to Millbank, will you?'

I feared then that he might try and take the paper back. I folded it, and tucked it behind the belt of my gown, and we rose. I said, 'You know my visits to Millbank have ended.'—Now we stepped into the hall, and closed Pa's study door. I said it was because of that, that I had grown well again.

He said, of course, he had forgotten it. Helen had told him many times, how well I had become . . . Again he studied me, and when I smiled and made to move away, he placed his hand upon my arm. He said, quite quickly, 'Don't think me interfering, Margaret. Of course, Mother and Dr Ashe know best how to care for you. But Helen tells me they have you swallowing laudanum now, and I cannot help but think that, after chloral—well, I am not certain about the effect of medicines like that, combined in such a way.' I looked at him. He had coloured, and I felt my own cheeks flush. He said, 'You've had no symptoms? No—waking dreams, or fears, or fancies?'

Then I thought, He does not want to take the money. It is the medicine he wants! He means to stop Selina coming! He means to take the drug himself and *have her come to him*!

His hand still lay upon my arm, the green veins with black hairs upon them; but now there were footsteps on the stairs, and then one of the girls was there—it was Vigers, with a pail of coals. When Stephen saw her he lifted his hand and I turned from him. I said I was perfectly well, he might ask anyone that knew me. 'You might ask Vigers. Vigers, will you tell Mr Prior how well I am?'

Vigers blinked at me, then moved the pail so that we would

not have to see the coals in it. Her cheeks had reddened—now we were all three of us blushing! She said, 'I'm sure you are well, miss.' Then she looked once at Stephen, and I also looked at him. He had grown awkward. He said only, 'Well, I'm very glad of it.' He knew, after all, that he could not take her. He nodded to me, then went up to the drawing-room. I heard the door drawn open, and then pulled shut.

I waited for that sound, then crept up all the stairs and came in here; and I sat and drew the money order out, and gazed at it until that white space where the figure must be put again seemed to expand. At last it might have been a pane of glass with frost upon it, and as I watched, the frost began to melt and thin. Then I knew that what I could make out, faintly, beyond the ice, were the crisping lines and the deepening colours of my own future.

Then there were sounds from the rooms below me, and when I heard them I opened my drawer and took out this book, and turned back the pages so that I might slip the order between them. But the book seemed to bulge a little; and when I tilted it, something slithered from it—something slim and black, it fell upon my skirt and then was still. When I touched it, it seemed warm.

I had never seen it before, yet I knew it at once. It was a velvet collar, with a lock of brass. It was the collar Selina used to wear, and she had sent it to me—it was my reward, I think, for all my cleverness with Stephen!

I stood at the glass and fastened it about my throat. It fits, but tightly: I feel it grip, as my heart pulses, as if she holds the thread to which it is fastened and sometimes pulls it, to remind me she is near.

6 January 1875

It is five days since I was last at Millbank; but it is marvellously easy not to go there, now that I know Selina visits me—now that I know she will soon come, and never leave! I am content to stay at home, to talk with guests, even to talk alone with Mother. For Mother keeps to the house, too, more than is usual. She spends her hours sorting her gowns for Marishes, and sending the maids into the attics to fetch trunks and boxes, and sheets to place over the furniture and rugs when we are gone.

When we are gone, I have written—for there is one advance, at least. I have found a way to make her plans a shelter for my own.

We sat together one night, a week ago—she with a piece of paper and a pen, drawing up lists; I with a book upon my lap, and a knife. I was cutting the pages, but had my eyes upon the fire, and suppose I sat very still. I didn't know it however, until Mother raised her head and gave a *tut*. She said, How could I sit there, so idle and so calm? We were to leave for Marishes in ten days' time, and there were a hundred things that must be done before we went. Had I even spoken to Ellis, about my gowns?

I did not draw my gaze from the fire, nor slow the gentle tearing of the knife. I said, 'Well, here is progress Mother. A month ago you were reproaching me for restlessness. It does seem rather hard of you, however, to be scolding me now for excess of calm.'

It was the tone I keep for this book, not for her. Hearing it, she put her list aside, saying, She knew nothing of calmness, it was my impertinence that she ought to be scolding!

Now I did look at her. Now I did not feel idle. I felt—well, perhaps it was Selina, speaking for me!—but I felt gilded with a lustre not my own, no, not at all my own. I said, 'I'm not a serving-girl, to be reprimanded and dismissed. I'm not any kind of girl, you have said it yourself. You still treat me like one, however.'

'That's enough!' she said quickly. 'I won't have such talk, in my own house, from my own daughter. And I shan't have it at Marishes—'

No, I said. No, she would not. For she wouldn't have me at Marishes, either—at least, not for a month or so. I told her I had decided to stay on here, alone, while she goes down with Stephen and Helen.

Stay here, alone? What nonsense was this?—I said it wasn't nonsense. I said that, on the contrary, it was perfectly sensible.

'It is more of your old wilfulness, that is what it is! Margaret, we have had arguments like this a score of times—'

'All the more reason, then, for us not to have another now.' Really, there was nothing to be said. I should be happy to be solitary, for a week or two. And I was sure that everyone at Marishes would be more content, with me at Chelsea!

She didn't answer that. I put the knife to the book again, and cut the pages faster, and when she heard the ripping paper she blinked. She said, What would our friends all think of her, if she was to go and leave me here? I said they might think what they liked, she might tell them anything. She might tell them I was preparing Pa's letters for publication—indeed, I might begin it, with the house so quiet.

She shook her head. 'You have been ill,' she said. 'Suppose you should fall ill again, with no-one here to nurse you?'

I said I should not fall ill; nor would I be at all alone, for there would be Cook—Cook might bring in a boy to sleep downstairs at night, as she had in the weeks after Pa died. And there would also be Vigers. She might leave me Vigers, and take Ellis with her to Warwickshire . . .

I said all this. I hadn't thought of any of it before that moment, but now I might have been letting the words fly from the book in my lap with each swift, easy movement of the knife. I saw Mother grow thoughtful—still, however, she frowned. She said again, 'If you should sicken—'

'Why should I do that? Look how well I have become!'

Then she did look at me. She looked at my eye, which I think the laudanum had made vivid; and at my cheek, which the fire, or perhaps the motion of my hand cutting the paper, had made burn. She looked at my gown, which was an old, plum-coloured gown I had had Vigers fetch from the press and make narrow—for none of my suits of grey and black are high enough at the throat to hide my velvet collar.

The gown alone, I think, almost decided her. Then I said,

'Do say you'll leave me, Mother. We mustn't always keep so close, must we? Won't it be pleasanter for Stephen and Helen, at least, to have a holiday without *me* in it?'

It seems, here, a shrewd thing for me to have said; yet I meant nothing by it, nothing at all. I should never have said, before that moment, that Mother had any opinion on the matter of my feelings for Helen. I should not have thought that she had ever watched me gaze at her, or listened when I said her name, or seen me glance away as she kissed Stephen. Now she heard the lightness and the evenness of my tone, and I saw a look upon her face—not quite relief, nor satisfaction, but something like them, something very like them—and I knew at once that she had done all those things. I knew she had been doing them for two years and a half.

And I wonder now how differently it might have been between us if I had only kept my love more hidden; or if I had never felt it at all.

She moved in her chair, and smoothed the skirt across her lap. It seemed not quite correct to her, she said. But she supposed that, if Vigers were to stay, and I was to travel with her, after three or four weeks . . .

She said she must talk with Helen and Stephen about it, before she could quite give me her consent; and when we visited them next, on New Year's Eve—well, I find I need to gaze at Helen now, hardly at all, and when Stephen kissed her at midnight, I only smiled. Mother told them my plan and they looked at me and said, How could it harm me, to be left alone in my own home, where I spend so many solitary hours already? And Mrs Wallace, who dined there with us, said it was certainly more sensible to want to stay at Cheyne Walk than to risk one's health by making a journey on a train!

We were home at two that night. After the house was locked I kept my cloak about me, and stood a long time at my window, raising the sash a little to feel the thin rain of the new year. At three o'clock there were still boats ringing their bells, and men's voices from the river, and boys running fast along the Walk; but for a single moment as I watched, the clamour and the bustle died, and then the morning was perfectly still. The rain was fine—too fine to spoil the surface of the Thames, it shone like glass, and where the lamps of the bridges and the water-stairs showed there were wriggling snakes of red and yellow light. The pavements gleamed quite blue—like china plates.

I should never have guessed that that dark night could have had so many colours in it.

Next day, while Mother was out, I went to Millbank, to Selina. They have put her back upon the ordinary ward, and so now she has prison dinners again, and wool to work at rather than coir—and her own matron Mrs Jelf, who is so careful of her. I walked to her cell, remembering how it had once been a pleasure to me to keep back my visit to her, to call on other women first, and save the gazing on her till I might gaze freely. Now, how can I keep from her? What is it to me, what the other women think? I stopped at the gates of one or two of them and wished them 'Happy New Year', and shook their hands; but the ward seemed changed to me, I looked along it and saw only so many pale women in mud-coloured gowns. Two or three of the prisoners I used to call on have been moved, to Fulham; and Ellen Power, of course, is dead, and the woman in her cell now does not know me. Mary Ann Cook seemed pleased enough to have me come—and Agnes Nash, the coiner. But it was Selina I went for.

She asked me quietly, 'What have you done for us?' and I told her all that Stephen had said. She thinks we cannot be sure about the income, and says I had better visit my bank and draw from it as much money as I can, and keep it safe till we are ready for it. I told her about Mother's visit to Marishes, and she smiled. She said, 'You are clever, Aurora.' I said the cleverness was all hers, it was only working through me, I was its vehicle.

'You are my medium,' she said.

Then she came a little closer to me and I saw her looking at my gown, and then at my throat. She said, 'Have you felt me near you? Have you felt me all about you? My spirit comes to you, at night.'

I answered: 'I know.'

Then she said, 'Do you wear the collar? Let me see it.'

I pulled at the material about my throat and showed her the strip of velvet that lay warm and tight beneath it. She nodded, and the collar grew tighter.

'This is very good,' she whispered—her voice was like a finger, stroking. 'This will draw me to you, through the dark. *No*—' for I had taken a step, to be nearer to her '—No. If they see us now, they may move me further from you. You must wait a little. Soon you will have me. And then—well, you may keep me close then, close as you like.'

I gazed at her, and my thoughts gave a tilt. I said, '*When*, Selina?'

She said that I must decide it. It must be a night when I was sure to be alone—a night after my mother had gone, when I had found the things that we would need. I said, 'Mother is leaving on the 9th. It might be any night, I suppose, after that one . . .'

Then I thought of something. I smiled—I think I must have laughed, for I remember her saying then: 'Hush, or Mrs Jelf will hear you!'

I said, 'I am sorry. It is only that—well, there is a night we might choose, if you won't think it foolish.' She looked puzzled. I almost laughed again. I said, 'The twentieth of January, Selina.—St Agnes' Eve!'

But she still looked blank. Then she said, after a moment, Was that my birthday . . . ?

I shook my head, saying, St Agnes' Eve! The Eve of St Agnes! '*They glide*,' I said, '*like phantoms, into the wide hall—*

'Like phantoms, to the iron porch they glide,
Where lies the Porter, in uneasy sprawl.
By one, and one, the bolts full easy slide,
The chains lie silent on the footworn stones,
The key turns! and the door upon its hinges groans . . .'

I said that; and she only stood watching, not knowing—not knowing! And at last I fell silent. There came a movement at my breast—part dismay it was, part fear, part simple love. Then I thought, Why should she know? Who was there ever, to teach her things like that?

I thought, *That will come.*

14 June 1873

Dark circle, & afterwards Miss Driver stayed. She is a friend of Miss Isherwood's, that came last month for Peter to see privately. She said Miss Isherwood never felt so well as she did now, & it was all thanks to the spirits. She said 'Will you see, Miss Dawes, if Peter cannot also help me? I find I keep so very restless, & am prone to such queer fits. I think I must be rather like Miss Isherwood, & need developing.' She stayed one and a half hours, her treatment being the same as for her friend, though taking longer. Peter said she must come back. £1.

21 June 1873

Development, Miss Driver 1 hour. £2.
First sitting, Mrs Tilney & Miss Noakes. Miss Noakes pains at the joints. £1.

25 June 1873

Development – Miss Noakes, Peter holding her at the head while I knelt & breathed upon her. 2 hours. £3.

3 July 1873

Miss Mortimer, irritation of the spine. Too nervous.
Miss Wilson, aches. Too plain for Peter's eye.

15 January 1875

They have all gone to Warwickshire—gone a week ago. I stood at the door and watched their luggage put into a cab, watched them drive from me, saw their hands at the windows; and then I came up here and wept. Mother I let kiss me. Helen I took aside. 'God bless you!' I said to her. I could think of nothing else. But when I said it, she laughed—it was such a curious thing to hear me say. She said, 'I shall see you in a month. Will you write to me, before then?' We were never parted for so long before. I said I would, but now a week has passed and I have sent nothing. I will write to her, in time. But not yet.

The house is stiller now than I ever knew it. Cook has her nephew here to sleep downstairs, but to-night they are all already in bed. There was nothing for them to do, after Vigers brought my coals and water. The door to the house was fastened at half-past nine.

But how quiet it is! If my pen could whisper, I would make it whisper now. *I have our money.* I have *thirteen hundred pounds.* I took it from my bank, yesterday. It is my own money, and yet I felt like a thief, handling it. I gave them Stephen's order; they were a little queer over it, I thought—the clerk stepping away from the counter for a moment to speak with a more senior man, then returning to ask me, Would I not prefer the money in the form of a cheque? I said, No, a cheque would not serve—trembling all the time—thinking they must see my purpose and might try and send for Stephen. But after all, what could they do? I am a lady, and the money is mine. They brought it to me in a paper wallet. The clerk made me a bow.

I told him then that the money was for a charity, and would

be used to purchase passages abroad for poor reformatory girls. He said—looking sour—that he thought that cause a most deserving one.

When I left him I took a hansom to Waterloo, to purchase tickets for the tidal train; and then I went to Victoria, to the Travellers' Office. They gave me a passport for myself, and another for my companion. I told them her name was *Marian Erle*, and the secretary wrote it, seeing nothing strange in it!—only querying me over the spelling. I have been imagining since then all the offices I might visit and the lies I might tell in them. I have been wondering how many gentlemen it would be possible to fool, before they caught me.

But then, this morning, I stood at my window and saw the policeman making his patrol along the Walk. Mother has asked him to watch the house more carefully, now that I am here alone. He nodded to me, and my heart gave a jerk; when I told Selina of him to-day, however, she smiled. 'Are you afraid?' she said. 'You mustn't be afraid of that! When they find me gone, why should they think to look for me with you?' She said it will be days and days, before they think of *that*.

16 January 1875

Mrs Wallace called to the house to-day. I told her I was busy with Pa's letters, and that I hoped to be able to work on, undisturbed. If she comes again I will have Vigers tell her I am out. If she comes in five days' time, of course, I shall be gone. Oh, how I long for it! I can do nothing, now, but long for it. Everything else is falling from me: I am drawing further and further away from this place, with every sweeping of the hand across the numbers on the pale face of the clock. Mother left me a little laudanum—I have taken it all, and bought more. It is very easy, after all, to walk into a druggist's shop and buy a draught of it! I may do anything now. I may sit up all night if I care to, and sleep in the daylight. I remember a game, when we were children: *What will you do, when you are grown, and have a house of your own?—I'll have a tower on the roof, and fire a cannon from it! I'll eat nothing but liquorice! I'll keep dogs in butlers' jackets—I'll let a mouse sleep on my pillow . . .* Now I have more freedom than I ever had at any time in my life, and I do only the things I always have. They were empty before, but Selina has given a meaning to them, I do them for her. I am waiting, for her—but, *waiting*, I think, is too poor a word for it. I am engaged with the substance of the minutes as they pass. I feel the surface of my flesh stir—it is like the surface of the sea that knows the moon is drawing near it. If I take up a book, I might as well never have seen a line of print before—books are filled, now, with messages aimed only at me. An hour ago, I found this:

The blood is listening in my frame,
And thronging shadows, fast and thick,
Fall on my overflowing eyes . . .

It is as if every poet who ever wrote a line to his own love wrote secretly for me, and for Selina. *My* blood—even as I write this—*my* blood, my muscle and every fibre of me, is listening, *for her*. When I sleep, it is to dream of her. When shadows move across my eye, I know them now for shadows of *her*. My room is still, but never silent—I hear her heart, beating across the night in time to my own. My room is dark, but darkness is different for me now. I know all its depths and textures—darkness like velvet, darkness like felt, darkness bristling as coir or prison wool.

The house is changed by me, becalmed. There might be a spell upon it! Like figures on a chiming clock, the servants go about their duties: setting fires to warm the empty rooms, drawing the drapes at night, and unclosing them next morning—there is no-one to gaze from the windows, but still the curtains are pulled. Cook sends me trays of food. I have said that she need not send me all the courses, that she might only send me soup, or fish, or chicken. But she cannot break herself of her old habits. The trays come, and I must send them guiltily back, the meat concealed beneath the turnip and potato, like a child's. I have no appetite. I suppose her nephew eats it. I suppose they are all dining very well, down in the kitchen. I should like to go to them and say *Eat! Eat it all!* What does it matter to me what they take now?

Even Vigers keeps to her old hours, rising at six—as if she too could feel the clamour of the Millbank bell in wakeful veins—though I have told her that she mustn't try to match my habits, and may stay in bed till seven. Once or twice she has come to my room and gazed strangely at me; last night she saw my untouched tray and said, 'You must eat, miss! What would Mrs Prior say to me, if she saw how you let your meals go?'

But when I laughed to hear it, she smiled. She has a very plain smile, and yet her eyes are almost handsome. She does not trouble me. I have seen her looking curiously at the lock upon the velvet collar, when she thinks my eyes are turned away; but only once did she go so far as to ask me, Was it a mourning-band I wore for my father's sake?

Sometimes I think my passion must infect her. Sometimes my dreams come so fiercely, I am sure she must catch the shape and colour of them in her own slumbers.

Sometimes I think that I could tell her all my plans, and she would only nod and look grave. I think that, if I asked her, she might even go with us . . .

But then, I think I will be jealous of the hands that touch Selina, even a maid's hands. I went to-day to a great shop on Oxford Street, to walk among the rows of ready-made-up gowns, to buy her coats and hats, and shoes, and under-things. I hadn't guessed how it would be, to do those things for her—to fashion a place for her in the ordinary world. I never saw in dyes and cuts and fabrics what Priscilla saw, and Mother, when I had to decide between them for myself; but, buying dresses for Selina, I grew light. Of course, I didn't know her size—and yet, I found I did. I know her height, from the memory of her cheek against my jaw; and her slenderness, from the thought of our embraces. I chose, first, a plain wine-coloured travelling-gown. I thought, Well, that will do for now, and we shall buy her other things when we reach

France. But as I held that dress, I saw another—a gown of pearl-grey cashmere, with an under-skirt of some thick kind of greenish silk. The green, I thought, would match her eyes. The cashmere would be warm enough, for an Italian winter.

I bought both dresses—and then another, a dress of white, with velvet trim, and a narrow, narrow waist. It is a dress to bring out all the girlishness they have subdued at Millbank.

Then, since she will not be able to wear a dress without a petticoat, I bought her petticoats, and also stays, and also chemises, and stockings of black. And, since stockings will be useless without shoes, I bought her shoes—black shoes; and buff-coloured boots; and slippers of white velvet, to match the girlish dress. I bought her hats—large hats with veils, to cover her poor hair until it grows again. I bought her a coat, and a mantle for the cashmere dress, and a dolman with a fringe of yellow silk, that will swing as she walks beside me in the Italian sun, and flash with light.

The clothes lie in my closet now, still in their boxes. Sometimes I go to them, and put my hand upon the card. I seem to hear the silk and cashmere breathing then. I seem to feel the slow pulse of the cloth.

Then I know that they are waiting, like me, for Selina to assume them—to make them quick, to make them real, to make them palpitate with lustre and with life.

19 January 1875

I have done everything, now, for the journey we will make together; but there was one more thing that I must do, to-day, for myself. I went to the Westminster Cemetery, and stayed an hour at Pa's grave, thinking of him. It was the coldest day of the new year. When a funeral party came I heard their voices, very clear upon the thin, still January air; and as we stood, the first few flakes of winter snow began to fall, until at last my coat, and the coats of all the mourners, were dusted white. I once meant to take flowers with Pa, to the graves of Keats and Shelley, in Rome; to-day I put a wreath of holly on his own grave. The snow settled on it and hid the crimson berries—though the points upon the leaves stayed sharp as pins. I listened to the clergyman's speech, then they started casting earth upon the coffin in the open grave. The earth was hard, and rattled like shot, and when the mourners heard it they gave a murmur, and a woman cried out. The coffin was a small one—I suppose, a child's.

I had no sense at all that Pa was anywhere near me; but this, in itself, seemed a kind of blessing. I had gone to say good-bye to him. I think I will find him again, in Italy.

I went from the cemetery to the centre of the city, and then I walked from street to street, looking at all the things I shall not see again, perhaps for many years. I walked from two o'clock until half-past six.

Then I went to Millbank, for my last visit there.

I reached the gaol long after the suppers had been served and eaten and cleared away—a much later time than I have ever visited before. I found the women of Mrs Jelf's wards at the last part of their labour. This is the kindest time of the day for them. When the evening bell is rung at seven, they put their work aside; the matron takes a woman from her cell and walks with her along the passages, collecting and counting all the pins and needles and blunt-edged scissors that have been used by the prisoners throughout the day. I stood and watched Mrs Jelf do this. She wore an apron of felt, to which she fixed the pins and needles; the scissors she put on a wire, like fish. At a quarter-to-eight the hammocks must be unfolded and tied up, and at eight o'clock the doors are fastened, and the gas shut off—until that time, however, the women may do just as they please. It was curious to see them—some reading letters, some learning their Bibles; one tipping water into a bowl, to wash with, another with her bonnet removed, and tying curls into her hair with a few poor lengths of wool saved from her day's knitting. I have begun to feel myself a ghost, at Cheyne Walk; I might have been a ghost to-night, at Millbank. I walked the length of those two wards and the women hardly raised their eyes to me, and when I called to the ones I knew they came and curtseyed, but were distracted. They used to put aside their work for me, gladly enough; but their last, private hour of the day—well, I can see how it would be rather different to them, to surrender that.

I was not a ghost, of course, to Selina. She had seen me cross the mouth of her cell, and was waiting for me when I went back to her. Her face was very still and pale, but there was a pulse ticking fast beneath the shadow of her jaw—when I saw that, I felt my own heart kick.

It didn't matter now, who knew how long I spent with her, who saw how near we stood. So we stood very close, and she spoke to me, in whispers, of how it will be tomorrow night.

She said, 'You must sit and wait, and think of me. You must keep to your room, you must have a single candle by you, with its flame shielded. I shall come, some time before the light . . .'

She was so earnest, so grave, I began to be terribly afraid. I said, '*How* shall you do it? Oh, Selina, how can it be true? How shall you come to me, through the empty air?'

She looked at me and smiled, then reached and took my hand. She turned my fingers and eased back my glove, and held my wrist a little way before her mouth. She said, 'What is there, between my mouth and your bare arm? But don't you feel me, when I do this?' Then she breathed upon my wrist, where the blood shows blue—she seemed to draw all the heat in me to that one spot, and I shivered.

'Just so will I come to you, tomorrow night,' she said.

I began to imagine then how it will be. I imagined her pulled long, like an arrow, like a hair, like the string upon a violin, like a thread inside a labyrinth, long and quivering and tight—so tight that, buffeted by rough shadows, she might break! When she saw me tremble she said that I must not be frightened—that if I was, it would make her journey all the harder. I had a sudden terror then of *that*—a terror of terror itself, which would tax and weary her, perhaps harm her, perhaps keep her from me. I said, What if I should spoil her powers, without meaning it? What if her powers should fail? I thought then of how it will be, if she does not come. I thought of how it will be, not for her, but for myself. I seemed suddenly to see myself as she has made me, I saw what I have become—I saw it, with a kind of horror.

I said, 'If you don't come, Selina, I shall die.' She has told me as much herself, of course; but now I spoke so simply and so dully, she looked at me and her expression grew strange, her face became white and stretched and *bare*. She came to me and put her arms about me, and placed her face against my throat. '*My affinity*,' she whispered. And though she stood very still, when she stepped from me at last my collar was wet with her tears.

There came the sound of Mrs Jelf, then, calling an end to leisure-time, and Selina passed her hand across her eyes, and turned from me. I curled my fingers about the bars of her gate, and stood and watched her fastening her hammock to the wall, shaking free her sheet and blankets, hitting the dust from her grey pillow. Her heart still beat as fiercely as my own, I know it, and her hands shook a little, as mine did; and yet she moved and worked tidily, as a doll might, tying knots in the bed-ropes, folding back the prison blanket to show a border of white. It was as if, having been neat for a year, she must be neat even to-night—be neat, perhaps, for ever.

I couldn't bear to see her. I turned away, and caught the sound of women, all down the ward, engaged upon the same routine; and when I looked at her again she had her fingers on the buttons of her gown, and had unloosed it. 'We must all be in our beds,' she said, 'before the gas is put off.' She said it self-consciously, not looking at me—still, however, I didn't call for Mrs Jelf. I said only, 'Let me see you'—I had not known I was about to say it, and was startled by the sound of my own voice. She also blinked, and hesitated. Then she let the dress fall from her, and removed the under-skirt and the prison boots and then, after another hesitation, the bonnet, until she stood, shivering slightly, in her woollen stockings and her petticoat. She held herself stiffly, and kept her face turned from me—as if it hurt to have me gaze at her, yet she would suffer the pain of it, for my sake. Her collar-bones stood out like the delicate ivory keys of some queer instrument of music. Her arms were paler than her yellowed under-clothes, and veined, from wrist to elbow, with a gentle tracery of blue. Her hair—I had never seen her naked head—her hair hung flat to her ears, like a boy's hair. It was the colour of gold when a breath has misted it.

I said, 'How beautiful you are!' and she looked at me in a kind of surprise.

'You don't think me very changed?' she whispered.

I asked her, How could I think that?—and she shook her head, and again she shivered.

There had begun to come, along the ward, the sound of slamming doors, the sliding of bolts, a crying and a murmuring; now the sound came closer. I caught the voice of Mrs Jelf—she was calling, at every door she fastened: 'Are you all right?' and the women were answering: 'All right, mum', 'Good-night, mum!' Still I gazed at Selina, not speaking—hardly breathing, I think. Then her gate began to shudder with the nearing of the slamming doors, and when she saw that she climbed, at last, into her bed and pulled the blanket high about her.

Then Mrs Jelf was there, twisting her key and pushing at the bars; and for a curious moment she and I stood hesitating, gazing together at Selina as she lay in her bed—like fretful parents at the nursery door.

'Do you see how neatly she lies, Miss Prior?' said the matron quietly. And then, in a whisper, to Selina: 'Are you all right?'

Selina nodded. She was gazing at me, and still shivering—I think she could feel my flesh, that was tugging at hers. 'Good-night,' she said. 'Good-night, Miss Prior.' She said it very gravely—for the matron's sake, I suppose. I kept my eyes upon her face as the gate was closed and the bars fixed between us; then Mrs Jelf swung the wooden door shut, put her hand to its bolt and moved on, to the next cell.

After a moment of staring at the wood, the bolt, the iron studs, I joined her, and walked with her along the rest of E ward, and then along ward F—she all the time calling in to the women, and they making her their quaint responses: 'Good-night, mum!', 'God bless you, ma'am!', 'Here's another day, matron, nearer my time!'

Roused and nervous as I was, I took a kind of comfort from the rhythm of her tour—from the cries, the steady slamming of the doors. At last, at the furthest end of the second ward, she turned the tap that closed the gas-pipes that fed the mantles in the cells; and the jets all down the corridor seemed to jump, then flared a little brighter. She said quietly, 'Here is Miss Cadman, the night-matron, come to take my place. How do you do, Miss Cadman? This is Miss Prior, our Lady Visitor.' Miss Cadman wished me good-night, then drew off her gloves and gave a yawn. She was dressed in a matron's bear-skin cloak, but had the hood set low about her shoulders. 'Have we any trouble-makers to-day, Mrs Jelf?' she asked, yawning again. When she left us, heading for the matron's chamber, I saw that her boots were soled with rubber and struck the sanded flags quite noiselessly. The women have a name for those boots—I remember this, now. They call them *sneaks*.

I took Mrs Jelf's hand, and found I was sorry to be leaving her—sorry to be leaving her *there*, while I moved on. 'You are kind,' I said to her. 'The kindest matron in the gaol.' She pressed my fingers and shook her head, and the words, or my mood, or her evening tour, seemed to make her mournful. 'God bless you, miss!' she said.

I did not meet Miss Ridley on my journey across the gaol—I had almost hoped to. I did see Mrs Pretty, talking on the tower stairs with the night-matron of her wards, drawing on a pair of dark gloves, flexing her fists against the leather; and I also passed Miss Haxby. She had been called to reprimand a woman who was making a stir in a cell on the lowest floor. 'How late you stay, Miss Prior!' she said to me.

Will it sound strange if I write, that it was almost hard to leave that place at last?—that I walked slowly, and lingered on the tongue of gravel, dismissing the man who had escorted me there? I have often thought that I should be turned by my visits into a thing of lime or iron—perhaps I have been, for to-night Millbank seemed to pull at me like a magnet. I walked as far as the gate-house and then stopped, and turned; and after a minute there came a movement beside me. It was the Porter, come to see who was hesitating at his door. When he recognised me in the darkness he wished me good-night. Then his gaze followed my own, and he rubbed his hands together—to keep the cold from them, perhaps; but also with a kind of satisfaction.

'She's a grim old creature, ain't she, miss?' he said, nodding towards the gleaming walls, the lampless windows. 'A terrible creature—though I say it, who is her keeper. And she's leaky—did you know that? There were floods, in the old days—oh yes, many times. It is this ground, this wretched ground. Nothing will grow in it, and nothing will sit in it straight—not even a great old, grim beast like Millbank.'

I said nothing, only watched him. He had taken a black pipe from his pocket and pressed his thumb into the bowl, and now he turned to draw a match along the bricks, and then to bend into the shelter of the wall—his cheeks grew hollow, and the flame rose and dipped. He cast the match from him, and nodded again towards the prison. 'Would you think,' he went on, 'that such a thing as that could wriggle about so devilishly on its foundations?'—I shook my head. 'No more would any soul. But the man that was porter here when I took on the job—now, *he* could tell about the wriggling, the floods! He could tell of cracks, like thunder in the night! Of the governor arriving one morning to find a pentagon split smart down the middle, with ten men running through the break! Of six more men drowned in the darks, from where the prison sewers had bust and let the Thames in. There was gallons of cement put into the foundations, then; but does that stop her from heaving about? You ask the warders, Is there trouble with the locks ever, because the doors have shifted on their hinges and got stuck? Are there windows that shatter and crack, with no-one by them? She seems quiet to you, I dare say. But some nights, Miss Prior, when there ain't a breath of wind, I have stood where you are standing now and heard her *groan*—plain as a lady.'

He put a hand to his ear. There came the far-off slapping of the water of the river, the rumble of a train, the ringing of the bell upon a carriage . . . He shook his head. 'She'll come down one day, I am certain of it, and take the lot of us with her! Or else, this wicked earth that they have set her in will give one great swaller, and we'll all go down like that.'

He drew on his pipe, then gave a cough. Again we listened . . . But the gaol was silent, the earth quite hard, the blades of sedge as sharp as needles; and at last the breeze became so raw we could not stay in it, I had begun to shiver. He ushered me into his lodge, and I stood before his fire until a cab was found for me.

While I waited there, a matron came. I didn't recognise her until she pushed her cloak a little from her face, and then I saw that it was Mrs Jelf. She nodded to me once, and was let out by the Porter; and from the window of my cab I think I saw her again, then, stepping swiftly along an empty street—eager, I suppose, to snatch up the dark and slender ribbons of her ordinary life.

What must that life be like? I cannot guess.

20 January 1875

St Agnes' Eve—it is come at last.

The night is a bitter one. The wind is moaning in the chimney and rattling the windows in their frames; the coals of the fire are struck by hail, and hiss. It is nine o'clock, and the house is still. I have sent Mrs Vincent and her boy out for the night, but keep Vigers here. 'If I should grow afraid,' I said to her, 'and call to you, will you come?'—'Afraid of burglars, miss?' she answered. Then she showed me her arm, which is very thick, and she laughed. She said she would be sure to make all the doors and windows very fast, and I must not worry. But though I heard her slamming the bolts, I think she has gone back to them now, as if to check their fastenings.—Now she is making her noiseless way upstairs, and turning the key in her own lock . . .

I have made her nervous, after all.

At Millbank, the night-matron Miss Cadman walks the wards. It has been dark there for an hour. *I shall come some time before the light*, said Selina. Already the night beyond my window seems thicker than I ever knew it. I cannot believe it will ever be dawn.

I don't want the dawn to come again, if she does not come first.

I have kept to my room since the light first began to fail at four o'clock. It looks strange to me, with its empty shelves—for half my books are packed in boxes. At first, I put them all into a trunk; but then, of course, the trunk could not be lifted. We must take only what we can carry, I hadn't thought of that before to-day. I wish I had, for then I might have sent a box of books to Paris—it is too late now. And so I had to choose which ones to take, and which to leave. I have taken a Bible where I might have taken Coleridge, and all because the Bible has Helen's initials in it—the Coleridge I suppose I can replace. From Pa's room I took a paperweight, a half globe of glass that has a pair of sea-horses fixed in it, that I used to like to study when I was a girl. I have all Selina's clothes packed in one trunk—all, save the wine-coloured travelling-gown and the coat, and a pair of shoes and stockings. These I have laid out ready upon the bed, and if I gaze at them now, through the shadows, it might be her lying there, in a slumber or a swoon.

I do not even know if she will come clad in her prison costume, or whether they will bring her naked to me, like a child.

There is the creak of Vigers' bed, and the spitting of the coals.

Now it is quarter-to-ten.

Now it is almost eleven.

This morning a letter came, from Helen at Marishes. She says the house is grand, but Arthur's sisters rather proud. She says that Priscilla believes herself to be with child. She says that the estate has a frozen lake in it, on which they have been skating. I read that, and closed my eyes. I had a very clear vision, of Selina with her hair about her shoulders, a crimson hat upon her head, a velvet coat, ice-skates—I must have been remembering some picture. I imagined myself beside her, the air coming sharply into our mouths. I imagined how it would be if I took her, not to Italy, but only to Marishes, to my sister's house; if I sat with her at supper, and shared her room, and kissed her—

I cannot say what would frighten them most—her being a spirit-medium, or a convict, or a girl.

'We have heard from Mrs Wallace,' says Helen in her letter, 'that you are working, and bad-tempered.—From that I know you must be well! But you must not work so hard that you forget to join us here. I must have my own sister-in-law, to save me from Priscilla's! But will you write to me, at least?'

I wrote to her this afternoon, then gave the letter to Vigers, and stood and saw her carry it, very carefully, to the post—now there is no recovering it. I addressed it, however, not to Marishes, but only to Garden Court; and I marked it, 'To be kept until Mrs Prior's return'. It says this:

Dear Helen,

What a very curious letter this is to write!—the most curious letter I think, that I have ever written to anyone, and a kind, of course, that—so long as I am successful in my plans!—I am likely never to be obliged to write a second time. I wish that I could make it very clever.

I wish you will not hate or pity me, for what I am about to do. There is a part of me that hates myself—that knows that this will bring disgrace on Mother, on Stephen and on Pris. I wish you will only regret my going from you, not cry out against the manner of it. I wish you will remember me with kindness, not with pain. Your pain will not help me, where I am going. But your kindness will help my mother, and my brother, as it helped them once before.

I wish that, if anyone should look for faults in this, then they will find them with me, with me and my queer nature, that set me so at odds with the world and all its ordinary rules, I could not find a place in it to live and be content. That this has always been true—well, you of course know that, better than anyone. But you cannot know the glimpses I have had, you cannot know there is another, dazzling place, that seems to welcome me! I have been led to it, Helen, by someone marvellous and strange. You won't know this. They will tell you of her, and they will make her seem squalid and ordinary, they will turn my passion into something gross and wrong. *You* will know, that it is neither of those things. It is only love, Helen—only that.

I cannot live, and not be at her side!

Mother used to think me wilful. She will think *this* wilfulness. But how could it be that? I am not willing this to happen, I am surrendering! I am giving up one life, to gain a new and better one. I am going far from here, as I was meant to—I think—always. I am

. . . hastening to get nearer to the sun,
Where men sleep better.

I am glad for you, Helen, that my brother is kind.

—There I sign it. The quotation pleases me, and I wrote it with a strange sensation, thinking, That is the last time I shall quote, like this. For from the moment Selina comes to me, I shall *live*!

When will she come? It is twelve o'clock. The night, that was bitter, is growing wild. Why do rough nights always grow wilder at midnight? She won't hear the worst of it, in her cell at Millbank. She might go into it unready, and be torn and bruised and baffled—and I can do nothing for her, except wait. When will she come?—she said, *before daylight*. When is the dawn? Six hours from now.

I shall take a dose of laudanum, and perhaps that will guide her to me.

I shall put my fingers to the collar at my throat and stroke the velvet—she said the collar would make her come.

Now it is one o'clock.

Now it is two o'clock—another hour gone. How quickly it passes, on the page! I have lived a year, to-night.

When will she come? It is half-past three—the time, they say, that people die, though it wasn't so when Pa died, it was plain day-light then. I have not been so wakeful, so determinedly, since his last night. I have not wished so hard as I then wished to keep him from going from me, as I have wished to-night for her to come. Does he really gaze at me, as she believes? Does he see this pen move on the page? Oh Father, if you see me now—if you see *her* searching for me through the gloom—guide our two souls together! If you ever loved me, you may love me now by bringing her whom *I* love to me.

Now I begin to grow afraid, which I must not do. I know she will come, for she could not feel my reaching thoughts and not be drawn by them. But *how* will she come? I imagine her coming faded, pale as death—coming ill or maddened! I have taken her clothes—all her clothes, not just the travelling-gown, but the pearl-grey dress, with its skirt the colour of her eyes, and the dress of white with the velvet trim. I have placed them about the room, to catch the gleamings of my candle-flame. Now she seems all around me, as if reflected in a prism.

I have taken her rope of hair, and combed it, and plaited it; and this I keep about me and sometimes kiss.

When will she come? It is five o'clock, and still the dark part of the night, but oh! the fierceness of my wanting makes me ill! I have been to the window and lifted the sash. The wind came and made the fire gust, blew my hair wildly about my head, cast hail against my cheeks until I thought my cheeks would bleed—but still I leaned into the night, searching for her. I think I called her name—I did that, and the wind seemed to echo it. I think I shook—it seemed to me I shook the house, so that even Vigers felt me. I heard the floorboards creak beneath her shifting bed, I heard her turning in her dream—she seemed to turn, as the collar at my throat seemed to grow tight. She might have started from her sheets, hearing me cry out—*When will you come? When will you come?*—until

I called again, *Selina*! And then again the cry was echoed and cast back upon me with the hail—

Except, it was Selina's voice I think I heard, and it was my name she called. And I stood very still, to catch it again; and Vigers was still, her dream gone from her; and even the wind seemed to still a little, and the hail to ease. And the water of the river was dark and calm.

But no voice came—and yet I feel her, I think, very close. And if she is to come, it will surely be soon.

It will be soon, it will be very soon, in the last hour of the dark.

It is almost seven, and the night is ended; there is the sound of carts upon the street, and barking dogs, and cockerels. Selina's gowns lie all about me, their brightness quite leaked away; in a moment I shall rise and fold them, and return them to their paper wrappings. The wind has fallen, and the hail has turned to flaking snow. The Thames has fog upon it. Now Vigers steps from her bed, to set the fires of the new day. How strange!—I didn't hear the Millbank bell.

She has not come.

Part Five

21 January 1875

One time, two years ago, I took a draught of morphia, meaning to end my life. My mother found me before the life was ended, the doctor drew the poison from my stomach with a syringe, and when I woke, it was to the sound of my own weeping. For I had hoped to open my eyes on Heaven, where my father was; and they had only pulled me back to Hell. 'You were careless with your life,' Selina said to me a month ago, 'but now I have it.'—I knew then what I had been saved for. I thought she took my life that day. I felt it leap to her! But she had already begun to tug at its threads. I see her now, winding them about her slender fingers, in the shadows of the Millbank night; I feel it still, her careful unravelling. After all, it is a slow and delicate business, losing one's life! and not a thing to happen in a moment.

The hands will stop, in time. I can wait for that, as she can.

I went to her, at Millbank. What else should I have done? She had said she would come, in the darkness—she did not come. What else could I do now, but go to her? I had my gown still on me, for I had never changed out of it. I didn't ring for Vigers—I couldn't bear to have her look at me. Perhaps I hesitated at the door, to find the day so white and large; yet I was sensible enough to stop a cab, and call to its driver. I think that, for myself, I was calm. I think my wakeful night had dazed me.

I think there was even a voice that came whispering to me as I drove. It was a toad's voice, very close at my ear—it said, 'Yes, this is right! This is better! Even for four years, this is *proper*. Did you really think there was another way? Did you really think it? *You*?'

The voice seemed familiar to me. Perhaps it had been there

from the beginning and I had only closed my ears to it before. Now I heard the lisp of it and sat very steady. What did it matter, what it said to me? It was Selina I thought of. I imagined her pale, broken, defeated—perhaps, made ill.

What else could I have done, but gone to her? Of course, she knew that I would go, and was waiting.

The night had been a wild one; the morning was very still. It was early when the cab-man set me down at Millbank's gate. I found the tips of the prison towers blunted by fog, the walls streaked white where snow had snagged on them, and at the lodge they were raking the old coals from their fire and putting wood on it. When the Porter came to answer my knock I thought, for the first time, of how ill I must look, for his expression was strange. He said, 'Why, miss, I didn't think to see you here again, so soon!' But then he grew thoughtful. He said, he supposed that they had sent out for me, from the women's wards? and he shook his head. 'They will come down very hard on us over this, Miss Prior. You may be sure of it.'

I said nothing, could not guess what he meant, was too distracted for it. The prison, as I passed through it, seemed changed to me—but then, I had expected that. I thought it was I that had changed it, I and my own nervousness that made the warders nervous in their turn. One man asked me, Had I a paper? He said he couldn't let me pass his gate unless I had a paper from Mr Shillitoe. No warder had said such a thing to me before, in all my visits, and as I gazed at him I felt a rising, dull-edged panic. I thought, So they have resolved, already, to keep me from her . . .

Then another man came running, saying, 'That is the Lady Visitor, you fool. You may let *her* pass!' They touched their caps to me and unlocked their gate, and I heard them murmuring together when the gate was shut.

At the women's gaol, all was the same. I was received there by Miss Craven, who studied me oddly, as the Porter had; and then said, as he had: 'They have brought you in! Well! What do you make of it? I dare say you didn't think to find yourself back here so soon, and on such a day as this!'

I couldn't speak to her, but only shook my head. She walked quickly with me along the wards—they, too, seemed very still and silent, the women in them strange. I began to grow afraid, then. I was afraid, not of the matron's words, which meant nothing to me; I was afraid of how it would be, to look at Selina with the bars and bricks about her still.

We walked, and I put my hand upon the wall, to keep myself from swaying. I had eaten nothing for a day and a half. I had been wakeful, I had been wild, I had leaned weeping into the freezing night then sat very still before an ashen fire. When Miss Craven spoke again I had to peer at her to catch her words.

She said, 'You have come, I suppose, for a look at the cell?'

'The cell?'

She nodded: '*The cell.*' Her face, I noticed now, was rather flushed. Her voice had a catch to it.

I said, 'I've come, matron, to visit Selina Dawes'—and at that, her surprise was so great and so sharp, she put her hand upon me and clutched at my arm.

Oh! she said, did I really not know it?

Dawes was gone.

'Escaped! Gone clean from out her cell! Not a thing out of its order, not a single lock bust or opened, in all the gaol! The matrons cannot credit it. The women say the devil has been and took her.'

'*Escaped*,' I said. Then: '*No!* She hasn't done it!'

'So said Miss Haxby, this morning. So said we all!'

She went on like this, and I turned from her and shook, shot through with fright—thinking, Dear God, she has gone to me, after all, at Cheyne Walk! And I am not there, and she will be lost! I must go home! I must go home!

Then I heard again Miss Craven's words: *So said Miss Haxby, this morning . . .*

Now I put my hand upon *her*. What time was it, I asked her, that they found Selina gone?

It was at six, she said, when they came in to ring the women up.

'*At six?* What time then did she go?'

They could not say. Miss Cadman had heard a stir in her cell, around midnight; but when she looked in then, she said, Dawes was sleeping in her bed. It was Mrs Jelf that found the hammock empty, when the doors were unfastened at six. All they knew was that the escape was made at some hour in the night . . .

Some hour in the night. But, I had sat through all those hours, counting them off, kissing her hair, stroking her collar, feeling her close at last; then losing her.

Where had the spirits taken her, if not to me?

I looked at the matron. I said, 'I don't know what to do. I don't know what to do, Miss Craven. What should I do?'

She blinked. She was sure, she could not say. Should she take me up, to see the cell? Miss Haxby was there, she thought, with Mr Shillitoe . . . I said nothing to her. She took my arm again—'Why, you are shaking, miss!'—and led me up the tower staircase. At the entrance to the third-floor wards, however, I made her stop, and I flinched. The row of cells, like the others we had passed, was queer and very silent. The women stood at their gates with their faces at the bars—not restless, not murmuring, only still and watchful, and there seemed no-one there to command them to their labour. When I appeared with Miss Craven they turned their eyes on me; and one of them—Mary Ann Cook, I think—made a gesture. But I didn't look at any of them. I only went at last—slow and staggering, and with Miss Craven to lead me—to the arch at the angle of the ward, to Selina's cell.

Its doors were unfastened and flung wide, and Miss Haxby and Mr Shillitoe stood at them, gazing in. Their faces were so grave and pale, I thought for a moment that Miss Craven had confused the news. I was sure that, after all, Selina was there. I was sure that, in her defeat and her despair, she had hanged herself with the ropes of her hammock, and I had come too late.

Then Miss Haxby turned and saw me, and caught her breath, as if in anger. But then I spoke; and the wretchedness of my face and voice made her hesitate. Was it true, I said, what Miss Craven had told me? She did not answer, only moved a little to one side so that I might see for myself what lay beyond her—Selina's cell, quite empty, with its hammock hung out and the blankets neat upon it, its floor clean-swept, its mug and trencher tidy on their shelf.

I gave a cry, I think, and Mr Shillitoe moved to hold me. 'You must come away from here,' he said. 'This thing has shocked you—it has shocked us all.' He glanced once at Miss Haxby, and then he patted me, as if my surprise and my dismay did me some great and meaningful credit. I said, 'Selina Dawes, sir. Selina Dawes!'—He answered: 'Here is a lesson, Miss Prior! You had great plans for her, and see how she has abused you. Miss Haxby was right, I think, to caution us. But there! Who would have thought her quite so cunning? To escape, from Millbank—as if our locks were made of butter!'

I looked at the gate, the door, the bars at the window. I said, 'And no-one, no-one in all the gaol, saw her go, or heard her, or missed her, until the morning?'

Here he gazed again at Miss Haxby. She said, in a very low tone: 'Someone will have seen her—we are sure of it. Someone must have seen her go, and helped her passage.' She said there was a cloak, and a pair of night-shoes, that had been taken from the prison stores. They thought Dawes gone from the prison clad as a matron.

I had seen her drawn tight, like an arrow. I had thought she would come naked, bruised and trembling. I said, 'Clad as a matron?'—and Miss Haxby at last looked bitter: How else? Unless I thought, like the women, that the devil had borne her off upon his back!

She turned from me then, and she and Mr Shillitoe talked on in smothered voices. I still stared into the empty cell. I had begun to feel not dazed, but really ill. At last I grew so ill, I thought I might be sick. I said, 'I must go home, Mr Shillitoe. This has upset me, more than I can say.'

He took my hand, and gestured for Miss Craven to escort me out. As he passed me to her he said, 'And Dawes said nothing to you, Miss Prior? Nothing to suggest she had this crime in mind?'

I stared at him, then shook my head—the motion made me sicker. Miss Haxby studied me. He went on: 'We must talk another time, when you are calmer. Dawes may yet be recovered—we hope she will be! But whether she is recovered or not, there will have, of course, to be an inquiry—I should say, several inquiries. You may be called upon to speak about her conduct, before the prison committee . . .' He said, Could I bear that? Would I think again, if there was not some hint she gave—some sign, of her intentions—some clue, regarding who it was who may have helped her, or received her?

I said I would, I would, still hardly thinking of myself. If I was frightened, it was for her sake still, and not—not yet—for my own.

I took Miss Craven's arm, and began to walk with her along the line of watching women. From the cell next to Selina's, Agnes Nash caught my eye, and slowly nodded.—I turned my eyes from her. I said, 'Where is Mrs Jelf?' The matron said that Mrs Jelf had been made ill, by shock, and had been sent home by the prison surgeon.—But I was too ill myself, I think, to hear her properly.

Now, however, came another torment. On the staircase, at the junction of the wards below—at the place where I had once waited for Mrs Pretty to pass, so that I might run to the door of Selina's cell and feel my life fly to her—there I met Miss Ridley. She saw me and started, and then she smiled.

'Well!' she said. 'This is a lucky chance, Miss Prior, that sees *you* upon our wards, on *this* day! Don't say that Dawes has run to you, and you have brought her back to us?' She folded her arms, and stood upon her step a little more squarely. Her keys all shifted upon their chain and her leather boots creaked. Beside me, I felt Miss Craven hesitate.

I said, 'Please let me pass, Miss Ridley.' I still thought I might be sick, or weep, or fall in a kind of fit. I still thought, that if I could only get home, to my own room, then Selina would be guided to me from her lost place, and I would grow well again. I still thought that!

Miss Ridley saw my nervousness, and moved a little to her right—but only a little, so that I had to step between her and the whitewashed wall and feel my skirts brush hers. As I did it, our faces came close, and her eyes grew narrow.

'And so,' she said quietly, 'do you have her, or not? You must know it is your duty, to surrender her to us.'

I had begun to turn from her. Now the sight of her—the sound of her voice, that was like a bolt in its cradle—made me press near to her again. 'Surrender her?' I said. 'Surrender her, and to you, here? I wish to God I did have her—that I might keep her from you! Surrender her? I would as likely surrender a lamb, to the slaughterer's knife!'

Still her face was smooth.—'Lambs must be ate,' she said at once, 'and wicked girls corrected.'

I shook my head. I said, What a devil she was! How I pitied the women who had her to close the locks upon them, and the matrons who must take her as their model. 'It is *you* that are wicked. It is you, and this place—'

As I spoke, her features shifted at last and the heavy, lashless lids upon her pale eyes gave a quiver. 'Wicked, am I?' she said, as I swallowed and drew breath. 'Pity the women, do you, that must be fastened by me? You may say that, now Dawes has gone. You didn't think our locks so hard—nor our matrons, perhaps—when they kept her neat and close, for you to gaze at!'

She might have pinched or slapped me: I flinched, and shrank from her, and put my hand upon the wall. Nearby Miss Craven stood—her face shut, like a gate. Beyond her, I saw that Mrs Pretty had turned the corner of the ward, and had drawn to a halt to study us. Miss Ridley came close to me, raising a hand to her own white lip, to smooth it. She said she didn't know what I might have told Miss Haxby and the governor. Perhaps they thought themselves obliged to credit me, because I was a lady—she could not say. What she could say, was this: if I had fooled them, I had fooled no-one else upon those wards. There was something devilish queer about this flight of Dawes's, after my attentions to her—something very devilish queer, indeed! And if I was found to have played the slightest part in it—'Well,' she turned her eyes to the watching matrons, 'we keep *ladies*, too, upon our wards—don't we, Mrs Pretty? Oh yes! We have ways of making it very warm for *ladies*, here at Millbank!'

She said that, and her breath came hot upon my cheek—hot, thick, and mutton-scented. Along the passage I heard Mrs Pretty laugh.

I fled from them then—fled down the circling staircase, across the ground-floor ward, across the pentagons. For it seemed to me that, if I stayed another moment, then they would find a way to keep me there, for ever. They would keep me there, they would thrust Selina's gown upon me; and all the time Selina herself would be still outside—lost, blind, and searching, never guessing that they had me in her old place.

I fled, and seemed still to hear Miss Ridley's voice, to feel her breath upon me, hot as the breath of a hound. I fled; and at the gate I stopped, and leaned against the wall, and had to put my gloved hand to my mouth to wipe it clean of bitter matter.

Then, the Porter and his men could find no cab for me. There had come more snow upon the roads, and the drivers could not pass it; they said I must wait, and the way would be cleared by sweepers. But it seemed to me now that they sought only to keep me there, to keep Selina still lost. I thought, perhaps Miss Haxby or Miss Ridley had sent a message to the gate, that had reached there quicker than I. So I cried that they must let me out, I would not stay—and I must have frightened them, more even than Miss Ridley had, for they did it, and I ran, I saw them watching from the lodge. I ran to the embankment, and then I followed its wall, keeping very close to that one bleak way. I watched the river, that was quicker than I; and I wished I might take a boat, and make my escape like that.

For though I walked so swiftly, my journey was a slow one: the snow plucked at my skirts and made me stagger, and soon I grew tired. At Pimlico Pier I stopped and looked behind me, and put my hands to my side—there was a pain there, sharp as a needle. Then I walked again, as far as Albert Bridge.

And there I looked, not behind me, but to the houses of the Walk. I looked for my own window, which shows very clearly there when the leaves are off the trees.

I looked, hoping to see Selina. But the window was blank, with only the white cross of the sash upon it. Beneath it fell the pale front of the house, below it the steps and bushes, white with snow.

And upon the steps—hesitating upon the steps, as if uncertain whether to mount them or to shrink from them—there was a single shape of darkness . . .

It was a woman, in a matron's cloak.

Seeing that, I ran again. I ran, stumbling over the frozen ruts upon the road. I ran, and the air came so cold and so sharp I thought it would put ice inside my lungs, and choke me. I ran to the railings of the house—there was the dark-cloaked woman still, she had climbed the steps at last and was about to put her fingers to the door—now, hearing me, she turned. Her hood was high, she held it close about her face, and when I stepped towards her I saw her twitch. When I gave a cry—'*Selina!*'—she twitched still harder. Then the hood fell back. She said, 'Oh, Miss Prior!'

And it was not Selina, not Selina at all. It was Mrs Jelf, of Millbank.

Mrs Jelf. The thought that rose, after the first shock and disappointment of it, was that they had sent her to me to take me back to prison; and when she came to me I thrust her from me, and turned, and staggered, and made to run again. But my skirts were heavier than ever, now; and my lungs felt heavy, from the weight of the ice.—And, after all, where had I to run to? So when she still came, and put her hand upon me, I turned back to her and gripped her, and she held me and I wept. I stood and shuddered in her arms. She might have been anyone to me, then. She might have been a nurse, or my own mother.

'You've come,' I said at last, 'because of *her*.' She nodded. Then I looked at her face—and might have been gazing into a glass, for her cheeks were yellow against the snow, and her eyes were rimmed with scarlet, as if from weeping or constant watching. I saw then that, though Selina could be nothing to her, still she had felt the loss of her, in some queer and terrible way of her own; and she had come to me, for help or comfort.

She was the nearest I had, at that moment, to Selina herself. I gazed again at the blank windows of the house, then held my arm out to her. She helped me to the door, and I gave her my key, to place in the lock—I couldn't grasp it. We were quiet as thieves, and Vigers didn't come. The house, inside, seemed still to have the spell of my own waiting on it, and was very chill and silent.

I took her to Pa's room, and closed the door. She seemed nervous there, though after a second she raised a trembling hand and unfastened her cloak. Beneath it I saw her prison gown, very creased; but she was without her matron's bonnet, and her hair hung down about her ears—brown hair, with springing threads of grey in it. I lit a lamp, but dared not ring for Vigers to see to the fire. We sat with our coats and gloves still on us, and sometimes shivered.

She said, 'What must you think of me, for coming to your house like this? If I didn't know already, how kind you are—oh!' She put her hands to her cheek, and began to rock a little upon her chair. 'Oh, Miss Prior!' she cried—the words were stifled by her gloves. 'You cannot guess what I have done! You cannot guess, you cannot guess . . .'

Now she wept into her hands, as I had wept upon her shoulder. At last her grief, that was so strange, began to frighten me. I said, What was it? What was it?—'You might tell me,' I said, 'whatever it is.'

'I think I might,' she said, growing a little calmer at my words. 'I think I *must* say it! And oh! what does it matter, what happens to me *now*?' She raised her crimson eyes to me. 'You've been to Millbank?' she said. 'And know she is gone? Do you know, have they said, how it was managed?'

Now, for the first time, I grew careful. I thought suddenly, *Perhaps she knows*. Perhaps she knows about the spirits, about the tickets and the plans, and has come to ask for money, to bargain or to tease. I said, 'The women say it was the devil'—here she flinched. 'Miss Haxby and Mr Shillitoe, however, they think there may have been a matron's cloak taken, and matron's boots.'

I shook my head. She put her fingers to her mouth and began to press her lips against her teeth, and to gnaw at them, her dark eyes on me. I said, 'They think that someone might have helped her, from within the gaol. But oh, Mrs Jelf, why would someone do that? No-one cares for her there, no-one cares for her anywhere! There was only ever me, to think of her kindly. Only ever me, Mrs Jelf, and—'

Still she held my gaze, and bit at her lips. Then she blinked, and whispered across her knuckles.

'Only you, Miss Prior,' she said, '—and me.'

Then she turned from me, and hid her eyes; and when I said, '*My God,*' she cried: 'You think me wicked then, after all! Oh! And she promised, she promised—'

Six hours before, I had leaned calling into the frigid night, and it seemed to me that morning that I had not been warm since then. Now, I grew cold as marble—cold and stiff, yet with a heart that beat so wildly in my breast I thought it would shatter me. I said, in a whisper, 'What did she promise you?'—'That you would be glad!' she cried. 'That you would guess it, and say nothing! I thought you had guessed. Sometimes, when you came visiting, you seemed to look at me and know—'

'It was the spirits,' I said, 'that took her. It was her spirit-friends . . .'

But the words seemed mawkish, suddenly. I seemed to choke upon them. And when Mrs Jelf heard them she gave a kind of moan: Oh, if it had been, if it had been them! 'But it was me, Miss Prior! It was me that stole the cloak for her, and the matron's slippers, and kept them hid! It was me walked with her, through all of Millbank—and told the wardens it was Miss Godfrey with me, Miss Godfrey with a swollen throat, and a wrap about it!'

I said, 'You walked with her?'—She nodded: At nine o'clock. So frightened, she said, she had thought she would be ill, or begin shrieking.

At nine o'clock? But, the night-matron, Miss Cadman—she

had heard a row—that was at midnight. And she had looked, and seen Selina quite asleep . . .

Mrs Jelf bent her head. 'Miss Cadman saw nothing,' she said, 'but kept away from the ward till we were done there, then made a story. I gave her money, Miss Prior, and made her sin. And now, if they catch her, she'll go to prison for it herself. And I, dear God, will be to blame for it!'

She moaned and wept a little again, and gripped herself, and again began to rock. I watched her, still trying to understand what she had said; but her words were like some sharp, hot thing—I could not grasp them, I could only turn them about in a desperate, swelling panic. There had been no spirit-help—there had been only the matrons. There had been only Mrs Jelf, and squalid bribery, and theft. Still my heart beat. Still I sat fixed as staring marble.

And at last I said, *Why?* 'Why did you do those things—for *her*?'

She gazed at me then, and her gaze was clear. 'But don't *you* know?' she said. 'Can *you* not guess?' She took a breath, and trembled. 'She brought my boy to me, Miss Prior! She brought me messages from my own baby son, that is in Heaven! She brought me messages, and gifts—just as she brought you signs, from your own father!'

Now I could say nothing. Now her tears all ceased, and her voice, that had been cracked, grew almost blithe. 'They think at Millbank I am a widow,' she began, and, since I didn't speak or stir—only my heart beat wildly, wilder with every word—she took the stillness of my gaze for an encouragement, and spoke again; and so told it all.

'They think at Millbank, that I am a widow; and I told you once, that I had been a maid. Those things, miss, were untruths. I was once married, but my husband never died—at least, for all I know of it he didn't: I haven't seen him, for many years. I married him young, and was sorry later, for after only a little time I found another man—a gentleman!—who seemed to love me better. I had two daughters with my husband, who I cared for well enough; then I learned another child was coming—I am ashamed to say, miss, it was the gentleman's . . .'

The gentleman, she said, had left her; and then, her husband had beaten her and cast her out, keeping the daughters with him. She had had such wicked thoughts then, about her unborn boy. She had never been harsh, at Millbank, to those poor girls sent to the cells for murdering their babies. God knows how near she was, to being one of them!

She took a shuddering breath. I kept my eyes on her, still saying nothing.

'It was very hard for me, then,' she went on, 'and I was very low. But when the baby came, I loved him! He came early, and was sickly. If I had shown him just an ounce of hurt, I think he would have died. But he did not die; and I worked—all for him!—for myself, you see, I cared nothing. I worked long hours, in fearful places, all for his sake.' She swallowed. 'And then—' Then, when he was four years old, her son had died anyway. She had thought her life was ended—'Well, *you* will know how it is, Miss Prior, when that which is more dear to you than anything, is taken from you.' She had worked a little, in worse places than before. She would have worked, she thought, in Hell itself, and hardly minded . . .

And then a girl she knew told her of Millbank. The wages there are high, because no-one cares for the duties; it was enough for her, she said, that they gave her her dinners, and a room with a fire and a chair in it. The women had looked all alike to her at first—'even, even *her*, miss! Then, after a month, she touched my cheek one day and said, "Why are you so sad? Don't you know that he is watching you, crying into his hand to see you weep, when you might be happy?" What a fright she gave me! I had never heard of spiritualism. I didn't know, then, what her gifts were . . .'

Now I began to shudder. She looked, and tilted her head. 'No-one knows *as we do*, do they, miss? Each time I saw her, she had some new word from him. He would come to her at night—he is a great boy now, of almost eight! How I wished for a glimpse of him! How kind she was, to me! How I have loved her, and helped her—done things, perhaps, I shouldn't—*you* will know what I mean—all for his sake . . . And then when you came—oh, how jealous I was! I could hardly bear to see you with her! And yet, she said that she had power enough, still to bring my boy's sweet messages, and words from your own father, miss, to you.'

I said, dull as marble: '*She* told you that?'

'She told me that you came to her so often, to get word of him. And after your visits started, indeed, my boy came through stronger than ever! He sent me kisses, through her own mouth. He sent me—oh, Miss Prior, the happiest day in all my life! He sent me this, to keep about me always.' She put her hand to the neck of her gown, and I saw her finger tugging at a chain of gold.

Then my heart gave such a jerk, my marble limbs seemed to splinter at last, and all my strength, my life, my love, my hope—all flowed from me, and left me nothing. Until then, I think I had listened and thought: *These are lies, she is mad, this is nonsense—Selina will account for it all, when she comes here!* Now she drew the locket free, and held it; she prised it wide, and there came more tears upon her lashes, and her look was blithe again.

'See here,' she said, showing me the curl of Helen's pale hair. 'The angels cut this from his little head, in Heaven!'

I looked, and wept—she thought me crying, I suppose, for her dead child. She said, 'To know that he had come to her in her cell, Miss Prior! To think that he had lifted his dear hand to her, and placed a kiss upon her cheek, for her to give to me—oh, it made me ache to hold him! It made me ache, about the heart!' She closed the locket, and returned it to its place behind her gown, and patted it. It has been swinging there, of course, through all my visits to the gaol . . .

And then at last, Selina had said there was a way. But it couldn't be done on the wards at Millbank. Mrs Jelf must first help her get free; and then she would bring him. She would bring him, she swore it, to the place that Mrs Jelf lived.

She must only wait and watch, for a single night. And Selina would come, before day-light.

'And you mustn't think I would have helped her, Miss Prior, for anything but that! What could I do? If I don't help him come—Well, she says that there are many ladies, where he is, who would be glad to have the care of a little motherless boy. She told me that, miss, and wept. She is so kind-hearted and so good—too good to be kept at Millbank! Didn't you say it yourself, and to Miss Ridley? Oh! Miss Ridley! How I have feared her! I feared she would catch me, receiving kisses from my baby. I feared she would catch me being *kind* upon the ward, and so move me from it.'

I said, 'It was you Selina stayed for, when it came time for her to go to Fulham. It was you she struck Miss Brewer for—you, for whom she suffered in the darks.'

She turned her head again, with a grotesque kind of modesty—said, she only knew how ill she felt then, to think that she had lost her. How ill, and then how thankful—oh, how shamed and sorry and thankful!—when poor Miss Brewer was hurt . . .

'But now'—she raised her clear, dark, simple eyes to me—'But now, how very hard it will be, to have to walk by her old cell and see another woman in it.'

I stared at her. I said, Could she say that? Could she think of that, when she had had Selina with her?

'Had her with me?' She shook her head, saying, What did I mean? Why did I think she had come here? 'She never came to me! She never came, at all! I sat watching, through all the long night, and she never came!'

But, they had left the gaol together!—She shook her head. At the gate-house, she said, they had parted, and Selina had walked on alone. 'She said there were things that she must fetch, that would make my son come better. She said I must only sit and wait, and she would bring him to me; and I sat and watched and waited, and at last grew sure they had recovered her. And what could I do then, but go to her at Millbank? And now, she is not recovered, and still I have had no word from her, no sign, nor anything. And I am so afraid, miss—so afraid for her, and for myself, and for my own dear boy! I think my fright, Miss Prior, will kill me!'

I had risen, and now I stood beside Pa's desk and leaned upon it, and turned my face from her. After all, there were things that she had told me that were strange. Selina had stayed at Millbank, she said, to be released by her. But, I had felt Selina near me, in the dark, and at other times; and Selina had known things of me that I told nowhere, save in this book. Mrs Jelf had had kisses of her—but to me she had sent flowers. She had sent me her collar. She had sent me *her hair*. We were joined in the spirit and joined in the flesh—I was her own *affinity*. We had been cut, two halves together, from a single piece of shining matter.

I said, 'She has lied to you, Mrs Jelf. She has lied to us both. But I think she will explain it, when we find her. I think there might be a purpose to it, that we cannot see. Can't you think where she might have gone to? Is there no-one, who might be keeping her?'

She nodded. It was on account of that, she said, that she had come here.

'And I,' I said, 'know nothing! I know less, Mrs Jelf, than you!'

My voice sounded loud in the silence. She heard it, and hesitated. Then, '*You* know nothing, miss,' she said, giving me an odd little look. 'But it was not you I came to trouble. It was the other lady here.'

The *other* lady here? I turned to her again. I said, she surely could not mean *my mother*?

But she shook her head, and then her look grew stranger. And if her mouth had now dropped toads, or stones, I should not have been more frightened than I was by her next words.

She said, she had not come to speak with me, at all. She had come to see Selina's maid, Ruth Vigers.

I gazed at her. There was a gentle ticking from the clock upon the mantel—Pa's clock, that he would stand before and set his watch to. Beyond that, the house was perfectly silent.

Vigers, I said then. *My servant*, I said. *Vigers, my servant, Selina's maid.*

'Of course, miss,' she answered—then, seeing my face: how could I not have known it? She had always thought it was for Selina's own sake that I kept Miss Vigers about me here . . .

'Vigers came to us from nowhere,' I said. 'From nowhere, from nowhere.' What thought had I for Selina Dawes, the day my mother took Ruth Vigers to the house? How could it help Selina, for me to have *Vigers* close about me?

Mrs Jelf said she had supposed it a kindness on my part; and that I liked to have Selina's maid as my own servant, to remind me of her. Besides that, she had thought that Selina sometimes sent me tokens, in the letters that were passed between Miss Vigers and the gaol . . .

'Letters,' I said. Now I think I began to glimpse the whole, thick, monstrous shape of it. I said, There were letters passed, between *Selina* and *Vigers*?

Oh, she said at once, there had always been those!—even before I had begun my visits. Selina did not like to have Miss Vigers come to Millbank, and—well, Mrs Jelf could understand why a lady would not quite like to have her maid look upon her, in such a place. 'It seemed a very little thing to do for her, to take those letters, after her kindness with my boy. The other matrons will take in packets for the women, from their friends—though you must never say I told you, they will deny it if you ask!' *They*, she said, will do it for money. It was enough for Mrs Jelf that Selina's letters made her glad. And then, 'there was nothing harmful in them'—nothing save kind words and, sometimes, flowers. She had seen Selina weep over those flowers, very often. She had had to turn her eyes from her then, to stop her own tears coming.

How could that hurt Selina? And how could it hurt her, for Mrs Jelf to carry letters from her cell? Who *could* it harm, to give her paper?—to give her ink, and a candle to write by? The night-matron never minded—Mrs Jelf gave her a shilling. And by dawn the candle was burned away. They must only be a little careful, over the spilling of the wax . . .

'Then, when I knew that her letters began to have words for you in them, miss; and when she wished for a token to send, a token from her own box . . . Well'—here her white face coloured slightly—'you could not call it stealing, could you? Taking what was hers?'

'Her hair,' I murmured.

'It was her own!' she said at once. 'Who is there, to miss it . . .?'

And so it had been sent, wrapped in brown paper; and Vigers had received it here. It was her hand that had placed it upon my pillow—'And all the time, Selina said the spirits brought it . . .'

Mrs Jelf heard that, and tilted her head, and frowned. 'She said, the spirits? But Miss Prior, why would she say that?'

I didn't answer her. I had begun to shake again. I must have gone then from the desk to the fireplace, and leaned to rest my brow against the marble mantel, and Mrs Jelf must have risen, and come and put her hand upon my arm. I said, 'Do you know what you have done? Do you know it, do you know? They have cheated us both, and you have helped them! You, with your *kindnesses*!'

Cheated? she answered. Oh no, I had not understood—

I said I understood it all, at last—though I didn't, even then, not all of it, not quite. But what I knew already seemed enough to kill me. I stood still for a second, then raised my head, then let it fall.

And as my brow cracked upon the stone I felt the tugging of the collar at my throat; and then I sprang from the hearth, and put my fingers to my neck and began to tear at it. Mrs Jelf looked at me, her hand at her mouth. I turned away from her, and kept on plucking at the collar, working at the velvet and the lock with my blunt nails. It would not tear, however—it would not tear! but only seemed to grip me tighter. At last I looked about me, for something that would help me; I think I would have seized Mrs Jelf herself, and pressed her mouth against my throat and made her bite the velvet from me—except that I saw first Pa's cigar knife, and took that up, and began slicing at the collar with the blade of it.

Seeing me do that, Mrs Jelf gave a scream; she screamed that I would harm myself! that I would cut my throat! She screamed—and the blade slipped. I felt blood upon my fingers—astonishingly warm, it seemed to me, to have come from my cold flesh. But I also felt the collar, broken at last. I flung it from me to the floor; and saw it quiver, upon the rug, in the form of an *S*.

Then I let the knife drop and stood jerking beside the desk, my hip beating hard against the wood, making Pa's pen and pencil rattle. Mrs Jelf came nervously to me again, and seized my hands, and made her handkerchief into a pad to place against my bleeding throat.

'Miss Prior,' she said, 'I think you are very ill. Let me fetch Miss Vigers. Miss Vigers will calm you. She will calm us both! Only send for Miss Vigers, and have the story from her . . .'

So she went on—*Miss Vigers, Miss Vigers*—and the name seemed to tear at me like the blade of a saw. I thought again of Selina's hair, which had been put upon my pillow. I thought of the locket, which had been taken from my room while I lay sleeping.

Still the things upon the desk jumped, as my hip struck it. I said, 'Why would they do this, Mrs Jelf? Why would they do this, so very *carefully*?'

I thought of the orange-blossoms; and of the collar, which I found pressed between the pages of this book.

I thought of this book, where I wrote all my secrets—all my passion, all my love, all the details of our flight . . .

Then the rattling pens fell silent. I put my hand to my mouth. '*No*,' I said. 'Oh, Mrs Jelf, not that, not that!'

She reached for me again, but I broke from her. I went stumbling from the room, into the still and shadowy hall. I called, '*Vigers!*'—a terrible, broken cry, that went echoing about the empty house, to be smothered by a silence more terrible still. I went to the bell, and jerked it till the wire snapped. I went to the door at the side of the stairs and called into the basement—the basement was dark. I stepped back into the hall—saw Mrs Jelf gazing fearfully at me, the handkerchief with my blood upon it fluttering from her fingers. I started up the stairs, and went first to the drawing-room, and then to Mother's room, and Pris's room—calling all the time for *Vigers! Vigers!*

But no answer came, no sound at all save my own ragged breaths, the thump and slither of my feet upon the stairs.

And at last I reached the door of my own chamber, that was ajar. She had not thought to close it, in her great haste.

She has taken everything, except the books: these she

removed from the boxes which held them, and piled carelessly upon the carpet; in their place she took items from my dressing-room—gowns and coats, and hats and boots and gloves and brooches—things, I suppose, to make a lady of her, things that she has handled in her time here, things she has cleaned and pressed and folded, and kept neat, kept ready. She has taken these—and, of course, the clothes I bought Selina. And she has the money, and the tickets, and the passports marked *Margaret Prior* and *Marian Erle.*

She even has the rope of hair, which I combed smooth, to coil about Selina's head to cover the marks of the prison scissors. She left me only this, to write in. She left it neat and square, and with the cover wiped clean—as a good maid would leave a kitchen-book, after taking out a recipe.

Vigers. I said the name again—I spat the name, it was like a poison in me, I felt it rising in me, turning my flesh black. *Vigers.* What was she, to me? I could not even recall the details of her face, her look, her manners. I could not say, cannot say now, what shade her hair is, what colour her eye, how her lip curves—I know she is plain, plainer even than I. And yet I must think, *She has taken Selina from me.* I must think, *Selina wept, for the wanting of her.*

I must think, *Selina has taken my life, that she might have a life with* Vigers *in it*!

I know it, now. I would not know it then. I thought only that she must have cheated me; that she must have had some grip upon Selina, some queer claim that had forced her to this.—I still thought, *Selina loves me.* So when I went from the room I went not down to the hall, where Mrs Jelf still waited; I went to the narrow stairs, the attic stairs, that lead to the servants' bedrooms. I cannot remember when I last climbed these stairs, before to-day—perhaps, when I was very young. There was a maid, once, I think, who caught me gazing at her, and gave me a pinch that made me cry; and after that, the staircase frightened me. I used to tell Pris that a troll lived at the top of it, and that when the servants went to their rooms they went, not to sleep, but to be maids for him.

Now I climbed the creaking stairs, and might have been a

child again. I thought, *Suppose she is there, or comes and finds me?*

But of course, she was not there. Her room was cold and quite empty—the emptiest room, it seemed to me at first, that it was possible to imagine: a room that held *nothing*, like the cells at Millbank, a room that had made nothing a substance, a texture, or a scent. Its walls were colourless, its floor quite naked but for a single strip of rug, worn to the weave. It had a shelf, with a bowl, and a jug that was tarnished, and a bed, with yellowing sheets, that were twisted and bunched.

All she left behind her was a servant's tin trunk—the trunk she came with, it has her initials hammered in it, very roughly, with the point of a nail.—*R. V.*

I saw them, and imagined her hammering the letters into the soft red flesh of Selina's heart.

But if she ever did that, then I think Selina must have parted the bones at her breast, to let her. She must have grasped her own bones and, weeping, eased them open—just as, now, I lifted the lid of the trunk, and wept to see what lay inside it.

A mud-brown gown, from Millbank, and a maid's black frock, with its apron of white. They lay tangled together, like sleeping lovers; and when I tried to pull the prison dress free, it clung to the dark fabric of the other and would not come.

They might have been put there in cruelty; they might have been cast there only in haste. Either way, I saw the message of them. There had been no trickery on Vigers' part—only a sly and dreadful triumph. She had had Selina here, above my head. She had brought her past my door, and up the naked stairs—all while I sat, with my poor shielded candle. All while I waited through the long hours of the night, they were here, lying together, speaking in whispers—or not speaking at all. And when they heard me pace, and moan, and cry out at my window, they had moaned and cried out, to mock me—or else, they had caught the terrible straining of my passion, and the passion had become theirs.

But then, that passion was always theirs. Every time I stood in Selina's cell, feeling my flesh yearn towards hers, there might as well have been Vigers at the gate, looking on, stealing Selina's gaze from me to her. All that I wrote, in the dark, she had later brought a light to; and she had written the words to Selina, and the words had become her own. All the time I lay in my bed, turning, turning with the drug on me, feeling Selina come, it was *Vigers* that came, it was *her* shadow on my eye, *her* heart that beat to match Selina's—while mine struck out some weak, irregular rhythm of its own.

I saw all this; and then I went to the bed they lay on, and turned the sheets, looking for marks and smudges. Then I went to the bowl upon the shelf. There was still a little cloudy water in it, and I sifted it with my fingers until I found a hair that was dark, and another, quite gold. Then I cast the bowl to the floor, and it broke in pieces, and the water stained the boards. I took the jug, meaning to smash it—but it was of tin and wouldn't break, I had to beat it till it buckled. I seized the mattress, and then the bed; the sheets I ripped. The tearing cotton—how can I write it?—it was like a drug upon me. I tore and tore, until the sheets were rags, until my hands were sore; and then I put the seams to my own mouth and tore with my teeth. I ripped the rug upon the floor. I took the servant's trunk, and pulled the gowns from it and tore at them—I think I would have torn at my own dress, my very hair, if I had not gone panting to the window at the last, and put my cheek against the glass, and clutched the frame, and shivered. Before me, London lay perfectly white and still. The snow still fell, the sky seemed pregnant with it. There was the Thames, and there the trees of Battersea; and there—far-off to the left, too far to catch from my own window a floor below—there were the blunted tips of Millbank's towers.

And there upon Cheyne Walk, his coat very dark, was the policeman, making his day's patrol.

Seeing him, I thought one thing—it was my mother's voice, rising in me. *I have been robbed*, I thought, *by my own servant!* Only let me tell that policeman, and he will stop her—*he will stop her train! I'll have them both at Millbank! I'll have them put in separate cells, and make Selina my own again!*

I went from the room, and down the attic staircase, down to the hall. There was Mrs Jelf, pacing now, and weeping—I put her from me. I drew open the door, and ran along the pavement; and then I cried out to the policeman, in a quivering shriek that was a voice unlike my own, that made him turn and come running and say my name. I clutched at his arm. I saw him gazing at my hair, which was wild, and my face, which was terrible, and—I had forgotten this—the wound upon my throat, that I had twisted and made bleed again.

I said I had been robbed. I said, there had been thieves, in my own house. They were now upon the train, from Waterloo to France—two women, with my clothes on them!

He looked at me strangely. He said, Two women?—'Two women, and one of them my maid. And she is terribly cunning, and has abused me, cruelly! And the other—the other—'

The other escaped, I meant to say next, *from Millbank Prison!* But instead of saying it, I took one quick icy breath and put my hand to my mouth.

For how should he suppose that I knew that?

Why were there clothes, for her to dress in?

Why was there money ready, why were there tickets?

Why was there a passport, made out in a fanciful name . . .?

The policeman waited. I said, 'I am not sure, I am not sure.'

He glanced about him. He had removed his whistle from his belt, I saw—now he let it fall upon its chain and bent his head to me. He said, 'I think you shouldn't be upon the street, miss, so confused. Let me walk home with you, and you may tell me all your story there, where it is warm. You have hurt your neck, look, and the cold will make it smart.'

He held his arm for me to take. I drew away from him. 'You mustn't come,' I said then. I said I had been wrong—there was no robbery, nor anything strange at the house at all. I turned, and walked from him. He kept pace with me, reaching for me, murmuring my name—yet also unable, quite, to put his hand upon me. And when I seized the gate and shut it on him, he hesitated; and while he did that I ran quickly into the house, and closed the door and slid the bolt, and stood with my back pressed to it, and my cheek against the wood.

He came, then, and pulled on the bell, I heard it ringing in the darkened kitchen. Then I saw his face, stained crimson by the glass at the side of the door: he cupped his hands, and peered into the darkness, and called for me and then for a servant. After a minute of this he moved away again; and after another minute with my back pressed to the door, I crept across the tiles into Pa's study and peeped through the window-lace, and saw him standing at the gate. He had removed his note-book from his pocket, and was writing in it. He wrote a line, then checked his watch and glanced once more at the darkened house. Then he looked about him again, and slowly moved away.

Only then did I remember Mrs Jelf. There was no sign of her. But when I went softly to the kitchen I found the door unfastened, and suppose she took her leave that way. She must have seen me run and seize the policeman, and gesture back towards the house. Poor lady! I imagine her sweating with terror to-night, to hear the constable's tread outside her door—just as last night she sat, as I did, weeping at nothing.

18 July 1873

A tremendous row at the circle tonight! There were only 7 of us gathered, namely me, Mrs Brink, Miss Noakes & 4 strangers, 2 of them a lady & her little red-headed daughter, the other 2 sitters gentlemen, that I think had come only for fun. I saw them looking about themselves, & think they were looking for a trap-door or wheels on the table. I thought then they might be grabbers, or that the idea of grabbing might come to them later. When they gave their coats to Ruth they said 'Now miss, keep our things from being spirited away while we sit here & we will give you half a crown.' When they saw me they made me bows & laughed, one of them taking my hand & saying 'You must think us very rude, Miss Dawes. We were told you were handsome, but I was sure you would turn out very fat & old. There are, you must admit, a great many lady mediums answering that description.' I said 'I see only with the eyes of the spirit sir' & he answered 'Well, then I am afraid there is a great deal wasted every time you look in the glass. You must let us use our fleshly eyes on you the more to make up for it.' He himself had a very poor set of whiskers, & an arm that was slender as a lady's. When we sat he took pains to sit at my side, & when I said we must join hands to pray he said 'Must I take Stanley's hand? May I not rather hold both your hands?' The lady with the daughter I thought looked quite disgusted then, & Mrs Brink said 'I think our circle is not a harmonious one tonight, Miss Dawes. Perhaps you ought not to sit for us.' I should have hated however, not to have sat then.

The gentleman kept very close beside me while we waited, saying once 'This, I think, is what they call congenial spirits.' Finally he did take his other hand from his friend & he put it upon my bare arm. I said at once 'The circle has been broken!'

& he answered 'Well it is not Stanley & I that have broken it. I can feel Stanley's hand now, he is holding tight to the tail of my shirt.' When I went into the cabinet he rose to help me but Miss Noakes said 'I am to help Miss Dawes tonight.' She fastened me with the collar & then held the rope, & the gentleman's friend Mr Stanley seeing that said 'Lord, must you do that? Must she really be tied like a goose?' Miss Noakes answered 'It is for persons like you that we do this. Do you think that any of us enjoys it?'

When Peter Quick came & put his hand on me they all sat very silent. When he went out however, one of the gentlemen laughed, saying 'He has forgotten to change out of his night-gown!' Then, when Peter asked if there were any questions for the spirits, they said they had a question & it was this, could the spirits give them any little hint as to the whereabouts of buried treasure?

Then Peter grew angry. He said 'I think you have come only to mock my medium. Do you think she has me come across the Borderland only for your sport? Do you think I labour, only to have 2 little flash boys like you laugh at me?' The first gentleman said then 'I'm sure, I don't know why you have come' & Peter said 'I have come to bring you marvellous tidings, that Spiritualism is true!' Then he said 'I have also come to bring you gifts.' He went to Miss Noakes & said 'Here is a rose Miss Noakes, for you', & then to Mrs Brink, 'Here is a fruit, Mrs Brink', it was a pear. He went all about the circle like this until he reached the gentlemen, & there he waited. Mr Stanley said 'Well, have you a flower or a fruit for me?' & Peter answered 'No I have nothing for you sir, but I have a gift for your friend & here it is!'

Then the gentleman let up a great shriek & I heard his chair scrape on the floor. He said 'Damn you, you devil, what have you put on me?' What it proved to be was a crab. Peter had tipped it into his lap & the gentleman feeling its claws moving over him in the darkness, he had thought it was a kind of monster. The crab was a big one from the kitchen, there had been 2 of them in pails of brine & they had needed plates with 3lb weights on them to keep them from crawling out – of course,

I did not know this until later. Peter came back into the cabinet while the gentleman was still calling out in the darkness & Mr Stanley had risen to find a light, & I only guessed what it might be because when he put his hand over my face it smelt so queer. When they took me out at last the crab had had a chair tipped on it & its shell was quite busted, its flesh showing pink but its claws still moving, & the gentleman was brushing at his trousers where they were stained with brine. He said to me 'That was a nice trick to play on me!' but Mrs Brink said at once 'You should not have come here. It was you that made Peter so unruly, you have brought low influences with you.'

But when the 2 gentlemen had left, we laughed. Miss Noakes said 'O Miss Dawes, how jealous Peter is of you! I think he would kill a man for your sake!' Then while I stood & took a glass of wine, the other lady came to me & made me stand aside. She said she was sorry the gentlemen had turned out so nasty. She said she had seen other young lady media who would have let men like that turn them into coquettes, & she was glad that I had not done that. Then she said 'I wonder Miss Dawes, if you might take a look at my little girl?' I said 'What is the matter with her?' & she said 'She will not stop crying. She is 15 years old, & I should say she has been crying just about every day since she was 12. I tell her she will cry her own eyes clean out of her head.' I said I must look closely at her, & she said 'Madeleine, come here.' When the girl came to me I took her hand, saying 'What did you think of what Peter did tonight?' She said she thought it was marvellous. He had given her a fig. She is not from London but rather from Boston, in America. She said she has seen many Spiritualists there, but none that were so clever as me. I thought her very young. Her mother said 'Can you do anything with her?' I said I was not sure. But as I stood wondering, Ruth came to take my glass, & when she saw the little girl she put a hand to her head, saying 'O, but look at your pretty red hair! Peter Quick would like another look at that, I know.'

She says she thinks she will do very well, if she might only be got for a little time away from the mother. Her name is Madeleine Angela Rose Silvester. She is to come back to us tomorrow, at half past 2.

I cannot say what time it is. The clocks have stopped, there is no-one here to wind them. But the city is so still, I think it must be three or four—the silent hour, between the running of the late cabs and the rattling of the carts to market. There is no breath of wind, no drop of rain, upon the street. There is frost upon the window but—though I have waited, with my eyes upon it, for an hour and more!—its waxing is too secret and too soft, I cannot catch it.

Where is Selina now? How does she lie? I send my thoughts into the night, I reach for the cord of darkness that once seemed to bind her to me, quivering tight. But the night is too thick, my thoughts falter and are lost, and the cord of darkness—

There never was a cord of darkness, never a space in which our spirits touched. There was only my longing—and hers, which so resembled it, it seemed my own. There is no longing in me, now; there is no quickening—she has taken all that and left me nothing. The nothing is very still and light. It is only rather hard to keep the pen upon the page, with my flesh filled with nothing. Look at my hand!—it is the hand of a child.

This is the last page I shall write. All my book is burned now, I have built a fire in the grate and set the pages on it, and when this sheet is filled with staggering lines it shall be added to the others. How queer, to write for chimney smoke! But I must write, while I still breathe. I only cannot bear to read again what I set down *before*. When I tried that, I seemed to see the smears of Vigers' gaze upon the pages, sticky and white.

I have thought of her, to-day. I thought of when she came to us, and Priscilla laughed and called her plain. I thought of the last girl, Boyd, and how she wept, saying the house had ghosts in it. I suppose she never heard those things. I suppose that Vigers came to her, and threatened her, or gave her money . . .

I thought of Vigers, lumpish Vigers, standing blinking while I asked her who brought orange-blossoms to my room; or sitting in the chair beyond my open door, hearing me sigh and weep and write my book—she seemed kind to me, then. I think of her bringing my water and lighting my lamps, carrying food from the kitchen. No food comes now, and my clumsy fire smokes and spits, and falls to ashes. My slop-pot sits unemptied, turning the dark air sour.

I think of her dressing me, brushing my hair. I think of her great servant's limbs. Now I know whose hand it was that had the wax about it that made that spirit-mould; and when I remember her fingers I see them bulging, yellow at the joints. I imagine her placing her finger upon me and the finger growing warm, and softening, staining my flesh.

I think of all the ladies she has placed her waxen hands upon and stained—and of Selina, who must have kissed her fingers as they dripped—and I am filled with horror, and with envy and with grief, because I know myself untouched, unlooked-for and alone. I saw the policeman return to the house this evening. Again he rang upon the bell, and stood gazing into the hall—perhaps at last he thinks me gone to Warwickshire, to join Mother. But perhaps he does not, perhaps he will come back again tomorrow. He will find Cook here then, and make her come and tap upon my door. She will find me strange. She will fetch Dr Ashe, and perhaps a neighbour—Mrs Wallace; and they will send for Mother. And then—what? Then tears or staring grief, and then more laudanum, or chloral again, or morphine, or paregoric—I never tried that. Then the couch for half a year, just like before, and visitors walking tip-toe to my door . . . And then the gradual re-absorption into Mother's habits—cards with the Wallaces, and the creeping hand upon the clock, and invitations to the christenings of Prissy's babies. And meanwhile, the inquiry at Millbank; and I might not be brave enough, now Selina has gone, to lie on her behalf, and on my own . . .

No.

I have returned my scattered books to their old places on the shelves. I have closed my dressing-room door, and turned the latch upon my window. Upstairs, I have made all tidy. The broken jug and bowl I hid away, the sheet and the rug and the gowns I burned in my own grate. I have burned the Crivelli portrait, and the Millbank plan, and the piece of orange-blossom I kept in this book. I have burned the velvet collar, too, and the handkerchief, spotted with blood, which Mrs Jelf let fall upon the carpet. Pa's cigar-knife I put carefully back upon his desk. The desk has a film of dust upon it, already.

I wonder which new maid will come, to wipe that dust away? I could not have a servant stand and curtsey to me now, I think, without shuddering.

I have taken a bowl of cold water and washed my face in it. I have cleaned the wound at my throat. I have brushed my hair. There is nothing else, I think, to tidy or to take away. I am leaving nothing out of place, here or anywhere.

Nothing, that is, except the letter I wrote Helen; but that must remain, now, in the rack at the hall at Garden Court. For when I thought I might go there, and have their maid return it to me, I remembered how carefully Vigers had carried it to the post—and then I thought of all the letters she must have taken from the house, and all the packets that must have come here; and all the times she must have sat, in her dim room above my own, writing of her passion as I wrote of mine.

How did that passion seem, upon the page? I cannot imagine it. I am too weary.

For oh, I am so terribly weary at last! I think, in all of London, there is no-one and nothing so weary as I—unless perhaps the river, which flows on beneath the frigid sky, through its accustomed courses, to the sea. How deep, how black, how thick the water seems to-night! How soft its surface seems to lie. How chill its depths must be.

Selina, you will be in sunlight soon. Your twisting is done—you have the last thread of my heart. I wonder: when the thread grows slack, will you feel it?

1 August 1873

It is very late, & quiet. Mrs Brink is in her room, her hair all down about her shoulders & a ribbon tied in it. She is waiting for me. Let her wait a little longer.

Ruth is lying on my bed with her shoes kicked off. She is smoking one of Peter's cigarettes. She is saying 'Why are you writing?' & I tell her I am writing for my Guardian's eyes, as I do everything. 'H*im*' she says, & now she is laughing, her dark brows coming together over her eyes & her shoulders shaking. Mrs Brink must not hear us.

Now she is silent, gazing at the ceiling. I say 'What are you thinking of?' She says she is thinking of Madeleine Silvester. She has been to us 4 times in the past 2 weeks, but she is still very nervous &, after all, I think she might be too young for Peter to develop. But Ruth says 'Only let him put his mark upon her once, she would come to us for ever. And do you know how rich she is?'

Now I think I hear Mrs Brink weeping. Outside, the moon is very high – it is the new moon, with the old moon in her arms. They still have the lamps on at the Crystal Palace, & the dark sky makes them shine very clear. Ruth is still smiling. What is she thinking of now? She says she is thinking of Little Silvester's money, & what we might do with a share of money like that. She says 'Did you suppose I wanted to keep you at Sydenham for ever, when the world has so many bright places in it? I am thinking how handsome you will look, say in France or Italy. I am thinking of all the ladies that will like to gaze at you there. I am thinking of all the pale English ladies that have gone to those places, in high hopes that the sun will make them well again.'

She has put her cigarette out. Now I shall go in to Mrs Brink.

'Remember,' Ruth is saying, 'whose girl you are.'

Acknowledgements

Thanks to Laura Gowing, Judith Murray, Hanya Yanagihara, Julie Grau, Sally Abbey, Sally O-J, Judith Skinner, Simeon Shoul, Kathy Watson, Leon Feinstein, Desa Philippi, Carol Swain, Judy Easter, Bernard Golfier, Joy Toperoff, Alan Melzak and Ceri Williams.

The writing of *Affinity* was partly funded by a London Arts Board New London Writers Award, for which I am also extremely grateful.

Sarah Waters was born in Wales in 1966 and now lives in London. Her first novel, *Tipping the Velvet,* was also published by Riverhead.